Her Eight
Limbs of Love

LOUISE BEKER

ISBN: 13: 978-0-473- 32210-6

First published in New Zealand by
Angelos Publishing Limited 2015
Auckland, New Zealand

Cover Design: Damonza.com
Editor: Nina McSweeney
Photography: Gezz Media Ltd

www.louisebeker.com
info@louisebeker.com
www.facebook.com/louisebeker.author

Printed and bound in New Zealand by
BookPrint Ltd

In loving memory of my Dad,

who inspired my love of nature, adventure, friendship and peace.

Forever in my heart.

'He who is happy within, who rejoices within, and who is illuminated within, that Yogi attains absolute freedom.

The Bhagavad Gita

Chapter One

As Sasha watched Evangeline Thornton lying quietly on the mat, she observed her eyes closed and limbs splayed out wide. Her belly rose and fell in a soft small motion and she was still and serene. On one level this qualified as a successful yoga session: the woman's mouth wasn't moving as she lay in corpse pose, which was nothing short of a miracle.

Mrs Thornton was a *yabberer*.

Without fail, Evangeline would begin to yabber as Thomas, her butler, guided Sasha gracefully down the majestic hallway, flanked by Edwardian dressers with vibrant flower-filled vases atop them. Twice weekly, Thomas would lead Sasha past the statues of naked Greek men - she assumed they were Greek and also naked, although she daren't look too hard in her trek along the grand passage.

Mrs Thornton's yabbering was always a screeching high-pitch. 'Tomuusss,' she would shriek in her soprano-like range. 'Through heeere,' she shrilled every lesson.

Thomas, clad in a ridiculously old-fashioned butler's suit at the unsociable hour of six in the morning, would always turn to Sasha tight-lipped and nod his head mysteriously, his eyes gleaming with some form of pride. Imaginatively, Sasha decided that the glance and gentle tilt of his head could be interpreted as *you're so privileged*. Although she didn't fully agree.

Religiously, Thomas would usher her silently past the annoying loudly-ticking great-grandfather clock, straight into the opulent living area, the size of which was larger than her entire Camden apartment.

It's a ballroom, not a living room! Sasha thought.

The first thing that always struck her upon entering *Ballroom* was the size of the great gilt-edged mirror suspended on the opposing wall.

How on earth did they hang that? She often wondered.

In quiet moments, Sasha would fantasize about the giant object falling unceremoniously from its perch: a God-almighty crash, the tinkling of a million fragments of glass exploding, vestiges of eighteenth century dust hovering above it like wispy clouds and Evangeline shrieking *Tommuuss,* compelling him to lift the gigantic antique back onto the wall in some herculean manner. But Thomas was no Hercules. He was thin, aging and balding.

The second thing Sasha would notice about the oversized room was the heat. They'd surely siphoned half of the London power grid for several hours to get it toasty warm for the winter temperatures. Amusingly, the siren shriek for Thomas would occur like clockwork fifteen minutes into the lesson, as Evangeline huffed and puffed her way through Sun Salutations.

'Tomuusss, turn the heating down now, pleeease. Tomuuss!'

Thomas would morph soundlessly into the monstrous room and oblige within fifteen seconds. Sasha often wondered if he sat childlike on the floor in the hallway, waiting patiently for instruction. She also happily noted that at least Evangeline used the word *please.* The British were so frightfully polite, unlike her homeland Californian natives who could be bold and sometimes a little brash.

Sasha had left the sunshine state bound for England a number of years earlier. In the case of push-versus-pull the former had won, by quite a margin. Push was quite a hazy word, though, and ran reasonably close to *fled*. Fled was actually more on the mark as a description. She had definitely fled. Sasha really hoped in London there could be a whole new life for her, because Los Angeles was certainly too small a place. You couldn't hide if you needed to. And that's what she needed: to hide. It wasn't the illegal robbed-a-bank kind of hiding. It was more the *recover-your-ass-whipped-heart* type of concealment. Run from shame.

As it transpired, a new and improved life had been waiting for her in England's great city. But to her credit, she had been very instrumental in it's creation. Her name had likely helped – Sasha Devine. It was catchy. And she'd managed to wrap her yoga branding successfully around it.

Devine Yoga – Divine Life.

Over the years she'd become the go-to yoga instructor for London's rich…and rich. Who did one call when they wanted the best in private yoga instruction? *Sasha Devine,* of course. Her name was trendy and spiritual. And so many people these days seemed to want *spiritual*; they wanted fixing or enlightenment, or the fast track to the great Creator. The world seemed very full of unhappy and materialistically driven people, speeding about aimlessly in empty bodies, separated from any deep sense of meaning. And no class was spared in the great global disconnect from the soul, most especially the wealthy.

So what was more marketable than a *Divine Life?* *Devine* was such a Godly kind of name. Sasha was Californian-cool and capitalizing on that. Years ago, she'd realized that people were oft to be drawn to catchy branding. After all, the human mind blew at times like a fickle breeze. One that tumbled restlessly on the wafting winds of whom you knew, or whom you *could say* you knew. Aspiring to heavenly new heights with an *It-Instructor* was likely a good investment. And as it turned out, Sasha was considered this by a lot of very wealthy people.

Evangeline Thornton was one of them.

Momentarily, Sasha leaned fractionally forward from her cross-legged position on the expensive new cream woolen carpet that *Ballroom* had been covered in last year.

'It used to be Persian,' Evangeline had yabbered to her at her first lesson.

Carpet-dropper. Sasha watched the unkind thought whizz into the universal ether before she could snatch it back.

Mrs T had, in fact, undergone a metaphysical transformation of earthshaking proportions a year earlier. A.K.A...*her husband had an affair*. Natural and New Age were suddenly in vogue, so the Persian had been ruthlessly ripped out. Sheep were in and so was yoga.

'My father went to Indi-aaah when I was a girl,' she once blathered, shrieking the 'aaah' in India as she did.

When Sasha enquired if she'd traveled with him, Mrs T had eyeballed her ferociously and shrilled, 'of course not!'

Sasha had avoided asking any questions since.

Instead, she received a steady stream of inventory on the house: 'My great grandpaahh (paahh with shrieking inflection) brought this back from the first world war; this was from my first trip to Geneva; I found that vase in a beautiful boutique in Beverly Hills – oh, I just love Los Angeles. Don't you just love Los Angeles?'

No I don't, so shut-up and get in Downward Dog.
Sasha never said these things out loud, of course. She'd also give herself a frightfully hard time after these momentary lapses of kindness.

Observing the strong but not overweight body lying in relaxation at the end of the lesson, Evangeline Thornton looked more like a wax statue one might find shoved in the back of a cupboard at Madam Tussaud's. It was her best version of *surrendered*. She never quite seemed to make it all the way there.

Her perfect makeup may have hidden a multitude of sins and chemically supported skin, but there were few clear signs of her true age. Not a scrap of a gray hair on her mature head either, indicating a frequent salon visit – frequent enough to battle the ravages of regrowth. Her blonde tresses were wrapped up tightly as could be in an immaculate top-knot bun. And despite Mrs Thornton's hair being kept long in her quest for immortal youth, it was never to be seen beyond the constant constraint of the binding over her crown. How harshly all the little muscles on the back of her neck were being pulled, Sasha thought.

Evangeline's physique of rock suited her personality. She was one tough cookie and the sole remaining heir to a crisp dynasty fortune. Her granddaddy was the deceased potato king. Although he wasn't the founder of the original chip, he knew a good thing when he tasted one and by the year 1930 he was competing fabulously in the snack industry. He'd had enormous vision. And as a result of that, Mrs T now had a ruddy great mirror hanging in a room that could host a Wimbledon tennis fixture, with a big old house wrapped around the both.

God bless the humble potato.

Sasha was about to bring Evangeline back from her silent reverie - surely a mental to-do Harrods shopping list - when she noticed the Modigliani painting again. It often caught her eye. It was hanging further down *Ballroom* and she felt overwhelmed with a desire to take a closer look at it. She adored art, more so the Impressionists, but here was an original Modigliani.

Modigliani, Sasha sighed. Not too loud, she hoped, as she spent a moment speculating on whether Mrs T genuinely appreciated such a legendary work. Odds were high she barely noticed it - likely only several times a year when the finest silverware was wheeled out of storage and into *Ballroom* for some sumptuous party with the Aioli and Dip family dynasties.

'And gently rolling onto your side...' Sasha said quietly, bringing the session toward a close.

Evangeline dutifully obeyed.

'And...' she continued.

'That was wooonderful, Sa-Shaah.' Mrs Thornton trilled, sitting up abruptly as she did so.

Never ever lets me finish. Never.

'Superb. I feel *sooo* relaxed. Wonderful. Tommuusss,' she said, springing to her feet at haste.

Thomas dutifully appeared again as if he'd just beamed in rapidly from the transporter room on The Enterprise.

'Tom-muusss, please give Sa-shah her payment and prepare my shower, thank you,' she said as she promptly exited *Ballroom* with barely a backward glance.

Prepare my shower?! Sasha squirmed inwardly at the stone-age instruction. Had they not yet joined the twenty-first century?

'Of course, Maam.' Thomas nodded his head again. Actually it was more of a nod-tilt. And still as mystifying as ever. He handed Sasha a cream-colored-something with that *you're so privileged* look again. It was an envelope of exceptional quality embossed with *Lady E. Thornton.* Fortuitously, her ex-husband was a

Lord. He was also now happily and scandalously living with a blonde twenty-five years his junior. Lord Thornton was due to pay a small principality as a divorce settlement to top off her *crisp fortune*. So Evangeline was set for life...and likely several incarnations beyond.

Sasha felt that deep down Mrs T didn't care a jot about the money, despite her pompous disposition. She just wanted back old *Harold F the Third* and probably the status too...not to mention repair of her shameful loss of face. Sasha knew these things because Evangeline used to be a brunette up until four months ago.

Rolling up the two quality yoga mats she'd brought along, she slid them into a special carry bag and zipped it up. Thomas directed her back down the grand hallway, past the flowers and Greek nudist colony to the main entrance door. For a moment it seemed he was actually going to say *goodbye* for the first time in forty-seven visits. But he simply opened the rather wide door in a courteous manner, throwing her his legendary enigmatic look before disappearing back up the passage at a graceful speed, undoubtedly to warm Lady Thornton's shower to the perfect temperature.

As Sasha descended the steps of the elegant residence located opposite Hyde Park, she didn't notice the great expanse of parkland stretched out before her; the trees devoid of foliage. Nor did she pay attention to the people walking determinedly to Knightsbridge Underground Station to catch the tube to work. Instead, she was thinking about Evangeline and realizing the only person Lady Thornton had meticulously applied all that make-up for in the early hours of the morning, was for her - the yoga instructor. Shaking her head sadly in understanding, a cellphone beep announcing a text message was audible from somewhere in her sports bag.

Pausing on the pavement, she removed it from a small side pocket, her face forming a puzzled expression as she considered the unusual message.

Hastily texting a response, Sasha headed in the direction of Hyde Park station to meet her friend.

***

Fiona O'Brien was a Personal Trainer at an exclusive Knightsbridge club. Fortuitously, Sasha had bumped into her best friend directly after teaching a yoga class at the upmarket gym. The *bumping into* had been a literal affair, a moment never forgotten in her vault of fond friendship memories. Fiona's impact was sudden – colliding with her after opening a door. Actually, it was more the glass of water in her hand that had smashed directly into Sasha's chest.

'So sorry!' Fiona lilted in marginally detectable Irish, assessing Sasha's wet shirt momentarily. 'Over here.' she added, guiding Sasha to the water receptacle in the reception area, where she filled another glass and promptly hurled it over her own tight white lycra top and petite exercise-chiseled frame.

Sasha gawped open-mouth in shock at the woman dripping in front of her.

'Well, it's only fair,' Fiona smiled broadly, flashing perfectly white teeth. Her enchanting green eyes gleamed mischievously. 'New yoga instructor, right?'

'Yes, I am. Sasha Devine.'

'That's a holy kind of name. I'm Fiona O'Brien. It's a pleasure to meet you,' she said, extending her hand. At which point, *Sleazy Ian,* the club manager, walked out of his office to see what was going on and blatantly ogled their damp shirts and enhanced looking breasts.

'Wet t-shirt competition?' She winked at Sasha, whose face broke from surprise to a broad beaming grin.

'I have to be somewhere. But I'll see you around,' Fiona added, throwing her a relaxed smile before sauntering sexily past Ian. 'Just meeting the new lady...Sir.' *Sir* rolled off her tongue with a blended strain of *employee* and *sex kitten.* Although, his sexual interest was the last thing Fiona desired.

It was the only thing he desired.

Fiona was one of few staff at the club who could ever get away with a prank like that around Ian. Mostly because she had the audacity to willfully apply her sexuality when she felt like it. She understood her attraction value, and also that the club manager was a pompous sexist ass. But his weakness for women, in particular, Fiona's voluptuous breasts and toned body, kept him well and truly on the back foot. Sasha watched his dark eyes follow the personal instructor's backside and long swinging auburn ponytail all the way out the exit.

Fiona's charming upbeat personality and winning way was infectious and from that moment on their friendship had never looked back. Café catch-ups were a frequent fixture where they downloaded all their client highs and woes, amusing experiences and gossip. Sasha was more accustomed to get-together text messages from her friend that were themed around *Tea.* So she was more than a little curious as to what had inspired the most recent, *Koffee, ma bitch?*

Such a straight-up and mercurial way with words was the kind of rapid-fire wit and charm that had secured Fiona the job at the swanky gym - that or shoving her fine ample breasts in the face of *Sleazy Ian*...which she didn't actually do, but he'd sure daydreamed about it. Having been hired on the spot Fiona had reached the glaring conclusion it had nothing to do with her degree in Exercise Science.

Arriving at their regular coffee spot, Sasha smiled at

the distinguished Italian café owner as she entered 'Basilio's' lavish premises. 'Ciao, Basilio,' she said with a wave of her hand.

Basilio's was their usual gathering place and, as usual, was already dotted with patrons eating breakfast at the classy establishment. The floor was covered with black and white marbled tiles and ornate tables and chairs, and the walls were hung with fine Italian art that made her feel romantically transported to its country of origin. She spied the gorgeous cakes and pastries on display at the counter, along with Basilio's smiling face and twinkling eyes.

'Che piacere vederti, Bellisimo,' he replied, ambling graciously toward her in his very stylish made-to-measure gray suit and greeting her with a kiss on each cheek. In Italian he'd just said something like *how nice to see you, beautiful.* Fiona had told her so on a previous visit, being more the expert on Italian language...and Italian men for that matter.

Hugging her warmly, Basilio guided Sasha to a free table at the front of the café by the window. 'The usual, Bella?'

'Si.'

'E bell'amico?' he added, referring to Fiona joining her.

'Si.'

Basilio smiled brightly. There was wisdom in his kind eyes and sixty-two year old still-handsome face, sporting the ring of a long-term marriage. He shone with the soul of a man who really lived and loved, joyfully and unconditionally. For a moment Sasha felt herself resting in his benevolent energy as she watched him disappear behind the counter.

The gentle tinkle of the doorbell announced the arrival of Fiona as she bounded in like a young exuberant puppy. Bundled up in a hooded pink fluffyon-the-inside coat that extended to her hips, it allowed her trademark tight black exercise pants to reveal a good amount of her exceptionally toned rear. Rising happily to greet her, Sasha embraced Fiona with a warm hug.

'Hey, Sash!'

'Fee. How are you?' she smiled, watching Basilio magically appear once more from behind the counter as she took a seat.

'Frosty cold,' Fiona grimaced. 'I need warming up fast. How do you get a decent cup of coffee around here?'

Basilio beamed at the audible remark as he stepped gracefully toward their table.

'Ciao, Fiona.'

'Ciao, Basilio,' she responded, greeting him with a kiss on each cheek.

'Mama Mia, you are looking as fit as ever, Bella,' he said in the most charming Italian accent. 'The usual?'

'Thank you. Si,' Fiona said, thumping herself into the chair as she watched the elegantly dressed gentleman walk away.

Sasha observed her carefully, noticing the unmistakable glint in Fiona's eye. 'Okay, so what's up with you?'

Fiona's fascination-filled gaze had now shifted to an overweight man eating a cream cake. 'What do you mean?' She replied, wrenching her attention back to Sasha.

'For three years I get nothing but English pleasantries about tea: *Tea and scones*; *Tea, Vicar?*; *Cuppa char* and the like,' Sasha explained. 'But this morning it's as if you woke up in the Bronx. So what's up?'

'I don't know what you mean?' Fiona repeated, denial evident.

'Come on, *Koffee, ma bitch*?' Sasha's brow crinkled

11

visibly. 'Who is he?'

'I have no idea what you're talking about.'

'Of course you do.'

'It's that obvious?'

'No. The condom sticking out of your pocket kind of gives it away.'

'What?!' Fiona looked down, hastily patting the sides of her pink jacket as if putting out a fire.'

'I'm kidding.'

'You ruddy cow.' She playfully swatted Sasha on the shoulder.

'So who is he?'

'I can't hide anything from you, can I.'

'Honestly, I don't think you ever really try, Fee. You're like the world's worst liar. Besides, the after-sex glow on your face is a giveaway.'

'Okay, I'm busted,' she shrugged with a grin. 'I went to a gig after work at our local bar last night and the hot drummer came home with me...again.

'Again?'

Fiona nodded her head sheepishly, with just a hint of pride.

'Yes, we've been hooking up a bit lately. I can't resist. He's drop dead gorgeous - tall, dark…'

'Not a gangster-type by any chance?' Sasha interrupted, winking.

'You're hysterical,' Fiona grinned sheepishly. 'Damn, those drummers are good with their hands, though.'

'Amazing you've been able to keep him a secret this long. What's the drummer's name?'

'Umm…it's…umm...'

'God, do you even know it?!'

'Of course I do, but it's under wraps until it's confirmed we're an item. Don't want to jinx things.'

Sasha's eyes narrowed suspiciously. 'You like him a

lot, don't you?'

'No.' Fiona squirmed, the lie evident. 'Where's Basilio with that coffee? I have a hangover to die for.'

Don't you think it would have been better to confirm you were an item before you slept with him?'

'Maybe,' she shrugged with indifference.

'God.' Sasha pulled a face.

'Don't be a prude. You could do with getting laid, Sash. Besides, I didn't think yoga practitioners were supposed to judge?'

'Well, I try to practice *awareness*.'

'Try?' Fiona wrapped her long immaculately painted red nails on the table. 'Trying is not doing, my friend.'

'Spoken by the queen of *doing*,' Sasha added lightly.

'And damn proud of it. Doing equals success. Success equals money.'

'Really? And who defines what success is?' Sasha replied. 'Isn't that a fairly subjective thing? Do you think someone in a war-torn or drought-stricken part of the world would agree with you? Because I'd imagine their idea of success would simply be having a glass of fresh water a day.' Sasha continued calmly. 'Given that up to eighty percent of the planet's population merely subsist or survive, I'm not sure your theory is held by the majority.'

Fiona slid the glass salt-shaker she'd been toying with in her hand toward the middle of the table, straight into the pepper shaker, creating a clinking sound. 'Touché. You sure know how to keep things real. And sober.' Fiona paused thoughtfully. 'Thank God *my* definition of success and capability includes drive and motivation, though.'

'That's very *manly* of you, Fee.' Sasha winked. 'Have you ever considered another career, like the military?'

Fiona shook her head with a grimace. 'Same boring

clothes every day. No freedom. Not to mention dangerous...there are far too many lush single men in uniform. Even I have my sensible limits.'

Sasha chuckled.

'Actually, I'd suspect the military to be more in alignment with *you*,' Fiona added enigmatically.

'What on earth do you mean?'

'No offence, but aside from your lonely puritanical state, you seem quite bound by rules, don't you – a lot of *dos and don'ts* - especially lately. Not obviously. But I see you assessing stuff in your head, like you have some internalized authority ordering you about.'

Sasha's outbreath made a whistling sound. 'Phew. That's very psychoanalytical, Fee.'

'Amazing what a bit of alcohol does to the noodle,' she winked, tapping her head.

'I guess in some ways you're right,' Sasha replied reflectively. 'I do subscribe to an internal authority. But I prefer to call it *deep inner listening* and that's part of my yoga practice.'

'I call that *uptight.'*

'You can call it what you like,' Sasha glanced down at the table, observing the touch of defensiveness in her own voice. 'It's simply about self-awareness and a practice that supports that.'

'A practice. You mean a few stretches? What people see in taking stretch classes is a great mystery to me. Aside from the fact that it clearly keeps *your* body in shape.'

'It's a lot more than stretches, Fee. And there's a lot more going on with yoga than just keeping your body in shape. There's a whole kind of...philosophy...behind it.'

'A philosophy, huh. Never knew that about yoga. You never said.'

'You never asked.'

Fiona drummed her nails absentmindedly on the table again. 'So not rule-based then?'

'No. The core of true yoga philosophy is really about *eight limbs*.'

'Eight limbs, huh. Like you have an invisible and extra set of arms and legs?' she joked.

Sasha chuckled. 'No, you clown.'

'Okay. So, it's like you're an octopus...or you're secretly like a Marvel super action-hero? Because, you're like that to me...my hero.' Fiona leaned across and playfully rested her head on Sasha's shoulder, astutely lightening the tone of their conversation.

'That's nice, but no. It's an eight-limbed *Path.*'

'Like the yellow brick road?'

'On a more multi-dimensional level...kind of.'

'You're blinding me with science, Sash. So the stretching is just a part of it.'

'Absolutely. The body postures are like *one limb* of the pathway. And technically they're called Asanas.'

'See, that word just disturbs me.' Fiona said, shaking her head.

'Why?'

'Imagine if people went around saying they're off to *Ass-ana practice.* You'd wonder if they were away kissing someone's butt, or doing something equally intimate.'

'Really, Fee.' Sasha rolled her eyes.

'I'm kidding,' she smiled. 'Tell me more about this *path to enlightenment*...which I'm currently blinded from due to excesses of sex and alcohol.'

'If I thought you were genuinely interested...'

'I am.' Fiona interrupted. 'Genuinely. Cross my heart,' she added, drawing the symbol over her chest. 'It's time I left *the dark side* and opened myself to new frontiers. Besides, it's ridiculous that I've known you this long and have no real idea what yoga is about. And

I'm a fitness instructor for crissakes.'

'In fairness, Fee, I have no idea how to use the latest equipment in the weights room. So I think we're even.'

'Yes, but aside from recommending a client to yoga for extra flexibility, I don't really have a clue about it.' Reaching across, Fiona placed her hand on top of Sasha's and leaned in with a serious look, whispering, 'and it's time.' At which point they both broke into laughter.

'Maybe it is. Besides, you might find it helpful.'

Throwing an easy-come easy-go kind of shrug, Fiona responded, 'you never know. Just don't expect to see me doing cartwheels or standing on my head any time soon.'

'I won't hold my breath.'

'You know, in fairness to myself, I do know yoga is about balance – and I guess that's mentally and emotionally, as well as physically.'

'Pretty much,' Sasha replied. 'Yoga is basically dedicated to creating *union* between a person's mind, body and spirit.' She thought hard for a moment. 'It really supports a yoga student to develop themselves as an individualized being, intimately connected with the whole of creation.'

'Ahh…,' Fiona feigned a strained expression, 'could you break that down a fraction more for me? Soften the blow.'

Smiling, Sasha continued. 'It's about creating balance and self-awareness, so you can live in peace, good health and harmony, with the greater whole…with all of life.'

'Bingo. There's the balance.' Fiona's lips curled into an easy grin. 'And so, you have these eight limbs that take you there…like the yellow brick road of yoga?'

'Kind of. It's really a structural framework…a guide.'

Fiona glanced up thoughtfully at the ceiling. 'And

this guide was designed by…don't tell me…God?'

'You're funny, Fee,' Sasha chuckled.

'Just checking.'

'It's in Patanjali's Sutra.'

'Sound's like a dessert or a surgical procedure,' Fiona winked.

Sasha shook her head in mock exasperation. 'Thousands of years ago, the foundations of yoga philosophy - the eight-limbed blueprint - was written down in *The Yoga Sutra* of Patanjali.'

'Begs the question - what's a Sutra?'

'A Sutra is an *observation* that contains a *general truth*. A scientific principle, so-to-speak.'

'Science. Not God then?'

'Perhaps it's both, really.'

'Now you have me curious. Continue, Master,' Fiona said cheekily.

'Okay. So this sacred text describes the inner workings of *the mind*, and provides the eight-limbed pathway for controlling the restlessness of the mind, so you can enjoy lasting peace.'

'Peace, and controlling my darn restless mind …hmm…so I would no longer feel drawn to consuming alcohol to excess, having random sex with strangers and eating all the wrong food?'

'I can't really answer that for you.' Sasha smiled. 'But I believe you would definitely become more self-contented and healthy, though. And that would affect your choices positively.'

'I thought I *was* self-contented.' Fiona said, reflecting for a moment. 'But, I guess needing men and booze is not quite there, is it,' she paused. 'So these eight limbs…are they like a ladder?'

'Not really. No one element or *limb* is elevated over another in a hierarchical order. They're really more like stages. Each is part of a holistic focus, designed to bring a person to completeness as they connect more with *The Divine.'*

'The 'Divine'…being?' Fiona pointed skyward with a cheeky glint in her eyes.

'If you like, yes. God. Source. The Universe. The Divine. Look, from my perspective they're all different names for the same thing.' Sasha reached over and took Fiona's hand, pointing her finger back toward the center of her chest. 'And I think you'll find that here.'

Glancing down, Fiona peered suspiciously at the finger pressed against her. 'Very funny. So what's the *first* limb?'

'The first limb is Yama.'

'Meaning?'

'Universal Morality.'

Fiona's enthusiasm deflated. 'I'm not a big fan of morality, Sash.'

'Well, replace that with *Wise Characteristics* if that's easier.'

'Much. Thank you.'

Sasha paused to consider her words and continued. 'There are *five* Yamas. And rather than a list of *dos and don'ts*, they advise us that our fundamental nature is compassionate, generous, honest and peaceful.'

'Oh, really?' Fiona raised her brow. 'So if I look over at that man eating his third cream cake in a row and my mind says *that fat guy needs to work out*…then I've a bit of work to do on my *Yamas*…except the *honest* bit, of course.'

A feeling of sudden inner discord rattled Sasha's insides. As much as she loved Fiona's sense of humor, there were times she longed to be able to hold a serious conversation for more than a few minutes. 'Something like that. How about we pick this up another time,' she added, closing the subject down.

'I'm just kidding.' Fiona explained. 'I just get all

bent out of shape about people overeating. One cream-cake…maybe. But three in a row? A travesty for the human temple.'

Sasha nodded absentmindedly. Their yoga conversation was clearly over.

'How about we gossip instead? I can't handle any depth this morning.' Fiona watched Sasha suppress a smile. 'Okay, I can't handle any depth at all. Who's your next client?'

'Melody Trenton at nine-thirty.'

'Christ, that vain beanpole.'

'Yes.' Sasha had to admit, her client was vain. No doubt about it. She nodded her head in a slight admission of agreement.

'Social-climbing giraffe. Let's not talk about her this morning,' Fiona paused. 'How about Mrs T's ass?' She said, using the nickname, *Mrs T*, that she'd come up with for Lady Thornton from day one of her being mentioned.

'Mrs T's *ass?*' Sasha looked momentarily confused.

'You really do need a stiff espresso. Tom! Tom-*Ass.*'

Laughter tinkled out of Sasha like cubes of ice landing in a glass. 'He's the same, really.'

'No sweet goodbye again today, then?'

'No, just that unusual nod thing.'

'He's so *frightfully British*.' Fiona said in a plum voice.

'Yes he is. I do feel a bit sorry for Evangeline, though.'

'Sorry? Sorry?! For the bloody potato-chip queen?'

'A little.'

'Why? It's not as if she's been left on the bones of her ass.'

'No, but…'

'Just on Tom's ass.' Fiona giggled.

Sasha ignored the remark.

'Don't tell me I've broken one of the *Yamas*. Why do you feel so sorry for these people? You should have been a personal trainer.'

A flicker of unease swept through Sasha.

'Yoga makes you soft.' Fiona added.

'No.' Sasha's response carried a splattering of defensiveness. 'It can help you think more broadly. And become a more compassionate human being.'

'Nope. It makes you soft. Why do you feel sorry for Lady Thornton?'

'Well, she's been left by the man she loved.'

'Loved? I think it was his money and title she loved.'

'Look, it doesn't matter what she loved about him. She's been left by him and she's sad.'

'How many times do I have to tell you - you have to grow some thicker skin, Sash. Besides, it's not like she's wallowing around and crying on your shoulder, is it. She sounds rude and self-absorbed which is actually closer to the honest truth, and probably why Lord-ruddy-Thornton is now banging some young blonde.'

Sasha held up her hand to signal enough. 'That's not fair.'

Fiona stared her down. 'Do you think Mrs-damn-Thornton would care a jot about *your* heart if it were broken?'

Sasha paused to consider.

'You shouldn't even have to think about that. No! No is the answer to that question.'

'You don't know that, Fee. Stranger things have happened.'

'Well I won't be placing a bet on it.' She softened visibly. 'Not that I ever want to see your heart broken.'

'Sei mai stat il cuore spezzato?' Basilio said, quietly stepping toward them with a coffee in each hand. His brown eyes searched Sasha's with curiosity for a moment before he carefully placed a cup down in front of her.

For a second she was taken aback by the strange knowing look on his face and recoiled slightly. 'What?'

'Cosa, Basilio?' Fiona interjected. 'Cosa? What?'

Basilio placed the second coffee down and smiled softly, patting his chest. 'Spezzato…have you ever had your heart broken, Bella?' His eyes bored a little too knowingly into Sasha's.

'This lady is the heartbreaker, Basilio,' Fiona said lightheartedly. 'Look at her…bellisimo!'

'Si. Such beautiful blue eyes; such a pretty face.' There was tenderness in his voice. 'Mama mia, sono il cuore spezzato.' He clasped both hands dramatically to his chest and held an anguished expression on his face.

Fiona leaned forward, gently pinching both her friend's cheeks. 'Mama Mia, she break-a-my-heart too!'

'Oh, spare me.' Sasha rolled her eyes as they grinned at her.

'Divertitevi…enjoy!' Basilio said, glancing once more at Sasha with kindness in his eyes before turning and moving gracefully back towards the counter.

Sasha realized his question about whether she'd had her heart broken was actually rhetorical. Basilio already seemed to know what the answer was.

'Hey, Miss deep-in-thought.' Fiona interrupted, watching her friend's faraway gaze. 'Where did you just go?'

'Oh…Melody. I was just thinking about her lesson today,' she lied.

'Do you think if you get her to bend enough, she might snap in two…like a twig?' Fiona continued. 'I don't fancy that would do her matching bra 'n' knickers modeling prospects any good…'

But Sasha wasn't really listening. As Fiona's voice drifted further off into the distance, she remembered what heartbreak felt like and recalled a fraction of the chest-ripped-open ache inside her that occurred barely a week before she hastily boarded a plane. And departed California for good.

Chapter Two

There were no walls around the platform. Just a wooden ceiling and the slated floor that Holly was becoming more familiar with as each grueling day drew on. Her back was now infinitely familiar with the hard surface beneath her. In fact, there were probably groove lines embedded in her skin, much like scars after surgery. And some form of surgery it was, too. Not like a gross procedure in a makeshift emergency operating area in some war-torn zone, though - where the Doctor might punch their fist into an artery gushing blood. No. This was more refined: a pre-selected procedure, full of subtle incisions; the psychological repair of her human blueprint, with every deep and extended breath – and by the most masterful physician of all.

The temperature was ruthless. So perhaps it wasn't the smartest thing to do, being here at this time in the year. But there was something quite enticing about a tropical environment. All heat and thunder and lightening. Besides, it wasn't as if great planning had been at play, or that it seemed like a good idea at the time; it was the only idea at the time.

So here she was. Waiting for it. Splayed out like a starfish, head tilted to one side and staring out at the rich green of the foliage beyond the borders of her current self-imposed incarceration. Until it began - the tone that echoed out across the multiple bodies lying similarly prone and silent. There was something almost…holy…about it. But was it actually the sound that was holy? Or was it the vibration it seemed to create as it rippled throughout her body? Maybe it was him. Maybe *The Guru* commanded forth the sacredness via the purity of his evidently very spiritual self. Or maybe it truly was just a sound; just a long-held note that, for some reason, made her feel good.

'Ommm…' There it was again. It traveled steadily across the platform for an extended length of time measuring some fifteen seconds. It was as if tangible particles were being carried on a mystical wind, interacting enticingly with all they touched as if they were some form of vibrational medicine.

Her head rolled back into position, staring at the wood-slated ceiling before her eyelids fluttered shut. She waited for the third sublime chant, as if a needle filled with some sweet drug was about to be injected into her veins.

'Ommm…'

Holly forgot about the thin mat and the firm floor beneath her. And for a number of blissful moments of time, she forgot about where she had come from.

Or where she was headed.

***

At nine fifty-five that morning, Melody Trenton was almost ready for her seventh private yoga lesson. Almost. But not quite. Opening the door to her spacious two-story home, located in the heart of Primrose Hill, she greeted her yoga instructor.

As Sasha watched the door swing open, she was struck once again by Melody's salon-immaculate long dark hair. It fell down to the top of her *perfect butt-crack,* as Fiona succinctly described it. Further blessed by the Gods, she also had flawless olive skin, impeccable white teeth, and nauseatingly stunning cornflower-blue eyes…along with the most *outstanding rack* - as her bosom had been so aptly described by many a man.

The six-foot tall model was deemed sufficiently exotic looking, spectacular and flawlessly proportioned, by her agency - and the rest of the world who cared about such things - to become a top lingerie model. Something Melody herself was less than contented with at the ripe age of twenty-four. *I have to diversify before I get too old,* she'd declared on several occasions.

'Sasha…you're very early,' she said coolly. Her teeth were blinding as she stood at her opened door posing catalogue-like in the most trendy pink yoga ensemble purchasable, with her tanned body looking positively *Amazonian.*

Sasha checked her watch. 'Not really. Just by a minute.'

'Come in,' Melody gestured. 'I'm just blending a quick smoothie for breakfast.'

And lunch, you rake. Sasha thought. 'That's fine.' *But darn stupid right before a yoga lesson.*

Trailing after the pink stick insect, she followed her toward the kitchen which extended off an open-plan living area that was entirely black and white in style and screamed *boring-ass unimaginative.* Unsurprisingly, these were also Fiona's descriptive words.

The room also contained a grand piano that took up far too much space and which the glamor-puss didn't have the first clue how to play.

'I just did a shoot yesterday.' Melody said, shrugging

her shoulders as though that explained why she was making a smoothie three minutes before she was due to start her lesson.

Nodding her head in acknowledgment, Sasha watched the younger woman pour several scoops of white powder into the blender and add apple juice and various green powders. She had to admit, the concoction looked healthy.

Ripping a handful of leaves off a bunch of spinach that rested wilting on the counter, Melody stuffed them into the blender and threw in raw broccoli for good measure.

'Was it a late-night?' Sasha watched in quiet horror as a large amount of dark chocolate sauce was then squeezed out of a plastic bottle into the mix.

'No.' Melody shrugged her shoulders indifferently again, annoyingly for the second time, sniffing and pressing the back of a finger under her nose - disturbingly as if she'd just snorted cocaine. 'It was great,' she added without elaborating.

Flicking the blender switch on, a loud noise erupted, mulching the mixture until it was a thick murky brown liquid. The machine ground to a halt filling the air momentarily with silence. Melody filled a large glass with the goop then sat the blender jug in the sink without bothering to rinse it. Likely some poor cleaner would later spend an hour, irritated as hell, chipping dried green-brown crap off the glass.

'You gotta alkalize.' Melody exclaimed, lifting the glass in a *cheers* gesture before drinking.

'Sure.' *And now I'll need an oxygen mask to get through your yoga lesson,* Sasha thought.

Gulping a few large mouthful's, Melody sat the half full glass back down on the breakfast bar and stared at Sasha glassy-eyed. 'You know, have you ever considered modeling?'

Sasha felt aghast. It was as if particles of Melody's vanity had just blown off her body and stuck to her like blood-sucking little insects. 'No, I haven't,' she responded, fighting the agitation that had just begun to rummage through her body.

'Oh, because you're quite pretty.'

'Thank you.' She searched the floor awkwardly for some sign of comfort.

'That long honey-blonde hair...' she continued, the locust-like swarm bombarding Sasha's sensitive receptors as Melody eyed her neatly tied ponytail hanging mid length down her back. 'And you're tall with good bone structure. How tall are you?' She checked her up and down as if assessing her height and physique in an expert manner.

'I'm five-foot nine.' Sasha replied, her discomfort increasing rapidly under the steady bulbous-blue gaze.

'Oh.' Melody shrugged indifferently for the second time. 'And how are old are you?' It was a sort of smirk-smile on her perfectly formed face.

Thankfully, Sasha's cellphone began vibrating from her sports bag pocket at precisely that moment, causing the imaginary carnivorous insects to fall instantly from her body and hit the floor like thousands of tiny dried leaves in autumn. 'I'm sorry. I thought I'd switched that off. Do you mind if I take this while you...finish your smoothie.' Reaching into her bag she threw Melody her secret *I hope-a-bird-craps-on-your-head-today* smile. It was her best version of vengeful. Reserved for the chosen extra-irksome few.

'Oh. Of course,' she beamed back superficially; flicking a pointed glance down at the jeweled watch on her wrist to indicate her time was now being wasted.

Sasha lost no time in gaining physical distance from Melody. Pacing hastily toward the center of the living room she announced her name to the caller and listened to the unfamiliar voice.

'Uh-huh,' she replied in her casual Californian accent, glancing back at Melody who had seated herself at the breakfast bar whilst hoovering the remains of her goop. The glass was now positioned vertically above her mouth but the remaining contents were glued to the side refusing to slither out.

'Well, yes, I do have one early morning weekly appointment available.' She listened to the caller's decisive manly reply. 'I'm sorry, no. But I do have one evening currently available also.' Sasha regarded Melody uneasily, observing her pat the base of the gunked glass and give up on the remaining slime as she placed the smoothie glass back near the kitchen sink – unwashed - adding to the cleaners *pain-in-the-ass* list. She then proceeded to inspect her long and perfectly manicured nails.

'Uh-huh. I see.' Sasha paused. 'Yes, six-o-clock would work. Thursday morning,' she listened to the caller's response. 'Yes, that will be fine. Look, I'm currently with a client. I can call you back, or you could text me your address details, please.' She paused again. 'Great. I'll confirm all of that when I receive them.' Another pause. 'Uh-huh. Thank you, Mr Huntington. I'll see you then.' Sasha disconnected the call and spun to face Melody who was no longer examining her nails. She was watching Sasha walk back to the kitchen as if she were suddenly the most interesting person on the planet.

'Mr Huntington?' Melody's voice had become rather high-pitched and loaded with snoopy intrusiveness.

'Uh-huh.' Sasha replied with finality, returning her phone to its pocket and removing the yoga mats from their special bag.

'Which Huntington would that be?'

Sasha kicked herself inwardly. It was a blunder of

large proportions to reveal a client name. 'That would be my *client-confidential* Mr Huntington,' she replied quietly. Avoiding eye-contact, she took the mats to the center of the living room, unrolling each of them with a simple flick.'

'Well its not very confidential if you take the call in my living room in front of me, is it?' Melody responded in a bitchy voice.

'I wasn't aware you were listening. I'm sorry.'

'Well, you might be sorry. Although, that depends on which Mr Huntington you were speaking with,' she smirked, as if considering herself one of the cleverest people within a fifty-mile radius. 'It wasn't Lucas by any chance, was it?'

'Out of the thousands of Huntington possibilities?' Sasha threw her a small smile. 'That would be truly remarkable. Let's begin your yoga session.' She motioned Melody to relocate to the yoga mat.

'Oh, so it was Lucas.' She persisted in a snooty voice, exiting the kitchen area and moving toward her as fixated as a cat toying with a mouse.

'No. No, it was not Lucas Huntington…whoever that is,' Sasha added promptly. 'And now that it's past ten we really must be moving along with your yoga practice.'

'Oh.' Melody looked disappointed. And then annoyed. 'Well, we could have started on time if you hadn't taken that call.'

Okay - now I really hope a bird craps on your head. 'Look, I'm sorry about that. I'll extend the session accordingly.' *Despite having had to stand there and watch you make that ruddy putrid smoothie.*

Observing the pout form on Melody's million dollar lips as she lay down on the mat, Sasha felt sudden relief to be sitting cross-legged on the floor. But it wasn't because she had eventually silenced her less-than model client. Exhaling long and slow, relaxation finally seeped through her body. *How many Huntington's could it have been?*

Melody had not been quite so silly on this occasion. And Sasha felt the kind of inner discord that inevitably arose when she lied.

***

The first time the phone rang she didn't hear it. Fiona was finishing up with a private client at the club and her cellphone was stuffed in her sports bag in the changing room locker. The second time it rang she was enroute to the locker but detained by *Sleazy Ian*. Actually, it was more *cornered* than detained…or rather, *bench-pressed*. She made the monumental mistake of ducking in behind reception to help cover the desk for a few minutes, whilst Steph, the receptionist, shot off for a cigarette.

It was mid-morning-quiet and Ian must have noticed the scene through a crack in the blinds of his office window. He made his move as silent and swift as a ninja, creeping in strategically behind her. So when Fiona unfortunately relaxed into a bent position at the reception desk, she backed herself right up against him.

'Christ!' she said with a fright, spinning around at haste. Normally the fastest mouth in the west, she was now speechless - except for the second shocked 'Christ!!' that fired out of her mouth when she realized she'd just reversed onto his hardened anatomy.

In any other instance she could have laughed at the irony. *'Christ'* was another secret nickname for *Sleazy Ian* because his family name happened to be 'Christoph'. And despite him being reasonably good-looking (the Club had an unwritten *shallow policy* and never hired anyone who wasn't), his personality was so ugly it made his looks pale to insignificance. He was sexually slimy, despite most of the staff considering him relatively harmless.

Fiona and Sasha had quietly shortened his surname over a bottle of wine one night when Sasha decided *Christ* was a more fitting title for him: certainly not in the religious sense. It was more the type of blasphemous Christ one might express when having their finger jammed very hard in a cupboard door and experiencing the kind of pain that made you writhe. They also figured it was an excellent play on words because Christ suited his apparent belief about himself. 'Sleazy Ian...Christ, that's bloody perfect!' Fiona had laughed uproariously at the time.

She wasn't laughing now, though. No. She wasn't laughing at all. She was thinking as fast as humanly possible as he planted his hands firmly on the desk either side of her. She could see desire in his dark brown eyes – eyes that were now only a few inches from her own. And with his body pressed very close to her, particularly his noticeably erect penis jutting from his dress trousers, it was difficult to move.

God, I'm impaled.

'Shouldn't you be with a client, Fiona.' He drawled her name as if he'd just lathered whipped cream onto her chest with a view to licking it off.

'Steph needed a...pee break,' she blurted out, thinking fast on her feet. Ian hated staff smoking. She stalled for time. *Think, woman. Think!*

'A pee break?'

'Yes, a pee break!' she repeated, beginning to feel very annoyed and retrieving some personal power in the process.

'Well she should have asked me,' he said, attempting to breathe seductively onto her neck.

Christ!!

Fiona began to wriggle out of his grasp. 'She should

ask you for a raise while she's at it,' she added, sidling to the right, wriggling some more and grazing past his erection, to freedom.

'Oh?' he said, distracted and looking miffed she'd just escaped the closest physical proximity he'd ever reached with her.

'Yes. You seem to give those out readily.' She glanced down at his protrusion, maintaining her poise before flicking her long ponytail in the direction of his head and striding off.

Storming into the changing room Fiona ripped her sports bag out of the locker and slammed the door shut.

Unbelievable!

Unzipping the side-pocket, she yanked out her phone, noticing two missed calls from her friend. Sitting down heavily on a bench in the empty changing room, she rang Sasha straight back, popping the phone onto speaker so she could change her clothes as they chatted.

'Fee?'

'Where are you?'

'I'm driving. Hold on a second...' A faint scrunching sound could be heard in the background. 'Okay, hands-free sorted. What's up?'

'Christ is what's up!!'

'What?'

'Christ! Bloody *Sleazy Ian*!'

'Has he been living up to his name again?'

'He's a slime bag!' Fiona angrily ripped off her sports top, located her bra and flung it on.

'Doesn't sound like you, getting upset, Fee? I thought you found him quite harmless and could brush that stuff off.'

'Well, it's not so easy this time,' she said, securing the clasp on her bra.

'What happened?'

'He cornered me behind reception and shoved his

bloody great pole into me!'

'What?'

'He stood behind me without me knowing...and the next thing I'm near skewered by his goddamned erection!'

'You're kidding me?!'

'No, I'm not.' Fiona grabbed a t-shirt from the bottom of her bag and hastily threw it on.

'That's appalling. He's gone way too far this time.'

'Well, his penis did, I can tell you that.'

A small giggle burst unexpectedly out of Sasha.

'I'm not finding this funny at the moment, Sash.'

'Of course not.' She recovered herself to a suitably serious state. 'I'm sorry. It's terrible.'

'It's huge is what it is. He's hung like a horse,' she said with a blend of disgust and horrified fascination.

Sasha was forcing herself not to laugh as Fiona suddenly became aware of a shuffling sound in the locker room. 'Sash,' she whispered, spinning around to check the changing area and noticing one of the toilet doors was closed. *Bugger.*

'Fee? Fee, what's happening?'

Leaning down toward the bench, she whispered into the handset. 'Someone's in here,'

'What?'

'Someone's...bloody...in here.' Fiona stood bent-over and frozen with her ears pricked on high alert. She could hear Sasha's concerned voice in the background.

'Ahem.' The mystery person made a *clearing-my-throat-so-you-know-I'm-here* sound from behind the door.

'Christ!' she whispered into the phone.

'What?!' Is he in there?! Fiona, get out. Get out now!'

'Shhh,' Fiona whispered back into the phone.

'Ahem.' More clearing of the throat – possible

interpretation being *I just overheard you talk about a large penis.*

Shuffling sounds ensued before the toilet flushed and a gentle click of the door could be heard. Fiona stood transfixed, watching as an arm and a leg first appeared; then a face.

Oh, God.

'Hi Fiona.'

Diana Smithwood?! It was the client she'd just finished her personal training session with. Diana was editor for a popular woman's magazine. A well-groomed lady in her early fifties - very respectable and definitely not someone Fiona would ever want to be overheard by talking like she just had.

Diana smiled politely and somewhat apologetically at her. 'I'll just...' she paused, looking uncomfortable '...wash my hands,' she added, wandering past Fiona, still frozen in the center of the changing room.

Sasha's voice interjected on speaker in the background. 'Fee, are you ok? Christ!...what a pervert!'

Diana finished washing and drying her hands, peering occasionally at Fiona via the mirror with an embarrassed *wish-I'd-never-heard-any-of-that* look on her face. 'Well...' She finally spun around, pausing uncomfortably again and glancing at Fiona's t-shirt, 'I'll see you at our next session. Have a...good day.'

There was a half-smile forming on her face that Fiona couldn't decipher. Maybe it meant she *wouldn't* see her at their next session; that Diana was actually going to cancel her private lessons and write a damning magazine article about her being a Personal Trainer *Whore.*

Fiona looked down at her t-shirt, noticing it boldly stated the word 'Naughty' above a picture of a cat.

Fuck.

'What's happening, Fee? Fee?! Talk to me!' Sasha's

voice cut through the now silent room.

Fiona sighed heavily. 'It's okay, Sash. I'm now just officially London's greatest gym slut.'

'What?! Why? Who was that?'

'My client,' she said in a flat voice.

'Which one?'

'Diana Smithwood.'

'Diana Smithwood…the magazine lady?'

'Yes, editor of *City Woman* magazine,' Fiona said, slowly emphasizing *City* and *Woman.*

'Oh.' Sasha paused, now a little worried. 'Really.'

'Yes. Really.'

A long moment passed in silence. 'Well, it isn't so bad, Fee.'

'You think?'

'Umm…look, it could have been the editor of a religious magazine. And can you imagine what they'd be thinking right now?'

'Ahhh…that the bible story needs rewriting?' Fiona said with sarcasm.

A spontaneous chuckle erupted from Sasha.

'And I'm wearing that damn pink t-shirt you gave me.'

'No! Not the *Naughty Pussy* one?! Sasha's sides were almost bursting from holding back the laughter. 'Oh my God! I told you never to wear that in public,' she exclaimed, beginning to giggle.

'Oh yes, laugh away.' Fiona said drily. 'Not only do I have a naughty pussy, but apparently God's beloved Son wants a crack at it.'

Sasha could barely speak she was laughing so hard. 'I have to pull the car over. I can't drive.'

Tears rolled down her face. 'I can't believe you wore that t-shirt. I gave it to you as a joke.'

'I wasn't planning on wearing it in public, okay. I got excessively drunk last night, had mind-scrambling sex and grabbed the first item of clothing from my drawer this morning without looking.' Fiona began to smile at last. 'I'll tell you this, Sash, I can handle Sleazy Ian, but being seen in this ruddy t-shirt by the editor of City-bloody-Woman's magazine, whilst talking about a cock…well frankly, I think that's irreparable.'

'Somehow I doubt it, Fee.'

'Do you? All the same, I'm going to church this Sunday.'

Sasha could not stop laughing all the way home.

Chapter Three

Ten o'clock on Wednesday morning was one of Sasha's favorite private client appointments of the week. In terms of London travel it was a relatively short drive for her to the Buckley's gorgeous home in West Hampstead.

Jumping happily into her black VW Golf she drove north-west, away from her Camden apartment and directly up Haverstock Hill. Although the air was still very chilly outside, it was sunny and Sasha was in particularly good spirits.

Turning left onto Lyndhurst Road she reflected briefly on the previous day's lesson with Melody Trenton. The model had been rather nosy and really quite intrusive about the phone call from her prospective client, Lucas Huntington. Sasha could have kicked herself – how often did she ever take a call in front of another client. Never. Never except yesterday. She prided herself on client confidentiality. It was critical with the type of people she taught. And she could blame Melody and her algae-slime breakfast drink as much as she liked, but the simple fact remained it was a lack of good judgment on her part to have taken the call at that time. Not to mention a lapse in professionalism…and in front of her most nosy and information-retentive client.

Retentive until that smoothie passes through her.

Melody's prying had certainly made Sasha feel more curious about Lucas Huntington. After the lesson she'd driven back to her apartment like a possessed woman and promptly did what she always did.

Napped.

Later she pulled out her laptop from its secret hiding place in a drawer underneath her jumpers. *Who would ever look there? If some vagrant man tries to rob me he'll get distracted snooping in my knickers drawer first.* It was for this reason she always put her nicest panties at the top of the pile. *He'll never make it to the jumpers.* Having come to be more suspicious in life, it was not uncommon for her active imagination to think of odd scenarios such as this.

With the laptop recovered and powered up, she typed the name Lucas Huntington into the search bar and hit enter. *Bingo.* His profile appeared on the first page, listed under a modeling agency site. *Must be him.*

Clicking onto the website and scrolling down the page, a picture of the man's washboard abs came into view. Saliva particles formed uncontrollably in Sasha's mouth. *Phewee.* Leaning closer to the laptop screen she sucked in air at the sight of his six-pack. Visions of convenient yoga position adjustments formed rapidly in her mind. *Downward Dog...rotate hips back...grasp inside thigh. Grope butt.*

Sasha shook her head in dismay at herself. Her hormones were getting out of check lately and her thoughts were beginning to trail along closely behind them.

A car horn tooted loudly, jolting her brusquely from more pleasant thoughts. Daydreaming had kept her vehicle immobile at a green light. She was seriously beginning to suck at the sensory control required for the Yama, Brahmacharya.

Darn those Yamas, she sighed. Perhaps it was time

she hit her spiritual books again to redirect her wayward mind back to higher thoughts?

Planting her foot on the accelerator, tires smoked as the car launched back to life at speed and screeched around the corner.

It could not have been the same Lucas Huntington that Melody was so intrigued by. He'd sounded like a more mature adult man on the phone – not some shagable twenty-one year-old sex God. In fact, the man she'd spoken to had sounded serious. Disappointingly, she would have to steel herself for teaching someone who probably had the effect of watching paint dry, not Mr Glamor-Boy from the Internet photos.

A smile creased her lightly tanned face once more as she turned onto leafy Frognal Lane. Pulling her Golf in carefully by the curbside, she parked in front of a property hidden entirely from roadside view by a tall fence and long-established trees.

Exiting the vehicle with her yoga mat bag bundled safely under her arm and slinging her sports bag over her shoulder, Sasha made her way to the front gate and pressed a button on the intercom.

Within seconds, a woman's voice crackled through the speaker. 'Sasha? Is that you?'

'Yes, Amy.'

'Wonderful, darling. Come on in.'

The intercom buzzed and Sasha watched the gate swing slowly open, revealing an impressive front lawn. It was immaculately mowed and surrounded by landscaped garden, only too fitting for the splendid sand-colored brick two-story mansion that stood before her.

Pausing on the pathway, Sasha admired one of her favorite London views. It was a scene she never tired of. Perhaps it was because she knew the interior of the magnificent family home was so filled with love.

Amy Buckley was deserving of much of the credit for this. She was as beautiful, nurturing and feminine, as a woman could be. Sasha always felt so good in her presence.

Amy had been a florist in her former single life, until she met Ben. He'd popped into her shop in Hampstead one day to collect some flowers for his sick mother and been smitten from the moment she first graced him with her sweet smile. For months he found many excuses to buy flowers from her until he eventually plucked up the courage to ask her on a date. It was the first of many. And many became marriage.

Ben was probably the best looking and nicest computer geek Sasha had ever met. He owned his own computer software company that specialized in avionics. She didn't understand entirely what that meant, but gathered that Ben was financially successful and also extremely clever. He must have been – he was smart enough to pursue Amy's beautiful heart.

Sasha had only met her husband once before, when there had been a bomb scare one morning in Central London near his company office. Naturally, Ben left the city immediately and headed straight home. He'd crept quietly into the conservatory where Sasha was instructing Amy who was, at-the-time, on her back in Fish pose and oblivious to her husband's presence in the room. Placing a finger over his lips to indicate Sasha shouldn't say a word he completely surprised his lovely wife by pouncing on her and showering her with kisses and hugs. Sasha often recalled the moment. She'd never seen a couple more in love and was deeply touched by Ben's unabashed display of affection for his wife.

They had children too – Thomas, now seven, and Emily...a very cute curly-blonde-haired four year old. Both were the cherub variety. However, Sasha seldom crossed paths with the kids. They were usually at school, or a nanny would look after them so Amy could have her yoga session in uninterrupted peace. But it was evident she wouldn't have minded a jot if the children barged in on her lesson. They never did. The entire family seemed to operate in some mysterious synchronistic harmony, the engine room of which was Amy's large and angelic heart.

'Sasha, darling,' Amy exclaimed warmly, opening the door and greeting her with a long-lost-friend kind of hug. She could have metamorphosed out of a magical garden with her looks – slim and petite, elfin-shaped face and features, and even a short crop of hair that revealed her perfect pixie-like ears. But it was Amy's magnificent smile and enchanting green eyes had apparently bewitched Ben the most.

No wonder she was a florist. Her bouquets were probably sprinkled with fairy dust, too.

'Lovely to see you, Amy.' Sasha welcomed the warm hug, returning it in kind.

'I'm all ready for you. And the room is nicely heated.'

'Perfect.'

'I know I say it every week, but I *so* look forward to my yoga lesson with you.' Amy said, closing the door and floating gracefully through the tasteful Reception area, wearing flared and silky lilac yoga pants with a fitted lime-green top and looking something like *Twiggy does India*. She rocked the outfit.

Sasha glanced up at the chandelier in the lobby above her. It had a slightly pink hue and matched the dusky pink sky in a large painting that hung on the wall to her left. She doubted the color coordination was a coincidence. Nor were the spectacular seasonal flowers in the crystal vase on the hallstand to her right - dark-headed red roses, pink germinis and cream lisanthus, with burgundy oak leaf as the finishing touch - all impeccably arranged by Amy.

She still owned her floral business. Ben had bought the building outright after they married so it would always be there for her. Now staff ran the shop, but she still popped in several times a week, mostly just to reconnect with her beloved flowers and her deep need for creativity.

As they turned left down a hallway and wandered through a large living area, Amy led them toward a gorgeous conservatory style room at the back of the house. The ceiling and exterior wall were mostly glass, allowing a flood of light in. The room looked out onto a large brick patio that contained, among other things, large potted tubs overflowing with lovingly grown herbs of every description.

'Isn't that sunshine glorious, Sasha.' Amy drew to a halt in the center of the room where the rays of light could land on her.

'Yes, it's a perfect morning.'

'It's so lovely at this time of year to see such blue skies.'

'It is wonderful.' Sasha replied, beginning to remove the yoga mats from their bag. 'And it sure beats the early morning rising at five in the cold and dark.'

'Gosh, that must be tough, Sasha. I've barely risen at five in the morning since I was a florist, except for one of my babies. God knows that's a challenge. And I don't even have to leave the house!' She smiled brightly.

'You get used to it. Actually, I like the early morning starts. It's more…peaceful.' Sasha flicked one of the mats, rolling it out onto the lush taupe-colored carpet and crouching down to adjust its angle.

'I bet it's not pitch black in California at that time.'

'Well, not quite as much, but I can hardly recall.'

'Don't you miss it?'

'What?' Sasha didn't look up.

'Home? Don't you miss home?' Amy sat down in a white wicker chair, crossing her legs and tucking her chin into the palm of her hand, peering at her thoughtfully.

'Sometimes.' Sasha glanced up, hesitating for a second. 'But…I like it here.' Her hand fumbled into the bag to retrieve the second mat.

'Is there someone special for you here? A nice man?'

Standing up, Sasha flicked the second mat, rolling it perpendicular to the other and avoiding eye contact. 'No.' She finally looked up at Amy and half-smiled. 'I don't really have the time.'

'I understand.'

'You do?' Sasha looked at her with surprise.

'Of course. Before I started dating Ben I was all about my floral business. Nothing else mattered. And I didn't have the time either…or so I thought.'

'What do you mean?'

'Well, looking back I can see more clearly that I was just…' She paused, looking wistfully off into the distance.

'You were what?' Sasha turned fully to face her.

'I was…afraid.' Amy hesitated. 'I wanted to believe in this perfect man for me, but deep down I didn't entirely have faith in that at all. I didn't believe.'

'Really? I find that hard to imagine. You seem so…optimistic.'

'Ben really brought that out in me.'

'Oh?'

'I wasn't a pessimist, though. I was just happy in my own little world…with my flowers.' She lifted her head out of her chin. 'And then Santa fell straight down my chimney. Only, I couldn't see it to begin with.'

'You couldn't?' Sasha replied with curiosity.

'Well, lots of men came into my shop to get flowers. It was a blur of them. So I didn't even notice Ben to begin with. But then he just kept coming in. For a while I actually thought he was quite obsessed with his mother, buying her all those flowers,' she chuckled. 'Although, as it turned out he was quite obsessed…with me.'

Sasha could have sworn Amy blushed a little. She was the sweetest person she'd ever known. 'And what a wonderful thing that turned out to be.'

'It certainly did.' Amy rose gracefully from the chair. 'I fall more in love with Ben every day, which almost seems impossible, but it's true.' She looked over at Sasha. 'I hope you have a beautiful love like mine some day.'

'I'm not sure everyone is quite as lucky as you.'

Amy's face creased into a troubled frown as she walked toward the mats, her green eyes blazing. 'Well I wish they were. You must never give up on love,' she said, lying down on her back and positioning herself in Savasana.

Sasha felt a wave of sadness pass through her and for a moment felt deeply uncomfortable. It was possible she already had.

***

'Sasha!'

'What is it, Fee?' she said, answering her cellphone as she pulled into the Knightsbridge club car park later that day to teach her five-thirty yoga class.

'You're not going to believe this, but Ian has hired a new trainer.'

'I didn't think another personal trainer was needed at the club?'

'He specializes in weights.'

'Oh. Well, that's good. No competition for you there.'

'I guess not. Although I strongly suspect a lot more women are going to start taking up weights.'

'He kept that a secret. I wasn't aware they were looking for a new staff member?'

'I wasn't either. But you know Christ.'

'Yes, he's a universal mystery.'

Fiona chuckled. 'Sure is one who likes the element of surprise. You know, he's truly blessed us this time.'

'Really? How so?'

'Think - Hollywood Hot meets Sports Pro...but Brazilian.'

'What?'

'Sizzling, my friend. Very very cute.'

'Cute man?' Sasha repeated, a little distracted as she opened the vehicle door.

'Are you on drugs or something, Sash? What else would I mean?!'

'I'm not sure. That a meteor just hit the club?' She smiled, collecting her sports bag from the passenger seat and exiting the car.

'You're very close to the mark. He's flaming gorgeous, with a burning toosh. So stick your head into the weights room and you might spot him.'

'Does this mean the drummer's days are numbered?'

'No way. My drummer rocks. Actually, I was thinking Rodrigo looks more like a bit of you.'

'Oh...Rodrigo, huh. You don't seem to have a problem remembering Mr Brazil's name.'

'Honey, you won't either when you clap eyes on him.'

'We'll see. I'm surprised Christ installed a good-looking guy, though. I would have thought he'd prefer a new woman to rub up his ego - not some male competition to deflate it.'

'Yes, I thought about that too, Sash. But he's clever, our Christ. I'm betting he's thinking more women will flock to join the club when they hear about Rodrigo.'

'Flock?' Sasha said, arriving at the club entrance and pushing on the door.

'Go and check him out!'

'I think you've hyped him up too much and I'll be disappointed. Anyway, I don't have time to go snooping about in the weights area.' She looked over at reception, noticing it was the usual peak-time busy with lots of people milling about. 'I'm here to teach my class. And besides, you know the club rules.'

'What - no personal involvements with members or other staff?'

'Exactly.'

'So do you think I should have reminded *Sleazy Ian* of that when he was rubbing his penis up against me? I mean, that's reasonably intimate, wouldn't you say?'

Sasha giggled at the sarcasm in Fiona's voice. 'It is. But I seriously don't think Christ is capable of any relationship that could be considered a deep personal involvement.'

As Sasha made her way past the busy reception area toward the locker room, a female club member frowned disapprovingly at hearing her words.

'That's for sure. But he certainly could make some woman very happy with the size of his almighty appendage.'

'That's *not* the kind of image I want in my mind before I teach my class.'

'Well it could help your Downward Dog positioning,' she guffawed. 'Hey, are you still on for a drink Friday evening?'

'Yes, sure.'

'Okay, great. Our usual bar. And good luck with your class.'

'Thanks.' Sasha was about to end the call as she reached the locker room door, but then remembered something. 'Hey, Fee.'

'Yep. Still here.'

'You don't happen to know of a Lucas Huntington by any chance?' She pushed on the door and entered the locker room where there were a few women in various stages of changing.

'The hot young model?'

'Yes he is hot. But not him. I'm thinking it must be a different one.'

'I can't think of another notable Lucas Huntington at the moment. Why?'

Placing her bag down on a bench, Sasha opened one of the lockers. 'He's a new client. I'm seeing him first thing in the morning.' She lowered her voice.

'I've got no idea, other than the hottie model, sorry Sash. But I can dig around a bit if you like?'

'Thank you, but no. It's fine. I'll meet him in the morning,' she said, shoving her sports bag into the locker and securing the door.

'Why so curious?'

'Oh, it's a long story, but Melody Trenton overheard me on a call with him and she really perked up at his name.'

'Nosy bitch.'

'A touch.'

'Well she probably thought you were talking to the sexy model guy.'

'Maybe. But for some reason I didn't get that feeling at all.' Sasha exited the locker room, observing the members milling about in the reception area.

'Whoever he is, he must have bags of money or status for that Trenton leech to know him.'

Peering through the group of exercise devotees, the broad back of a tall man in one of the club's staff uniforms caught Sasha's attention.

'No,' she said distractedly, tracking *broad back man*

with her eyes. 'The distinct impression I got was that she *wants* to know him.'

'Well sadly for her, she's not the one who will be staring at his crotch at six in the morning now, is she.'

Sasha didn't respond. She was still absent-mindedly watching the rear of the man in the staff uniform. He moved toward the entrance and exited out the door without a backward glance.

'Sash?'

'Uh-huh?'

'Where did you just go?'

'Oh,' Sasha said with surprise. 'Oh!' She exclaimed with the realization. 'I think I just saw Rodrigo.'

'You think? Trust me, honey, you'd know if you saw him.'

'Well it was just his back.'

'That's a shame!'

'It's okay.' Sasha headed into the yoga room where men and women were beginning to assemble for her class. 'I'll see him another time.'

'And when you do,' Fiona added mischievously, 'trust me, you'll be hooked!'

Chapter Four

'In every situation, we should endeavor to adopt a considerate attitude and do no harm; to be non-violent. This is the first Yama – Ahimsa,' the Guru was explaining.

In actual fact, he wasn't really called 'The Guru.' But Holly and several other yoga students had coined the phrase after a few days at the retreat. The man had a mysterious *something* about him. Maybe it was all those years of meditation and yoga practice, but whenever his gaze happened to light upon her, she felt disturbingly known - right through to her very core. This bothered her because she had the sneaking suspicion she didn't know herself that well. And recent events would imply she didn't know herself at all. So it didn't seem fair that someone could look into her eyes and apparently deeply understand her. It didn't seem fair at all.

It wasn't as if he was sinister in any way. It was quite the exact opposite. The Guru exuded a warm and benevolent nature. And he was clearly very wise. Yet on occasion, when he laughed, it was as if a veil were drawn back upon him, revealing the simplicity of a five-year-old child and leaving her to view him as a great contradiction.

'Harm can be done through actions, but also through thoughts,' he added.

Darn. He'd just looked at her. Not only that, he held eye contact with her for several seconds. That wasn't good.

'Ahimsa is practiced through acts of kindness and thoughtful consideration to other people, and your own self...' A chuckle bubbled out of his mouth, revealing that sweet inner child again as if it were a jewel on display.

Holly was never sure whether to feel impressed or embarrassed in these moments. If she thought about where she'd come from, the later was probably the best option. But as the days at the retreat rolled slowly by she felt curiously charmed whenever the giggling youngster appeared.

'...by deed, and also in your mind,' the Guru finished.

At least, she hoped he was finished. Holly shifted uncomfortably in her seat.

He was staring at her again.

***

Leaning forward, Sasha adjusted the heating in the car to full whilst keeping her eyes fixed on the showery road ahead. It was five-forty in the morning - cold, raining, and her hair was damp from sprinting to the vehicle from her flat via a puddle or two. This had subsequently left the slightly flared bottoms of her fitted black yoga pants wet. Frowning, she felt the sodden ends now coolly grazing her ankles.

She was heading north-west for the second time in as many days. However, this time, the direction was towards Belsize Park and the home of Lucas

Huntington.

The night before, she'd surfed the Internet once more in the vain hope of finding out some information about her new client. But she was detained, yet again, looking at pictures of Lucas the sex-God-model.

You had me at Huntington, she smiled, looking dreamily at his tanned six-pack.

Maybe Melody *had* been referring to him - he *was* a model colleague of hers, after all. So it was logical. But the younger woman had also carried a steely kind of look in her eyes that screamed *Aspiring* when the name 'Lucas Huntington' was mentioned. Sasha considered that a twenty-one year old younger male version of Melody, who was not even half as successful, was unlikely to have made the model's eyes pop out of her head quite the way they had. Having mulled it over, she concluded that the man in Melody's mind must have been someone who was a little outside of her current social orbit and league. It would have to be someone that would benefit her career, reputation and social standing, in some way. It had only taken a single yoga lesson with the woman to work out the way she ticked. Or rather, had taken one minute of meeting her: Melody had excitedly announced upon opening her door how wonderful it was to be taught by the '*It* Yoga Instructor.'

'We meet at last. I know some of the kind of clients you work with so you just had to be my teacher!' She'd gushed.

Turning left onto England's Lane and driving in the direction of Lambolle Road into the heart of Belsize Park, Sasha considered she was perhaps being harsh towards Melody. She really needed to make more of an effort to extend some generosity of spirit toward the young model. After all, she was only twenty-four and already a reasonable amount of fame and fortune had been thrust upon her. That had to be a challenge for any ego, particularly a younger one.

I need to be more mindful of the yoga Yamas, especially Ahimsa. I haven't been very kind in my thoughts lately.

A memory of the mean words that had flowed through her mind toward Melody at her last lesson were now echoing loudly back at her. A troubled expression formed on Sasha's pretty, asymmetrically-perfect face and in her bright blue eyes as the wipers scraped rain relentlessly from the front windscreen of the car in a steady mesmerizing rhythm.

Is wishing for a bird to crap on someone's head so wrong? She wondered. *Or is it just honesty and self-compassion in the face of someone being painfully annoying?*

Turning the car right onto the next road she sighed heavily. True yoga practice could be tough. Few of her clients really understood the gravity of the art and science they were party to. It required so much more than the seemingly simple form of stretching the body, holding poses and toning oneself to a mint condition. Yet she understood, too, that yoga was an organic process – subtle - and that transformation of a life and spirit occurred in it's own mysterious way and time. The fact her clients had chosen to engage that process, regardless of intention or ability, meant they were on that path. They were moving toward a deeper awareness of themselves, truth and life, no matter how physical, fickle, or superficial their conscious intentions initially were. Clients sought her out for many reasons, and regardless of *why*, she was entrusted with the responsibility to be the best example and guide she could be.

People are where they are. I can never experience life through their eyes because I haven't lived as them.

It's unfair of me to judge Melody. Hell, it's not as if I'm perfect - I've made some monumental stuff-ups in life.

Sasha recoiled inwardly as one of her last Californian memories surfaced with the sting of a scorpion's tale. Heaviness weighed upon her as she turned her car onto Lucas Huntington's road. Slowing the vehicle to a crawl she squinted through the dark, checking the numbers on the letterboxes before spotting the correct address and pulling in directly by the curb in front of a large detached house.

Streams of falling rain distorted a clear view. He must have turned the outside lighting on for her as the entire frontage was well lit. The home was a magnificent three-story period property, built with red brick. It looked gorgeous from the exterior with a tall white-pillared entranceway, and she could see large bay windows jutting out on each of the first two floors. Solid brick pillars were positioned either side of the gateway along with a black wrought-iron fence marking the front boundary.

Silencing the engine, Sasha removed the ignition key, pausing to center herself. It wasn't often she felt nervous before meeting a new client, but for some reason she did this morning. Reaching across to the passenger seat and slipping her hand inside her sports bag, she located a small hand towel and dabbed her face, wiping the rainwater that still dripped from her hair. Returning the towel to the bag, she fumbled on the floor of the passenger side, locating an umbrella before gathering her yoga mat bag and opening the door to the cold and rain. However, the five-second walk to the front entry of his house really didn't warrant needing shelter, so flinging the umbrella back on the passenger seat she shut the car door quickly behind her.

Sprinting hastily through the open gate, she bounded up the flight of six stairs. Hesitating before her fingers pressed against the cool steel doorbell, Sasha grabbed the small towel from her bag once more and was just about to wipe her face dry when the sound of a click was audible. The door swung open.

A tall man with unsmiling lips and dark hair stared at her. 'You're wet,' he stated in a disapproving tone. 'Come on in.' He looked tired and...*angry?*

Taken aback momentarily, she hastily dried her face, stuffing the towel quickly inside her sports bag and extending her hand. 'I'm Sasha. It's a pleasure to meet you.'

'Lucas,' he replied, his piercing blue eyes puncturing her like bullets as he extended his arm reluctantly and gave her several firm handshakes. 'I thought the loft room upstairs might be best,' he added, devoid of emotion and closing the door firmly behind her.

'Sure,' she responded, quickly slipping off her wet trainers and following him down the reception hallway to the foot of an elegantly sweeping set of stairs. Maybe he wasn't a great morning person. The disposition of her clients often varied before sunrise.

Pausing at the base of the steps he avoided direct eye contact. 'It's two flights. I'm sorry,'

'No problem.' She glanced to the right of the stairs into a large living area and could tell the place had been gutted and modernized at some point. The walls were painted a bright white and the floor was a dark-toned and highly polished wood that extended toward a large open-plan kitchen. The roof was high, she noticed, casting a quick gaze around. There were floor to ceiling windows at either end that undoubtedly allowed a flood of light in during the daytime.

Moving off up the stairs, she trailed after him. Lucas was a tall man – he had to be at least six foot two. Although subdued, his movements were decisive and his presence rather mysterious and a more than a little charismatic. Garbed in dark track pants and a t-shirt, his bare feet looked oddly out of place on such a distinguished character. Imaginatively, Sasha slipped a pair of tweed slippers onto his feet.

Rounding the second flight of stairs she noticed his upper body looked strong and solid but his posture was slightly hunched as if something ailed his stomach.

The second floor revealed another very large living and entertainment area with the same wooden flooring. Peaking through the open double doors she observed several leather sofas and gorgeous black and white rugs on the floor and a large flat-screen television fixed to the wall.

All very…manly.

An audible sigh escaped his mouth as he started up the second flight of stairs. 'Did you have far to travel?' he said without looking around.

'Not at all. It's just fifteen minutes away at this time of morning.'

'You have early starts every day?'

'Mostly. During the week, that is.'

Reaching the top of the stairs he turned hard left in silence. There were four doors off a wide hallway and he moved toward the first one on the right. Sasha followed him through the slightly ajar door into the room. It was a large loft area with several wide skylights and the same refurbished wooden floor and white walls. Aside from a heater that felt like it had been switched on for some time, along with several lounge chairs by the far wall, there was also a screen at the far end of the empty room that partially obscured stacked boxes.

'It's perfect,' Sasha said out loud.

Turning to face her, he looked her in the eyes directly for the first time since they'd met at the door. 'Really?' he said with uncertainty.

'Absolutely.' Sasha felt herself stepping into teacher

mode and began to take charge. 'Look, I have a couple of short forms for you to fill in before we begin. If you don't mind?'

'What are they?'

'Disclaimer and general health forms. Nothing too heavy,' she smiled, ignoring the tone of suspicion in his voice. 'Why don't you take a seat,' she motioned.

'Fine.'

As they wandered toward the chairs, Sasha removed a clipboard and pen from her sports bag. 'There you go,' she said, handing them to him as he sat down. 'I'll just set up the mats and give you five minutes.'

Strolling back to the door, she closed it properly so the room would retain heat. And returning to the center of the loft and unzipping her yoga bag she laid out the mats as Lucas worked through the forms.

He's actually handsome, in his own way, she thought, taking a subtle sideways glance at him as his radiant blue eyes bored intently into the paperwork. He had short, thick black hair, a pale face with the faintest of scattered freckles and a strong jawline. Tiny little dimple dents were set in his cheeks. Despite an attractive amount of unshaven stubble, his skin looked pristine. And postural hunch aside, he was in good shape. She couldn't help feel a little curious as to why he'd decided to take up yoga.

Does look quite jaded, though. Slightly dark rings of a soft pencil-sketch tone were apparent under the jewels that were his eyes. *And perhaps he has a few anger issues, too,* she thought, reflecting on his demeanor as he opened his front door.

'All done,' he said decisively, putting the pen and clipboard down on the nearby chair.

'Oh, really?' Surprised at the speed he'd filled in the forms, she moved back to the free chair, collecting the clipboard and sitting beside him. He remained quiet as she scanned the document. *Hasn't written much at all.* He'd signed the disclaimer, indicating no injuries on the health form, and simply put a tick in the 'conditions' section beside the word 'stress.' Intuitively deciding he wasn't the type of man to joke with about being a mystery, she gently invited elaboration. 'So you're suffering from some stress at present?'

'Suffering?' He said, taken aback.

'I mean…that you're under some pressure at the moment.' She altered her tone to a softer one. 'Work?' She enquired. 'You haven't filled that part in.' *You've hardly filled any part in.*

'I guess.' He didn't look at her.

'And workwise you're a…?'

'Stockbroker.'

'I'm sure that has its stresses.'

'Some.' The response was uttered with finality.

Sasha decided a different tack was in order. She placed the clipboard down on her knees. 'What made you decide to explore yoga, Mr Huntington?' Formal was probably the best approach.

'It was…recommended to me.'

'Okay, that's great. And what would you actually like to achieve from your yoga practice?'

'I'm not sure. It wasn't really my idea.'

Sasha considered his words, ignoring the slight negativity. 'It sounds like stress reduction would benefit you. What else?'

He was staring at the mats on the floor and avoiding eye contact with her.

'Aside from the obvious physical benefits,' she added.

'What are those?' He replied, looking ready to spring off the chair and exit the room any moment.

'Body tone, flexibility, weight reduction, posture, circulation, skin condition, improved sleep, general health and immune system enhancements - to name a few. And quality of breathing...one of the benefits I rate the most highly.'

'Why's that?' His blue eyes fired several rounds of ammunition into her. Ignoring the fact that they were also attractive as they annihilated, she continued.

'Good breath technique can be great for stress reduction.' She smiled reassuringly. 'Yoga helps promote inner peace and calm. Does any of that sound of value to you?'

'Inner peace, huh...' Appearing cynical, he turned away again. It seemed that he was considering something. Sasha waited patiently. He looked down at the floor, running a hand through his hair and suddenly standing up. She was half-expecting him to send her home.

'Well let's get on with it,' he said in a cool and matter-of-fact voice.

'Of course.' She didn't hesitate. 'Let's start you in Savasana,' she added, guiding him towards his mat.

'What's that?'

'Corpse pose.'

'Corpse?' he said with distaste.

'Relaxation pose - it's one of the core Asana's. 'Asana' - meaning *posture*. If you'd like to lie down on your back, take your feet to the edge of your mat and your arms to the sides at a forty-five degree angle...with your palms facing up.'

He followed her instruction. 'We'll begin with some simple abdominal breathing.'

Sasha adjusted his legs slightly, returning to the top of his head where she pushed his shoulders away from his ears and moved alongside him. 'Now, close your eyes.' He followed her instruction. 'I'd like you to bring your awareness down into the base of your stomach and begin by taking a few nice deep full breaths through your nose, drawing the breath down into your abdomen as it rises and exhaling long and slow as it falls.'

She watched his stomach but it didn't move. 'Okay. If you can bring your full focus right down into your abdomen, please. I need you to feel it expanding like a balloon as you inhale fully, Mr Huntington.' She waited patiently as he finally followed her instruction, completing a long slow exhalation.

Then almost startling her, his deep voice cut suddenly through the pendulum pause of his breath. 'I think if we're going to do this, you should call me Lucas.' His eyes remained closed; his voice factual and cool.

Sasha peered down at him inquisitively. Despite his tone, and the realization there was a lot of work to do, the first great step had been made.

***

It was almost daylight as Sasha drove back to her apartment in Camden. She was tired. The session with Lucas was demanding - not so much in his ability to follow instruction, but more his general demeanor.

Like wading in treacle.

He'd been quiet, aloof and hadn't smiled once. The man obviously had a lot on his plate and it was a good thing he'd taken up yoga. It looked like he might stick at it for a while, too. He'd booked two of her few remaining weekly regular timeslots, so she'd be seeing him every Monday evening as well as Thursday mornings. Thankfully, he appeared peaceful and more relaxed by the end of the lesson. Progress, not perfection, was all she could ask for. At least he'd reached a state of deeper breathing. *I'll trust that helps him with his day in some way.*

Turning her Golf right, off Stratford Villas, she

eventually parked on a quiet residential lane in the heart of the Camden Square conservation area. Camden was such a central location. She loved it.

In a short walk she'd arrived at her front entrance, which was a lot easier without rain hampering her. At Lucas's home, Sasha had noticed the pelting sound of water on the skylights gradually subside before the end of his yoga session.

Her key slipped neatly into the lock and she pushed on the door, entering the contemporary flat that had been her home for several years. It was spacious for a one-bedroom place, with lots of natural light. All modern, it had an open-plan fashionable fitted kitchen and slick new bathroom that included a shower and bath. One of her favorite ways to relax was taking a long candlelit soak in a tub, so she'd rented the apartment almost on the strength of that alone. But the appeal of having a deck area outside with some space and privacy was what had tipped the balance.

Removing her slightly damp trainers she padded barefoot across the hardwood flooring to the ranch slider doors and looked out at her little patch of grass beyond the deck, smiling as she took in the view. It wasn't much land, but it was home. Sighing with relief, she observed the neat section of lawn and reflected on her morning so far.

The lesson with Lucas had definitely unsettled her. Uncertain as to why, she wanted to clear the feeling that sat in her body before her next client lesson. There was well over an hour before her next teaching session, and despite having not yet eaten she felt a distinct urge to sit down for twenty minutes and do some meditation - that or take a nap. And although the nap was tempting, the meditation was sure to give her a freer mind and a better level of focus as she taught throughout the day.

Collecting the yoga mat and cushion that sat propped

by the wall, she rolled the mat out onto the floor in the center of the room and placed the cushion down, sitting promptly upon it without hesitation. Crossing her legs carefully into lotus position, Sasha lengthened her spine, closed her eyes softly and brought her awareness down into the base of her abdomen.

Several minutes passed as she began to focus more deeply on her breathing, allowing the outer world to fall away. It was difficult, surrendering. Her mind seemed more committed to being busy. She watched its steady stream of flowing thought, doing her best to practice non-attachment. Faces from her week appeared: Melody …Lucas…Fiona. Recollections of conversations buzzed in like commercial sound bites; disjointed chunks of dialogue and the expression of anger in Lucas's eyes. *So much anger.*

Yet all of the images and words were utterly and irrevocably gone - all belonged to the past, whether it was a week, a day, or an hour gone by. There was no bringing back any of it. It existed only in her attachment to it – her attachment to time and physicality.

Feeling discomfort in her body, a wave of resistance arose in her: resistance to being still…resistance to letting go of her incessant mind and its jumble of meaningless words and emotion-making associations. Feelings arose and vanished in her. The freight train of her mind slowed further and further until eventually it drew to an eerie and somewhat terrifying halt; suspended momentarily at a terminal that existed nowhere…*nowhere. Now-here…now here,* a voice whispered. There was only a void of empty space around her. Stillness…breath...life. *Now here.*

Sasha had disappeared into nothingness and at the same time, everything - the inexplicable contradiction of spiritual experience. The vastness of existence was the much broader backdrop from which her everyday dramas and dreams played out. She was falling; losing touch entirely with time, becoming temporarily present to the immensity of each moment; to the magnitude of life itself.

Sitting in a state of quiet timeless peace, it seemed as if hours had passed. Although in total, it was a mere twelve minutes. The sound of a pin dropping could have been heard. But it was sudden rain falling heavily outside again that stirred her to return to the physical density of her apartment and the ornately embroidered green cushion she sat upon. And as the beauty of being mindless faded rapidly in the downpour, the old freight train of her mind roared back to life with a vengeance she'd forgotten it was capable of.

'You'll pay for this! You little bitch!' It screamed, ripping through her serenity.

Gasping, she opened her eyes, rapidly blinking from the sudden light. But it wasn't her own freight train she was hearing. It was a hatred-filled voice from her past; a dark locomotive in steady pursuit. And after all these years she still hadn't escaped it.

Chapter Five

'Where the hell are you, Sash?' Fiona sounded impatient, as well as being a number of drinks into some Friday night revelry.

'Not far away,' she replied, straining to hear her friend against the background bar noise. Picking up her pace Sasha made her way to the Convent Garden bar, carefully negotiating the cobbled pavement in her high-heeled boots.

'Well, you've missed Happy Hour and Dave's about to start playing soon. Love you to meet him before the band begins their first set.'

'Oh, so he has a name now, does he?'

'The keepers always have names.'

'And he's a keeper after a few weeks?'

'What can I say…the man has great hands.'

'Well perhaps I need to elevate that on my list then.' Sasha yelled into the phone with a smile, turning down a lane and dodging Friday evening merrymakers as she went. 'Somewhere above less important things like: kind heart, good person and…'

'Filthy fricking rich!' Fiona interjected, breaking into raucous laughter at her own humor.

Sasha shook her head and rolled her eyes.

'Although I'm suspecting in Dave's case it's just his soul that's rich.' Fiona added.

'I hope he can't hear you!'

'He's gone to the bathroom.'

'Well as long as he treats you well and makes you happy.'

'After a few dates I can honestly say…honeymoon heaven.'

'I'm not sure I would call those dates.'

Fiona hiccupped once and proceeded to shout to someone in the background about drinks.

'Who are you there with?' Sasha said, doing her best to speak loudly into the phone so she could be heard.

'Just a few of the club staff, mostly.'

'Great.' She pushed on the bar door entering the packed establishment where people were milling around in after-work groups. 'Usual spot?'

'Of course,' Fiona shouted. 'Can hardly hear you?! It's so noisy.'

Navigating her way through the crowd, Sasha moved toward a table near the center of the bar by a beam. 'That's because I'm right behind you,' she yelled, before disconnecting the call.

Pulling the phone away from her ears, Fiona checked the screen in confusion before spinning around. 'There you are!' She launched herself at Sasha with a big hug. 'I was worried you weren't going to make it.'

'Worried?'

'Well there's a very interesting person here this evening you should meet.'

Sasha stared blankly at Fiona who was pulling a face and nodding her head as if playing charades and urging her friend to get the answer. Glancing around the bar, now slightly confused, Sasha observed the dark décor and Tudor-style look of the place that was visible above the bobbing heads. The ledges were dotted with ancient looking bottles and various other paraphernalia. 'You mean, Dave?'

'No, silly.'

'Umm…I've no idea. Someone interesting?' Sasha said, furrowing her brow. She was even more confused watching Fiona's eyes intensify in expression, whilst her head gestured weirdly as if she were loose at the neck. 'Fee, I haven't got a clue what you're on about. Who do you mean?'

'Here are your drinks, ladies.' She heard the deep accented voice and watched a pair of strong masculine hands cut between them holding several glasses of white wine.

Spinning about, Sasha turned to see the devilishly handsome and muscled Brazilian, Rodrigo. He towered inches above her, casually dressed in a light blue t-shirt and jeans that fitted like he should be modeling for underwear commercials.

'Apologies. Did I interrupt something?' His accent only seemed to enhance his multitude of other assets. Rodrigo smiled with teeth that looked designed for the Hollywood screen, a chiseled jaw and green eyes that radiated self-assuredness and a zest for life. He glanced toward Fiona before peering warmly at Sasha who had gone weak at the knees, absorbing the heady kind of chemistry he seemed to emit as his inquisitive eyes locked on hers.

Ignoring his question, Fiona removed one of the drinks from his hand. 'Rodrigo, I'd like you to meet my very best friend and yoga instructor extraordinaire, Sasha Devine.'

'Sasha, it's a great pleasure to meet you.'

Was it possible he could speak in slow motion? The words drizzled out of his mouth like honey. She wanted him to say them again, they sounded so good. He looked as good to match. The t-shirt that his chest begged to be touched in hugged his sizeable pectoral muscles and biceps. His gorgeous after-shave drifted up her nasal passage, urging her to plant her nose into the delicate area below his sandy-colored hair and the ears above his tanned neck. His teeth gleamed from behind sensual and ever-so-kissable lips. She was both entranced and speechless. In the silence that ensued, Fiona gently removed the second glass from Rodrigo's hand. Sasha peeked across at her, catching the *are-you fricking-nuts, say-something-you-daft-wench* look etched on her face.

'She works at the club, too,' Fiona finally blurted out in a mostly chivalrous act, jerking Sasha out of her dumbstruck state.

'Yes, you mentioned that earlier.' Rodrigo smiled again. It was like standing in the blast radius of a bomb. Sasha considered ducking for cover, lest her face be seared.

'It's very nice to meet you, Rodrigo,' she said, finally engaging her brain. But there was something enchanting about saying his name. It rolled off her tongue and out of her mouth like an extension of herself. Strangely, she wanted to say it again.

Rodrigo...Rodrigo.

'I haven't seen you about at the club?' he added.

For a second, Sasha kidded herself there was a note of disappointment in his voice. She was clearly beginning to hallucinate and was therefore in critical need of a drink.

'I just teach classes there a couple of times a week.' She raised the glass, hastily gulping down several large mouthfuls as if it were water.

'You like Chardonnay.' It was a statement. Not a question. He looked amused and well in control. Did he know the power of his testosterone-fueled body?

'Big week. Need to unwind.' Sasha blurted out her response before quickly finishing the other half of her drink. Fiona observed the guzzling with surprise.

'Very quickly, I see,' he added.

Do you also see how nervous you're making me, you Brazilian...stud.

'Sash darling, you must be thirsty. I'll get you a water.' Fiona had a smartass tone in her voice. 'Like I did when we first met, remember. It was such a *hot* day.'

Did she really just emphasize the word *hot* like that?

'No, no. Stay here. I'll get you water.' Rodrigo insisted, smiling broadly.'

'Great, thank you.'

Sasha's eyes followed him steadily as he disappeared to the bar, his head sticking up above most of the other patrons. Turning, she caught the bemused expression on Fiona's face.

'Oh, give me a break, Fee.'

'I'm not saying anything. Mouth is zipped.' Fiona whizzed her fingers past her lips.

'And exactly how long would that be for?'

'Ahh...about two seconds! So who just got a big crush on Mr Brazil?!' She burst out laughing.

'Probably every woman in this bar.' Sasha stuck her nose in the air with her best *I'm ignoring you now for the rest of eternity* look, adding, 'including you!'

'Are you serious?!' Fiona's expression was both incredulous and insulted. 'Of course I have a ruddy crush on him. How could you consider I wouldn't? I just about wet my pants when he passed me my drink.'

Glancing at each other momentarily, they burst into laughter at exactly the same time.

'I see what you were trying to tell me.'

'Told you. Didn't I.' Fiona grinned.

'So why didn't you let me know Rodrigo was going to be here this eve?'

'It wouldn't have made any difference. You'd have still near passed out when you laid eyes on him. In fact, it looked like you almost did. Besides, I didn't know he would join us. A couple of the other trainers dragged him down here, apparently.' She paused. 'I was right, though. Wasn't I?'

'Right about what?'

'That you'd be hooked.'

'I'm not sure *hooked* is the right word. I think *impressed* is more accurate. Besides, we just met. I don't know anything about him at all,' she replied.

'But you might want to…know him, I mean.' There was a devious expression on Fiona's face.

'I think I'll just abide by the club rules and get to know him as a work colleague.'

'Whatever.' Fiona chipped back, unconvinced.

'You know I don't get involved with players, Fee.'

'You don't get involved with anyone,' Fiona quipped. 'Anyway, who says he's a player?'

'Well…look at the guy.'

'I am looking. Trust me.'

'Trust…exactly my point…he sure looks like the type for that,' Sasha added with a touch of sarcasm.

Fiona snorted at her friend's words and eye-rolling. 'He seems nice to me. And just because lots of women might look at him it doesn't mean he's looking back.'

'Maybe.' Sasha took another sip of wine.

'You have trust issues, Sash. That's not fair on a man.'

'Probably not,' she responded, glancing across the bar at the back of Rodrigo's head. 'But all the same, I don't think I'll be taking a risk on one of Brazil's finest.'

'Whatever.' Fiona repeated a second time. But the expression on her face remained unconvinced.

***

She was drinking far too much wine as the night

progressed. They'd all drunk too much. But Sasha was having great fun.

'Good to see you letting your hair down, Sash.' Fiona yelled into her face whilst jumping up and down to the sound of Dave's drums.

It was true she could be quite serious and didn't often drink much, preferring to stay in control and respect the yoga Niyama, Sauca – maintaining the purity of her physical body. This meant that Sasha seldom drank alcohol, let alone to excess. But the previous day had felt pretty heavy after her meditation and another abnormally disturbing ending. So it was great to be blowing off some steam and forgetting about everything for a while. She was in great company with her workmates – they were sticking together as a group and having lots of fun.

Rodrigo seemed okay, too. He didn't spend the evening surveying women in the bar as she expected. It was really more the other way round. *Understandable that they would all want his babies,* Sasha thought.

In fact, it could have been coincidence, but it seemed that an awful lot of women were accidentally bumping *into her* while she was in conversation with him. And it was certainly a fact that many women bumped into him. He had three patches of alcohol spilled on his t-shirt – two on the front and one on the back. She only knew about the damp patch on his back because she'd almost fallen over at one point in the night and grabbed onto him in her semi-slide to the floor. Whilst clinging to the back of his t-shirt she discovered it was soaking wet. In her descent, he'd turned and grabbed her arm, almost capturing her in a romantic dip and preventing her planting herself on the wooden floorboards in an embarrassing fashion. He had such a strong manly grip – which admittedly felt good.

Liar!

She was forced to correct herself. *It felt sensational!*

The moment in his arms contained the kind of satisfaction acted out by actresses in scenes of old black and white movies, where they'd light up a cigarette after a romp in the sack with a legendary screen hero. She wished she could eject a plume of smoke artistically from her mouth at that precise moment. Or at least, right after he rescued her back onto her feet, smiling as he surveyed her eyes with a penetrating stare. *He did, didn't he? Stare directly into my eyes?*

'Jesus, why didn't you get in there first, Sash!' Fiona whispered into her ear at one point about his wet t-shirt patches, regrettably spraying small particles of spit as she did so. She wasn't the most elegant drinker on the planet. 'Those women are stealing our move.'

Ignoring the comment, Sasha changed the subject. 'When am I going to meet Dave?' she asked.

'Any second now, hopefully. They're due to have a break.'

'He's great on the drums, isn't he.'

'I know.' Fiona looked over at him with a slushy look on her face. Sasha watched Dave glance back with a grin and a wink. 'That's not all he's great on.'

'Get a room.'

'Why do you need a room?' Rodrigo said overhearing Sasha's comment and directing his question to Fiona. He'd returned, unnoticed. Leaning in warmly behind Sasha with several more drinks, his South American accent sent another rush of chemicals throughout her body.

Fiona started to laugh. 'Because I'm a saucy minx!' she said, dancing off through the crowd in the direction of the band.

An awkward self-consciousness stirred within Sasha as Rodrigo sidled in beside her, his sizeable bicep sliding past her shoulder. It was a sudden reminder of his masculine physicality, his scent and the unwanted effect it had on her. Animal attraction molecules were bubbling up from some mysterious underground cavern inside her, located somewhere beneath her navel and the juncture at the top of her legs. *Damn.* Her internal cocktail cabinet needed closing down fast. It was the kind of dangerous chemical weaponry that could result in serious personal damage. She knew the track wild and rampant biology could lead down. *I don't need more lessons like that.*

Sasha was sure she'd now mastered one of the greatest self-preservation strategies in the human psyche. Control. It served her well and had become her friend.

'Fiona is like a Latino,' Rodrigo smiled down at her. He was flirting with her. *Was he flirting with her?* The wine was creating mental confusion.

'In what way?'

'All fire and passion. Look.' He pointed towards where the band had just finished. Fiona had clambered onto the stage and was planting a big kiss on Dave's lips – which he looked pretty happy about. 'She should have been born in Brazil.'

Brazil rolled off Rodrigo's tongue like a red carpet invite. Hearing him say it made her want to jump on the next plane with him to Rio, hole up in some romantic little bungalow on a beach and dance and make love into the night. But her weak thoughts also dismayed her.

'So are all Brazilian's generally fiery and passionate?' Sasha found it difficult to look at his eyes at close range. It was easier to avoid their fascinating green intensity and the feeling that seemed to twinkle on their surface. And it was better for the purposes of *control* to look anywhere but directly into his eyes. But all the same, she didn't. Instead she smiled at him, purely spontaneously. *Damn.*

'Not always.' He smiled back. 'But we are a passionate people. It is a little different here in England, yes?'

'It's a little more...reserved, I guess.' *And I like it that way. I don't like messy uncontrolled emotion.*

'Where are you from, Sasha?'

'California.'

He raised his eyebrows. 'Los Angeles?'

'Yes.' She took another sip of wine.

'So, why England?'

'Well you tell me.'

He chuckled. 'Ah yes, why would I leave beloved Brazil for this cold country.' He hesitated. 'My parents. My father does some business out here occasionally and they still keep a home in London. So I thought I'd take the opportunity to live in another part of the world for a while.'

'And how are you finding it?'

'Freezing,' he grinned, completely disarming her. Thankfully Fiona appeared again, dragging her drummer lover behind her.

'Guys, I want you to meet Dave,' she said, enthusiastically barreling in between them. 'Dave, this is my best friend, Sasha.'

'Nice to meet you.' He said, extending his hand to her, then Rodrigo. He was just a little taller than Sasha with wavy black hair that was wet at the nape from sweating at the drums. His upper body was solid and stocky with well-defined deltoid muscles that were currently being hugged by a classic fitted black t-shirt.

'Nice to meet you too, Dave.' He was instantly likeable. His feeling brown eyes shone with an easygoing approachability. Rodrigo began to chat with him about drumming and Fiona scrunched in beside Sasha.

'How's it all going over here?' She smiled

mischievously.

'It's good. All good.' Sasha answered in a quiet voice.

Fiona gave her a nudge using her elbow. 'I bet. So umm…any interest.'

Beginning to feel worried about the words that were spilling more loudly out of Fiona's mouth, Sasha glanced down at her watch. 'Look, sorry, I really need to be heading off now,' she added quickly, hoping Fiona's topic of conversation wasn't appearing obvious.

'That's a shame. It's just getting fun.'

'It is. But I have something on in the morning and don't want a late night.'

'What's on?' Fiona asked pointedly.

A nervous feeling rippled through Sasha. 'Oh, there's just somewhere I have to be.'

'Well, what time? Let's all meet for breakfast in the morning.' Her voice was loud enough that Dave and Rodrigo could hear. Both men turned to face them, Rodrigo's green eyes considered Sasha carefully.

'No. Honestly, Fee. I'm sorry, I can't.' Feeling very sober all of sudden, she reached for her coat from the back of a nearby chair and hastily bundled it on.

'Are you leaving, Sasha?' Rodrigo peered at her.

She spent a moment fantasizing about him being disappointed before dismissing the crazy notion and throwing him her most confident Californian look. 'Yes I am. I've a busy morning, but you three have fun. It was great to meet you. Dave, sorry I have to dash so soon, but I'll see you another time.'

Sasha knew it was a hasty departure, but felt compelled to leave. It was suddenly becoming very claustrophobic in the bar. Besides, it was the truth. She did have a morning commitment. Something important. And she had no intention of breaking it.

Chapter Six

'In Karma Yoga, the emphasis is upon selfless action.' The Guru spoke slowly, allowing them to absorb every word carefully, as if one might be instructed to chew a single mouthful of food thirty-two times before swallowing.

Holly had long been interested in the subject of Karma. Actually, for several years. Mostly, this was because she was innately diplomatic and did not have the penchant to strike back in any way if upset by another human being. Her nature was deeply peaceful, as inspired by her parents' example.

Any *hurt* she had felt as a result of another's words or actions, was usually of the emotional and psychological variety – as people could be inclined to inflict upon occasion. In the event of this, though, it was never Holly's nature to strike back in any way or form. Instead, she was prone to try and understand what may have prompted the barb or selfish action.

So a year ago, when she was providing some personal training instruction at a gym, it so happened that her client raised the subject of Karma. And Holly became rather entranced by the conversation.

Up until that point, she'd never actually considered that the word *Karma* was anything more to do with fate, or a form of destiny. It was never a concept she thought worth delving into beyond that. Yet the seed planted by the client that day - the kernel of words that burrowed into her brain - turned out to be quite a bountiful one. The dialogue, at the time, had inferred that in the heart of Karma lay the philosophical notion that a scientific *Law of Cause and Effect* was really the engine behind the principle.

On the one hand, this information had given her hope that she was able to create a positive future for herself through her actions. Yet as a result of events that had occurred recently, it also caused her to feel a degree of foreboding. Some things could not be undone. A mysterious universal hand could only balance them.

Holly sighed heavily as she felt the beads of perspiration forming on the side of her face.

Concentrating on philosophy in the heat of the afternoon was proving to be quite a challenge. But it was also possible she just didn't want to hear it.

'Karma Yoga transcends concerns of success or failure, egoism and selfishness...' That's what he'd just said, she thought, concentrating harder. 'It removes gross impurities of the mind and, through service, develops the hand of generosity.' He'd emphasized the word, *service*. It was weird, but he looked directly at her as he did so.

Holly was sure of that.

***

A little before nine-thirty on the Saturday morning, Sasha pulled into the car park, easing her vehicle into a narrow spot and switching off the ignition. She had a hangover and was feeling way below average. It wasn't the ideal way to start something...*purifying*.

Staring over at the rear entrance to the building she could see it looked a bit ramshackle and in need of a good paint job. What it probably needed more, though, was to be demolished and replaced entirely. But that would likely require an act of God, or some philanthropic benevolence by a generous human being.

Nervously drumming her fingers on the steering wheel, she stalled for time, unable to go in. There was still five minutes to think about showing up. She could always turn the car around and go home. *Keep running from my shadow.* But hadn't she been doing that for years? And was it working? Not really. Her life had become a lie, and she wasn't even sure she knew who she was anymore.

Her need to satiate her dehydrated body was becoming undeniable and her hands shook ever so slightly. Sasha liked to think it was her wine-soaked and sleep-deprived body causing the tremors - not fear. It was hard to say which was more dominant at present, though.

Reaching across to the passenger seat she grasped onto her water flask as she viewed the building with deep suspicion. Aside from the back door, slightly ajar, it looked dilapidated and the small windows gave the appearance of a creepy old prison. She sighed heavily. There was no way to avoid it any longer. The only way forward was straight down the middle. And maybe, just maybe, she could cleanse her past and make it go away for good.

Unscrewing the water bottle she savored a long drink as if it were the last gasp of air before total oxygen deprivation. Refastening the lid, she placed the flask absentmindedly back in her sports bag and glanced over at the passenger seat to a tattered piece of paper. The address and telephone number that she'd hastily scribbled down a number of weeks ago now leapt boldly out and taunted her.

Tears formed unexpectedly, stinging the back of her eyes. The letters and numbers on the paper were appearing blurry through her dewy haze. She recalled how she'd been feeling lately at the end of her meditation sessions – with so much fear and anxiety. It wasn't how one expected to come out of a meditation. It was supposed to bring her deeper peace. Instead, it seemed to trigger the opposite.

Several weeks ago she'd had enough of being held hostage to deeper emotions and had promptly gone to her laptop to look up the necessary details, jotting them down quickly. It had taken her a while to call and make the arrangements. But now here she was.

There was never a great time for this – there never would be, Sasha thought. It had to be now. The path was inevitable. She finally knew this to be true. It was time.

Opening the car door she froze briefly in her seat, her legs stirring ever so slowly before connecting her feet with the cold gravel outside. In years past, Sasha had learned to avoid indulging her feelings excessively - slamming a door on them had become a habitual response. Initially this was for survival, but over time it had seeped into her general way of being. So it was with some surprise and dismay that she felt her insides succumb to a feeling of total vulnerability. Tears prickled up in her eyes. There was a once a time in her life they had flowed from her like the Ganges, requiring the force of sheer will to end them. But now here they were again, inconveniently seeping out…after so many years.

Sasha clasped a hand over her mouth in despair in an effort to damn the torrent. But as several heaving sobs wracked her chest, salt water began to stream steadily and uncontrollably from her eyes and she finally surrendered to the buried feelings.

***

It wasn't until the next day that Sasha began to cheer up with the help of Fiona's humorous company.

'So talk me through these roast vegetables,' Fiona winked.

'What?' Sasha glanced across the table with puzzlement, searching her friend's cheeky green eyes.

It was Sunday. Sunday's could be tough. Although Sasha enjoyed her own company and was accustomed to it, nothing ever quite prepared her for the subdued silence that seemed to permeate the day - especially in winter. Sunday's were a powerful reminder that the majority of humankind seemed to have a family, a partner, or somebody else they could wile away the day with. Fortunately, on this afternoon she had Fiona. They were now happily tucked away in a busy Camden bar where a musician had just finished playing a set on his guitar.

'Your yams.' Fiona replied as if her words and their meaning were obvious.

Sasha glanced back at her blankly.

'The bloody limbs. You know?' She waved her arms about as if flying.

'Oh. You mean the Yamas.'

'Well I don't mean your Sunday dinner, sweetheart. Of course that's what I meant.'

'Ha!' Sasha chuckled. 'Okay.'

'There are five, right?'

'Well done. Yes, five Yamas, and they're all about moral virtues. The idea is to incorporate them into your daily life. And they can guide you in purifying your nature.'

Fiona grimaced. 'Not possible in my case. What's

the first?'

'The first Yama is Ahimsa. It's about having compassion for all living creatures. So no cruelty or violence to any creature or person in any way whatsoever.'

'So calling that guy eating lots of cream cakes the other week '*fat*' was…'

'Cruel and violent? Yes.'

'Oh.'

'But don't beat yourself up about it, Fee.'

'No, I won't,' she added unconcerned. 'And *compassion for all living creatures*. Cats and dogs are safe then?'

'Absolutely.'

'Cockroaches?'

'Technically, they should be safe too.'

Fiona grimaced. 'So you shouldn't…' She made a stomping motion with her foot.

'Not really.'

'But God can turn a blind eye on occasion, surely.'

'You'd have to take that up with the Creator, yourself.'

'Okay. So put your weapons down with Ahimsa.'

'Exactly.' Sasha smiled. 'It's about kindness, consideration and doing no harm.'

'Sounds admirable. Righto. Roll on number two.'

'Two, is Satya.' Sasha paused. 'That's to do with speaking the truth.'

'I like it - do it all the time. Usually too much.' Fiona winked, picking up her glass of cider and taking a mouthful.

'That's a great example of Satya right there.'

'Cheeky, Sash.'

'Actually, sometimes it's not always best to speak the truth, because it can cause unnecessary harm to someone. And you want to avoid harming another. So in terms of Satya, we have to consider what we say, how we say it, and in what way it could affect others.'

'Christ. Sounds complex. I think it's fair to say I officially suck at Satya.'

Sasha giggled. 'I think the easiest way to figure it out is if the truth has negative consequences for another then it's better to say nothing.'

'Unless you're in court and you're forced to tell *the truth, the whole truth, and nothing but the truth.*'

'You're funny, Fee.'

'Ain't that the truth.'

'Okay smarty pants. The third Yama is Asteya.'

'A stay-a at your place tonight.' Fiona said, winking again.

'Oh, God.' Sasha shook her head. 'Why did I start this?'

'Because I make you laugh. Continue, oh Master.'

'Okay. Asteya relates to physical stealing, but it also means that if you're in a situation where someone entrusts something or confides in you, you don't take advantage of him or her.'

'What if it's pleasurable though?'

Sasha shrugged her shoulders and screwed up her face. 'Not sure what you mean.'

'Well…' Fiona leaned across the table lowering her voice. 'Let's say Dave's told me what turns him on. But he's *not* horny…and I am. Can I use that information to…,' she whispered, pointing down between her legs.

Sasha pulled a confused face.

'For God's sake, Sash. To get him going! Not that I need to, because...well, you know…'

'No. I know what?'

'He's good-to-go *all* the time. I mean it's *me* we're talking about here, sister.' She blew on her fingers, throwing Sasha a cocky look.'

'Oh - my - God.' Sasha rolled her eyes. 'Well, with

Asteya whatever you are seeking should be freely given, that's how you know.'

'Trust me, my friend. It's freely given in the end.'

'Well, as long as it's not inconsiderate behavior demanding his attention. You figure that one out for yourself.'

'Don't you mean *demanding his erection?* '

'You're hysterical.' Sasha said drily.

'Okay.' Fiona made a serious face. 'Stealing is a no-no regarding Asteya. In summary, if it's not freely given, you're stealing. Whatever it is. Got it?'

'You got it.'

'Cool. What's number four.'

'Oh, you're going to love this one.' Sasha smiled.

'It's sex, right?' Fiona peered intently across the table back at her. 'Has to do with sex.'

'In some ways.' Sasha picked up her glass of pineapple juice and took a sip.

Fiona slammed her hand down on the table, rattling her glass of cider. 'Well don't keep me hanging in suspense!'

'Cool your jets, sister. Four is Brahmacharya. Sense Control.'

'Oh. I don't like the sound of this. It's that darn *abstinence* thing, isn't it.'

'Yes, but it doesn't necessarily imply celibacy.'

'You'd think so in your case.'

'Fee!' Sasha playfully swatted her on the shoulder. 'That's not fair.'

'Well. You ran for the hills from the hottest man on the planet the other night. What's a girl to think?'

'I did not run for the hills. I had something on in the morning.'

'It should have been *him* you were on.'

'Stop it.'

'Rodrigo, Rodrigo...' Fiona made fake moaning

sounds.

'Oh, God.' Sasha rolled her eyes again.

'Don't *Oh God* me. I'm telling you, you could be *in* with that guy.'

'Rubbish.'

'I'm just saying.' Fiona shrugged her shoulders, opening her palms out as she did so.

Sasha cleared her throat, ignoring her. 'So Brahmacharya is really suggesting responsible behavior with sexual energy in regard to your goal of moving toward the truth.'

'Sex is great. It's also my goal. That's the truth, and I'm always moving toward it,' Fiona quipped, her expression serious.

'You're moving toward your *Higher Truth,* Fee. Not sex!'

Fiona stared back at her blankly. 'I don't understand. What could be a higher truth than great sex?'

'Look,' Sasha explained with slight frustration, despite knowing that Fiona was just being funny, 'it's about using your sexual energy to connect more with your *spiritual self.*'

Fiona's expression remained vacant. 'My spiritual self? See, I struggle with that. What the hell is my *spiritual self*?'

Sasha considered the question. 'Well, I guess it really revolves around your belief system and your daily life structure. It's your *consciousness*. And how you connect with The Divine, God, the Universe - whatever you want to call it - in everything around you.'

'I'm sorry. This ties in with sex and the Brahma-yama thing, how exactly?'

'I think, ideally, it's about utilizing your sexual energy and sexual activity to come into greater union with The Divine.'

Fiona considered Sasha's words seriously before

responding. 'I do that.'

'Really?'

'*Oh God, Oh God, Oh God!*' Her expression was ecstatic. 'Surely that counts in terms of my union with the Divine.'

Sasha sighed. Then smiled. 'Must be time to move on to the last Yama.'

'Don't be like that, Sash. I know, I know. Brahmacharya is basically saying *use your sexual energy wisely.*'

'Basically.'

'And in an ideal world, it's probably best to preserve it unless you're in a committed relationship and in love with someone…and that helps the union with…' Fiona pointed skyward.

'And the union here.' Sasha pointed to Fiona's heart. 'In theory, yes.'

'In theory?'

'Well… ' she paused, looking down at the table. 'I've never really experienced that yet, so I can't fully testify it's the truth,' she said quietly.

'Oh.' Fiona was silent for a moment. 'You will, Sash. One day. You will.'

'Maybe.'

Fiona hesitated, reflective as she picked up her glass. 'I think I'm finally doing okay with that one.'

'Really?' she smiled. 'That's lovely to hear. I guess it's about progress, not perfection. That's good enough for…' Sasha pointed skyward.

Fiona smiled softly. 'I'm sure it is,' she paused. 'So how about you hit me with Yama five, since I'm doing so well.'

'Okay. The fifth and final Yama, is Aparigraha.'

'Sounds like a bad Spanish cocktail.'

Sasha giggled. 'Key words to note here are *Greed* and *Hoarding.*'

'They would be no-no's, I take it?'

'That's right.' Sasha smiled. 'Aparigraha means to take only what is necessary. And never take advantage of a situation or act greedy.'

'So the whole desire to acquire wealth is also kind of…uncool?' Fiona added.

'Pretty much. For a yogi, the collection or hoarding of things implies a lack of faith in God and themselves to provide for the future. And really, we should only take what we have earned; if we take more, we're exploiting someone else.'

'I think you're right. But let's face it, consumption and hoarding are heavily promoted on the planet.'

'Yes, they are. I wish more people would let go of their attachment to material things.' Sasha sighed, fidgeting with her glass. 'What are we doing to this earth, and to each other…all for the sake of having *more.*'

'Well people are going to have to let go at some point, aren't they. There's only one exit in life, after all - the *Travel Light* exit. You can't take shit with you on that flight.'

A tiny smile curled the corners of Sasha's mouth. 'Yes. But I'm not sure everyone does travel so light at the end. And maybe some do *take shit.*'

'Ha!' Fiona chuckled. 'You mean a suitcase full of regrets, a vanity bag of hurt and some bummed-out toiletries?'

'Anyone ever told you, you have a way with words, Fee?'

'Every fricking day.' She smiled, picking up her glass and finishing the apple-flavored remains at the bottom.

'So are we good with Yama Five?'

'I believe a summary is in order.' Fiona said, placing her empty glass back down.

Glancing across the table and taking in her friend's perfectly high cheekbones, slim arching nose and porcelain-colored skin, Sasha noticed how Fiona's skin tone made her auburn hair flame even brighter. 'Everything changes, Fee. Impermanence is the one true constant. That's my summary.'

'Sobering,' Fiona said quietly, appearing thoughtful and twiddling with her glass before adding, 'you know, I think I'll have another.'

Chapter Seven

Lucas Huntington had her curious. There was no doubt about it. It wasn't so much his probable lonely existence, rattling around in a large three-story home, or his successful career as a stockbroker. Nor was it his very limited communication that made her inquisitive about his armored self. It was the sense of broody emotions lurking oceanic-like behind his crystal clear blue eyes that she wondered about. He was hiding something. Sasha was sure of it.

A career like his could develop the type of mask he wore. She figured he'd have to be quite detached from his feelings - ambitious and driven. That could make a person rather remote. Although, from the brief amount of time she'd spent with him, it looked like he was comfortably professional, more so than comfortably personal. While it was true that some people could take a while to get to know, the angry man lurking beneath was still somewhat evident – it had leaked out again en-route to his second yoga lesson that Monday evening.

Sasha had been following him once more in the silent climb up the staircase when he tripped, banging his toe heavily on the adjacent step and allowing an uncontrolled angry 'Fuck!' to escape his lips. Which was odd, because he really didn't seem like the *Fuck* sort - and certainly not the vehement *hell hath no fury as the scorned by a stair* type of man.

For a few seconds she stood behind him, stunned, not knowing whether to intervene supportively or to burst into completely inappropriate laughter. But the sight of the tall clean-cut and formal businessman allowing a ranting *'fuck'* to escape his lips just seemed entirely wrong.

'Are you okay?' She finally located the most suitable words.

Remaining stationery whilst ignoring his bruised toe, he barely glanced at her. 'I'm fine.' The response was flat.

Of course that's all he'd say.

However, after hesitating and clearing his throat, Lucas surprised her by uttering a quiet 'thank you,' before continuing on solemnly up the stairs.

Sasha considered it a mild breakthrough.

Entering the warmed room she unzipped the yoga bag, pulling out the mats to set them up and feeling instantly more relaxed at being back in the instructor seat. Observing him discreetly, she watched him finally look down to assess the damage to his large toe.

'How were you after your first lesson...Lucas.' She decided to use his first name. The *F-word* had suddenly humanized him.

'Oh,' he ran a hand through his short crop of neatly cut hair, 'good.'

Good was favorable. She glanced up at him encouraging elaboration. 'Really?'

'I slept better.'

It was a matter-of-fact response, but also the first time he'd really looked her in the eyes. She saw fatigue staring back at her - not the sleep deprivation kind, despite his comment. It was more a world-weary and worn-to-the-bone exhaustion. She knew the look well – it had often been staring vacantly in the mirror back at her a number of years ago. It was a *barely-functioning-on-the-top-side-of-life* kind of look - where one just made it through each day, as if existing in some deep-seated despair that this was your life; where one had gone *beyond shock* and was undergoing a labored trudge down an endlessly long, inescapable and dark tunnel. It was possible he had fallen from an exalted height, or maybe life had dropped him to his knees and he was finding his way back up. A look could speak volumes. She was reminded of this in the brief moment he emptily told her he had slept better.

She risked a smile. 'Sleeping is good.' There was no response, so she continued. 'Shall we begin?'

'Yes, let's.'

'I thought we'd start straight into Sun Salutations this morning. You can follow me initially.'

'Sure.' He stepped onto his mat. Sasha had run her own mat parallel and slightly ahead of his, so he could follow her directly for a period of time until he got into his own rhythm. She stood at the head of her own mat and he followed her positioning.

'Begin by bringing your awareness into the souls of your feet and feeling the earth beneath you,' she said. 'Connect with your breath, expanding the inhalation into the base of your stomach. Lengthen and slow the exhalation.'

She heard him breathe out heavily with an uneven sound.

'Inhale into prayer position.' He coughed slightly and she turned to look back at him. 'Everything okay?'

'Sure.' He sounded prickly again.

Registering his discomfort she followed a hunch. 'The word *prayer* is a problem for you?'

After several moments of silence, he finally responded. 'I don't believe in God, so I don't relate to the word prayer...or it's power for that matter.'

Longest sentence he's spoken. Interesting one, too.

'I understand.'

'Do you?' He fired back in a challenging tone.

'Yes I do, actually,' she said calmly, recognizing the importance of her response and glancing back at him before facing forward once more. 'Let me rephrase. Inhale, placing your palms together in front of your chest.'

Sasha began a slow Sun Salutation sequence, staying in a rhythmical flow and continually reminding him to return his awareness to the in and out breathe. Once it seemed he knew the routine she stopped demonstrating, focusing solely on his technique and adjusting him slightly from time to time. 'Good. Lunge right leg back, press into your heel. Breathe. Lift your chin slightly; lengthen out through the crown of your head.' He seemed to be picking it up very fast, although she noticed he was pushing himself hard into poses and perhaps exceeding his stretch limit. His face appeared strained at times.

'Can't we do this faster?' he asked at the end of a Sun Salutation sequence, frustration evident. The request surprised her. 'Lets get your technique correct first.'

He flashed an annoyed stare. 'You said it was good.' Pausing in a standing position, his blue eyes pierced hers like flying knives.

'It is good.' She walked to the top of the mat to face him. 'But you've only just begun to learn yoga. Technique is important. You can return again and again to a strong practice if you have the patience to master the fundamental form well.'

'I don't feel like I'm doing enough.'

'That's interesting. What exactly do you feel you're not doing enough of?'

'A hard work out...sweating...you know what I

mean.'

'Oh, sure. You mean the gym-cardio, bust-your-ass kind of work out?' Sasha thought he might almost break a smile, but it didn't happen.

'Well, yes. Isn't this supposed to get you fit?'

'It's not just about your fitness. It's almost a reversal of the exercise philosophy you probably have.'

'Which is...?'

'To drive yourself; to exert high pressure on the body and all your joints and limbs through strenuous cardio-vascular exercise.'

'Well otherwise what's the point then?'

'Partly...inner balance.'

His face crumpled in confusion. 'I don't get it.'

'With yoga, your body can transform in ways you wouldn't imagine. But you must listen to your body. Allow it to yield in its own time. Lengthen through the exhalation. *Sink* into a pose rather than *pushing* into it. Pushing is your ego exerting its will.'

Shaking his head, he still appeared confused and somewhat frustrated. 'Couldn't we just try going faster?'

'You have a real need for this?'

'I guess,' he shrugged his shoulders.

'And what exactly is the hurry?' She couldn't resist.

A blank look appeared on his face. 'Like I said, fitness...and it's more exciting - more of a challenge going faster.'

'Really. And is that how you do life, too...fast?'

'Most of the time,' he replied crisply.

'And how's that working for you?' The remark slipped out of her mouth before she could catch it.

'Okay, I guess.' He said, looking around and gesturing with his hands as if his house was testimony to the benefits of speed and being driven.

'I see,' she said simply.

'Look, I'm just asking if we can do this salutation thing faster. Okay?'

Sasha reconsidered the request, glancing up through the skylight and observing faint stars twinkling in the black evening outside.

'I'll tell you what,' she said, 'you give me twenty more rounds of Sun Salutation now, with regulated breathing and strong technique and then we'll increase the speed.'

'Okay, deal.' He responded as if he'd just signed a contract.

'Good,' she replied calmly.

'Great. Then let's get on with it.'

They eyeballed each other for a moment before Sasha looked away. 'Okay,' she added, walking back to her mat before turning to face him directly. 'We'll begin then. Toes spread wide, feet pressed firmly into the mat, spine nice and long.' She watched him adjust his posture. 'And inhale, pressing palms together…'

Determination formed inside her. There would be no speeding up of Sun Salutations. Lucas didn't know it, but he would be struggling to get past twelve rounds keeping his breathing regulated and technique correct. She was one hundred percent certain of this.

What she wasn't sure about, however, was whether he'd retain her services after the lesson was done.

***

Her challenge for Lucas to complete the twenty rounds of Sun Salutation had worked. By round eleven his breathing was very irregular. His legs looked heavy and he wasn't dropping into the poses so well. He exhibited signs of tiredness and much mental distraction.

By the end of round twenty he'd slowed to a

pedestrian pace and looked beyond ready for a break. In her most diplomatic way she suggested a resting pose at the end of the sequence. He happily agreed and there was no further mention of speed.

By the time he was relaxing in Savasana pose in the final ten minutes of his lesson, Lucas looked peaceful. The tense face and jaw she'd observed on arrival had softened. There were few signs of tightness being held in his shoulders and arms. In fact, he could well have been a different man than the sullen one who had greeted her at the door. She knew she'd pushed him hard in the practice, but the lesson had served its purpose – he stopped challenging her and settled into listening and following instruction with greater respect. And although she suspected his controlling self would surface again, for now, he seemed more content to take instructions. It was for his benefit – she figured he'd have another excellent sleep ahead. In fact, it appeared he'd already drifted off on the floor in front of her. The movement in his ribcage had widened out and his mouth had opened slightly. She watched his head roll off to one side and considered adjusting it back to center.

No, I'll let him rest uninterrupted for a while.

Lying there asleep he seemed almost…vulnerable, soft and accessible. His armor was no longer visible. She could lay bets that his colleagues at work never saw him remotely near this current state. But of course, his defensive covering would undoubtedly be there again by morning.

Progress, not perfection. That was what she'd been taught. The words had become her personal mantra. Yet she was still excessively hard on herself at times. Lucas was likely that way too, she thought.

Glancing down at him once more from a cross-legged seated position off to his side, she observed one of his hands begin to twitch unexpectedly.

He must be in a deep state.

Sasha deliberated once more about adjusting his head position and inched slightly nearer. His breathing had become more audible. He was clearly snoozing, so it probably wouldn't be a good idea to move his head. All the same, it was becoming fascinating watching him utterly disarmed and napping. She shuffled closer, peering down at him, but not expecting what happened next.

Leaning forward within an arm's reach of Lucas, she watched him suddenly gasp as if catching a deprived breath. His head and neck pressed towards the floor as if he were reeling back from something. Within moments of that movement, one of his arms flung itself reactively off the floor. Her body was unfortunately positioned right in its path and she didn't have enough time to recline back from her *Nosy-Leaning-In* pose.

Before Sasha realized fully what was happening, Lucas's arm had hurtled up and careered directly into her face.

'Aagghh!' She yelped, rolling backwards onto the wooden floor, as the bridge of her nose began to sting fiercely from the strong blow of his knuckle.

Responding with a similar shocked sound, Lucas awoke rapidly in a state of confusion. His reflexes were now on high alert and apparently spoiling for a fight. 'What the fuck?!' he yelled angrily, sitting up with clenched fists before noticing her lying semi-curled up on the floor.

Sasha's hands had instinctively moved up to cover her face and watering eyes. She was stunned, but also entirely embarrassed and kicking herself for getting within such close and evidently dangerous reach of him.

'Jesus,' he exclaimed, looking down at her as if coming out of a dream. He quickly moved to her side. 'What just happened?!'

Slowly removing her hands, he could see the bridge of her nose was already looking red and slightly swollen. Crouching over her, his blue eyes were a mix of anger and concern. 'You were sleeping, I think,' she explained. 'And I moved closer to…adjust your head.' It was a reasonably accurate explanation. 'I think you must have been dreaming and were startled. Your arm just flew off the floor…and my face happened to get in the way.' As her eyes watered further from the blow, involuntary tears ran down her cheeks.

'God, I'm so sorry.'

'It's okay,' she replied, slowly sitting up and suddenly overcome by a strange sense of humor in the midst of her discomfort. 'I get this all the time.'

'You do?' He looked at her, baffled.

She smiled. 'I'm sorry. That's not funny, really. I'm just…kidding.' Her voice broke off and she held a hand gently over her wounded nose.

His expression became stern. 'Forgive me if I don't find it quite so comical.'

Sasha moved to stand up as he extended his hand to assist her off the floor. Gladly, she took it. 'I'll be fine. It's just a bump on the nose,' she said, returning to her feet.

'And probably a couple of black eyes,' he interjected in a worried voice. 'Come with me, you need some ice on that right away.'

'I…' she looked down at the mats.

'Don't worry, I'll collect those later. Lets get you down to the kitchen.'

It seemed that he was suddenly back in charge again and in his element. Conceding, she followed him out the door and gingerly down the staircase. It was the first time he'd walked beside her as they moved slowly and silently down the steps, eventually reaching the ground floor.

'I hit you pretty hard, I think. I feel terrible. I'm really very sorry,' he said with genuine remorse.

'Well, technically, you were unconscious at the time.'

'Please don't joke about it,' he said with serious look on his face as he directed her politely through another open-plan living area, past a large breakfast bar and into the modern kitchen. It was immaculate. Not a scrap of any clutter or cookbook nestled in a corner - just an expensive looking set of utensils in a holder sitting forlornly near a La Cornue's Grand Palais oven.

That's probably worth more than my entire apartment, she thought, noticing the extremely posh kitchen range.

'Here,' he directed, pulling out an elegant barstool and scraping expensive Italian marble tiles as he did so. 'Take a seat.'

She watched his long body move to one of the double doors of his fridge, opening the more narrow of the two and rifling through it before emerging triumphantly a moment later holding up a bag.

'Peas,' he said, surprising her by exposing his first smile. 'No home should be without them.'

Chuckling, she felt relieved he'd lightened up. 'That's entirely true.'

Closing the freezer door he returned to the kitchen bench, proceeding to bash the block-like plastic bag against it, until the hard chunks of bound vegetables eventually began to break up. Having loosened the peas he moved back beside her, immediately tilting her head in an upward position. 'I've never hit a woman before,' he said quietly, gently placing the icy bag over her nose.

Although her vision was impaired by the cold plastic protrusion now resting across her face, she could hear the dismay in his voice and knew his rare smile had disappeared.

'It was an accident, that's all.' Her voice was soft. But upon hearing no response she slowly peeled the freezing bag from her face. Sad blue eyes gazed back her. They made her feel unexpectedly...strange. 'Lucas, it was just an accident,' she added.

'I guess,' he said, backing away to lean against the opposing bench and crossing his arms as he stared at her thoughtfully. 'Are you going to be okay? Driving home this evening, I mean. Will you be okay to drive?'

'Of course.'

'Because I could always drop you back and arrange for your car to be driven to you,' he said with care and concern.

Sasha was surprised by how the tone of his voice affected her. She hastily whipped the bag of peas back onto her nose, shielding her eyes. 'I'll be fine. Thank you, all the same.'

It was several seconds before he spoke again. 'Where in the States do you come from?' He asked.

'California.'

'How long have you been in England?'

'Years,' she said, grateful to avoid his eyes and sensing what was coming next.

'What brought you over here?'

'A new beginning,' she replied candidly. Amazing how much easier it was to tell the truth with frozen peas covering your face, she thought.

The silence was awfully long.

'I see,' he said finally.

Do you? Do you really? Do you know what it's like to run from shame? She doubted it. But that wasn't his fault.

'I should get going.' She began to remove the icy bag.

'No, don't.' He took several steps toward the stairs. 'Your nose could do with a few more minutes. Stay there. I'll go get your things.'

Protesting was a waste of time. Besides, she knew he was right and thanked him instead.

But Lucas didn't hear her. He was already moving toward the staircase and Sasha was left feeling peculiar as she waited in the kitchen alone.

Chapter Eight

'What is truth?' The Guru surveyed the room, thankfully without looking at her this time. 'We all have different truths, so is truth not changeable?'

Holly found the question very deep, and was far too hungry to delve into it at this point. Her belly rumbled for about the sixth time in half an hour.

'Truthfulness is the result of our mind, speech and actions, being unified and harmonious.' His liquid brown eyes continued moving slowly around the group of students. 'Truth results in greater personal integrity and strength of character.'

God, if only she'd popped a snack in her pocket. *Some almonds...almonds would be nice.*

'Begin by becoming more aware of what you're doing. Ask yourself if it's harmonious with all parts of you. And does it do any harm? If you aren't sure, then hold back.'

Thankfully he was looking at another student. Holly began daydreaming about ice cream. She'd been doing that a lot lately. Was it the just the heat?

Perhaps.

Weeks of super healthy food was making her fantasize about a decadent triple scoop ice cream — with three different indulgent flavors. She'd choose chocolate, of course. Banana too. And definitely butterscotch...

'What often seems to be the truth – what is obviously the truth and what you know is the truth...is often not the truth at all.' He giggled, causing his five-year-old self to morph instantly back into the room and fully capture her attention. Jimmy - that's what she'd decided to call the infant persona of The Guru. Tuning back in more deeply, she listened to what Jimmy was saying.

'Truth is tricky. It is buried under layers...lots and lots of layers.'

Jimmy was really growing on her. He seemed easier to hear than the adult Guru, for some strange reason. But she noticed that, disappointingly, Jimmy had rapidly disappeared as quickly as he arrived. The Guru was back. And those ancient soulful brown eyes were actively searching the room now, which bothered her.

'Why would you attempt to bend truth?'

His eyes found hers

'Dig deeper for the real truth in your life.'

He was speaking directly to her, she was certain of it. But surely one could keep the odd secret?

'You will find the truth in the stillness of your being.'

I wish Jimmy would come back, she thought.

***

'What in God's name happened to your face?! Fiona exclaimed loudly as she strode confidently into Basilio's café the next day.

Sasha watched a half-dozen patrons turn and stare at her. 'It's just a bump on the nose. Nothing serious.'

'God, woman. It looks like you've been bashed!' Fiona grabbed onto Sasha as she stood up to greet her, giving her a tight hug before pulling away to examine the damage on her face more carefully. 'Who the fuck did this to you?'

'Shhh, Fee. Quiet. People can hear you.' Sasha sat down lowering her head to avoid the stares.

'Do you think I give a crap about that?' Fiona retorted, sitting down. 'Look at your nose, and those goddamned black eyes.' She gazed back at her flabbergasted.

'Fee, your language is appalling. This is Basilio's nice establishment, remember.'

Fiona glanced around unconcerned. 'Okay, okay. But hurry up and tell me what happened.'

'It was just a small mishap giving a yoga lesson?'

'What…you fell on your nose?'

'Not really.' Sasha smiled. Fiona generally had that effect on her.

'Let me guess, you were doing Downward Nose pose and you hit the floor?'

'Stop it,' she chuckled.

'Which client?'

'Lucas Huntington.' Sasha scratched her chin nervously.

'Mr Mysterious?'

'Yes.'

'Well how the hell does he look?'

'Fine.'

'So what happened?' Fiona's expression was still one of mortification.

'He fell asleep in the final Savasana pose. I leaned over to adjust him and…'

'He decided to punch your lights out?' Fiona interjected.

'No, Fee. Sometimes people get startled when they're waking up from a sleep or a dream.'

'Well it clearly wasn't a wet one, that's for sure.

You'd have had a far more exciting end to your day. And look a damn sight better.'

Sasha started to giggle. 'You're too much. He flung his arm up. My face got in the way, okay. End of story.'

'Oh. My. God. I'm still stunned. Your beautiful face looking like you hit a ruddy power pole.'

'Yes, was a bit of a shock to me this morning, too,' she responded sheepishly.

'Those are two mean looking bruiser eyes, Sash. How do you explain them to all your wealthy-prestigious clients?'

'Well, it added some entertainment and drama value to Lady Thornton's lesson this morning, I can tell you.'

Fiona raised her brow in a question.

'Oh my God, Sash-aaaaaah!' Sasha quietly imitated the drama. 'I think she easily got above the two-thousand hertz range.'

Fiona's face remained blank and emotionless, with a mere flicker of understanding.

'Extremely high-pitched, Fee,' she explained. 'Like, *break-a-dozen-crystal-glasses* kind of high-pitched.'

'You should get special ear insurance. And she should pay for it.'

'Well I probably charge her enough, to be fair.'

'So what about Lucas? What did he say? What did he do after he smacked you about?'

'Bella, someone smacked that beautiful face of yours?!' They hadn't noticed Basilio approaching. He gently placed several cups of coffee on their table, appearing full of concern.

'Basilio, we haven't ordered yet.' Sasha looked surprised.

'I ordered for you. I see your face as you arrive.' He shook his head, tut-tutting. 'Mama mia…coffee is on me.'

'Thank you, Basilio. That's so kind of you.'

'I have many Italiano friends. You just say the word, Bella. We will sort this *beast* out,' he grimaced, pinching his fingers together as if crushing an ant as the word *beast* rolled off his tongue.

'That really won't be necessary, Basilio. I'm fine. It was just an accident during a client lesson.'

Bending toward her and tilting Sasha's face up, his kind eyes carefully assessed the damage. 'Mama mia…sgradevole.'

Sasha glanced across at Fiona for translation.

'Terrible,' she interpreted, nodding in agreement.

Basilio frowned with care and concern in his eyes. 'Bella, you must date nice Italian boy who will look after you.'

She smiled back at him as he released her face. 'That's very sweet, Basilio. But honestly, it was just an accident.'

'There are no accidents in life, Bella.' He said with a serious tone. 'Things always happen for a reason.'

'And yours is a bad cosmetic one, sister.' Fiona chuckled.

'The bruises will be gone in one week, tops.' Sasha added dismissively.

'Two.' Fiona indicated with the peace symbol. 'And they'll turn that shitty yellow color and you'll look like an alcoholic with a jaundiced liver.'

'Thanks. That makes me feel a whole lot better.'

'No problem,' Fiona winked. 'That's what fabulous friends like me are for.'

'I'll leave you both to drink your coffee,' Basilio added.

'Thank you,' they responded in unison.

'And Bella, please look after that beautiful face of yours in future.' He blew her a kiss before walking gracefully back behind the counter.

'So.' Fiona turned her attention back on Sasha. 'You

never finished telling me what luscious Lucas said and did after he realized he'd planted his fist in your face.'

'Well...actually, he responded much like you.'

Fiona appeared puzzled.

'I think his exact words were *what the fuck*?!'

She chuckled. 'Really? That's what *Mr Serious, aloof, and alone-in-large-mansion* said?'

'Yes.'

'Profound. He's growing on me.'

'Thought you might approve.'

'He has some edges. Interesting.'

Sasha smiled, glancing down at the table in recollection. 'Yes, he's...surprising.'

'In what way?'

'Well he was quite caring, really.'

'How so?'

'Oh. He walked me downstairs to his kitchen and then put a bag of frozen peas on my face.'

'Peas...romantic.' Fiona's voice was thick with sarcasm. 'You had me at *bag of frozen peas*.'

'Oh, come on, Fee. It's not like that.'

'Forgive me, I thought I just saw a chink in your lonely sexless armor.'

'You always bring things back to sex.' Sasha said feigning disapproval.

'That's because *everything* comes back to sex.'

'No it doesn't.'

'Of course it does.'

'Does not.'

'Does.' Fiona chuckled softly. 'And whilst you've pointed out sexual energy should be used wisely and I'm now also aware that some might consider *not* having sex motivating and a good thing for many reasons, I'm not sure if that brings you happiness at the end of the day.'

'But you're implying sex does.'

'Well, I happen to think you getting laid might bring *you* a bit more happiness.'

'But I am happy.' Sasha responded with surprise.

'No you're not.'

'What are you saying?'

'You're. Not. Happy...Sasha.' Fiona emphasized each word before leaning closer and giving her a prod in the ribs. 'Not really. You're not. You're in the *no sex* camp. And you've been there a long time.' She paused. 'Sometimes I get the feeling you judge that part of yourself...that level of freedom. It's like you've slammed a lid down on a fundamental part of you. And maybe you have a good reason for that, but I think whatever that reason is, it's well past its sell-by date, and it's there through fear. Not love.'

'Well maybe I'm just waiting for the right man, Fee. Besides, there can be good reasons for fear. And maybe fear is a useful friend.' Sasha replied, beginning to feel a tiny bit defensive.

'I agree. I really do. But not when it becomes your ruler. Not when it's your guide. And that, for me, is the distinction.' Fiona sighed heavily. 'And honestly, that's what I get about you.'

'You do?'

'Yes I do.' She gazed thoughtfully at Sasha. 'With respect, and the *Brahma...char* thing aside, I think you could do with loosening off your reigns a little.'

'I feel fine.'

'I think if you were feeling fine you'd have stuck around and let a very hot Brazilian man flirt with you the other night.'

'What. Rodrigo? He wasn't flirting with me. Let it go.'

'He was.'

'He was not,' she hesitated. 'Was he?'

'Am I part Irish, and is the pope Catholic?'

Sasha's mouth formed a barely noticeable frown. 'Well maybe my life isn't all about sex. Maybe I want more than some flash in the pan hot Brazilian man. Maybe I want...real love.'

Fiona responded softly with surprising care. 'Sash, darling. If you want real love, you'll have to take a risk every now and then and let someone in. Don't think I don't see you.' She hesitated. 'It's like something is bugging you deep down. And when I think about it, it's been there the whole time I've known you.'

Sasha felt a curious mix of anxiety and unexpected hope but said nothing.

'I've never asked you about California...your past, anything much really,' she continued. 'Heck, I've never even seen pictures of your folks. I'm not sure how good a friend that makes me after all this time that we've known each other.' Fiona glanced down at the table. 'I know I joke a lot, but I care about you. And if there's ever anything you need to talk about...someone to talk to...I'm here for you. That's all I'm saying.'

For a few moments Sasha considered opening up. Fiona wouldn't judge her half as much as she judged herself. Surely. But one could never be certain about people. Not really. After all, she thought she knew someone well once before. But it turned out she didn't at all.

Love and Fear...Love and Fear...Love and Fear. The two words were cycling around and around in Sasha's mind in those few seconds before coming to rest soundly on *Fear*.

'That's sweet of you, Fee. Thank you.' It was all she could say. They were the only words she could find.

***

'Good Lord, Sasha! Whatever happened to your

face?!' As she opened the door, the words flew out of Melody's mouth with pitch-perfect dramatic tension and just the right amount of gushy sympathy. She was even marginally believable, like a C-grade actress.

Sasha was pretty certain Melody didn't give two hoots about her bruised face. In fact, as she watched her glance across the road, she realized it was likely that Melody was more concerned with what people in her immediate neighborhood thought about the black-eyed woman on her doorstep.

'Come in. Quick, quick. Get out of the cold, darling.'

Suddenly she'd made it into her *darling* book. *Definitely. She's worried about the neighbors.* Sasha glanced up in the hope birds were flying in the area.

As the gangly model strutted catwalk-like into her kitchen, she suddenly stopped and bounced up and down exclaiming. 'I've already had my breakfast smoothie this morning. Aren't I good?' Looking ever so skinny like a pogo stick, Melody spun about, the glare of her blinding white teeth distracting Sasha momentarily. But her teeth weren't half as transfixing as her sudden regression into childhood.

'Yes you are. But it really wasn't a problem.' Sasha had just lied outright – yet again. She couldn't believe what a fibber she'd become. And it was certainly becoming a bad habit where Melody was concerned.

Satya Satya Satya…she could have whipped herself with the word. Honest communication was considered the bedrock of any healthy relationship when it came to Satya. Deceptions and mistruths were not great when it came to the second Yama. However, she'd also been taught that if the truth had negative consequences for another then it was better to say nothing.

I'm glad you got your lazy backside out of bed early enough to respect my time and had your silly chocolate-infused smoothie before I arrived. And if you'd have

done that last week, I wouldn't have taken that call.
Then you wouldn't have overheard my conversation and
been so annoying – you nosy, rude, self-involved...

'It really wasn't a problem,' Sasha repeated. It was
truly the best response she could give.

'So how was your new client last week?' Melody
tweeted joyfully like a canary, interrupting her stream of
thought.

'Sorry?'

'Lucas Huntington.' She stared at her pointedly.

'I...' Sasha was taken completely off guard and had
no idea what to say. 'I...'

'Because *I know* which Huntington it is,' she
smirked.

'I'm not sure what you're talking about.'

'I have spies *everywhere*,' Melody laughed,
sounding almost sinister.

Sasha fantasized about the woman's nose growing
longer, like a sad pointed carrot with warts appearing on
it, before shaking off the crazy image.

'What?'

'Lucas Huntington. Stockbroker extraordinaire...and
very eligible bachelor, I might add,' Melody finished,
flicking her foot back with a girly skip.

Sasha wondered how, out of a city of millions, that
Melody had come to such a grand conclusion about one
stockbroker. And also began to understand why she was
so cheerful. 'I think you must have the wrong person.'

'No I don't,' she added girlishly. 'I have it on very
good authority he's just started taking yoga lessons.'

'Whose authority would that be?'

'One of my spies, silly.' Melody giggled as she
walked through to the living room. 'Executive assistants
aren't always so good at guarding electronic diaries...as
it turns out.'

Sasha was gob-smacked and really had no idea what

to say.

'And 'S D' would be your initials, I gather.' She flashed her bright white teeth again, although this time they looked like they belonged inside the mouth of a rabid dog.

'Look, I really don't know what you're talking about. And besides, my client information is confidential.'

'Well this particular information is now confidential *between us*.'

Sasha didn't like her tone. She didn't like the look on her face. She didn't like any little part of Melody in those few very challenging moments. Her blood was boiling and she felt the strangest and strongest impulse to walk over and...slap her. *Ahimsa Ahimsa Ahimsa.* Instead, she took a deep breath. 'I think we should begin your lesson now.' Sasha began getting the mats out.

'Sure,' Melody smirked. 'But I don't see what the big deal is about - admitting he's your client.'

'He's not my client.' Sasha lied again. She was even more annoyed to be put on the spot.

Melody suddenly changed tone, becoming creepily angelic in a split second. 'Don't panic, Sasha. I'm simply interested in finding out more about him. I've wanted to meet the man for six months since we briefly crossed paths at a charity gala event. He's quite hard to keep track of, you know.'

'No. I wouldn't know.'

'Oh, don't be like that. I think you really should know more about who some of your clients are.' Melody lay down on her back on one of the mats with a contented looking smile on her face.

'What does that mean?' Sasha glanced down with suspicion.

'Nothing.' There was Miss Flippant again - bandying about that annoying word which actually meant *everything,* not nothing.

'Nothing?' she looked down at the rake-like woman whose arms and legs looked almost too long for her body. Yet she still appeared to have curves in the places that counted most, at least in terms of her bank balance.

'It's just that sometimes people aren't really what they seem.' Melody said with her eyes shut.

Sasha felt unexpected fear seep through her body.

'I don't know what you mean?'

'Well,' she guffawed, sounding like a hyena. 'I mean exactly what I say. But don't worry, Sasha. Your secret is safe with me.'

Sasha remained silent. She was suddenly unsure exactly what and whose secret was being referred to. And one thing she felt certain of was that no secret was safe with Melody.

Chapter Nine

The next day, Sasha noticed how cold it was as she sprinted from her car to the club entrance. The weather was freezing with the sun having taken cover beyond a mass of somber gray cloud. Surely the temperature in London had plummeted a further five degrees over the past week. It certainly felt that way. Early morning lessons were a challenge, but in a few weeks time the days would slowly begin to get a little lighter and warmer.

Exhaling heavily, she watched the steam of her breath colliding with what felt like sub-artic conditions. Sasha seldom thought about California these days, but summer sun and beach memories tumbled unexpectedly through her mind as her legs carried her at pace across the car park. Thankfully, she was able to dismiss the thoughts as fast as they appeared. Sentiment was a dangerous thing and suited only to the indulgent, she thought, nearing the club entrance.

Yoga had helped her gain an understanding of a deeper truth - the past was over. The true beauty in life was the moment being lived. If only her subconscious mind would catch up with that fact.

Pushing heavily on the glass door, a cool winter breeze almost blew her through the entrance, unfortunately causing her to career straight into a club member.

'I'm so sorry!' Sasha exclaimed.

A tall platinum blonde spun about to face her. 'That's quite okay,' she responded, a surprised smile forming on her attractive face at the sight of two black eyes staring back at her.

Sasha had never seen the woman at the club before. She was likely another new member. No doubt hearing about the good-looking Brazilian instructor had spurred her to join. The club seemed to have had an influx of new female members the past few days. Still, she couldn't blame them. There was nothing like great eye candy to motivate a good workout.

I bet she's not here to take my yoga class, Sasha thought, watching *Long-Legs-Blonde* strut off in the direction of the changing room.

Heading straight for the yoga studio to set it up, she passed several members on her way in as they straggled out, perspiration from their aerobics class still evident on their faces. The studio area felt like it was at a good temperature, but all the same she moved toward the thermostat at the far end of the room and boosted it up a notch. Yoga was best conducted in a warm space. She'd had the luxury and good sense to train in a tropical environment and well understood the advantages of heat during a practice.

Busying herself unrolling mats in a nice even layout and spacing across the floor, Sasha moved nimbly around the room. She'd almost finished when she happened to glance up at the floor-to-ceiling mirror covering the main wall and caught sight of the tall and now familiar figure of Rodrigo staring back at her in the reflection. He was leaning inside the door entrance, quietly watching her, his arms crossed over his chest and one leg slung casually in front of the other.

'How long have you been standing there?' she fired

out, inwardly startled, but hiding the fact as she flicked the last mat onto the wooden surface.

'Long enough.'

'Long enough for what?' Her nerves were rattled as she listened to his entrancing accent. Once again his shirt was clinging to his taut muscular chest, emphasizing the most impressive looking pectoral muscles she'd ever seen on a man before.

'Long enough to notice your two black eyes.'

For the first time since they'd manifested on her face Sasha felt extremely self-conscious about her bruises. 'Oh, those,' she said dismissively, wishing she had more yoga mats to distract her from his gaze. 'They're nothing.'

Rodrigo peeled himself off the wall, much like a sexy model in an aftershave commercial might.

Oh God, surely he's not coming over here.

Watching him warily, he approached in long slow strides.

Darn. Just my luck. She glanced down at the yoga mat as if that would save her.

'They don't look like nothing to me,' he responded barely meters from her now.

'Well, a bang on the nose will do it.'

'And that's how you did it?' He pulled up a few feet short of her. It was too close.

'Well actually, a client hit me, accidentally.'

He was staring at her. She found herself looking at his lips. *His lips. His insanely gorgeous kissable lips.*

'They must have hit you very hard,' he said, suspicion evident in his voice.

It was a surprising thing, but at that moment, Rodrigo did something that made her want to pass out and drop backwards like a plank. She'd occasionally seen soldiers do it when they were forced to stand to attention for long periods of time at formal military events. They'd lose consciousness and just fall...not in a crumpled-like heap, but more like a stiff corpse, which must have been hellish on their skulls. Sasha imagined that's how she'd collapse at the moment that great hunk of Brazilian handsome reached out and gently placed his hand on her chin, tilting her face up and stepping a whole foot closer. A whole foot. That's exactly what he did. It placed him little more than a foot away in her estimations. But she wasn't estimating, not really. She was spinning. In fact, her mind had vanished entirely. She was just a pulsating body full of hormones, flushing heat and strange feelings.

Striking green eyes were staring at her. They held a deep and arresting tenderness that threw her completely. The touch of his hand was so soft it was more like a caress. She stood breathless and speechless as he looked down at her face with an expression that revealed an unidentifiable side of him.

'Was your client a he or a she?' He finally said, breaking the ethereal silence.

'A he,' she replied quietly.

Rodrigo remained silent. This was surely the moment to fall backwards onto the floor. The intensity of him standing this close caressing her face was too hard to handle.

Okay, so maybe it's not exactly caressing, she admitted to herself.

'I don't like men who hit women.' His voice was gentle...protective. *Was he being protective?* He barely knew her.

'It was an accident.'

'Uh-huh...' he smiled. 'There are no accidents in life.'

Basilio had said exactly the same thing to her recently. In fact, he'd had a similar caring look on his face at the time. She found herself feeling abnormally unarmored. There was a peculiar longing in her to draw closer.

'You think so?'

'I know so. Everything happens for a reason.' His voice sounded throaty. He was being sexy with her. It honestly seemed that way. And did he mean he'd met *her* for a reason? That was a crazy thought – they barely knew one another. But it was hard not to think it. She could almost feel his breath on her face...if she just leaned a little closer.

'Well, I guess I got in the way of his knuckles for a reason,' she finally responded, adding a smile to mask her discomfort.

But he didn't smile back. In fact, she felt him suddenly vanishing, as if a magic spell had just rapidly worn off. He appeared to be considering her comment. Had she said something wrong? Was the mention of another man enough to pop their dreamlike bubble? She wanted to take her words back. If only she could stuff them back inside her mouth, right away. Yet, alas not. Disappointingly, his hand slid from her face and fell to the side of his body.

As if on hideous cue, the platinum blonde that Sasha had bumped into on arrival now stuck her very attractive, pert-nosed face into the room.

'Rodrigo...are you ready for me?'

Looking over at her, he smiled warmly.

Had the magic simply relocated? Sasha wondered.

'Of course, Danielle. I'll be there right away.'

Danielle. Long-Legs-Blonde has a name. And he knows it already, of course.

'You know, you really need to be more careful, Sasha,' Rodrigo said, turning back to face her.

Searching the ground for comfort she avoided his penetrating stare.

'A woman with eyes as beautiful as yours should

take good care of them,' he added, before walking past her and disappearing out the door with the leggy blonde.

Remaining glued to the spot, Sasha barely moved an inch until her first students arrived.

***

When Lucas opened the door the following morning, Sasha wasn't sure how he'd react to the sight of her bruises. For a number of seconds he simply stared at her.

'Christ.' He finally shook his head. 'I'm so sorry.'

'It's fine, honestly.'

'It's not fine at all.' His tone was solemn. 'Come in, it's freezing out there.'

Closing the door she removed her shoes and followed him toward the staircase. However, instead of leading her up the steps as he'd done previously, this time he slowed his pace to walk alongside her.

'How's the rest of your work been this week?' He finally broke the silence half way up the stairs.

'Great, thank you.'

'So you haven't missed any as a result of...' he pointed a finger awkwardly toward his nose.

'Oh. My face. God, no.' She smiled.

'Because if you did I must reimburse you for any missed lessons.'

'That's kind, but no. It's fine, truly. Actually, I think the look has added a bit of winter color,' she remarked as a light afterthought.

'You shouldn't joke about it.' There it was again - the deep wariness that had been present in him a week earlier.

She immediately changed the subject. 'So how've you been feeling since the past few lessons?'

'Honestly?'

'Yes, the truth.'

'I've been aching in places I didn't know I had.'

She chuckled softly. 'Yoga can have that effect.'

'You never warned me.'

'Well now you know why.' Glancing at him, she noticed how much his face changed when he lightened up a little.

'I sure do.'

'You did take my bait on the twenty rounds of Sun Salutation.'

'And you taught my ego a great lesson.' He nodded, conceding.

They reached the room entrance where he politely opened the door, allowing her to enter first. Wandering across to one of the chairs, she placed her bag down and removed the yoga mats.

'Sasha…?'

A strange tingling sensation occurred in her body at the sound of him saying her name. It bothered her. She turned, clutching the mats a little nervously.

'Yes?'

'You talked about yoga creating inner peace and calm.'

'Yes, I did.'

He was serious again. 'How does that work? How exactly is all this…these poses,' he gestured to the center of the room, 'supposed to help?'

'That's a great question,' she smiled, regaining her poise. 'Asana practice consists of physical poses. And it's the most commonly known aspect of yoga, particularly for those who aren't familiar with the other seven limbs of Patanjali's Yoga Sutra.'

'So physical yoga is actually only one of eight limbs of the practice?'

'That's right. In reality it's more the third stage.'

'The first two, being?'

'The Yama and the Niyama limbs.'

'Which are?'

'In short, the Yamas are your attitudes toward others and the world around you. And the Niyamas are how you treat yourself…your attitude toward yourself.'

'Interesting.'

Wandering to the center of the room, she unrolled one of the mats before continuing. 'The third limb, Asana – or moving the body into postures - has widespread benefits. As I mentioned, health, strength, balance and flexibility are some. But on a deeper level the practice of Asana, which in Sanskrit means 'abiding' or 'staying', is used as a tool to calm the mind and move the yogi into their essence of *Being.*

'Okay, great. So it's a tool, but how's it working?' He watched her unroll the second mat.

'Aside from freeing the body of tension and stress, the challenge of poses and the way they open the body offer a person the opportunity to explore and control all aspects of their emotions, concentration, intention and faith.'

'And how exactly does it do that?' He took a few steps nearer, following her to the center of the room with curiosity.

'To some degree, the physical practice acts as a…' she hesitated, '*binding agent*, bringing a person into greater harmony with all the *unseen aspects* of their being.'

'Unseen aspects?'

'Yes. The forces that shape our lives through our response to the physical world.'

'Our response to the physical world,' he repeated, pausing reflectively for a moment. 'And our own *internal forces* behind that?'

'Uh-huh,' she nodded. 'So the Asana practice becomes a way of exploring our mental attitudes and it strengthens our will as we learn to let go, moving into a state of grace and stillness that comes from creating balance between the material world and the spiritual essence of who we are.'

'That sounds very deep,' he said, more abruptly than he intended. 'And it also seems to assume everyone has this...*spiritual essence*.' He stared at her.

'That's because *we do* all have it. Some may just not be aware of it, accessing it...or believe in it.'

'I'm not sure I agree with that. But what is this *spiritual essence* you refer to anyway?'

'I guess you could describe it as *consciousness*.

'Which is what?'

Sasha considered her response. 'You know that part of you that can stand off and neutrally observe yourself in a situation?'

'I do.'

'Well, you could almost define it as that. I mean, if you think about it, it's not as if that witnessing aspect of yourself is located anywhere specifically, is it?'

Lucas paused to think. 'I figured it was my brain, but actually, it's not just located there...it's bigger.' A small smile rippled across the surface of his face. 'Huh. I've never considered that...my *witnessing self*.'

'And when I say that, I'm referring to the part of *you* witnessing *you*. Not your mind having thoughts about things.'

'I get it. You mean my *Self* observing myself.'

She smiled. 'Yes, and you could say that's your mind, but it's not really, is it. It's kind of...*everywhere.* And the more you become aware of that part of yourself, the more it feels like you extend *everywhere*. You're not just this flesh and blood...thing.'

Moving quietly onto his mat he considered her words.

'Part of the beauty of Asana practice is that it's

grounding. It reattaches us to our bodies. So instead of our mind taking us on a merry roller coaster ride, we reconnect ourselves to the responsibility of living a life guided by the wisdom of our body.'

'So my body can guide and teach me?'

'Yes. Yogically speaking, the needs of your body are the needs of the divine spirit which lives *through* your body.'

Lucas pondered her words for a moment. 'So what you're saying in effect is...God is within?'

Sasha looked quietly back at him. 'Ultimately, I really think that's something only *you* can decide or discover for yourself.'

'I see.' He hesitated, looking into her eyes. 'And is that your experience...of God?'

'Sometimes, but not always, because my personality - I guess you could say - gets in the way. It's a journey. Look, we should probably get started.' Their conversation was getting too personal.

'Of course. I'm sorry, I didn't mean to pry.'

'Not at all.' She smiled at him, feeling awkward.

Lucas remained deep in thought for the rest of his lesson. He was thinking hard. And when she was just about to leave his house he surprised her with where his thoughts had taken him.

***

'I can't. I'm sorry,' Sasha responded, resting on the handle of Lucas's front door for a sense of security.

Leaning against the hallway wall, he folded his arms casually against his chest. In that moment she saw the kind of confidence that had undoubtedly projected him to a very high level in his career. He had a very determined side to his nature. She suspected he wasn't going to let things go. 'Because I'm your student?' he replied.

'Well, yes…partly.'

'You know, technically I employ you. And that's not putting me off.' A half smile appeared on his face. Admittedly she found it attractive. In fact, Sasha had been finding Lucas much more appealing since he'd placed the bag of peas on her face, if she was truly honest with herself.

She chuckled, causing a glint in his blue eyes to appear.

'I don't want to scare you off, because the yoga is genuinely helping me.'

'Is it?'

'Yes. A lot. For starters, I'm sleeping better than I have in months…or possibly years.'

'I'm glad to hear it,' she said, a little intrigued.

'Look,' he paused. 'I'm heading out of the country tomorrow on business. I'll be away for a week or so.'

'Oh,' she replied, a little thrown.

'I'm sorry it's such late notice. I only found out last night. But I've arranged for my assistant to ensure your payments continue while I'm away.'

'That's not…'

He held up a hand in protest. 'My point is, you temporarily *won't* be my teacher. So before we resume lessons again, I'd love to take you out for dinner.' Lucas saw the look of reservation form on her face. 'Or lunch,' he added. 'Besides, I still owe you for the two black eyes.' He smiled broadly. It was the happiest she'd seen him look since they'd met, which disarmed her. She didn't have a clue how to let him down or what to say.

'Great. I'll take that as a yes,' he said, picking her yoga bag up off the floor and handing it to her.'

'Thank you.' Her smiled disappeared, replaced by a troubled frown as she took the bag from him and twisted on the door handle. 'But you know, it's really not a good idea. It's totally against my professional policy and practice. I'm sorry, Lucas.'

Cocking his head to one side he surveyed her eyes and the indecision on her face. 'That's not a *no,* though, is it?'

'It's a…'

'Yes.' He interjected, leaning his arm across her and placing his hand on the door to prevent it opening further. 'One dinner, Sasha. That's all I'm asking. Nothing more.' His tone softened as his body leaned closer to hers.

'Lunch. One lunch,' she added firmly. 'That's all. Okay?'

'Deal.'

'You seem to like making those,' she countered, pulling the door open and watching his arm fall away.

'Yes, I do.'

'I'm not sure they'll always work out so well for you,' she said, unable to resist the parting shot.

'Like I told you, I do okay,' he smiled, trailing behind her out the entrance in his bare feet. 'I'll call you.'

'Goodbye, Lucas.'

'I'll see you, Sasha,' he said, enjoying watching her long honey-blonde ponytail swing from side to side as she exited out his front gate.

Chapter Ten

Greed was a funny thing, reflected Holly. People generally associated it with the acquisition of money, power or things. But according to The Guru, it could surface in ways that were not always obvious.

Holly found the latest lesson about the Yama, Aparigraha, to be hugely fascinating. She'd never considered the concept of greed beyond the bounds of material possessions. But a major light bulb had suddenly just switched on for her.

'Language can also be a place where greed creeps in. Talking too much, interrupting, and dominating conversations without allowing for others to participate are all examples of this,' he said.

Thankfully, Holly favored a quiet approach to life, so she felt relatively safe with the subject. If The Guru looked at her in this class, she could comfortably stare straight back at him. Her parents had taught her to share. And listen. Except when she was really hungry. Then it was hard to concentrate on anything. Unfortunately, the philosophy lesson in her training course fell directly before she was due for a meal. And aside from that, the four hours each day of physical yoga practice ensured she required a steady stream of food.

Sugar. I'm craving sugar, she thought, ducking her head down in case The Guru happened to be able to read thoughts.

'Greed's pay-off is emptiness,' Jimmy suddenly said, startling her. She knew Jimmy had just taken over the lesson because that special giggle occurred again right before he spoke.

Thinking about it, Holly realized she wasn't a particularly materialistic human being at all. Accumulating things made her feel almost uncomfortable. Sure, she loved beauty and would never turn down the gift of a five star luxury stay if the heavens rained it down upon her. And it was also true she liked to maintain and present herself well, and travel. But she was simplistic at heart.

She sighed. Jimmy had vanished as quickly as he'd arrived, leaving The Guru to pick up the dialogue. 'Thoughts can be a source of greed, too. Envy and jealousy can clutter the mind and turn into obsessions.'

Holly didn't feel particularly envious as a human being, but she did notice she'd become quite driven lately - a current of ambition and determination had begun to flow liberally through her veins. It was a relatively recent phenomenon, perhaps stemming from being psychologically kicked in the guts, so-to-speak. Regardless of how her inner drive had been born, she realized it was possibly a cover up for something else.

An image of a plump apple pie straight out of the oven began to form in her mind. It was a welcome distraction that she could almost taste. Licking her lips, she felt dismay descend upon her.

It was unlikely she would find any pie in this place.

***

A week flew by. Sasha had barely crossed paths with Rodrigo again, which was quite a blessing as he had a knack of unsettling her. In fact, after watching him exit the yoga room the previous week with the platinum blonde, she decided it was better to avoid him completely. His cocky self-assuredness around her had become…annoying. She was reminded of this in their brief encounter several days earlier as she'd exited the changing room.

At the time, Rodrigo was in the reception area surrounded by a bevy of adoring female fans. Deciding to dodge him, Sasha was sneaking around behind his flattering flock and heading toward the yoga room. He had his back to her, so it was unlikely he'd notice. Unfortunately though, she was barely three meters from the studio entrance when *Sleazy Ian* stuck his head out of his office. 'Sasha,' he said in a loud voice.

Spinning about, she faced him uncomfortably. 'Ian?'

'A word with you.' He gestured inside his office.

Christ.

Glancing cautiously back at Rodrigo, she realized he'd turned to check things out and his gaze was now fixed upon her. He towered almost a full head in height above his entourage and was staring at her through those penetrating green eyes with a half-smile etched on his face. It wasn't the *smile-with-your-mouth* variety - it was the smile through your eyes, as if you know an intimate secret about the person you're looking at. *Infuriating. Arrogant man.* She was not about to join his worshipping groupie gang anytime soon.

Spinning away from Rodrigo, expressionless, she traipsed after Ian into his office, leaving the door wide open. No sensible woman spent time in Ian's office with the door closed. That would be way too risky. Instead of walking behind his desk, he sat on the front edge of it, so there was no object between them. She was at that moment struck by the amount of product in his hair. It was standing firm and so slicked-up at the front that gale force winds were unlikely to budge a single strand of his jet-black locks.

Regrettably too, because of Fiona's comments embedded in her brain, it was difficult to avoid glancing down at the pouch in Ian's trousers that hid his sizeable manhood. Sasha hated herself for the sneaky little look. It was one of those unfortunate psychological responses that the brain could have to the words *don't* and *no. Don't look at his great big penis.* So, of course, she did. It was just for the tiniest and most discreet split-second, though. It didn't count as an ogle. But still, it was a horrid moment for her. She cringed.

'Take a seat, Sasha.'

As that would place her in direct line of his trousers, she hastily declined. 'I'll stand, thanks. I have a class to teach in a few minutes.'

'Sure.' He added, nodding his head as though he'd just given her permission to do exactly that.

'What's up?' she said, utilizing her bold Californian background. Offence was always better than defense with *Sleazy Ian*.

'I've heard a few disturbing *rumors* lately.' The word *rumors* rolled off his tongue with the kind of glee reserved for an evil snitch.

'Rumors about what?'

'Staff fraternizing with other staff.'

'Really?' She was genuinely thrown. 'What staff?'

'I can't say.'

'I don't see the point in having a conversation with you about this then.'

'Well...' he shrugged his shoulders. 'It's a friend of yours...'

'A friend of mine?' She crossed her arms instinctively. 'What are you talking about?'

'Your friend…Fiona.' He rubbed his hand slowly up and down his trouser thigh as he said her name.

Sasha's heckles rose in a nano-second. 'I can assure you, Ian, Fiona is *not* fraternizing with anyone at this club. Staff or member.'

'Really? And how would you know that?' He leaned forward. It could have been her imagination, but his trouser pouch had grown larger.

'Because I know for a fact she's…seeing someone outside of here.' Sasha faked an air of calm.

'Is that right.' He looked annoyed. 'And whom would that be?'

'I honestly don't think that's any of your business, Ian.'

Tapping one of his feet on the floor with agitation, he stared at her. Sasha could tell he was rattled. But frankly, so was she.

'It may very well be my business.' He paused. 'So let's hope she stays a…good girl. You know the club has strict rules, don't you, Sasha.'

Good girl? Good God! Slimy toad. 'Of course I do.'

'So I wouldn't like to see her, or you for that matter, step over that line and force me to do something I'd rather not.' Ian smiled smugly, surveying Sasha's body full length as he did.

Anger boiled up inside her. 'Well I wouldn't want to see *you* get caught stepping over that line either,' she blurted out. Unfortunately she couldn't take the comment back.

His eyes narrowed. 'I have no idea what you mean.' Standing up, he turned his back on her as he walked behind his desk. 'Be careful, Sasha. The fitness industry in London is smaller than you think.' He spun to face her briefly, ogling her breasts one more time before sitting down and perusing papers. 'Don't let me keep you from your class,' he added without looking up.

For several seconds Sasha considered giving him a piece of her mind. Then she realized that losing her cool would be potentially harmful not only to herself, but Fiona, too. There was Satya challenging her again with the discernment of what truth to speak and when. She bit her bottom lip. It was better to say nothing. In this case, silence was golden.

Every dog has his day, she thought, hastily leaving his office. But as Sasha headed once more in the direction of the yoga room, her belly was a cauldron of emotion. She was finding it challenging to stay in a healthy place of detachment. Disturbingly, Ian was growing more of an appetite for power.

Skirting the edge of the reception area, she caught sight once more of Rodrigo with the group of women still clustered adoringly around him.

Probably pawing at him.

Blanking the image immediately, her chin jutted into the air as she strode off. She was far too angry to stop at the Brazilian's harem and exchange pleasantries.

Rodrigo noticed Sasha's speedy departure from Ian's office. But glancing across, all he could see was the look of cool detachment stamped on her face.

***

It was Friday morning when Lucas finally phoned her. As the week passed, she decided he wasn't going to call; that he'd changed his mind, or recognized it wasn't a good idea - because it wasn't. It was foolish of him. And it was more foolish of her to accept his invitation. She should have flatly declined at the time he'd asked and left it at that. Besides, it wasn't as if she hadn't been in this type of position before. And where had that led to?

Disaster and pain.

Had she learned nothing?

Having taught locally that morning she was at her flat considering breakfast when he called.

PC Lucas Huntington appeared on the phone screen. Sasha used *PC* to code all private clients on her phone in a group. It certainly wasn't a secret encryption for *Pretty Cute* – which Fiona had joked about. Although, he was rather attractive. He'd also been growing on her more with the breaking down of some of his British upper-crust and reserve.

I should ignore it. I should ignore his call and when I teach him yoga on Monday, just invent a lie...a blinding white lie...since I'm already appalling at Satya.

'Hello,' she finally responded, overriding her inner dialogue and answering the call anyway.

'Hi Sasha. It's Lucas.'

She knew that, but didn't want to sound like she was waiting in anticipation. *I was waiting in anticipation, though. I don't know why, but I was.*

'How's your week been?'

'A wonderful week, thanks,' she said, feigning super positivity. 'And you?'

'Good. Very productive, thank you. I'm phoning about dinner,' he said, cutting straight to the chase.

'You mean, lunch,' she corrected him.

A long pause containing the unmistakable weight of him thinking, filled the air. 'Yes, of course. Lunch is fine. I fly back this evening. So how about tomorrow or Sunday?'

'Sunday works.'

'Great. Sunday it is. I'll pick you up.'

No, that doesn't feel right. You're my student. And you're certainly not a date. 'Thank you, but I'd be happy to meet you somewhere.'

Another long pause ensued. 'It's no problem, Sasha.'

'Look, I'm sure it's not, but I'd prefer to meet you,

all the same.'

More lengthy silence filled the air. 'Okay then. How about Hampstead Heath? A stroll if the weather is reasonable. And lunch.'

'That sounds nice, thank you.'

'Great. I'll confirm where to meet on Sunday morning.'

Or you could have your Secretary call me. Then Melody-bloody-Trenton can ask me all about it at our next yoga session. The unkind thought tumbled unrestrained from her mind, troubling her.

'Sunday it is. Goodbye, Sasha.'

Click. The call ended with a mixture of relief. *The rules of engagement*, she berated herself. *Never accept invitations from your male clients.*

Shuddering inwardly, she filled her kettle and switched it on, beginning to feel the gnawing of hunger.

Time was a funny thing, she thought, moving to her fruit bowl and collecting a whole pineapple. Over half a decade could pass and yet parts of that still seemed as if they were yesterday. Placing the pineapple onto a wooden chopping board, she moved toward her utensils draw to retrieve a knife.

She'd stolen something – something that belonged to someone else. You couldn't bend the truth far enough to hide that fact. Even if the details could somehow vindicate her, she'd still taken what belonged to another. And she'd ruined something that hadn't been hers to ruin. Learning about the Yama, Asteya, had really just confirmed what she knew to be the truth. And even if she *had* known that permission from another was needed, it was doubtful it would have ever been given. Therefore, she'd stolen.

The ugliness of that still resided in her; the indelible shame.

Forcibly pushing the uncomfortable feelings away,

she reached into the draw and took hold of the thick black handle of a sharp knife, the flash of its silver blade momentarily holding her spellbound. Surely she'd been punished enough for her crime, she thought.

Holding the knife up near her face she spent a moment scrutinizing it, spellbound by it's razor edge.

Years denying her happiness. Living with mistrust of her instincts; closed off to parts of life that the average person took for granted. Love. Family. Companionship.

Her heart pounded loudly in her chest. Had she hidden enough from her past? Had she outrun it? Had enough time lapsed?

Glancing trancelike at the knife, tears began to well up in her eyes. The blade taunted her – it always taunted her. It was only with the force of will she slowly lowered it down to her chest as a single large tear, intact and complete, fell from one of her brilliantly blue eyes and landed, *plop*, directly onto the blade.

Watching the salty water break up as it found its silvery ending, her shattered tear slid reluctantly toward the handle, now scattered and broken – no longer whole, nor connected with its perfection.

Just like me.

Could she find it again – that unbroken self? The innocence that she'd been?

Sasha wasn't sure anymore. But if she just stuck with her yoga, if she followed the eight-limbed path, maybe – as Fiona had unwittingly described it – she could follow the yellow brick road to someplace new; someplace safe. And maybe, she would find the emerald city and her heart again.

Chapter Eleven

'You missed a great night last night.'

'Really?' Sasha looked across at Fiona sitting opposite in the booth and observed the noticeable circles under her slightly speckled green eyes. They weren't dark like a bruise, but were still clearly evident against the pale skin of her friend's face. Fee was looking tired a lot lately. 'It sounds like what I missed is a hangover.'

'Spoil-sport. The place was packed and the band was going off,' she responded bluntly.

'I'm sure it was fun.'

'That's the second Friday night in a row you haven't come along,' Fiona said, scrutinizing the distant look on Sasha's face. 'What's up?'

'Nothing's up. I've just…had a lot on.'

'I'm thinking that maybe you're avoiding someone.' Fiona reached for the long stem on the glass of wine. It was her first drink for the evening as they sat in the quiet Camden bar waiting to catch a movie. 'Although, I can't for the life of me think why.'

'I'm not avoiding anyone.'

'Well, what is it? And what's this secret thing you go and do on Saturday mornings that is wrecking your social life?'

'I don't do anything *secret* on Saturday mornings,' Sasha's defensiveness suggested the opposite.

'Why can't you tell me then? If it's not a big deal.'

'It's not a big deal. I do a bit of extra yoga teaching, that's all.'

'Uh-huh.' Fiona quietly observed the changing expressions on her friend's face and felt bothered she was withholding something from her.

'And where do you do this yoga teaching?'

'Just local.' Sasha shrugged her shoulders dismissively, gazing down at the mottled wooden table full of scratches and clear evidence of being well used. 'Hey, I think Ian is seriously beginning to get out of hand,' she added, changing the subject quickly. Fiona noticed but said nothing.

'Beginning to?'

'Okay. He's getting worse. And I mean... disturbingly worse.'

'Houston, we have a problem.' Fiona's voice became formal. 'A large rocket in our leader's pants is getting out of control.'

Sasha frowned. 'It's not funny, Fee. He's changed. It used to be harmless, but he's on some sort of power trip now. It's...disturbing. There's this whole other vibe about him.'

'You can see why I got so angry the other week.'

'I can now. We need to be careful.' Sasha hesitated. '*You* need to be careful, Fee. He implied you were *fraternizing* with another staff member - but I think he just did that to find out if you're dating someone.'

'I'm having great sex with someone. I hope you told him that.'

'I certainly did not. And I'm being serious.' A frown furrowed Sasha's brow. 'I think he's a bit obsessed with you.'

'A bit? No kidding, Sherlock.' She took a large mouthful of wine. Sasha watched her with concern.

'I don't mean to sound like your mother, but you're

looking a bit dark under the eyes, Fee. Either you're not getting enough sleep or your liver isn't functioning well. Do you think you might be overdoing the drinking a little?'

Fiona eyes grew large in her head as she gaped at Sasha in shock. 'Are you serious? I'm bloody Irish. Compared to the average punter at Catholic Mass, I'm a lightweight when it comes to drinking booze.'

'Okay. I'm only saying because I care about you.'

'I know. Like I only bring up your non-existent sex life for exactly the same reason,' she smiled, changing the rare edgy tone between them. 'But now that I know about Brahmacharya, I understand you're channeling your energies...in other creative ways. Unless of course there's some other yoga purifying wisdom-thing I'm not yet aware of?'

Sasha smiled. 'There is actually. But I doubt you'd like to hear about it.'

Fiona raised her brow. 'Oh, really. Is it another Yama-pajama rule?'

'Close. It's one of the Niyamas.'

Fiona sighed heavily. 'Let me guess - the Niyama is the Yama's wingman? Or rather, wing-limb.'

'That's clever. Yes, Niyamas are the second of the eight limbs.'

'Well hit me with it, sister. What's a Niyama? And how many of them are there?'

'There are five. And a Niyama is about how you treat yourself and your attitude towards you.'

'Great. I should pass them with flying colors.' Fiona caught the amused look in Sasha's eyes. 'Or, maybe not.'

Chuckling, Sasha continued. 'The first Niyama is Sauca.'

'Sounds very culinary.'

'It's about cleanliness.'

'That's easy. I'm a clean-freak.'

'Outer and *inner* cleanliness.'

'Oh.' Fiona slowly nodded her head in understanding as she watched Sasha eye the wine glass in her hand.

'Uh-huh. So outer cleanliness relates to body, environment or surroundings. And there are also yogic cleansing practices to detoxify and cleanse the physical body for *inner* cleanliness.'

Fiona shook her head defiantly. 'Detoxify is a dirty word, Sash.'

'I thought you'd see it like that. Incidentally, Sauca also includes detoxifying the mind.'

'Oooh…twice-foiled. My mind is a sewer.' She paused, sliding her glass away. 'I've officially failed the first Niyama.'

'It's not a test, Fee. Remember, it's just a blueprint for a healthy and peaceful life. A guide.'

'Marvelous.' Her voice was filled with sarcasm. 'But surely to God I must be good at some of these Niyamas. What's next?'

'Santosha. Which basically means *contented*.'

'Yes!' Fiona raised her arms above her head in victory. 'I am contented!'

Sasha grinned. 'It's about finding contentment with what you have, who you are…and practicing humility and modesty.'

She dropped her arms back down as a defeated expression washed over her face. 'Well, one out of three isn't bad. Continue, my teacher.'

'The third Niyama is Tapas.'

'Don't you eat those in a bar over a drink?'

Sasha began laughing. 'Yes. But in this case it's referring to keeping in good condition through disciplining your body, speech and mind. For example, only eating when you're hungry and maintaining good posture.'

'I think I'm okay at Tapas.'

'I agree.'

'And number four?'

'Svadhyaya.'

'If I can't say the word then I'm hardly going to be able to do it, am I?'

'Svadhyaya involves self-enquiry and self-examination.'

'Navel-gazing. Go figure.' Fiona fired back, picking up her glass and finishing its contents.

Sasha ignored the comment. 'It also includes studying sacred texts. Basically, as your knowledge about yourself grows deeper, so does your connection and union with all things.'

'Yes, but what does that all mean, Sash? Really. What?

'Well, for me, I think it means having a deeper experience of life and love - recognizing that love is the most important guiding principle in life.'

'But that's all so *general*. You mean that I love the shop owner who sells me a loaf of bread and the tailor and the postman...and...trees. I suppose I have to hug trees, or something like that?'

'Do I hug trees, Fee?'

'No, but...you're always so damned *nice*. And sensible. Doesn't it get painful being so sensible?'

'I'm not always sensible.'

'Could have fooled me.'

'Well clearly I have. I've done some very stupid things in my life,' Sasha let slip before hastily continuing. 'Look, love as the guiding principle in life is not guided by your head. That would be *thinking* love. I believe having connection and union with all things has more to do with *feeling* love - in your heart. I'm sorry, that's probably an obvious statement.'

'Obvious works well for me.' Fiona paused. 'It's

getting heavy, though. Phew. Lets move on, my brain is fried. We must about be at the fifth almighty Niyama.' She glanced up at the ceiling. 'Please God, let this be a simple one,' she whispered.

Sasha looked down at the table, suppressing a smile. 'Isvarapranidhama.'

Fiona's face went blank. 'Are you kidding me?'

'No. I'm not.' Sasha suppressed a giggle.

'Well this has got to be a doozy.'

'It's about living with an awareness of The Divine.'

'Go figure. Saying the word is about as easy as the concept.'

'It's really not that bad when you break it down. Is-vara-prani-dhama.

'I bet understanding God and the workings of the universe are like that, too. I feel so relieved.' Fiona said sarcastically.

'Isvarapranidhama encourages you to let go of your false sense of control and to connect to God; The Divine…that which gives you a sense of wholeness and sacredness.'

'Now you see,' Fiona paused thoughtfully, 'alcohol does that for me.'

'Oh, Fee…' Sasha rolled her eyes.

Fiona grinned at her. 'Don't worry. I hear you, my friend. I may come on like a comedian, but I'm as deep as…umm…a deep lake.'

'Of course you are.'

'I kind of get it. It's another level of loving everyone and everything around you. You progress to seeing and feeling God in all things.'

'Great interpretation.'

'Good. Time for another beverage?'

Sasha smiled, glancing down at her watch. 'Not for me, thank you. Dave must be due any minute. Shouldn't he be here by now?'

'Yes. But he sent me a text earlier. He's bringing a friend along with him.'

'A friend?'

'Uh-huh,' she replied, avoiding eye contact.

'I hope you guys aren't trying to set me up with someone?' Sasha responded suspiciously.

'Not at all,' Fiona said, a little too lightly as she launched up out of her chair. 'I think I've definitely got time for another drink.'

'Fee...Fee?!' Sasha shouted after her. 'We have to leave soon for the film.'

But Fiona was disappearing to the bar at haste.

***

The movie theatre was pleasantly dark, affording Sasha some relief as she watched the large screen without absorbing a scrap of dialogue. A car chase scene was unfolding in a blaze before her but she remained oblivious to its context or meaning. Instead, during the moments of intense film drama, she stole a glance down at the man's hand to her left. It was resting on his thigh, with his fingers splayed slightly in a relaxed manner. Her awareness shifted to his chest, snugged up in a stylish shirt and fitted navy woolen jumper. His right arm was so close it almost touched her. Every tiny little move he made seemed to ripple out and magnify her sense of him. He exuded an air of quiet command. Of course he would, though – with an army of women at his beck and call to boost his ego. And then there was his powerful physique and all that South American...*passion*.

Earlier that evening, Sasha had watched Dave enter the Camden bar with Rodrigo in tow. She'd been sitting alone in the booth waiting for Fiona to return from the bar and almost fell off her seat at the sight of him. She wanted to slither under the table and dissolve into the floor. This could not be happening. He was the last person she wanted to be out with - some cocky womanizing Brazilian. She certainly didn't want to sit with him at the movies.

'Hello, Sasha. It's nice to see you,' he'd said, sliding his tall frame into the seat beside her, causing her to bunch along.

'And you, Rodrigo.' It was just a small white lie.

Fiona had returned sheepishly to a discreet and annoyed stare from her and managed to dodge eye contact for the rest of the evening by focusing on Dave. Which forced Sasha to converse with Rodrigo, much to her great discomfort.

Now here she was. Sandwiched in beside his warrior-like, super handsome self. *Mr Brazilian Adonis.* It was odd, considering he was such a good-looking man, but for some reason she was beginning to feel a little repulsed by him - in the moments she wasn't super attracted to him. She wasn't exactly sure why she wanted to flee in his presence, but he seemed to represent the type of danger faced by a gazelle on an African plain when in close proximity to a cheetah. Her extinction would be imminent if she dropped her guard for one second in his company. Unfortunately though, halfway through the movie something quite horrid started to happen: tingling sensations occurred in her stomach and chest. They were disconcertingly and butterfly-flutteringly good. And she couldn't seem to shut them down.

The last thing she wanted was to join the Rodrigo Fan Club of women, like some silly love-struck teenager. But *darn* he smelt good. And *darn* he looked good. His physicality was a distinctly unfair advantage, as was her vicinity to his muscular shoulder. If she could just rest on it for a tiny moment...lean on that strong and sexy limb; if she could just take a few minutes to lay her head against him; absorb his manly energy.

She sighed heavily, the action causing her chest to noticeably rise and fall. Rodrigo quietly observed the movement, despite his attention on the screen. He was aware of her, she could feel it and it melted her insides. Breathing heavily again, she tilted her head slightly to the left. It was really just meant to be a half-look; a subtle glance. But he turned his head fully to meet her, like the cheetah watching its prey. And he waited - he waited for her to look back at him.

There was enormous conflict inside her - his powerful energy confronting her own defiant boundaries and need to stay primed to run for safety. But it was an ashamedly quick battle as she found herself conceding. Surrendering to the moment, she turned fully to face him. And as vehicles crashed and exploded on the screen, his eyes locked onto hers with deep curiosity. The intensity both confused and disoriented her, causing her to tremble. How could he display such disarming tenderness and transparency? It gripped her momentarily, causing the tingling in her body to amplify. It was as if an electrical current had been switched on, swirling energy in her chest all the way down to her womb. Miraculously, however, her mind and nerves suddenly got the better of her.

Be careful, Sasha. Ian's words drifted back, disturbing her and dousing the moment. It reminded her of who she was, where she was, and also her haunting past. Breaking the connection, she turned to face the screen again.

Surely he wasn't interested in her. *Surely not.* And surely she wasn't attracted to him. *Disaster.* It must have been a trick of reflected cinema light and some sad and ancient biological reproductive drive in her for

Neanderthal Man. An image suddenly appeared to her of a child clad in a loin-cloth running wild across a plateau, club in hand. She shook it off, concentrating hard on the screen for the remainder of the film.

As the credits finally rolled and the cinema lighting came on, Sasha wanted to flee home as fast as her legs would carry her. Instead, she remained quiet as the others discussed the merits of the movie on the way out.

'Let's pop into a bar for a drink,' Fiona declared enthusiastically as they exited the theatre into crisp air and clear skies.

'Don't you think you've drunk enough the last few days, babe?' The comment flew out of Dave's mouth, surprising Sasha.

'I'll drink what I want, when I want,' Fiona responded sharply, clearly annoyed.

'You've been hitting the bottle pretty hard lately.'

'Have not.'

'You have. Too much. But I'm not going to argue with you.'

Fiona's face flamed with anger. 'You know me a short time and you think you can tell me what to do?!'

At this point Rodrigo dived into the conversation. 'How about we all go for dessert? Look, there's a place over the road, there,' he pointed.

His husky South American accent hit Sasha's body like a tidal wave of energy. It was time for her to run, literally. 'I'm sorry to leave you all but I'm going to head off.'

'What?! Because you have another mysterious yoga class to teach in the morning?!' Fiona spat out with irritation. 'Can't you just have some fun and get a bit of a life for a change!' Her words whipped through the air, landing on Sasha like a scolding iron. It was one of the only times in their relationship that Fee had ever spoken harshly to her and the blow was thudding.

'I'm just…a little tired,' Sasha answered, reeling from the tone in Fiona's voice and pulling her black woolen coat more tightly around her for comfort. 'I did enjoy the movie, though.'

An awkward silence fell upon the group for a few seconds. It was tense.

'I did too.' Rodrigo finally added. 'It had some great action.' She watched his strong jaw move and a smile light up his face, which made her feel better. 'Are you sure we can't tempt you to come for dessert, Sasha?'

'No. Thank you all the same. I'll get going,' she said, watching Fiona staring forlornly at the footpath as Dave reached out to hold her hand.

'Let me walk you to your car,' Rodrigo added.

'I'm fine, thank you. I walked from home this evening. I don't live far away.'

'Well I must accompany you. You can't go alone at this time of night.'

'Honestly, it's not far. Barely five minutes away.'

'One hundred meters on your own in a city at night is far enough. I insist,' he said firmly.

Sasha realized there was no point in declining the offer. He was right. Besides, she was feeling vulnerable and flat all of a sudden. Logic prevailed. 'Okay,' she agreed.

'When I come back, I'll meet you guys over the road at the dessert place,' Rodrigo added.

'Okay, great,' Dave responded, moving towards Sasha and embracing her with a warm hug. 'It's nice to see you again, Sasha.'

'And you, Dave,' she smiled, despite sadness weighing upon her. Fiona didn't budge from her position on the pavement. 'I'll see you, Fee,' Sasha said gently, resisting their usual farewell hug before turning and walking away.

***

'Did you honestly enjoy the movie?' They'd been strolling in silence for several minutes before Rodrigo spoke.

'Of course,' she responded.

'Not all women like action movies.'

'Well I happen to be one of the ones that do.'

'I thought your taste would be more,' he searched for the word, 'artistic.'

She smiled. 'I like most films. Growing up in Los Angeles…it's hard to avoid them.'

'Ah…Hollywood,' he paused. 'Where all your dreams come true, yes?'

'Not always.' Sasha watched the pavement, listening to the sound of her boots as she steadily walked ahead.

'You didn't have enough of a dream in Los Angeles to make you stay there?'

'No. I guess not.'

Rodrigo thought carefully before he spoke again. 'Everything okay with you and Fiona?'

She glanced at him for the first time since they'd set off. 'Honestly? I'm not sure.'

'She didn't seem her usual self. She was a little…tense,' he replied.

'I don't think she appreciated the references to her drinking. I'd basically made a similar comment to her earlier in the night. '

'Ah.' He nodded his head in understanding. 'And that made her angry.'

'Probably. I'm really not sure. She has been drinking a lot. Lately, much more than usual. And she's not the kind of person who takes kindly to…'

'Truth?'

'Well, it was *my* truth really. *Opinion* may be a more accurate word. Fee can be bloody-minded at times.'

Sasha hesitated before looking at him. 'Or maybe you'd consider it *passionate.*'

'Well,' he smiled, 'passion can also be bloody-minded...and a foolish thing.'

'Yes, it can be,' she replied reflectively.

'Have you ever done a foolish thing, Sasha?'

Picking up her pace she rounded a corner. Rodrigo increased his already long stride to keep up. 'Everyone makes mistakes. It's very human,' she said dismissively.

'No. Not a mistake. I said *a foolish thing.*'

'I'm not sure there's a difference.'

'But of course there is,' he said in a serious tone, which made her feel nervous. 'A mistake is something you did that you never realized would be harmful...you never intended or foresaw the consequences.'

'And a foolish thing?'

'I think there's more of a knowing deep down inside that something's not good; that it's not the best action or choice to make. But you ignore the warning signs, or act naively.' He shrugged his shoulders. 'So I think a foolish thing is more preventable.'

'That's a good distinction. I never thought of it like that.'

He stared at her. 'So have you?'

'Have I what?'

'Ever done a foolish thing?'

Christ, she thought, wishing he'd drop the subject. Thank goodness they were near her home. 'Hasn't everyone,' she responded casually.

'I'm not so sure.' He glanced at her. 'You know, you're more enigmatic than I realized.'

'Oh? Why's that?'

'I can't figure you out.' He smiled. 'Are you the serious woman or the fun one?'

'The fun one would ask you what you prefer me to be.'

'That doesn't sound fun. It sounds…' He spun his hand in the air.

'Dizzy?'

'Yes, dizzy,' he laughed.

Sasha seized the moment of distraction. 'How about you – have *you* ever done a foolish thing?'

'Of course!' His grin was ear-to-ear and infectious.

'Like what?' She couldn't help but smile.

'Ah, let me see. Well…,' he paused, 'when I was about twelve I had a big crush on my friend's sister who was three years older than me. One day, when I was at their family home and we were all swimming in the pool, I grabbed her in the water and kissed her.'

'Really?'

'Yes.' He smiled at the memory. 'In front of her parents.'

Sasha started laughing. 'You're kidding me.'

'No. Not at all. True story,' he grinned, drawing a cross over himself.

'Well, what did they do?'

'Her parents? Nothing. But she…she slapped me so hard my cheek was red and sore for days.' He chuckled at the memory.

'A foolish thing, then?'

'Yes,' he said, peering into her eyes as they walked under a streetlamp. 'It was certainly no mistake. It was a very foolish thing – both preventable and naive. But the heart…' He sighed heavily. 'Ah…the heart is wired so. It is wired for foolish things. Is it not?'

Sasha slowed her pace, nearing the entrance to her flat. 'I guess it is. Maybe until we learn.'

'Learn?'

'Whatever we need to learn.' Sasha looked back at him thoughtfully. 'This is me.' Stopping in front of her door she reached into her jacket pocket for her set of keys.

Rodrigo looked at the door then back at her and smiled softly.

'So, did you learn something - back then?' she added with curiosity, hastily fumbling her way through the keys in search of the right one. But he was standing barely two feet in front of her. Looking up at him, she unexpectedly found it difficult to breathe. A light on at the corner of her building allowed her to make out the shape of his face, his strong jaw and eyes that were glued to hers.

'Of course. It has affected me to this day.'

'Really?'

'Yes. I've never ever dated a woman older than myself. And probably never will.'

Sasha chuckled softly, helping her to breathe again. The street seemed so quiet. Everything was still as they stood so close to one another. She felt drawn to him. He was radiating some sort of addictive chemical. It wasn't fair - it wasn't fair for a gazelle to be fascinated by a cheetah. It was a deadly game. Rodrigo didn't move a muscle. It was as if he was waiting for something. She sensed it; watched it - wanting to lean into him. If she did...if she just tilted her head slightly towards him...maybe he would lean in too.

But instead she found herself thanking him for accompanying her. Chastising herself inwardly, she finally located the correct key for her door and gripped onto it. 'That was kind of you to walk me home.'

'It was my pleasure.'

He was standing so steady. Barely moving an inch forward, nor back. Forcing herself to turn toward the door, she inserted the key into the lock.

'Goodnight, Rodrigo.' She pushed the door open, glancing back as she switched on the light inside.

'Goodnight, Sasha.'

It was the first time since leaving California that she

wished she could just let go; she wished she could be honest; wished she could hear something different.

Rodrigo walked several meters up the street but stopped to look back one more time. He watched her carefully and didn't move until she'd securely closed the door behind her.

Chapter Twelve

Breath work was fabulous. Holly always felt so amazing after a burst of Kapalabhati. *Respiratory breathing,* as The Guru had described it. She preferred to describe it as *how to feel one hundred percent serene and brilliant...in two minutes flat.*

Okay, so maybe there was the odd occasion it could take longer. But regardless, it was a blast. And her skin positively glowed afterward.

The Guru was busy pointing out that Pranayama was a pretty critical limb in the eightfold path of yoga. 'Prana refers to the life force or energy that exists everywhere and manifests in each of us through the breath.'

What an amazing concept, Holly thought. It's like our *universal soup* - kind of like a fish's equivalent of the water that they swam in.

'Ayama means to *stretch or extend*,' he continued. 'Prana flows out from the body. And Pranayama will teach you to maneuver and direct Prana for optimal physical and mental benefits.'

Like what benefits? she wondered.

The Guru looked at her. 'You can go for months without food, days without water, but only moments without breath.'

It was almost as if he'd tapped her brain and mysteriously knew what response to make to her thought.

But were his words...like a threat? Or was he being profound?

'Breathing is life. Breathing affects all our actions, and our thoughts too,' he added.

Perhaps it does, she considered his words. She hadn't thought about food for the last hour.

'Mastering the breath will help you master yourself.'

It was barely audible, but Holly was certain she heard him chuckle.

***

Hampstead Heath was one of Sasha's favorite London Parks. It had been from the moment her feet first trod upon the hilly and rambling tract of land a number of years earlier. The Heath included areas of ancient woodlands that, when first explored, made her feel as if she'd tumbled down a rabbit hole into a magical world, much like a modern-day Alice in Wonderland.

Now standing in front of the stately Kenwood House, soaking up the late morning winter sunlight as it gently touched her face, she felt cozily warm, bundled up in a thick woolen coat, scarf and gloves. Before her, swept a gracefully sloping hill that rekindled a sleeping memory. She'd once taken a morning stroll by the pond at its tree-shrouded base. At the time, it had been mid-winter and the surface water thickly frozen over with ice. With amusement she'd observed dozens of ducks in hilarious ice-skating antics, sliding at speed on the glassy surface, crashing and careering into one another like a comedic version of live animal skittles.

'A penny for them?'

'Oh!' Sasha jumped as she felt a hand connect with her thickly covered elbow.

'I'm sorry. I startled you,' Lucas said, watching her surprised expression as she spun about.

He too was wearing a long black coat. And on top of his head was a blue woolen hat, which didn't seem to fit his corporate aloof image. The beanie made him appear like a football fan – more comfortably human and accessible, with just a hint of thug.

'You looked far away,' he added.

'Oh. I was a little closer than that,' she replied, tilting her head toward the base of the hill. 'Just recalling seeing ducks skidding about on the frozen pond a few winters ago.'

Lucas smiled softly as he followed the movement of her eyes. 'Yes, they're a funny sight all right. Have you visited the Heath much?'

'I used to. A lot. Years ago, when I first arrived in London. I loved it.' Visibly inhaling, ethereal wisps of steam drifted from her mouth as she exhaled. 'I still love it. I just don't make the time to come here so much anymore.'

'Life gets to be like that, doesn't it,' he said, surveying the land around them. 'But you of all people should know to make the effort.'

'Me of all people?'

'Of course. You are a yoga instructor. You seek balance in life, do you not?'

'I do. But perhaps the old adage is true – you teach best what you most need to learn.'

'Is that so,' he said, turning to gaze at her inquisitively. 'After the way you drilled me through Sun Salutations I'd have picked you to be masterful at the art.'

'I did drill you a little, didn't I,' she conceded.

'You sure did.' He smiled, bringing a flood of

lightness to his normally serious face and making him appear like a different person. 'Shall we walk?'

'Before we both freeze here…yes, lets.'

'There's probably more mud in that direction. We'll go this way,' he gestured toward the opposite track. 'I've booked a restaurant for lunch. But we have plenty of time to get lost on the heath before then.'

'I have a hunch you know your way around here very well.'

'Clever hunch. I've lived in the area for years. We…' He stopped suddenly, searching for words. 'I mean…I…used to walk around here a lot.'

Well accustomed to hiding parts of her own history, Sasha pretended not to notice. 'And did you always know you wanted to be a stockbroker?'

'Not at all. Actually, I think the direction was more an act of rebellion.'

'Rebellion?'

'Yes.' He appeared thoughtful. 'It certainly wasn't deemed an appropriate path for me by my father.'

Curiosity filled her as she searched his face. 'Really. And what do you think would have been an appropriate path - for him?'

'I couldn't be sure.' A faint smile spread across his face. 'Probably a high-ranking military career. Full of…' he searched for the words, 'pomp and ceremony. So I could return the hero and pick up the family mantle.'

'Families…the pressure, huh.'

'Is that why you left California? Family pressure.' He paused. 'I'm sorry. I'm prying again. That's terribly impolite of me.'

'Not at all.' Sasha smiled. 'My parents were part of the *flower power* era - all very authentic Californian. I was raised to be free. So no pressure there.'

'That must have been nice.'

'It was. But sometimes I think it would have been better to grow up with a few more boundaries.'

'Really?'

'Sure. Without them, I tended to drift along at times. Occasionally in the wrong direction,' she added as an afterthought.

Lucas took his eyes off the dirt track as they walked, staring at her momentarily. 'The wrong direction?'

She felt like kicking herself. 'Well, not so much wrong. I mean a *less-focused* direction. You know, like getting easily...sidetracked.'

He looked away, absorbing his winter barren surroundings as they walked further along the trail. 'Sidetracked, huh. Sometimes I wish I could get a little sidetracked.'

'Oh, trust me. You don't,' she said, glancing down at the worn footprints in the damp ground as they began to weave their way down the hill.

'No, I do. Honestly. Life gets to be terribly dull just fulfilling material and practical obligations.'

'Don't you mean *aspirations*?'

'No. I mean obligations.'

'Why do you consider them obligations? It's not as if someone is holding a gun to your head demanding that you have...the best house in Belsize Park...or something like that.' Sasha added, uncertain about his home being the best in Belsize Park, but figuring it must be pretty close. And besides, the words just happened to spill straight out of her mouth, as forthright Californian remarks were still inclined to do.

He considered the question. 'I guess they're not truly obligations, anymore. Probably just ingrained thought and...habit.'

'The family pressure again?'

'That may have been its origins. But then I think it became something else. I guess I can't blame my past these days. Yes, the sense of obligation may have been passed on initially, but then I claimed that way of being for myself. It's like being handed a baton in a relay that I hadn't considered *not* being a part of. And I never noticed the transition point. Suddenly I was just carrying this…rather weighty thing.' Furrowed lines formed in a corrugated fashion on his forehead. 'So regardless of any efforts on my part at *rebellion*, here I am, still being very much a Huntington – my father's son.' A half-chuckle escaped his lips. 'God help me. Here I was smugly thinking I'd managed to get away.' He paused. 'As if we can ever outrun our genetics.'

Sasha listened carefully. 'Perhaps you did, though.'

'Get away? No. I definitely did not.'

'Why do think that?'

'Because I married a woman who embodied my family and their ambitions,' he hesitated, checking her reaction. 'I just didn't realize that initially.' Looking directly into Sasha's surprised eyes a spark of electricity momentarily whipped through her body. 'But people can just plain surprise you, can't they?'

'Yes. They can,' she responded quietly with understanding. 'Sometimes I wonder if you can ever really *know* another person.'

'Or if you can ever really *trust* one,' he added, picking up his pace on the track.

'But you trusted your wife? You must have. At least for a while.' Curiosity was getting the better of her. She increased her pace on the muddy trail to keep up.

'I did, of course. Otherwise I'd never have married her. But she was different initially. More natural.' He reflected for a moment. 'Or perhaps so phony I couldn't tell. It was my…heritage…and family name she inevitably loved. Not me, I'm afraid.' His voice quietly trailed off.

'I'm sorry to hear that. What happened? she replied,

instantly annoyed at herself as the question rolled straight off her tongue. 'Now I'm the one prying. I'm sorry.'

'It's fine. It's all history now anyway. She...she left. When she realized I wasn't interested in following in my father's footsteps. I guess being with a stockbroker wasn't part of her worldly goals. And...' He stopped himself.

'And what?'

'Nothing. It's nothing. This is all way too heavy for a pleasant Sunday morning stroll.' He looked across at her and smiled. 'You're supposed to be educating me more about yoga.'

'Yes, I am.' She returned the smile. It was probably better they change the subject anyhow. 'Now that I understand a little more why you're drawn to it.'

'And why am I drawn...to yoga?'

She could have sworn she saw a softening in his eyes. Her pulse quickened. 'I'm guessing, but I'd have to say, to find and experience some form of freedom. Mostly from your mind.'

'And you think yoga will help me get there?'

'Yes. I do.'

'How?'

'Well to start with, it can support you greatly in becoming more aware of yourself – your thoughts and feelings. And ultimately, that guides you to *now* - this moment. Living in the moment is the least complicated way to be.

'It sounds refreshingly simple. I tend to spend my life in the future, predicting markets and such. Strange really, the movement of money and stocks and shares...as if it really means anything at all.' His voice softened. 'Sometimes I envy men with trades – working with their hands.' He turned his palms up, examining them for a moment as if they didn't quite belong to him.

She listened carefully and was surprised to feel him touch her arm as they walked. 'So how does *simple* work for you?'

Sasha felt thrown by the question. 'Like I said earlier – you teach best what you most need to learn.'

Silence hung in the air momentarily. 'Well. I need to learn. So tell me all about it.'

'What would you like to know?'

'You mentioned something about the yoga pathway. *Limbs*, if I recall.'

'That's right. Excellent memory. The eight limbs.'

'The eight limbs,' he echoed. 'Breathing must surely be one of them, yes? You've focused a little on that. It seems pretty critical. And I've heard as much.'

'Yes, breathing is important,' she said relaxing. 'In yoga, the various types of breathing methods are referred to as Pranayama. But I haven't started teaching you that fully yet.

'And Pranayama is a specific limb?'

'Yes. It's the fourth limb.'

'Why's that?'

'Pranayama is about how we relate to our breath, or spirit. Through awareness and exercises, our breathing is regulated and controlled. And the aim is to strengthen and cleanse the nervous system and increase the source of our life energy – or *Prana*,' she explained.

'That's it?'

'Partly. But that's a very simple description. Pranayama generally goes hand-in-hand with the Asana practice…holding poses; the third limb. The two together are considered the highest form of purification for the mind and self-discipline for the body. The practices produce a physical sensation of heat, called Tapas - deemed the *inner fire of purification*.' He was listening attentively, so she continued. 'The heat purifies the *Nadis*, or subtle nerve channels in our bodies. And that allows a greater state of health, along with calming the mind.' She looked over at him with a smile. 'Have I lost you yet?'

'Not at all. You explain it very well. I was just thinking about achieving a calm mind. It sounds great.'

'Yes, it is. The deep yogic breathing soothes the nervous system, the mind, and can help reduce cravings and desires.'

'Desires?' He smiled.

'Yes. The tendency to grasp at the world outside of you to fulfill an inner sense of need.'

'Hmm,' he murmured, considering her words.

'The absence of cravings and desires – whether they be food, people or things – helps set the mind free and allows for greater concentration,' Sasha explained.

'In order to access another limb?'

'The journey is about becoming more mindful and living with an awareness of every moment of life. But yes, it does lead onto other yoga limbs.'

'Sounds like a handy way to be. I could do with that – being aware in every moment. What an amazing thing…it sounds remarkably like *really living*.'

'It is really living,' she echoed, observing his brow knit together in reflection.

'And Pranayama…it comes after…?'

'The Yamas, the Niyamas and Asanas.'

'Well my body certainly knows about the Asanas.' He faked a grimace. 'You know, I wasn't entirely honest about my physical discomfort the day after all those Sun Salutations…the ones you made me do in a row,' he added cheekily.

'I did not make you do them,' she responded back playfully, swatting her hand into his upper arm. It was the kind of thing a schoolgirl would do when flirting with a boy she liked. And it was also an entirely spontaneous gesture. She suddenly felt exposed.

'You did.' He relieved her discomfort with a nice smile. 'You were like a military sergeant dishing out orders. And you loved it.' He gently tapped her arm back in return as they headed down a steeper incline.

'Perhaps a little.' A relaxed feeling seeped through her like warm liquid. Returning the smile, she pressed her thumb and forefinger together. 'Just a tiny bit.'

'I concede, though, I had it coming to me. And the fact I could hardly walk the next morning was punishment enough for my arrogance.'

'You were just very determined.'

'No.' His glance drifted down toward the ground. 'I was arrogant.'

The shamed expression on his face caused a ripple of compassion to move through her. 'Well, wait until I start teaching you Pranayama. I'll drive you relentlessly. Then you'll really feel like you're at some military academy.'

'My father would be thrilled,' he added with a touch of sarcasm.

Sasha was about to respond when the heel of her right foot connected with a particularly muddy spot on the track. Before she knew what was happening, her entire right leg had skidded out in front of her. As she instinctively moved to correct her balance, her left foot slipped forward. The slope of the hill was so steep that regaining her footing was a near impossible feat, and whilst Lucas was quick, he couldn't save her from landing heavily on the wet track. Although he did manage to grab the arm of her coat as she flew backwards. But in reacting to accommodate her fall, and grasping onto her coat, he also lost his balance. Sasha was in mid flight when she saw his leg fly into the air to her left, just as her backside hit the hard ground. Her body was beginning to slide south on the steep gradient as he crashed down beside her. Still clutching her coat, the momentum and drag caused his body to roll toward her. Sasha felt a stinging blow to the left side of her face as Lucas's right elbow landed heavily upon it.

'Christ!' he exclaimed as they slid several meters and drew to a halt.

From somewhere further down the hill, Sasha could hear several people laughing, she assumed at them. They must have made an amusing sight and she might have laughed too, except for the smarting pain around her cheekbone and left eye.

Lucas hauled his body off the ground from somewhere partially above her. 'God. Are you okay?'

The sunlight seemed glaring. As she blinked, several tears squeezed their way out of her aching left eye. 'I think so. Mostly. Except my cheekbone and this eye,' she said, pointing sheepishly at the left side of her face as she glanced up from her horizontal position.

'Oh, God. Your eye. Not again,' he said with dismay. 'I'm so sorry.'

'It's okay.' She sat up, the back of her coat covered in mud. 'I still have one that works.'

'This is terrible. I can't believe I've given you another black eye. You've barely got rid of the last two!' He stood up annoyed, his coat looking like he'd been wrestling cattle at a rain-soaked rodeo. 'Come on, let's go find some ice.'

Grabbing hold of his outstretched hand, he drew her back up onto her feet. 'We could try the surface of the duck pond,' she joked.

'Can you stop being a comedian when I've just hurt you!' he suddenly snapped. The words were as crisp as an under ripe green apple, blatantly reminding her of his shadowy personality twin. A bucket of cold water thrown in her face would have had a more welcome effect.

Gently disengaging her muddy-gloved hand from

his, Sasha trailed after him as he turned and trudged sullenly back up the hill.

***

It was Monday when Theresa Slater contacted Sasha from the office. Explaining she was Lucas's personal assistant, she politely cancelled his Monday evening yoga lesson, due to apparently *unforeseen circumstances.*

Sasha decided that the unforeseen circumstances were another black eye *he felt responsible for, that he didn't want to face.* But it didn't seem appropriate to say that to Theresa. It was certain to make her spin in her tenth floor corporate chair and would somehow make its way into the eager ears of Melody Trenton.

Examining her latest cosmetic accident in her bathroom mirror, Sasha wondered, what if there really were no accidents in life? What if she'd been dealt this strange series of black eyes for a reason? And if that were the case, why?

Surely it was just random chance. Yet the sneaking suspicion that she hadn't evaded her past stayed with her for the rest of the day and long into the night.

Chapter Thirteen

'Saaasha!' Lady Thornton shrieked as if she'd just seen a ghost. 'What on earth happened to your eye this time?'

'It's nothing, honestly.' Sasha responded quietly as she entered *Ballroom* for Evangeline's Tuesday morning lesson.

'But, dear girl,' she trilled, 'this is the second time you've had a black eye in a matter of weeks. In fact, you had *two* last time.' Moving closer, she examined Sasha's face carefully before adding in a slightly accusing tone. 'Was it…your boyfriend?'

The suggestion was positively mortifying and Sasha cringed internally. 'It was just a fall and another clunk on the head,' she responded sheepishly, bowing her head slightly as if it would somehow mask the bruise around her left eye, or the shame of having to admit she was still single after so many years.

'Well, you seem to be *falling over* an awful lot lately. Are you sure it's nothing else?' Evangeline glared suspiciously at her for a moment, appearing briefly like a crusty old schoolteacher.

'Absolutely. Out walking.' Sasha shuffled her feet nervously, feeling suddenly like a six-year-old being hauled in front of a classroom for stealing the teacher's apple. 'You know…the old slide and fall routine,' she added, her arm extending out in a comedic descriptive gesture.

Lady Thornton didn't see the humor. 'Quite,' she responded in an ominously icy voice. 'But what do you think people in the neighborhood say when you consistently show up here looking like some beaten housewife?'

'I hadn't considered...'

'Quite.' Evangeline repeated, cutting her off abruptly for the second time. 'Well I can't have it. I can't. It simply won't do.' Spinning away, she strode several steps towards the center of *Ballroom*.

Sasha could see Lady Thornton's expression in the giant gilt-edged mirror. She looked unreasonably strained; even a little angry. Was it possible she had visions of her neighbors watching the entrance to her house around-the-clock, as if she were tabloid-worthy fodder? Was she really filled with that much self-importance, or that deeply paranoid?

'I'm just not sure...' Evangeline continued, her words heading in a direction that didn't seem like a great one. It was Sasha's turn to cut her off.

'It won't happen again. I promise. I'm so sorry,' she interrupted.

For a moment, Lady Thornton's face appeared thoughtful in the mirrored reflection. She paused for a number of seconds before turning around. 'Good.' Taking several steps toward Sasha she appeared to be uncertain of what else to say. 'Because I've been through quite enough scandal already. I'm sure you understand,' she said with finality, avoiding eye contact and surprising Sasha entirely by reaching out and tentatively giving her a pat on the back of the hand. 'People talk, Sasha,' she whispered, as if those very same people were in the room listening attentively. 'Gossip can't be avoided in life. And there's a lot at stake here.'

'Absolutely. I do understand.' Although Sasha wasn't entirely sure she truly did understand – especially what the *lot at stake* was. But she did know what humiliation felt like. Without thinking, she reached out and gently touched the hand that Evangeline had just patted her with.

Lady Thornton blinked several times as if she'd just stepped out of a space shuttle having visited another planet. 'A lot at stake,' she repeated solemnly. 'Let's...' she gestured royally as she spun about '...do yoga.'

Sasha pursed her lips together to suppress a smile. 'Of course,' she answered, hastily removing the two yoga mats and unrolling them onto the lush carpet. 'Today we'll start in Savasana.'

Evangeline silently and dutifully obeyed, accustomed as she now was to lying face up with her legs splayed to the edges of the mat and her palms turned toward the ceiling. She closed her eyes, or rather, clamped them tightly shut as if she were locking out the world, along with a multitude of other sins.

'Gently relaxing your jaw and all the muscles in your face...'

'Sasha.' Evangeline said quietly.

'Yes, Lady Thornton?' She responded with curiosity. Evangeline had never spoken during a lesson. She'd never said a word; never interrupted a session in progress at all - except for her premature and hasty exits. Sasha watched the older woman's face. It looked weathered and she seemed so tired. Her lips were pursed, her eyes closed, but twitching ever so slightly. Evangeline appeared to be fighting to hold something in...or perhaps to prevent something from spilling out.

The response was taking forever. Sasha waited patiently, watching her face. The woman's body looked like it was in a partial phase of rigor mortis before she finally spat out the stuck words.

'Have you ever been…left…by anyone?'

Sasha hesitated, observing Lady Thornton's lips quivering ever so slightly. 'I'm not sure I could describe it that way,' she paused. 'But I have felt tremendously let down before by someone I trusted.'

Another long silence ensued. Evangeline was certainly struggling to spit something out. But Sasha sensed it was very important that she be patient; something critical to the wellbeing and health of her client was happening – some organic form of inner healing.

'Did it…hurt…a lot?' Lady Thornton coughed slightly, as if clearing her throat. But Sasha realized this had more to do with the difficulty she was having with expressing herself so honestly and the vulnerability that came with that.

'Of course. It was devastating,' Sasha said quietly. 'It was the kind of pain and shock that makes it hard to get out of bed or eat, for weeks on end…and where your world feels utterly and totally shattered. Everything was…meaningless. It was hard to function.' She stopped short of describing herself as a vaporous trail drifting behind the image of her body. It was possible she'd said far too much. But it was the truth – if a truth like that could ever be described in a way that did justice to the hurt inside. She had no idea how Evangeline would respond - if at all.

'But you did. You kept going…?'

'Yes. Of course I did.'

Lady Thornton swallowed hard, causing her epiglottis to move up and down as if it were an elevator moving at top speed. 'Why?' she enquired, ever so quietly.

Sasha wasn't sure how to respond. In that moment, she felt an overwhelming sadness for Evangeline. She felt her pain and suffering, her deep sense of loss and shame; the self-torture occurring inside her mind. All the *ifs, buts and maybes*. She felt it all, and knew exactly and completely what it was like for her: how one could get so dropped to their knees that nothing anyone could say or do would ever make them feel like they could stand straight again, let alone walk. She also knew that the simple word spoken, that single question – *Why?* - uttered to another human soul, beyond the shackles of pride, was Lady Thornton's doorway home.

The silence was begging for a response. When it eventually came and Sasha did move her lips, the words tumbled out effortlessly, but strangely as if they belonged to another and as if they were being poured straight through her mouth. 'Because that's all I *could* do,' she said softly, disappearing into some faraway land. 'After feeling like all the air had been punched right out of my lungs, they began to slowly fill up again, totally of their own accord...because I certainly didn't feel like I wanted them to. And despite the shock and grief in my heart that numbed my existence entirely, some part of me, way deep down inside, wanted to embrace life again. So I did. I accepted the will of my lungs and I began to breathe. And every day I became a little stronger. Until one day, my lungs and I were breathing in union, and I felt a desire to trust again.'

Even if I haven't made it all the way there yet, she thought.

Feeling herself returning from a strange and sad trance, Sasha glanced down momentarily, observing with surprise that Evangeline's body was no longer locked up and frozen. Her stomach and chest appeared to be shuddering up and down. And as Sasha looked more closely, she saw tears carving colorful trails through the woman's thick makeup and down the sides of her face.

'Lady Thornton?' Sasha gently touched her hand, and was surprised to feel that very same hand grasp her own tightly in return.

'It hurts so much.' Evangeline whispered. 'Oh, God, Sasha...it just hurts so much,' she managed to stutter, before bursting into large and uncontrollable sobs.

***

Fiona had cancelled their regular coffee catch-up early that morning via a text. She said it was to do with a client booking, but Sasha was sure it was a lie in order to avoid her after their awkward farewell outside the cinema. She also sensed the issue went deeper than a mere friendship blip. Fiona was not her usual bright self. She'd been drinking a lot more than normal and dark circles were beginning to show up under her eyes as if charcoal had been rubbed beneath them.

It was probably safer for Sasha to skip grabbing a coffee at Basilio's. Better than to risk explaining another black eye on her face coming from the same man and the subsequent possibility of some D-grade Italian Mafia mob – likely consisting of Basilio's second cousins and nephews - being set upon Lucas. Sasha didn't feel confident about his odds. So instead, she decided to pop into the club and try to locate Fiona. It was one of the most likely places to find her.

Upon entering the building, Sasha found the gym reception area bustling with people coming out of classes or leaving for work. Making her way quickly to the locker room to check if Fiona was around, she pushed through the door into the changing rooms. However, the first person she laid eyes on was *Long-Legs-Blonde* - Rodrigo's number one groupie.

Danielle...God, look at her perfect...everything. She was scantily dressed in skimpy underwear - bits of white string and lace - and looking every inch like a Playgirl Centerfold with her long blonde hair cascading over her shoulders.

'God,' Sasha muttered under her breath as she began her search around the locker room. But upon completing the short circuit past the toilets, shower cubicles and the changing area, it was clear that Fiona was not around. Heading back towards the exit door, she was about to leave when a familiar voice cut off her easy departure.

'Sasha?'

Freezing in her tracks, Sasha spun about to see *The Centerfold* beaming broadly at her.

'Hi...Danielle, isn't it?'

'Good memory.' Danielle said, taking several long gazelle-like strides toward her, thankfully now wearing clothes, and peering curiously at Sasha's black eye. 'You're Rodrigo's friend, aren't you?'

Perplexed for several seconds at the direct and searching comment, Sasha finally prized her jaw open. 'Well I wouldn't say we're...' She stopped mid-sentence, noticing Danielle's intent gaze. It was possible it was a trick question. 'Yes,' she added decisively.

'Oh, that's great. Because I wondered if I could ask you a few things about him.'

'Things?'

'Yes. Just simple stuff.'

'Simple stuff? Like what?'

'Oh,' she laughed. Sasha was certain it sounded false and Danielle was hiding something. 'I'm curious, is he a *good* friend?'

'I'm not sure I understand what you mean?' Her confusion began to fade as she gathered her wits. Suspicion oozed up in Sasha's stomach as she watched Danielle flick her hair nervously.

'Well. He's Brazilian...and they tend to be pretty...' she hesitated, '*forward* with women.'

'I'm really not sure what you mean. And if you have anything you need to know about Rodrigo, you should probably ask him yourself,' Sasha replied, managing to retain a courteous tone. Then turning toward the exit door she went to leave, but was promptly stopped in her tracks.

'Has he ever hit on you?' Danielle fired out.

Prickling immediately at the question she turned to face her fully. 'Danielle, I really have no idea what you're suggesting.'

'Oh come on, *you know*, Gyms...lots of testosterone ...and men...they're always trying to get into your pants,' she declared, shrugging her shoulders nonchalantly.

Sasha stared back at her in stunned silence for a several seconds before replying in a crisp voice. 'No. I *don't know*. I'm really not sure what else to say.'

Danielle searched her face carefully as if gauging something. 'It's just that...' She stopped herself.

'Just that what?'

'Just that...' She seemed to be having difficulty spitting the words out.

Figuring out what Danielle was trying to say, Sasha decided to speak it for her. 'It's just that you're interested in Rodrigo and you're not sure if he flirts with other women like he does with you,' she said in a flat voice. She almost felt sorry for Danielle, knowing what it was like to fall under the mighty Brazilian's spell. The man was powerfully magnetic in a way that was almost unearthly.

Danielle threw her a strange look. 'Not exactly, I...'

'He's *Brazilian*. Okay!' Sasha responded matter-of-fact and annoyed. 'I have to go,' she said crisply, grabbing the exit door handle.

'What happened to your eye?' Danielle added hastily.

'Nothing.'

'It doesn't look like nothing. And it's the second time…'

'That's really *my* business,' Sasha interrupted, restoring quiet control to her voice before leaving the locker room at speed. Fuming, she made her way to the reception area, her mind preoccupied with her conversation with Danielle. Rodrigo must have been sending the woman flirtatious mixed messages - which was probably how a clever man such as him operated. *Long-Legs-Blonde* was clearly besotted with him. It seemed he was an expert at getting under female skin.

'Sasha?'

And right on cue, there was Rodrigo's distinctive accent.

Oh, God. My day can't get any worse.

It was the legendary man himself. Milling about in the reception area; his tight polo shirt clinging to his muscled body. Regrettably, biceps had never looked so good. And for a couple of seconds he appeared to be positively beaming with surprise at unexpectedly seeing her, until he caught sight of her bruised eye.

'Hi.' Sasha made a small gesture of a wave and ducked her head. What was she thinking coming to the club?! The man was a notorious flirt and to be avoided – most especially because she was attracted to him *and* he was bad news. She now had two options: whip into the yoga studio, or make a loop around and duck back outside to the car park.

Definitely option two. I need to get the hell out of here fast.

His eyes followed her as she weaved her way strategically to the exit. Within seconds of escaping, she finally reached the door and pulled firmly on it. However, it barely opened a couple of inches before being slammed firmly shut again. A large male hand above her head was now pressed against the pane of glass and preventing the door from opening.

'Leaving in an awful hurry.' His Brazilian accent lilted in her ears.

His body was almost touching hers. She shivered inwardly. It was unfair, the chemical sensation he had upon her. Glancing up at his tanned and ridiculously handsome face she felt her cheeks flush ruby red. His green eyes elicited the effect of walking in an enchanted forest. He gazed down at her with some kind of fascination - a look that was closely followed by dismay as he examined her blackened eye socket more closely.

It was definitely time to go. 'What are you doing?' she said, glancing up at the hand that was still forcing the door shut.

'What are *you* doing?' He slammed the question right back at her as if it were a tennis ball in fast flight over a net.

'I'm trying to get to my car, actually.'

'Why? What's the hurry?'

'I have a client to get to.'

'Looking like that?'

'What do you mean?'

'It can't be good for your business showing up all the time with black eyes, Sasha.' The words and her name seemed to drizzle right out of his perfectly formed lips. She could see his flawless white teeth and almost feel his breath as he stood glued next to her.

'My business is good and works just fine.' Her body flexed rigid and upright.

'Even when you look like a domestic violence victim every time you show up on your clients' doorstep?'

What was up with everyone saying stuff like that to her?! 'I'm not...a domestic violence victim.' She suddenly felt very uncomfortable and sick inside at his words.

'Could have fooled me.' A flicker of annoyance flashed across his face. 'Who is this…clown who keeps doing this to you.' He tilted her chin up to inspect her face as if the answer could be found on her bruised skin. Strangely, she felt like swooning at his touch.

Stop it, stop it. He's a ridiculous flirt!

'I've had two unfortunate client accidents in a short space of time, that's all. Look, I've got to go now,' she said, pulling on the door again. But once more, he pressed his hand hard against the glass pane. 'Let me out,' she added firmly.

'Tell me who is doing this to you.'

'Let me out the door, Rodrigo.' She gritted her teeth. 'We're blocking the exit.'

'No.' He shook his head. 'Once, is maybe an accident. Twice…is a problem.'

'It's nothing, okay. You're completely mistaken. Total accident both times.'

'Why are you being so defensive?'

'Because you're blocking the damn door.' Sasha responded angrily. 'Do you want to create a scene and get Ian out here?'

'You're angry?' A smile began to form on his face.

'No, I'm not.'

'You are. You're angry…with me.' His head reeled back as a look of surprise formed on his face.

'I'm late, Rodrigo. That's all. And you're making me late,' she fired back with annoyance.

Pausing momentarily, he searched her eyes. 'I see,' he said, appearing thoughtful.

'Ahem.' From behind them, the sound of a woman clearing her throat broke their locked gaze.

'Sorry, do you mind if we leave?' Three gym patrons were gawking back at them, two rather apologetically. However, the third, regrettably, was Danielle. And she was looking far more fascinated than apologetic.

Oh, damn, Sasha thought with exasperation.

Unfortunately, things got worse. Ian leaned his head out of his office. 'Rodrigo. Sasha. Now.' He pointed to the interior of his office.

Suddenly feeling anxious and rattled she looked up at Rodrigo in quiet desperation. 'I can't,' there was a pleading look in her eyes. 'I just can't do this today.'

Rodrigo removed his hand gracefully from its pressed position on the door. Sasha watched the warmed imprint of his fingers on the glass with relief as they slowly dissolved back to oneness with the clear pane.

He wavered, his expressionless unreadable as his eyes drilled into hers. Then yanking on the door, Rodrigo unexpectedly held it open for her. 'Go.' His head gestured toward the cool and soothing winter world outside. 'I'll deal with Ian.'

'Thank you,' she whispered begrudgingly as she bolted for freedom like a bird released from captivity.

Chapter Fourteen

'What is the purpose of detaching ourselves from our senses?'

Holly stopped fidgeting in her cross-legged position and began to ponder the question.

'Are the senses not good?' The Guru asked.

They seem to be, she thought, as her mind drifted toward a decadent chocolate mud cake, thickly slathered with chocolate icing.

'Of course they are.' He smiled.

Holly sighed with relief; it was so great to hear him on the same page as her for a change. She sat up tall and listened with extra special attention.

'How could we delight in a beautiful sunset? Or feel our internal warning signals of danger?' She nodded her head in agreement as he continued. 'How else could the sound of a beautiful piece of music touch us so deeply, or a great work of art stir our hearts?' The Guru suddenly stopped speaking and appeared thoughtful, pausing for the longest moment.

'The problem, however, is that your senses can become so pleasurable that they control you, instead of you controlling them.'

Darn, she moaned internally. She should have known there would be a catch.

'Maybe you enjoy the taste sensation so much that you've become a little obsessed with food.' His finger-waving routine had started up again.

Her shoulders slumped as she slunk down low on her cushion so her head would be less visible amongst the other students. He was bound to look at her now...just bound to.

'And maybe that very same obsession with food is just a cover-up for something else,' he giggled. Jimmy was back, but for some reason that didn't make her feel happy like it normally did. In fact, she had the distinct feeling of wanting to leave the class.

'Maybe you're addicted to caffeine, or sex!' The increased volume and tone of his voice shocked her - The Guru never got angry. And Jimmy was clearly only making a very brief appearance today, she reflected.

'Why? Why such addiction?' He promptly smiled like a bipolar angel might and transformed rapidly on the spot to a man exuding great peace. 'Know this...' he hesitated, raising a finger to the heavens.

Holly waited in great suspense for his masterful explanation.

'It does not matter why.'

You're fricking kidding me,' she thought.

Another lengthy pause ensued as Holly grappled with confusion and frustration.

'Detachment is key,' he added.

Oh God, she shook her head in exasperation, watching her mud cake slide sickly into a black abyss.

'Pratyahara, the fifth limb, is the practice of withdrawing the senses – of removing their connection to the brain. This disconnection can occur during breathing exercises and meditation, during the practice of yoga postures, or any activity that requires deep concentration. And this,' he said glancing around slowly at everyone, 'will assist you greatly.'

***

'You honestly believe that? That the same man hit you twice in the face within a few weeks and you think that's an accident?'

'Of course.' Sasha crouched down and unrolled the second mat onto the ground. It was raining outside, yet again - more incessant late winter rain.

Amy smiled. 'If I wasn't worried about you, I'd think that it was kind of cute, in a warped sort of way.'

Sasha looked up at her and smiled. Amy was sitting perched in her white wicker chair looking every inch a queen. 'No need to worry, Amy.'

'Perhaps some kind of unconscious force made him do it.' A devilish smirk appeared on her elfin face. 'Or it's his equivalent of a pick-up line. He might be shy and doesn't know how to connect.'

'Giving a black eye would be a pretty odd way to go about it.'

Amy ignored the quip. 'Or it could be love, you know - cupid striking you in the face, literally. Stranger things have happened. Is he handsome?'

'Well…' Sasha shrugged.

'Oh he *is* handsome.' Amy chuckled. 'What's his name?'

'Not important.'

'It is to me. Go on, give this old married woman some excitement.'

'You're not old, Amy.'

'Yes, but I'm sheltered now.'

'Sheltered?'

'Yes, sheltered.' Amy sat up tall in her chair, her eyes gleaming. 'You must understand, Sasha, that for years, every day, I would prepare beautiful bouquets of flowers for people and events of every description. I was always in the thick of romance and intrigue. And there was always a story behind every bunch of flowers that walked out the door,' she said, her expression full of wispy sentimentality. 'Often I'd receive snippets of a tale to go with every blessed arrangement I put together: It's for our wedding anniversary; their dog died; my mother has been amazing; I've waited for her all my life...'

'Waited all his life...charming.' Sasha said, the cynicism evident.

'Yes, Sasha! It actually *is* charming. Don't you see, romance abounds everywhere, if you have the eyes to see it. But you must first *believe* in it.' Amy's passion was endearing.

Sasha stood upright from laying out the mats. 'These days, I think I need to *see it* to believe it,' she said calmly.

Leaning back in the chair, Amy appeared thoughtful. 'I guess I was so very blessed to be able to see it, every day: human hearts, reaching out and connecting with one another through beautiful flowers. And then, of course, I have Ben...the eternal romantic.'

'Yes. You're very blessed, Amy.'

'Your turn will come, Sasha. Good things always happen to good people. Eventually.'

'I must say, I've heard that a lot. Although I can't say I always see it in life...but I do like your optimism and enthusiasm.' Sasha smiled. She meant every word. Amy was such a tonic to her serious world.

'So tell me, what's his name? You said he was a client?'

'Yes, he is.'

Launching up out of the chair, Amy's silky yoga pants flowed gracefully around her as she moved toward the mats. 'Well, for goodness sake, woman, don't keep me in suspense any longer. It's just a name.'

Sasha watched Amy's effervescent energy with quiet bemusement. She really did help her relax.

'It's...' Sasha hesitated. 'It's...Lucas.'

'Lucas?' Amy said with surprised delight. 'I've always loved Lucas as a name. So has Ben. What's his family name?'

Sasha didn't feel like divulging her clients' names to anyone. Especially as she'd already blown Lucas's name into the open with nosy Melody Trenton and created a monster in the process. But there was something so trustworthy about Amy; her open face and spirit. There was so much goodness in her. There was just no hiding anything from her.

'Umm...it's Huntington. Lucas Huntington.'

Amy's eyes glazed over for a moment. 'Huntington?' A look of confusion formed on her face.

'Yes.' Sasha watched Amy's reaction with some surprise. 'I know what you're thinking.'

'What?' Amy replied, perplexed.

'You're thinking it's that sexy young model. But I'm sorry to disappoint you. It's not.' Sasha smiled.

'Oh, yes. The sexy model guy, okay.' Amy hesitated, considering her words carefully. 'It's a very distinguished kind of name, isn't it...Huntington.'

Sasha thought Amy would be joking with her by now. But the devilish elfin look seemed to have vanished rather fast. She appeared to be thinking hard about something.

'I think there's a bit of a distinguished family background,' Sasha added.

'Really? Interesting. So how long has he been a client of yours?' Amy sat down cross-legged on her mat and stared up at Sasha.

'Over a month now.'

'And do you like him?'

'Kind of. He's…intriguing.'

'Intriguing? In what way?'

Sasha looked down at Amy, sitting somewhat obediently on the floor. 'Oh, he has a bit of that broody *Wuthering Heights* thing going on.'

Amy laughed. She laughed so hard any seriousness slipped right off her face. 'Wuthering Heights. That's so funny. And very clever.' She paused reflectively. 'But I don't recall Wuthering Heights working out so well for its characters.'

'Well, you've seen my face the past few weeks,' Sasha couldn't resist the humor.

'That's very true!' Amy chuckled. 'Aside from the black eyes, though, he hasn't made a move on you, has he?'

'No. There is some kind of *vibe* between us though.'

'A vibe. Really? Well you'll just have to keep me posted on how it all goes.'

'He's just a client, Amy. And I'm sure it will stay that way. Besides, he's way out of my league.'

Amy rolled back on the floor into Savasana, closing her eyes and taking a deep breath. 'He should be so lucky, Sasha,' she said firmly, a trace of a frown forming on her pretty forehead before it smoothed again. Amy appeared completely relaxed, but she wasn't feeling that way at all. Inwardly, her mind was busy pulling information together and she was experiencing some discomfort with where the pieces led.

***

'Honestly, Sasha. Must you really show up here with a black eye every week?' Melody's face was full of distaste and undisguised judgment as she stood on her doorstep gaping at the yellowing bruise.

Sasha already had to work very hard at practicing patience and tolerance with Melody – the Yamas, Niyamas and all the other limbs in the book were stretched every which way when connecting with the petulant model. But lately she'd been driving Sasha's spiritual growth to entirely new levels. Melody was turning out to be one of her most challenging clients ever. Sasha sucked in some cold air and shivered a little as she stood on the steps. Retrieving some personal strength, she ignored the tone and sidled indoors past *Her Royal Rudeness*.

'Really!' Melody declared, sticking her head outside and taking a furtive and suspicious glance around before shutting the door. 'You know, the paparazzi would love to get a photo of me with you standing bashed on my doorstep. And they'd delight in creating some silly story out of it.' She continued her tirade as they walked through to the living room. 'They'd say I have some beaten down-and-out sister I'm hiding that I don't support. Or some other sordid trash like that.'

'We don't remotely look like sisters, Melody.' Sasha responded drily. A sudden and unexpected deep sense of calm descended upon her as she realized how ridiculously self-absorbed and limited the young model's thinking was.

Melody guffawed as if Sasha had just said the most outlandish thing. 'Well of course we don't look remotely related! I mean, really!' She rolled her eyes to the heavens and paused. 'But you do know what I mean, don't you.'

Making a hasty beeline straight to the uninspired black and white living area, Sasha uncharacteristically dumped the yoga bag on the floor as she spun to face Melody. 'No. I don't know what you mean,' she said bluntly, losing her patience and a bit of her cool.

This seemed to rattle the younger woman, who

plastered a fake designer smile on her face in the time it would take to snap a digital pic. 'It's just that…I have a reputation to protect. I'm sure you understand.' Her eyelids batted all doe-like.

'Of course.' Sasha responded firmly, proceeding to ignore her as she roughly extracted the yoga mats from their carry bag.

Melody, accustomed as she was to having people generally fawn all over her, was somewhat taken aback. 'You honestly have no idea what it's like being chased around by paparazzi. It's a lot of pressure,' she clarified, despite not needing to.

Sasha decided to avoid any further dialogue lest she say something rude. Hastily rolling out the mats she quietly pointed to one of them so they could begin. But Melody seemed intent upon explaining herself - either that or she liked the sound of her own voice.

Sasha suspected the later.

'You have no idea what it's like being one of us.'

One of us? Seriously?!

Hell-bent on some kind of validation, Melody continued. 'Anyone of social standing, I mean. Take your client, Lucas Huntington, for example,' she declared, striding onto her mat. There was obviously some delight in the mention of his name. 'He'd know what I'm talking about. It's why we stick together - people like us. We understand the pressure.' Tossing her head defiantly, Melody rose to a standing position.

People like us?! So that's what all this is about… Lucas…again.

'In fact, you should ask *him* about it.'

Maybe she views him like a father figure? Sasha pondered. He must have been a good dozen or so years older than Melody, after all.

Regardless of why, Melody was strangely obsessed with the man. Sasha realized it was best to avoid conversation about him, or anything else for that matter.

'Let's start you in Savasana today, shall we? Some relaxation and breathing to begin with.'

'Hmmph.' Melody snorted in annoyance, lying down on the mat in a bit of a huff. 'You think we're all just fluff and money, I bet.'

Sometimes.

'Look, I don't think anything like that, Melody. It's my job to teach you yoga. So that's what I'm here to do. Otherwise, I prefer to mind my own business.'

'We care too, you know.' Melody prattled on as though she hadn't heard a word of what Sasha had just said. 'Why else would I attend charity gala events whenever I can,' she sniffed. 'In fact, I could do that sort of thing all the time,' she added, waving her hand around royally whilst lying on the floor.

Melody's energy was reaching for something. It was as if a long slimy tentacle was slithering over the yoga mat and wrapping itself around Sasha's body. She wondered how to shut her up so they could begin.

'That's the kind of lifestyle Lucas has. He's always supporting a charity...such a good man.'

Lucas's social influence must be important, Sasha thought, beginning to figure things out. Unfortunately, any kind thoughts were rapidly washing down a drain. Good God, the eight limbs were a challenge.

'But enough about Lucas,' Melody suddenly declared, her eyes still closed as she strategically changed direction. 'It's occurred to me I know very little about you, Sasha. Except that you're originally from California. And for some reason you're now living in London – which makes me curious. I always wonder what entices people to move about geographically in life, besides modeling.' Melody guffawed at her own humor and paused as if waiting for a drum roll. 'Some people relocate because they're running toward something. And others, well, they're often running *from* something,' she added, opening her eyes and staring laser-like into Sasha's. 'And for some reason I'm about one hundred percent certain that you're the later.'

Sasha felt the same deep uneasiness she'd had at Melody's last lesson. Mustering enough of a façade she faked a cool response. 'One hundred percent seems very confident.'

'Well I have every reason to be.'

'Oh?' Sasha's brow furrowed in stunned surprise.

'Like I said, I have spies *everywhere*.' Melody closed her eyes. 'And for the record, Sasha, it's something you should always keep in mind.' Her eyelids floated shut as a soft smile formed on her lips.

'What exactly do you mean?'

'You know,' Melody replied, pausing again for effect. 'I think it's time we started my yoga lesson. I could really do with the peace and relaxation I'm paying you for. I have a busy photo shoot to get to later.' Her shoulders shrugged as she lay in supine position on the floor. 'But let's just say that I understand it's not always easy to leave the past behind.'

A threat?

It sounded very much like a threat, or a loose attempt at blackmail. A rush of breath escaped Sasha's mouth as she exhaled long and slow.

Melody knew Sasha was too nice a person to push things and would fold in the face of maintaining professionalism. Which was true. So she'd been cornered into dropping the subject. But a deeply troubled feeling remained inside her.

It stayed with Sasha for the rest of the day and woke her in the night.

***

Arriving back in her Camden apartment that evening, Sasha felt uncommonly exhausted. Her exchange with Melody had rocked her. Although uncertain about what was being alluded to in the communication, there was a chance the nosy young woman somehow knew things about Sasha's past that should always remain hidden. If that were the case, it was a mystery how she'd ever found out. Of course, Melody could also have been bluffing...stirring the pot in order to could gain more information about Lucas. She seemed surprisingly obsessed with the man. Whilst it was true he had a captivating and magnetic side to him - one that affected Sasha also - he surely wasn't the only wealthy attractive man that a social climber like Melody could forge a relationship with. Nor was he the only man she could reinvent herself through as a charity socialite. She did seem hell-bent on him, though. And obsessive people could be prone to terrible and irrational human behavior. It was also increasingly evident Melody had a slight problem with drugs, as she often planted the back of a finger under her nose and sniffed throughout her yoga lesson.

One thing was certain - Sasha needed to monitor the situation carefully. It was becoming a little unsettling. And it was possible that, in time, she would have to cut Melody away as a client. It wasn't as if she needed the painful model, after all. But if Melody was capable and willing to make trouble for her and persist with threatening innuendo, then she definitely needed to find a way to let her go. And if Sasha could cut her ties with California at the drop of a hat, then getting rid of an annoying and potentially threatening client was really just a formality. But she needed to be careful how she went about it – Melody was one tricky and unpredictable lady.

It was disturbing, listening to the thoughts running

through her mind. Sasha was becoming more aware of how hardened her insides had become since she'd departed her homeland.

Not hardened...strong...and self-protective.

But she wasn't the same loving and naïve young woman she used to be, that was for sure. Caution and cynicism seemed to pervade everything these days. And a feeling of unease would too frequently lodge itself in her solar plexus and gut. Thank goodness she had yoga and meditation to keep her on a more even keel.

Flinging her yoga bag on the sofa, she headed straight for the bathroom. Having a long soak in a tub of nice hot water, followed by a good night's sleep, was probably about the best thing she could do for herself right now. It was definitely one of those times to shut the world out and be quiet and still.

As she turned the tap on and began to fill the tub, some of the anxiety of the day lifted from her shoulders as if weighty chainmail armor had been removed. Emptying the contents of a bag of salts into the water, she lit several strategically placed candles then picked up a bottle of lavender essential oil. Glancing at it thoughtfully, she hesitated before placing it back down.

Pratyahara, she reflected.

That single word provided her with renewed focus. Standing momentarily mesmerized, she watched the steaming water steadily filling the bath.

'Withdrawal of the senses,' she reminded herself, considering the Buddha's words: *Peace comes from within. Do not seek it without.'*

The words felt true for her. Silence had long been her greatest balancer in life. Where some would flee in terror from the void of a mute world, Sasha often craved it. Withdrawal of the senses meant tuning out external stimuli. She could utilize her bath time for that now. There would be no aroma of essential oils wafting through her olfactory canal; nor would there be any sound of music filling the silence and adding an enticing stream of lyrics and sound through her mind. Wandering out to the living room she switched off all the lights.

There will be darkness, too.

The only remaining form of visibility was the soft glow from the candles near the bath.

The tub was filled to two-thirds full. She switched off the taps, leaving space to top up hot water occasionally throughout her soak. Poking fingers through the surface several times to check the temperature, Sasha finally discarded her clothing on the floor and tentatively stepped in. Warmth encased and tingled throughout her, until eventually, as she sank beneath the water, her body acclimatized to the fluid environment and the sensation became neutral.

Sitting up slowly, she blew the candles out. All traces of light were extinguished and an inky blackness consumed her. Sinking back into the water, Sasha sighed heavily as she began to single-pointedly focus on her breathing. The external world was retreating. Aside from the occasional swash of water lapping the side of the bath, it was all so very quiet.

Peace is within. The Buddha's words drifted through her mind again.

Pratyahara...a bridge to get there, she thought.

Taking another long slow exhalation, Sasha closed her eyes. Submerging a little deeper into the water, she allowed her mind to soften and dissolve as stillness descended upon her.

Chapter Fifteen

She hadn't seen Lucas for over a week - not since their muddy joy-slide at Hampstead Heath. Only, it wasn't so joyful for Lucas. He was clearly annoyed. He'd also conveniently managed to avoid his yoga lessons since *the incident*, cancelling them under the guise of *Sudden-Business-Trip-Away* syndrome. But Theresa had called to confirm Monday evening yoga going ahead again. So Sasha was now back on the third floor of his Belsize Park mansion, observing him as he completed his yoga practice.

Thank God...almost time to go.

The entire session felt awkward. Lucas had barely said a word, avoiding eye contact with her completely. She couldn't fathom what was going on in the man at all. He blew hot and cold by the minute. On this occasion, though, it seemed his temperature was arctic.

'And when you're ready, gently rolling onto your side...and slowly coming up into a sitting position,' she said, finishing the lesson with relief.

His eyes were firmly closed as she recited a closing mantra.

'Namaste,' Sasha bowed her head with her hands in prayer position.

Namaste was such a deeply respectful and spiritually significant word.

The divine spark resides in you...

Momentarily she reflected upon Lucas.

Somewhere...beneath the permafrost.

Darn it, lately her mind was a wildly cynical thing. Exhaling sharply, she shook her head as if that would help clear the negativity crashing down on her like an avalanche. Glancing up at Lucas for a second, he was sitting upright with his eyes now open and peering at her inquisitively. He was in a cross-legged position, but as a result of current poor flexibility, his knees were jutting sharply into the air at a forty-five degree angle as if he were ready for flight.

Tight hip flexors.

He looked ever-so-slightly like an overgrown schoolboy. Sasha's face and features softened at the image.

'Why were you shaking your head just then?' He said, staring at her and startling her back to reality.

She hadn't realized she'd been doing that. 'No real reason. Random thought, I guess.'

'I see.' He paused, looking down at the mat for a moment as if gathering his thoughts. 'Sasha, there's something I need to say.'

She prepared herself for the termination of his yoga lessons.

He cleared his throat. 'Look...I'm very sorry for how I behaved the other week...at Hampstead.'

'Oh,' she said, slightly speechless and also surprised by the sizeable chunk of ice shelf that just slipped right off him.

'I was very rude.'

'Not at all. You were fine.' She dismissed his apology, despite the image of him trudging sullenly up the hill that flashed into her mind.'

'I think you truly need to become more receptive to apologies, Sasha.' His tone softened. 'I behaved appallingly, ignoring you all the way back up the hill, cancelling our lunch, and disappearing in a huff. It was childish and utterly wrong of me.'

Grappling with her response, it was clear his guard was down, which was was alarmingly attractive. 'Honestly, it's okay.'

'No, it's not. Because I like you.'

Did he just say that? He did, didn't he? I like you.

'And it's not how you treat someone you like…a lot,' he finished, subdued.

'Oh.' She looked down at the ground but there appeared to be none. She suddenly felt airborne. 'It's okay.'

'You said that before. You know, you bat off apologies like a cricketer hits sixes out of the park. It's not okay. Thank me for the apology,' he suddenly instructed. His tone had become all business-like, as if he were buying and selling shares on the stock exchange.

'Thank you?' It was a most confusing…order.

Untangling his lengthy limbs from sitting position, he stood up, extending a hand to help her up off the floor. An electrical current fired through her body, igniting a warm fluid sensation that permeated her core as his hand connected with hers in a firm strong grip. Hoisting her into a standing position, his hand clutching hers induced an instant femininity to arise within her and she fought the sensation of blushing.

'Yes,' he said, still holding her hand. It was hard not to notice his eyes - really notice them, more deeply than before. Their powder blue color was no longer like the sky, but vast and fluid like the shifting ocean. They held a disarming tenderness that caused her to stop breathing for several seconds. 'Thank me,' he repeated, his voice softening to match the look in his eyes. 'So I know you've absorbed what I've said. So I know you've accepted my apology.'

'It was just...' She couldn't concentrate on the words. Those unfathomable blue eyes were gazing into hers and they were compelling. Realizing all of sudden how desperately deprived she felt of a man's physical contact, her knees weakened as his masculinity and the feeling of his hand holding hers captivated her. He didn't seem to want to let go - his grasp was steady. Her palms were suddenly clammy.

Look away, look away, look away...

She searched frantically for an escape route – anything to prevent her from losing herself entirely in this hypnotizing moment.

'Thank me.' His free hand gently and unexpectedly reached up and touched her chin, tilting her head fractionally toward his face - forcing her to look fully at him; right into those intense baby blues. He took a small step closer.

Glancing at his lips, desire flamed instantaneously within her.

Run, run, run...

'I...' her words dissolved like vapor. She'd never let herself be attracted to a client – not since California. She told herself never again. Ever. And she'd policed that rigidly for years. This was impossible. It couldn't be happening.

But he was leaning closer. His breath was on her face, caressing her like the touch of a feather.

'Thank me...Sasha.' And there it was - the huskily sexy tipping point. His tone shifted to one of desire as the cool façade slipped totally from him. Ice now flowed like a river.

It was how he whispered her name; how his eyes seemed to cloud over mysteriously, revealing hidden depths as they bored into hers. It was the way his body moved in so close to hers that she could feel her heart pounding near his chest – the chest she now wanted to touch. It was how the hand on her chin found its way past her ear and underneath her ponytail, sliding smoothly onto the nape of her neck. And it was how, in that last separated moment, he drew his face down and pressed his lips sensually against hers.

It had been so long since a man had kissed her. Really kissed her. And with the kind of intimacy that made her fall right into him. She couldn't fight it and didn't want to. It was so hard being in control in every area of her life. And tiring. She kissed him back, throwing caution and the voices in her mind to the wind. Their tongues entwined sensually as heat became palpable between them. It was so utterly unexpected – not just the kiss, but also the attraction between them. They were such different people, occupying vastly different realities. The only overlap of similarity seemed to be the twice-weekly conjunction point of their lives where he was forced to be more in harmony with her through his yoga lesson. Outside of that there seemed no common ground.

Lucas felt her pull back for a second and pressed himself harder against her. She was outside of anything that existed in the box of his familiar life; the conformity and unconscious oppression of limiting walls pushing against him, and the meaninglessness he felt in their confines. He was so drawn to her. She was like a flower in bloom on a perfect spring day, fresh and vibrant: her soft silky skin, her beauty and some form of...*purity*. He wanted to pluck her from the garden of life and add the color and sweet fragrance to his own deadened plot.

He kissed her harder. She tasted salt from the dried sweat of his yoga session, felt his tongue searching her own, wanting him all the more. His hand slid from around her waist, outlining the shape of her buttocks and the graceful arc in the back of her leg. He squeezed, creating a swirl of hot energy in her womb.

As his mouth left hers, his tongue glided down her neck. She inhaled sharply with desire, the sensations overwhelming her passion-starved body. Her head thrown slightly back, eyelids opened fractionally, she vaguely observed the star-speckled night through the glass of the skylight. Desire pumping through her body forced her eyes shut. His teeth bit gently into her neck sending waves of pleasure rushing through her and deep into her pelvis. A sharp sigh escaped her lips.

'God...,' he murmured thickly, pulling himself away from her suddenly. His eyes were wild with longing and an abandonment she could barely recognize in him. He grabbed her hand, leading her to the door, backing her into the wall and pressing himself against her. She felt the throbbing erection between his legs. Warm liquid flowed readily to her pelvis and a gasp escaped her as his hips locked against her.

Hands found their way to her hair, pulling forcibly on the band that held it tied neatly in a ponytail. He slid it firmly down the length of her mane until it was entirely free. Dragging his fingers through silky strands, he drew her head back towards the wall as his tongue moved down the length of her neck, then back up to nibble on her ears. Her brain tingled.

She was totally lost in the moment. The yearning in her body unleashed. Her mouth sought out his, kissing him back, wild and wanton; elevating him to a fervent state. Before she knew what was happening, he opened the door, guiding her willfully off to one of the entrances in the hallway and shoving it open. The room was dark. Sasha couldn't see much except from light in the passage. It was likely a guest room. Who cared? He could have strapped her to his back and flown her to the moon and she'd have gone willingly in that moment. He pushed her heavily backward and she landed on a large bed, sinking into its softness before he sank onto her – all ardor, lust and unleashed manhood.

There was little wasting of time and little ceremony once he had her flat on her back. He ripped off his t-shirt, then hers, along with her sports bra underneath, then hungrily covered one of her exposed nipples with his mouth. She arched toward him, sliding her hands down over his buttocks. Drawing back momentarily, he paused, but only to peel off her fitted yoga pants. Lucas's own track pants followed. He was totally naked when he climbed back on her to taste her other nipple. She felt his smooth sun-barren skin and his throbbing hard erection rub against her.

Sliding his hand down to the newly freed gap between her legs, he began to explore her without hesitation. There was no going back now. She couldn't contain her pent up passionate state of arousal as the energy surged relentlessly from hidden depths. Her orgasm was a sweet explosive ecstasy.

He needed his own then. Wasting no time he mounted and entered her for a matter of seconds before a deep moan escaped him. Withdrawing quickly, he released himself elatedly over her. It was as rapid an exit as it was an entry, ending in a spent pile of sweat and heat.

Minutes passed in silence. Lucas lay beside her, his breath deepening but interjected by short sharp inhalations. Their bodies were a little distance apart, his arm lying partially across her chest and his hand open-palmed and loose near her neck.

A somewhat awkward emotional divide seemed to mist up, hanging tangibly between them. When he finally spoke, they were the last two words Sasha wanted to hear. They shattered the darkness of the bedroom with an unappealing reality. She was in no way prepared for them. And when they landed, they were like a fierce punch to her chest that temporarily arrested her heartbeat.

'I'm sorry,' was all he said.

***

I'm sorry.

Those two simple words, forming an apologetic expression, could mean a variety of things. True, they could be sincere and redemptive at their greatest and highest meaning. Yet they could also hang suspended like a cloud formation loaded with guilt particles that shaded the sun's light. They could be a semi-honest and rapidly ejected phrase, as if one had just plucked fruit from an unknown tree, permission not granted…then, oh dear, caught. Or they could be the voice of bitter regret, knowing an action would never be forgotten, yet seeking the grace of forgiveness all the same. They could be a polite gesture, too – as in, when one grazed past a chair knocking a coat off its back and had the good manners to acknowledge the fact.

Yet those two words could also be the worst kind of idiom - a meaningless throwaway declaration, removing any level of responsibility from the lips they were uttered from and, ironically, more hurtful than the connotation they represented. Inevitably, that robust and often-used midget sentence generally had something to do with an unintentional *accident*. It was for this reason they were words Sasha now despairingly wished she hadn't heard. The fact they were spoken at all indicated a type of regret that was rather disturbing under the circumstances – she, now lying naked, with his fertility sliding unceremoniously off her belly. Not only was the deed concluded with straightforward swiftness, it was also - more disconcertingly - unprotected. This left her

191

feeling uncomfortably and undesirably *used,* despite having been an X-rated willing party. So, *I'm sorry,* certainly seemed a rather perfunctory use of language with which to complete the act.

Of course, he could have been apologizing for the speed of their tryst and his lack of self-control - which would be warranted. Two minutes was considered really rather poor for male stamina, therefore, a shorter time-span - inexcusable.

But of course, those two dear words could also have resulted from the effect she had on him. And under consideration, this might warrant altering her interpretation to *flattering.*

Regardless, he fell quickly to sleep, splayed naked on the bed. Sasha hastily wiped herself down with his discarded t-shirt and donned her own clothes again – quietly jumping up and down to force herself back into the tube of clothing that was her yoga pants. She then made a speedy exit of her own – albeit without the similar levels of exertion or excitement that he'd displayed.

Although the romp had provided needed respite and release for the recent level of anxiety that hovered incessantly in her shadows, she was uncertain about the motivation that had prompted it in Lucas. Sure, he said he liked her. But didn't it also seem as if the majority of men could bandy about flattering lines like ping pong balls at an Olympic tournament - particularly if they thought it would get them into the sack with a woman?

He seemed a complex man. On the one hand, apparently wanting to outrun and escape his past. Yet on the other, deeply knitted to it, like strands of embroidered thread, crisscrossed and indelibly bound. She couldn't seem to shake the questions that ran rampant through her mind like a herd of frightened buffalo. Was it genuine attraction for her that had ignited the wild spark in him? Was it an innocent drive that compelled him? Or worse - perhaps it was actually, and horrifyingly, calculated. He was a stockbroker, after all. Critical analysis and strategy in the world of money and commodities would run second nature to someone like that. So it was possible the very same approach might also transfer to activities of the flesh. He certainly didn't seem the type to allow a deluge of feelings to run rife in his heart or life.

However, the thing was, that after their lusty encounter there was no contact between them for days. Sasha certainly wasn't about to drop her dignity any lower by being the first to communicate between them. And he, troublingly, had not made the tiniest peep of a word to her since then – which left *I'm Sorry* dangling with even more of a bitter taste, much like a barely ripe and skinless lemon shoved in her mouth. Not to mention a splattering of humiliation coming to land with a thud, as if an artist had just dipped their brush in shamefully red oil paint and coated it all over her.

By Wednesday afternoon, after yet another bothersome yoga session with Melody Trenton, Sasha was in a quandary about teaching Lucas the next morning. It was difficult facing her image in the mirror that week, so what on earth would it be like locking eyes with him again? She couldn't do it. Wouldn't do it.

After failing, yet again, to get hold of Fiona for the type of counseling session that would ensure humor and laughter, and having meditated upon the Yamas and Niyamas several times - rather unsuccessfully - for guidance, Sasha finally decided to act from the highest level of self-compassion she could muster and conceded to making contact.

No she didn't. Not really.

Actually, she hid.

And lied.

Relieved to reach the answer machine of Lucas's secretary, she left a garbled message cancelling his lesson due to a *migraine*. It sounded feasible, but utterly wrong – she'd never had a migraine before in her life. The layer of deceit also displayed a flagrant disregard of Satya. Not only was she an appalling liar, she was also now a very bad yogi.

Sasha imagined the lineage of yoga Guru's shaking their heads in despair; and the Buddha doing backflips away from her in disgust.

A friend was definitely needed.

She phoned Fiona three times that day, but disturbingly, she never answered.

Chapter Sixteen

'Do you understand the difference between love and lust?' The Guru said.

There was no sign of Jimmy.

Please God, don't look at me...please God, don't look at me, Holly repeated like a mantra.

'Brahmacharya is about chastity.'

She felt herself begin to tremble.

'But...' Jimmy appeared, thankfully, 'this does not mean the fun is over.' He waved a finger around the group with a big smile on his face. Today he was showing encouraging signs of...humanness.

'To be virtuous means holding the opposite sex in high esteem. Respect for someone helps sex become a spiritual act as well as a physical one. And with respect you will be able to join together on a much deeper level.'

Considering her recent past she sighed heavily in dismay.

'Meaningless physical contact can be both confusing and distracting.' He shook his head as if stating that was indeed a big no-no.

Holly found her cross-legged position was beginning to feel tense all of a sudden. She shifted about on her cushion.

'Avoiding this kind of behavior...avoiding meaning-less sex...can help you become more in tune with those who could be potential life partners.'

What did he just say? That sounded important. Holly chewed on her bottom lip for a second.

'When sex keeps you from becoming your best self, or keeps your partner from doing the same, this is NOT virtuous sex.' He was waving his finger about more vigorously now. And the smile on his face had vanished into oblivion.

Holly shuffled about on her cushion. There was something wrong with the darn thing, surely - she just couldn't get comfortable. Perhaps she should buy another one from the quaint little shop nearby. And they had those divine little toffees from God-knows-where. She couldn't decipher the language of origin on the packet, but they sure did taste good.

Darn. He was staring at her again. So much so, that several other students began to turn and look her way too. Surely her heart had just stopped beating.

'But...' he said, finally glancing away, as the thumping in her chest suggested the critical organ was working again, 'when both you and your partner move closer towards self-actualization...and there is a purity of love present between you...this is the way sex was meant to be.'

Holly forgot about the cushion, the divine sweets, and his beady-eyed stare. She thought about what The Guru was saying - and felt unexpectedly sad.

***

Friday drew on and there was still no contact from Lucas. It was possible he'd frozen to death on a polar expedition to his artic heart; dead well before reaching its frigid vascular chambers. Still, the silence was driving Sasha nuts.

The only way she was going to restore her sanity was by speaking with Fiona, which had to be face-to-face. But that would also mean revealing the truth – something she aspired to, although on this occasion preferred to lean away from. And knowing Fiona, any disclosure would require detail of the magnitude of a criminal investigation. Every sordid little feature; every thrown against the wall; every hands moving here and there grubby-little-facet. *'What? Where exactly were his hands? What did he do with them?'* she'd demand.

There was obviously something going on with Fiona. She was never one to not mince her words, most especially if she was annoyed or upset about something. Yet she'd been disturbingly quiet for much of the week, batting off attempts at contact with lame and random text excuses. Sasha felt increasingly bothered about it. Then worried. She had to find out what was going on. And there was one place she knew where to catch Fiona in person – especially on a Friday night. Just about always.

Happy Hour was over by the time Sasha made her way into the Covent Garden bar, dressed in smart fitted jeans, boots and a warm blue casual sweater. Her hair was tied back in a long ponytail and she'd applied a dusting of brown mineral powder to her face, bringing a bronzed appearance. There were some Californian things she couldn't do without - a healthy tanned look was one of them.

Live music rocked the small but heaving throng of end-of-week revelers at the bar. It sounded like Dave's band playing again, so Fiona was bound to be here. Sasha nudged her way through the crowd as politely as possible toward their usual area. Half way across the room, however, she spied a familiar and annoyingly good-looking head, towering above *the rest of humanity that didn't get the Adonis genes*.

Rodrigo. *Damn.*

She froze, considering what to do. After their last weird encounter, the prison-like entrapment at the gym entrance, he was best avoided. But she needed to persist and find Fiona. As Sasha reached the group from the gym, there was no sight of Fee. Instead, Rodrigo spun about, an expression of curious surprise evident on his striking facial features. Eyes as green as the fronds of unfurling fern leaves locked onto hers.

'Ah, Sasha,' he nodded with the look of someone surveying subject matter that suggested they were an expert on it. 'I almost didn't recognize you without your war tattoo,' he said, pointing loosely to his own eye with his beer-free hand.

Sasha batted off the comment, politely greeting the few gym people she knew and glancing around the bar area. 'Is Fiona here?'

'You know,' he leaned forward, ignoring her question as his muscled bicep, surely in a t-shirt two sizes too small, bumped into her shoulder, 'I've figured out who's been belting you up.'

'Stop it.' She frowned, shaking her head in annoyance.

He smiled. 'It's those blasted angels, isn't it.'

What a cryptic remark, she thought. Her head tilted back to view his undeniably handsome face, now sporting insanely sexy-looking stubble on an unshaved Friday night.

'They're rebelling…'

A small glint of challenge was detectable in his emerald eyes. Sasha countered with her best *not-a-clue-what-you're-on-about* look.

'…against their leader,' he added.

Her brow crinkled.

'The Divine One,' he winked.

Her pregnant pause, lengthy and loaded, hung suspended between them. 'Clever,' she responded unsmiling.

'Your parents are the clever people - such a unique name. And so perfect for a yoga instructor.'

Her pulse shot up at an alarming rate.

'I mean, what are the odds?' This time he dropped his shoulder and nudged her lightly with it, causing Sasha's heart rate to leap several more beats per minute. 'It seems you were destined for a spiritually *divined* path.'

'Unlike you,' she said, deflecting the attention quickly off herself as she snuck another glance at him from lowered lashes.

'How do you know my path isn't spiritual? And what exactly is that supposed to look like, anyway?' His face leaned in close to hers. A waft of alcohol fumes drifted by her nose and she realized that he was perhaps a little drunk. Which also meant she had the upper hand in the situation.

'Well, I don't think it looks like that,' she countered, tilting her head toward the bottle being raised to his lips.

A wry smile spread across Rodrigo's face before he completed the action of swigging back a mouthful of beer. 'Is that a judgment?' he said, folding his arms across his chest and leaning back, assessing her as if she were a piece of new gym equipment.'

'Not at all. It's...an observation,' she responded, beginning to relax a little, his Brazilian accent and tendency to smile the contributing factor.

'There's nothing wrong with letting your hair down every now and then, Sasha. In fact, why don't you, right now. Here.' He pushed the half full bottle of lager into her hand before she could speak. She thought he was offering her a drink. But instead, he placed his hands on her shoulders, spinning her body to face him fully, before reaching both his arms around to the back of her head. This brought her alarmingly close to his chest and neck. She inhaled sharply; the smell of his cologne assaulting her senses.

'What are you…'

'Shush,' he interrupted. Gently tugging her hairband he began to slide it slowly down the full length of her ponytail. She felt him stroke gently through her hair as if exploring the long strands inch by inch. Or was that simply imagination? Her heartbeat slowed. Everything became still and silent inside. The hairband slipped right off her silky ends and he combed his hands several times through her mane until her blonde locks were fully freed. 'There,' he said quietly, looking down at her, his hands still resting lightly on her back as she glanced up at him through part dilated pupils. 'That's better,' he said softly, gazing steadily into her eyes.

Sasha trembled inwardly. There was something so unnerving about Rodrigo. Not just his looks, charm and confidence. But every now and then it seemed a veil would lift and she'd catch a glimmer of something soulful behind the pools of emerald green. And whatever that was, it affected not only her heart rate and breathing, but also how she felt about herself. It was as if he knew a part of her better than she did. And that made her feel very uncertain around him. It was strange how someone could do that – step right inside your being, as if they were vapor passing through a wall.

Blinking several times as if coming out of a spell she noticed his eyes were still locked on hers.

'So…' She had no idea what to say. And also felt oddly glued to the floorboards. It was as if she was being held in place by a tractor beam. All the jostling and noise at the bar felt like another dimension away. 'You haven't seen Fiona tonight, then?' It was the only sentence that sprang to mind. The words felt awkward as they left her mouth – as if they didn't belong to her in that moment. And although softly spoken, they were enough to break the magic between them. As she took a slight step back, a small frown, virtually undetectable, crossed Rodrigo's face. Releasing his arms from behind her, she watched them hang back into place beside his strong frame.

'No. I haven't. I've barely crossed paths with her all week. Everything okay?'

It was the way he looked at her, the hint of seriousness, that made her want to confide in him. But she couldn't. Not really. The best course, as always, was to keep things quietly to herself. So she said nothing.

Watching her face carefully, he took a step back. 'I'll tell you what, how about you think about your answer while I go get us a drink.'

'Umm...I...'

'In fact, here, finish mine. While I'm at the bar,' he added, pressing his hand onto the warming bottle she was now clutching. The gesture caused a graze of skin contact between them and was almost...intimate. For the briefest moment, they seemed like a couple.

'Thanks,' she said in a barely audible voice. But he hadn't lingered for a response. Instead, he turned and deftly made his way through the crowd toward the bar.

***

Sasha finished the beer in her hand whilst chatting with a Kick Boxing Instructor she'd occasionally crossed paths with at the gym. Rodrigo returned holding a marguerite, which surprised her. It wasn't her usual drink – wine.

'Tequila goes better with your hair,' he smiled, handing her the drink and placing several more bottles of lager on a tall bar table nearby. 'And it's more fun.'

Chuckling, she felt herself finally relaxing from the small amount of alcohol now pumping through her veins. 'I guess it can be.'

'Ask any Mexican.' He flashed a brilliant smile. 'Cheers.' Glass chinked upon glass. 'Now where were we. What's up with Fiona?'

'I'm not sure, really. Ever since the…' she stopped in recollection at the difficult memory.

'Heated moment after the movies?' he offered.

'Yes.' She sipped nervously on her marguerite, realizing she was staring at the seam around the neckline of his pale blue t-shirt and wondering if he had any chest hair.

'You've fallen out?'

'I don't think so. But she's been…elusive. Which is totally unlike her.'

'Well, even the best friendships go through *patches*. I wouldn't worry about it.'

'Spoken like a true male.' The remark slipped from her lips before she could catch it. It wasn't meant to be negative, but it didn't come out quite right.

'You think we're all simple.' He smiled.

Sipping again on the drink, she could feel the tequila's rapid relaxing effects. 'Not at all. But I do think some men like to box things as *too complicated* so they can avoid whatever happens to be there.'

He chuckled. 'Maybe. Some men.'

'And which are you?' Her height felt as if it had increased by several inches. Standing tall and straight she stared up directly into the green of his eyes, now more curious about the man lurking behind them.

'I'm Brazilian, Sasha,' he responded, as if that explained it all. His sexy accent sent a vibration up her spine and caused tiny hairs to stand up on the back of her neck.

'What exactly does that mean?'

'Ahhh,' he sighed, smiling, 'Like I said, we have passion. The more heat and friction, the more we're likely drawn to something.' Sasha felt the emphasis on the word passion travel mysteriously into her pelvic region. Of late, it seemed to be becoming quite an active part of her anatomy. She swiftly crushed the image of an aroused Lucas. 'Brazilian men tend to move toward a challenge more than away from it. Particularly when it comes to women. At least, I do.' he added as an afterthought, the green of his eyes regarding her beyond his perfectly shaped nose.

Feeling discomfort, she broke the connection that seemed to be forming by lifting the glass to her lips and draining half of its contents.

'You look different,' he suddenly said, searching her face inquisitively as his arms folded back in front of his chest.

'Really.' She squirmed nervously. Was it possible he could tell she'd recently had sex?! Apparently some men were quite astute like that. The thought caused her to quickly bolt down the remains of her marguerite.

'Yes. But your drinking speed hasn't changed.'

A small smile reluctantly curled her lips. He surveyed her face with curiosity. 'Why don't you ask Dave what's up with Fiona?' His head gestured toward the band.

'Oh. I will. When he finishes his next set.'

'Well drink up, then.' He handed her one of the bottles of beer and took the empty glass from her hand. 'The band just started before you arrived. He'll be a while.'

Taking the bottle with uncertainty, she wondered if it was wise to continue drinking. Any more alcohol would only relax her further – not a good thing in her current sexy company. But God, it felt good to forget about events of the last few days. And since Fiona wasn't around to lighten things up, it was good to have Rodrigo's company. Besides, what was the harm in a few drinks? It wasn't as if avoiding alcohol stopped her from getting into trouble - she'd been stone cold sober the other night and ended up with a man in a passionate tryst!

At the thought, Sasha guzzled half her beer in rapid time and finished the rest of the bottle ten minutes later. Rodrigo disappeared only to return with more beers. Before she knew it, another bottle had vanished inside her. She was starting to feel a little drunk. But it felt so good to forget; so good to be in the moment. And it felt fantastic to have the attention of this flirting, flattering, Brazilian man. He must have complimented her at least three times in the last fifteen minutes – speaking in admiration of how she'd built a successful private yoga practice; he praised her lithe physique as he placed his hands briefly on the sides of her waist; and told her she had beautiful hair whilst stroking a hand through it. She was melting in his presence. It was now fully understandable why women at the gym always surrounded him - he made them feel good. It was no big deal for him to shower a woman with accolades. He could probably make the largest, flabbiest woman feel like a supermodel. There was nothing tight, controlling, or self-protective about him as a man. He loved making women feel great and knew utterly and completely how to do it. But the more she thought about it, the more Sasha realized it could only mean one thing:

She wasn't special.

This would have been a sobering thought if she hadn't downed another bottle of lager at speed. Drinking beer was turning out to be a lot more fun than she could recall. Except that she was beginning to lose her footing on the wooden floorboards. But there seemed to be enough people around for her to lean onto from time to time and help keep her composure.

'Dance with me, Sasha,' Rodrigo said at one point, full of happy animation.

'What, here?

'Of course!' He beamed.

'There's no room,' she said laughing.

'There is always room for dancing!' he replied, grabbing hold of her hand and guiding her to an area where there was more space.

Watching his body start to move in a rhythmical sensual way, she observed how graceful he moved for such a big man - so full of joy and ease as he danced. His happiness was infectious and she began to move her body, too. It had been a long time since she'd felt so free in her dance. Rodrigo's delight as he swung his hips and tapped his feet was giving her unlimited permission to let go in her body. Brazilians were renowned for their expertise and love of dance and he was no exception.

At the moment when she'd almost entirely lost all self-consciousness and was caught up in her body's own movement, he took both her hands in his and moved close to her. Initially, he was smiling and exuding fun, so it seemed okay that he was pressed against her a little. How could she resist such carefree innocence between them? It was the greatest pleasure being able to dance close with a man. His hands gripped hers as he pulled her even closer toward him. Pushing up against his t-shirt, she clung tightly to him watching beads of sweat form on his brow. His cologne was tantalizing the back of her nostrils as she began to move more fluidly and in harmony with his body. His hand moved onto her waist and slid down onto the back of her hip, pressing her closer as their pelvises began to lock tightly together. An amazing energy was forming between them as they swirled and gyrated sinuously as one.

Totally separated from self-control and feeling so free, Sasha began to experience herself as weightless as ether.

And then she looked up at him: looked into those deep, feeling, emerald eyes, that were no longer smiling and full of fun and lightness. They were smoldering and locked onto her, with heat and longing and desire. They were eyes wide open to life and sensuality.

Eyes wide open to her.

Reeling inwardly, she began to recoil back into her small internal cavern. But then Rodrigo did the most spectacular thing - he dipped her. He dipped her as if they'd been dancing together all their lives, and she felt all of it: each exquisite moment, as if it were a slow motion freeze-frame scene from a blockbuster movie. The splendor of his solid arm finding its way fully into the arch of her supple back; the look that rose up between them; the innate knowing she felt in the infinite strength and capacity he had to hold her; and the power and grace that united them as one as her back dropped and surrendered wholly and fully over his arm. She felt her lips part in ecstasy and her breath exhale for the longest sweetest moment.

Everything stopped. Her mind stopped. It was possible her breathing stopped. And she was almost certain her heart stopped. Nothing mattered in the timelessness she felt here. As Rodrigo leaned right over her, Sasha could almost feel his breath and the pounding in his chest.

And then it all changed.

Some stumbling oaf of a man bumped into them. Not much. But it was just enough to jolt them from the mysterious place they were visiting; enough to steal some of that magic.

Sasha felt the sweat on Rodrigo's back as she gripped onto his t-shirt. Her hands were wet and she clung to him as he slowly and gently lifted her upright.

Returning her to a standing position, his arms were wrapped fully around her. She felt precious and cocooned, as if no one else could touch her. A trembling of fear formed inside her as she took her next big in-breath and tentatively stared up at him.

He was gazing deeply at her with a searching intensity, but his eyes were filled with tenderness too. She didn't notice the music stop playing, so keenly was she watching his lips as they drew dangerously close. They were so near they were almost touching her own.

And then they did.

She felt their sweet softness and the heat of his breath as he kissed her, gently at first, then with passion. Searching for her. Feeling her. Finding her. And as he found her in that kiss, she moved toward him, stepping through fear and joining him in that magical place.

It could have been seconds or hours they were locked together. But with the band taking a break, the great exodus to the bar had begun and they were once more interrupted. First, someone bashed past Rodrigo. Then an elbow knocked her from behind in the ribcage.

'Ouch.' She pulled back from him and the sudden realization of what had just taken place dawned upon her.

'Are you okay?' he said, with a look of concern.

'Just…banged in the back by someone.' She took a step back, breaking contact and rubbing her forehead. 'Phew. What a night, huh.' It was suddenly hard to look at him. But she did catch the flicker of dismay in his eyes and see his forehead twitch before glancing away.

'Hey, guys!'

'Dave!' Sasha spun about with happy surprise, giving him a hug and a kiss on the cheek. Rodrigo shook Dave's hand, adding a manly pat on the shoulder in greeting.

'You two looked like you were cutting up the dance

floor,' he grinned at them both.

Grimacing inwardly, Sasha realized he must have seen them. Which meant he probably also saw the kiss.

'Then I lost sight of you. Did you hit the deck?'

Relief flooded her body.

'I dipped her.' Rodrigo responded, but he wasn't smiling so much anymore.

'Well, that explains the disappearance of one of the tallest men in the bar. You Brazilians have the moves, don't you.' Dave chuckled. 'Were you dropped?' He turned to look at Sasha who was feeling more uncomfortable as the seconds ticked by.

'No. He was…a gentleman,' she smiled, shifting her feet nervously.

Rodrigo was watching her but she couldn't read his face anymore.

'Good man!' Dave clapped him on the back. 'Bad look for a woman - getting dropped in a dip.'

A smile finally broke Rodrigo's emotionless features. 'Sasha's been looking for Fiona,' he added.

Dave's relaxed energy seemed to collapse instantly. 'She's not here.'

'Yes, we guessed. Any idea where she is? Didn't think she'd miss you playing,' said Rodrigo.

Shifting about uncomfortably, Dave glanced at the floor and ran a hand through his damp hair. 'We're not together, mate,' he responded quietly, before darting a sheepish look at Sasha.

'What?!' They replied in unison.

Dave sighed heavily. 'She dumped me.'

'I don't believe it.' Sasha looked at him with dismay.

'You two seemed great,' Rodrigo added.

'And she's been so happy,' echoed Sasha.

'Yeah. So was I.' A glimpse of sadness washed over his face.

'Did she say why?'

'No. And she's refusing to see or talk to me.'

'I don't understand.' Sasha couldn't believe Fiona would dump Dave over him challenging her about her drinking. Usually she'd simply bat off any comments with a cheeky comeback. The news was sobering. 'When did this happen?'

'Oh, it was a couple days after we were all at the movies together.' He glanced downward in recognition of the events of the night, scratching his chin awkwardly.

'Something's not right about this.' Sasha paused. 'Look, I'm really sorry, Dave. It's such a shame.' She gave him another hug. 'I'm going to head off.'

One of Rodrigo's feet slid gently in Sasha's direction. 'Now?' he said, watching her intently.

'Yes, I need to get hold of Fiona and see if she's okay.' Hastily gathering up her handbag and jacket she glanced back momentarily before leaving the bar. 'Thank you,' she said softly to Rodrigo. 'I had a...wonderful time.'

'It was my pleasure,' he responded simply.

But Sasha felt his eyes follow her all the way to the exit.

Chapter Seventeen

Fiona loved physical activities of most types. She always had. Ever since she was a little girl she'd displayed outstanding drive and motivation toward athletic performance and excellence. She could swing higher on jungle bars and jump further than most other little girls. And she'd sprint around parks as if there were a flame up her backside. Terrorizing neighbors on her tricycle and driving daredevil toward their ankles as they strolled the streets was a favorite pastime, causing her eyes to fill with a merry kind of mischief. She'd inevitably arrive in for dinner with mud and grass stains on her clothes. And having progressed to dolls, she had a habit of cutting her Barbie's hair and trouser legs short – her own version of *Sport Barbie.*

Yet, despite now having an attitude and training regime of a professional athlete - and possibly their language in more disgruntled moments, too - she'd managed to hide a yearning that ran very counter to her more masculine drives. Her greatest secret, tucked far beneath her conscious mind, was a subterranean ache for children. Very few people would have ever detected such a thing about Fiona. Perhaps once, in a time long passed, her great-granny might have. After all, it was she who'd discussed with the little girl what she might want to be when she grew up. Although at the time, the dialogue had been a one-sided affair.

'When I grow up, I want to have babies,' young Fiona had blurted out excitedly on a number of occasions. 'Lots of them.'

Given her tomboyish ways, anybody within earshot, including her own mother, would inevitably laugh. It was the family way. But one day, her great-granny didn't snicker - at least, not straight away. Instead, on a fated wintery afternoon when they were both alone and nestled in front of a glowering fireplace, *Grams* - as little Fiona had called her - fixed a beady brown-eyed gaze upon the cherub child and in a mere minute banished her dreams into the dead of night.

At the tender age of five, Fiona couldn't distinguish between the creaking sound of the rocking chair and the old woman's bones as her great-granny slowly leaned forward to peer at her sitting cross-legged on the floor. At the time, the young girl was cradling a log of wood in a vice-like grip, playing make-believe that it was a baby and attentively feeding her with an imaginary baby bottle - a twig - as she happily hummed away.

'What are you doing, child?'

Fiona's eyes widened with excitement. 'I'm feeding my baby, Grams.'

'Babies. Hmmph!' Granny's wizened face screwed up like a ball of paper about to hit the trash. She snorted distastefully. 'Stand up child. So I can see you.'

Fiona dutifully obeyed, clutching her baby log tightly.

The old woman extended boney hands toward her – one pinching into Fiona's little shoulders, as her other shaking limb grabbed onto the *wood baby*. Grams eyes squinted meanly at the little girl as she rasped. 'Babies suck the life from you and leave you hollow. That's what they do.'

If that wasn't enough of a fertility terminating

statement, the crone then leaned right in close to her great-granddaughter's face, wafting fumes of putrid breath, before delivering the final maternal-shattering blow. 'Devil's spawn. That's what they are,' she snarled, disturbingly as if she were the very same thing herself.

Horrified, Fiona fell into a wide-eyed frigid stupor. Grams then snatched the log of wood callously from her stubby little arms and hurled it straight into the fire.

'Burn in hell,' she cackled like an old witch, laughing heartily as if she'd just cracked the funniest joke.

Fiona balled so hard that tears appeared to squirt perpendicular from her eyes.

Great-Granny had downed several whiskeys that night. And whilst she may have felt entitled to a degree of bitterness, having birthed eleven offspring from being knocked up fourteen times (Great Grandpa Hugh was randy and always wanted a football team), her words and actions were inexcusable.

But a five year old regrettably lacked the skills to reason that.

As a child, Fiona had an extraordinarily vivid imagination. The poisoned words of *Grams*, along with her rancid smell - much like a dead carcass rotting in her guts and flowing liberally from the bitter woman's prune-like lips - had created the most hideous of scars upon Fiona's young psyche. After the dreadful event, she'd lain in bed night after night, fearing the devil to be lurking in her room, stealing her darling babes. She dreamed of her litter growing horns, or envisioned them all burning in hell. Sleeping fitfully for weeks, she'd wake in a sweat and shaking. No one knew. After all, she could never discuss Lucifer with anyone. It became her darkest secret, lying trapped in a psychological tomb somewhere in the cellular vicinity of her womb...with old *Grams* chortling away inside it.

Eventually, as traumatic events are oft to do, the memory drifted like silt to the bottom of Fiona's unconscious underworld. Yet the blueprint remained, buried and well forgotten, along with her dreams of ever *having babies.* She never understood why avoiding the path of motherhood seemed so imperative, she only knew it was - at any cost.

These days, the mere thought of babies would typically send a shiver of revulsion up her spine. She wasn't remotely maternal – that's what Fiona told herself. She was far too spirited and free to ever consider such a handbrake in life. The occasional boyfriend, having fallen in love with her array of charms, wit and Goddess-like body, and having made mere mention of wanting children, was inevitably rapidly and mysteriously ejected from her life.

But she hadn't progressed quite far enough with Dave to warrant banishing him. And he'd never mentioned the word *love* to her, even though she could tell he liked her a whole lot. There was just a really jittery feeling she had about him. And it started happening long before the incident at the movies.

Ending things with Dave hadn't happened because of his comments about her drinking. In actual fact, it was right of him to say what he had. She'd been overdoing her alcohol intake for quite a number of weeks…since she met him, actually. For some reason he made her feel nervous and she resorted to drinking as a coping mechanism. So ending their…whatever it was…seemed best because she couldn't handle the edgy sensation eating away at her insides. It made her feel out of control - and afraid. And Fiona wasn't the type of person to have fear come in and trample her life. She wasn't the type at all.

So within several months, he had to go. That was all

there was to it.

It did bother her that she wasn't bouncing back fast, though. Usually she could change gears pretty quickly, once she'd dispensed with the problem. And the problem was surely Dave – wasn't it? She didn't feel right with him. Sure, she'd felt a hint of that on occasion with other men, but despite being so drawn to him the anxiety she experienced was marked.

The sound of her cellphone ringing in the living room broke her deep train of thought. Leaving the mirror she'd been staring vacantly into, Fiona retrieved the phone but then saw Sasha's name showing on the screen. *Damn.* She exhaled heavily, sinking into her sofa and ignoring the call until the name stopped appearing.

She couldn't keep avoiding Sasha like this. She was her best friend and the person she always confided in the most. But what could Fiona tell her? That she was getting a major case of the jitters lately, after such a short time of seeing someone? That would make her a chicken. And she was no chicken. Fiona had graduated top of her class at school; she'd been a champion track and field athlete and ran close to the country's sprint record time; she'd breezed through her Exercise Science degree; and she'd sure as hell walked away from men who didn't treat her right.

But Dave *had* treated her right. Sure, they'd tumbled in the sack pretty quickly, but he'd been incredibly decent to her right from the get-go. He was warm, caring, a masterful and attentive lover, and he was a brilliant talented drummer. There was a beautiful soulfulness about him. And breathtakingly, he had that *steady-solid-man* thing going on. It was pretty rare in her world. He just stepped right in beside her like he belonged with her for the rest of their lives. No games. No bullshit. No pansying around because of 'hang-ups' over ex's or lost loves. Just Dave, being...Dave.

Who did that in this world? What man showed up like that - so real and honest?

Her phone beeped. Sasha had left a voice message - another one; her fourth this week. And Fiona was fast running out of excuses to avoid her.

Checking the time, she saw it was after eleven o'clock - odd for Sasha to phone her so late on a Friday night. She'd figured her to be in bed by now, preparing for her mysterious Saturday morning yoga...or whatever the heck it was she was sneaking off to. It was bothersome, all this recent *secretiveness*. Sasha did have a very private side like that, but lately it seemed more pronounced. And it wasn't Fiona's nature to pry on a deeper level. It was always easier just to keep things light and on the surface; let people be who and what they were...or wear whatever mask they wanted to. Didn't Shakespeare, express it best? *All the world's a stage and all the men and women merely players,* or something to that effect. She'd certainly met a few men who were players. *Worthy of Oscars,* she thought, *in the horror genre.*

Regardless, it was not proving so easy at present to *live and let live.* And she sure wasn't enjoying the feeling of the sand shifting beneath her feet and her world becoming uncertain in places it usually wasn't.

Shivering, she noticed the room had become very cold. Momentarily, Fiona had a flashback of sitting by an open fireplace. It was a strange image and one that made her shudder.

I hate fires.

Standing up, she made her way over to the heater, turning it up to high before heading straight to the kitchen. Whilst filling a bowl with crunchy cornflakes and dousing them with lots of milk, Fiona conveniently forgot about listening to Sasha's message.

***

The first thing Sasha did when she pulled the phone out of her handbag was to ignore the missed call from Lucas that showed on her screen, despite the sight of his name shocking her. The second thing she did was to postpone listening to the message he'd left for her at eight-thirty that evening. And the third thing she did was to call Fiona – who didn't answer, yet again. So she left her yet another voice message.

Frankly, Sasha was over being fobbed off. Fiona had managed to avoid her the entire week. They were best friends and it wasn't as if she'd done anything so bad as to warrant being shunned. Sure, she'd mentioned Fee's drinking, but that was from a place of caring and concern. It was possible she was snubbing Sasha because she wouldn't talk about where she was spending her time on Saturday mornings. But surely that was a minor issue. And surely some things could be kept private. Even between *besties*.

Ultimately, Fiona's sudden and large *mood swing* had nothing to do with her, Sasha felt sure of that. Dave's revelation he'd been dumped convinced her even more. But things still didn't stack up well. Something else was going on in Fee's world – that had to be the case. And whatever it was wasn't great, because she'd never seen her friend's cheery soul venture off the rails like this.

Having left a voice message there was nothing more that could be done this evening. And it was unlikely she'd hear back from Fiona tonight. But come tomorrow morning, if there was still no response, she was darn sure she'd be paying her a visit at her apartment to find out what was going on. It was uncharacteristic for Sasha to feel riled up, but she was worried and also unsettled by what had happened with Lucas. The thought of him reminded her…she still needed to listen to his message.

Walking purposefully toward the underground station she tapped a few digits on the keypad of her phone and waited nervously to hear what he had to say.

A heavy sigh was audible before he spoke.

'Sasha, I'm really so sorry I haven't been in touch earlier.'

So you should be.

'Look, my life is…complicated, at the moment.'

Oh, here we go. She waited for the shove off the cliff.

'We should talk.'

Just get on with it, and do it over the phone - so I don't have to see you again.

Another heavy sigh escaped his lips. 'I really like you.'

Hmm…unexpected. She stopped walking and listened attentively.

'And I'd love to see you again.'

Hopeful. She chewed her lip nervously.

'If you can forgive the time it's taken me to contact you…' His voice softened.

A small smile moved her lips.

'…not to mention those ghastly black eyes.'

Her heart expanded in her chest.

'Three of them from memory. If I recall rightly.' There was another long pause.

'I'd love to see you. This weekend…if you're free.'

A nervous tremor rippled through her body.

'So call me. When you get this message…okay.'

Her stomach churned.

'Talk soon.'

Silence. The message ended.

Sasha stared up at a few visible stars twinkling in the night sky. With a great deal of thought she considered returning his call, but decided against it, instead moving hastily in the direction of the underground station.

Along the way, she found herself tucking her phone back firmly in her handbag and left it there.

***

Having adjusted to the routine of Karma Yoga, Sasha had been steadily feeling better each time she left her Saturday morning class. It wasn't an obvious feeling. It was more a subtle change that seeped in gently over time, as if a great weight had begun to slowly lift from her shoulders.

She was certain her newfound intentionality was a key to the change. Clearly, the actions she was taking reflected her conscience and sincerity to make amends. Despite it being many years ago, her awareness now held deep understanding that the past was never truly over until the healing process was complete. For that to occur, she had to be proactive. And wasn't she tired of moving along in life with her little box of dark secrets bumpety-bumping along behind her? Tired of fear and shame? Certainly, the best course was to rewire and reroute her thoughts and begin to consider her life in a new frame – one based more on the person she'd become, not her past.

And her life had changed so much. Hadn't she transformed it markedly? Here she was now in London, with a thriving private yoga teaching practice. She was helping people – genuinely helping people. And she loved what she did.

Meeting amazing people was a bonus too. People like Amy Buckley, who inspired her to remember magic in life; to hope and trust, perhaps to even believe in love again some day. It was up to her to hold onto those kernels of light and grow them into something more bountiful. Yes, it required perseverance and discipline, but she had to start living outside the box she'd packaged so tightly around herself. At some point, she'd have to let people in, too. Yet sometimes it seemed hard letting go. It was like clutching onto the side of a cliff that had no bottom – some dark and endless abyss that would swallow every trace of her existence. If she were to let go, there would be nothing of her left. Not a smidgeon.

Exiting out back of the rickety old building and into the car park, sunshine lit her face, bringing her to an abrupt halt and causing her to close her eyes and savor the moment. Winter was beginning to lose its long craggy hold and traces of spring were cautiously emerging. That hint of warmth tantalizing her chilled body; the first leaves forming on naked trees; the odd early bulb resting on the head of a courageous stem.

Pulling her phone out of the side pocket of her sports bag she peered hopefully at the screen whilst making her way across the car park.

Still no message from Fiona.

Her heart sank.

She would go there. She would go to her place right now.

The driver's seat of her car felt more uncomfortably firm than usual. In fact, it was something she'd never really been aware of previously. Reaching for the ignition, Sasha hesitated before starting the engine. Sitting nervously for several minutes, she plucked out her phone and scrolled through the contacts.

Call him.

Until now, it felt like the best course to avoid contacting Lucas. But there was something plain to see: here she was having an issue with Fiona not calling her back, whilst conducting the same stubborn behavior with someone else. Nervously pursing her lips, Sasha scratched her forehead deep in thought. He'd made the first move. It was only fair.

The problem, however, was not in speaking with him. The problem, she reflected upon their sexual encounter, was where it might lead.

Chapter Eighteen

'Shirshasana,' he smiled, wandering gracefully around the platform amidst the scattered bodies and wide-eyed eager stares, 'is considered the King or Queen of yoga poses. To stand on one's head is like the world turning upside down...creating an expanded view upon things,' he chuckled. 'Or,' he paused for effect, 'the headstand can also be symbolically linked to an upheaval in perspective.'

It sounded like a warning to Holly - *an upheaval in perspective.* Was it really worth learning the blasted pose?'

Moving to the front of the platform, The Guru asked, 'why were you born?'

Not a fricking clue, she thought, *some hallucinogenic hippy sex trip by my parents? Mushrooms perhaps,* she pondered. *Mushrooms or weed.*

'What is your relationship to God...to The Divine?' he continued. As the word *Divine* exited his mouth, a broad smile seemed to stretch each corner of his lips so they almost touched ear to ear.

My relationship? Never met God. Not sure I ever will, she thought, reflecting on her food and chocolate addiction, not to mention previous sexual encounters.

'Upside down, with our feet hanging in the sky, we

can let our worries and attachments fall away, allowing our minds to open to bigger questions.'

Ahh...I see where this is going...

'Instead of attaching excessively to the Earth, one can ground their feet in the heavens...in The Divine... and be nourished with spiritual insights.'

Precisely. That's what I'm here for, Holly thought. *Spiritual insights. That and disappearing from the face of the planet for a while.*

'Can you make a commitment to bring your ideals and life to all its potential? Can you break free from your past?'

I can try. I can goddamned try.

'Are you ready, dear yogis? Are you ready for your world to turn...upside down?'

Yes, let's do it! Holly decided, wanting to scream to everybody...to life itself. *Let's master this fricking headstand! Let's turn everything on its head...because it's already a total mess!*

'Is yes your answer?!' The Guru exclaimed, with such surprising passion that a number of students flinched backward. His brown eyes grew beady and narrow as he carefully noted who was nodding their heads in agreement.

'Then have patience, dear yogis. Have patience and great compassion for yourselves,' he paused.

Holly, by now accustomed to his ability to make a grand point, knew The Guru wasn't entirely done.

'You will need it,' he smiled. 'In the mastery of the headstand, as in the journey of your life, you will need patience...and great compassion for yourself.'

***

Fiona lived quite close to Camden in Finsbury Park. Sasha swung her car toward the curb around eleven that morning, listening to the sound of her grumbling stomach that was now taking offence at her lack of breakfast. She'd overslept. Then awoke with a thumping headache and horrid hangover from her previous night's antics with Rodrigo. Managing to force down half a banana that morning before speeding out the door had been a much safer bet than any fatty food binge – her normal and unhealthy alcohol recovery plan.

Ignoring her body's pleas for more sustenance and taking a few minutes to gather her thoughts, Sasha felt a sense of dread as she wandered unenthusiastically to the entrance of Fiona's quaint city apartment. She'd visited here on numerous occasions, at times sleeping over having crashed out on the sofa after the usual shared bottle of wine too many, and in the wake of a great deal of laughter. And while she might have hoped for a sense of humor and some hilarity today, Sasha had the distinct feeling that wasn't the direction things would go.

Fidgeting nervously with the bunch of car keys, she rolled one continually between her thumb and forefinger as she climbed the small set of steps leading to Fiona's home.

The situation was uncomfortable, she thought, tapping on the door with a sense of unease. It was wrong to be feeling apprehension at visiting a dear friend. But then, Fiona had never attempted to avoid her before. Nothing like this had ever happened in their close to three-year connection. Her best friend emitted a great deal of personal power and always seemed to be in commanding control of her life, along with often finding something to have a giggle about. However, she'd rapidly ended things with Dave - and if there was one thing Sasha was sure of, it was that Fiona had really liked the amiable drummer. Despite being a highly independent lady, she'd gone to most of his band gigs and they'd spent much of their spare time together. A radiant glow emanated from her after their first weeks of dating. He was good for her and she seemed incredibly happy.

Maybe I've missed something. She's dumped guys before...but this is different, Sasha reflected. *Hmm...she was rattled at Ian's sexual advances a while ago, which is out of character for her, too.*

Normally, Fiona would brush off *Sleazy Ian's* innuendo and slimy ways like a feather. She'd laugh, or turn any seedy behavior or comment around with ease. And if that ever failed, Fee had an arsenal of hot-tempered emotion to fall back on. She had the talent - and possibly the DNA - of a flame-thrower. But recently, that fearsome inner dragon of hers had reared its head in unexpected ways.

Pressing the buzzer, Sasha waited expectantly as she heard footsteps approach from behind the door.

Click. The latch removed, the door drew slowly open, revealing a very different looking friend. Normally a religious applier of make-up when straight out of the shower, Fiona was dressed down with a surprisingly barefaced appearance. This was startling to Sasha for a number of reasons: one, she looked utterly pale and washed out, with *bags-to-carry-groceries-in* underneath her dimly sheened green eyes; and two, by eleven in the morning it was simply unheard of for her to grace the world publicly or privately without even a tiny splattering of mascara or a light dusting of powder. Fiona would rather run naked up the street than have her face be seen without some form of beautifying.

With respect to holistic folk, Sash...sod natural! I can face myself a hell of lot better in the morning without looking like I need a bag over my head. Sasha recalled her once saying in her usual straight up manner.

'But you're beautiful without make-up, Fee,' she'd responded. 'You're one of the lucky ones.'

'So what?' Fiona fervently announced with a fiery gleam in her eyes. Pointing dramatically to her own head she'd passionately declared, 'Beauty is the one great power we have, Sash! It's one of the few influences we have in life as women. People bang on a lot about all our other talents, but really, besides motherhood, what has the most impact? Beauty. What affects men more?' Sasha raised her eyebrows but continued to listen politely. 'And since men have set up the world to suit themselves the past few thousand years or so, it's got to be the fastest way to regain our power – hit them with beauty. I know that probably sounds like sell-out bullshit, but the fact is, you're going to get slammed either way – by women if you look good; and by men if you look bad, so sod it. Frankly, I'd rather take criticism with a bit of war paint on.'

She'd been surprisingly serious - a rare sight and sound. And as cynical as her words may have been, they were not something to be contested. Besides, Sasha reluctantly thought, Fee in her own rough-cut way had a fair point.

'I hear you, sister,' she simply responded in a respectful tone and left it at that.

Today, there were no signs of sultry eyelashes to greet her – just a strangely subdued expression of wariness…and preparedness, indicating Fiona had been waiting for Sasha to turn up on her doorstep.

'Hey, Fee.'

'Hey,' she answered, keeping the door half closed and leaning on the wall. Her face looked pasty white and the bags under her bloodshot eyes were even darker than before. Fiona's unmasked face matched her dull outfit of baggy navy-blue track pants, with a loose black jumper, revealing a bare white shoulder. Fee appeared more like a listless burnt-out housewife – one who certainly wasn't getting extra's from the postman or plumber.

'I thought I'd pop by. You've been pretty quiet.' Sasha pretended not to notice the uncharacteristic attire. 'Everything okay?'

'Sure.' Fiona looked unmoved.

Sasha peered momentarily down the hallway, feeling awkward at the absence of a warm welcome. 'Can I come in?'

Fiona hesitated, clearly uncertain. It was strange - she was usually so inviting. 'I guess,' she finally conceded, allowing the door to drift fully open as she padded bare-foot away, the sounds of her feet making a cute squeaking sound on the polished wooden floor.

Closing the door and trailing behind her into the living room, Sasha decided she might as well tackle things head on. 'I bumped into Dave last night at the bar.'

Fiona flopped heavily onto her comfortably lush black Italian sofa that took up most of the space in the warmly decorated modern city apartment. *Got to be a dark sofa, Sash, in case I spill the red – which, let's face it, is highly likely,* Sasha recalled her saying one night. Fiona had been waving about an opened bottle of Merlot at the time and guffawing at Sasha's first sight of the new furnishing. It was one of the few black items in an otherwise warmly decorated living room, filled with stylish colorful wall paintings, a bold red rug and several large elegant pots and glassware. They'd had so many cheerful nights here that it was hard to know who the woman before her now was. Fiona's forlorn expression caused her to instantly morph into a total stranger. Any trace of the animated joy that so often lit her face was nowhere to be seen.

'Bumped into?' Fee replied, her brow knitting

together and forming a small crevasse above her nose.

'Well, I dropped into the bar. I was hoping to find *you*…actually.' Sasha peered cautiously at her before continuing. 'But you weren't there, so I had a drink with…' It was difficult to say his name. A sudden vivid recollection of the deep and passionate kiss they'd shared caused her heart to race and a rush of blood to flow toward her pelvic region, making Sasha blush slightly. 'Rodrigo,' she mumbled after some hesitation. 'And a couple of the crew from the gym,' she added, to hide her misdemeanor.

'Oh,' Fiona added, the tiniest register of surprise peeping out from behind the hidden depths of her leafy colored eyes.

'Anyway, Dave popped over to say hello at the end of one of his sets.'

'Uh-huh.' Fiona pulled a knee up close to her chest, binding her arms tightly around it. Sasha waited for more of a response. There was none, so she continued.

'He said you'd ended things?'

'Yep.'

'Can I ask why?' Easing her way onto the furthest end of the sofa, Sasha instinctively reached for one of the soft lime-colored cushions behind her and clutched it onto her lap.

Fiona shrugged her shoulders, glancing away.

'I know you like him, Fee. A lot.'

'Well, I don't now.' Her tone was crisp and cool.

'Is that,' Sasha said, choosing her words carefully, 'anything to do with his comments about your drinking?'

'Jesus, Sash,' she responded sharply, still avoiding eye contact, 'you think a bit of a poke about my drinking is something I can't handle?'

'Not at all. Quite the opposite. That's why I'm a little confused…and…concerned.'

Stealing the briefest glance at Sasha, Fiona caught the expression of care on her good friend's face. She shrugged again. 'It was just time to move on. End of story.'

'Seems quite sudden.'

'Sudden is how these things usually go in our modern age,' she added, appearing reflective for a moment. 'You like someone – then you don't. One minute you think you know the direction of your life, then boom,' Fiona circled her hands expressively, 'the next thing everything changes…or disappears in a puff of smoke.'

Sasha stared at her inquisitively as an image of Amy Buckley drifted across her mind. 'Not always, Fee. If life were that unexpected and gloomy nobody would get married or have kids…and an awful lot of people seem to do that. And I bet half of them would tell you they're bored because life is so routine and predictable.

Fiona shifted uncomfortably on the sofa, drawing her other knee up to her chest and wrapping her arms around them both. Sasha was making a disturbing kind of sense, causing an uncomfortable feeling to arise inside her. She needed time and space to figure things out. 'It just didn't feel right, you know.' She shrugged her shoulders, finally looking directly into Sasha's eyes.

'No, I don't know. Why?' persisted Sasha. 'Did you want things to go differently?'

Shifting about uncomfortably in her seat, Fiona began to appear agitated. 'I…he… Look, I don't bloody know, Sash. It just didn't feel right, okay. I don't want to talk about it.'

Pools of moisture appeared to have formed in the back of her friend's eyes, shocking Sasha. She'd only ever seen Fiona cry once before – last year, when she'd tripped in the gym whilst giving a personal training session. Sasha recalled the event as if it were yesterday.

Having just finished teaching a yoga class, she heard a scream of agony from the vicinity of the cardio work-out area. Fiona had broken a fall quite dramatically on a rowing machine, snapping the ulna bone in her forearm. Later, Sasha wondered if Fee had actually only cried because she knew it would mean a rest period from her religious training regime, not because of the intense pain ripping through her arm. Despite having to wear a cast for five weeks, she was back on the treadmill within two days and working with her private clients within three days of her accident. And of course, she reveled in creating humor out of the event.

'The England cricket team has requested the use of my arm as a bat,' she said afterward, glancing down at her wieldy cast one morning at Basilio's while they waited for coffee. 'I've agreed, but only for a trade: I help direct the men into their training gear every morning...and they help me out of mine at night.' Their conversation ran down the sewers after that, but they'd laughed their heads off that morning.

Things were very different now. Whatever was broken inside of Fiona was causing a lot more pain than her arm ever did.

'Just leave me alone, Sash. I need to be alone,' she winced.

Looking across at Fiona wrapped up tightly in a ball on the sofa, Sasha recognized a wounded creature in the process of running to the wild to tend their wounds. She knew the look. And the feelings it hid. Taking a deep breath she reluctantly stood up to go. 'I understand,' she responded gently.

'Of course you do. You bloody yogis think you understand everything!' Fiona spat back resentfully. 'Except that you're no expert when it comes to relationships, Sash. At least I give men a chance!'

Sasha ignored the blow, thinking carefully. A lesion

inside was splitting her friend open. Fiona being Fiona, would fight to prevent that – and in all likelihood fail.

'That may be true about me and relationships,' Sasha conceded. 'But that has nothing to do with you, or now. Whatever you're going through, Fee, I'm here for you. For as long as it takes.' She moved toward the hallway, pausing at the doorway to the living room without turning back. 'I'm sorry you're hurting,' she added, fighting to contain the liquid in her eyes. 'You always have my support.' Biting down on her bottom lip, a single teardrop escaped down her face. 'And when you're ready to talk…if you want to, I'll be waiting.'

As Fiona heard the click of the front door closing quietly behind Sasha, she sat alone in the eerie silence of her apartment. The agitation inside her was increasing by the second and grabbing one of the cushions beside her, she flung it fiercely at the wall, knocking a painting askew.

'Fuck!' She yelled vehemently.

Her connection with Sasha had never been bad. It was wrong it had become this way. Yet she'd caused it by willfully pushing her away. If only she could talk; communicate what was going on inside of her. The problem was, she didn't know what that was.

A strange murky feeling seeped up from somewhere in the pit of Fiona's stomach. 'Fuck!' She yelled again, this time in sheer frustration. Rolling helplessly onto her side, she curled into a tighter ball as a dense heavy fog rolled in over her mind.

'What's happening to me?' she trembled, as fear bubbled up like one of Mother Earth's muddy geothermal episodes. Gripping her folded legs vice-like, pangs of ancient pain crept terrifyingly to her surface. And for the first time in almost twenty-five years, Fiona began to recall a deeply buried place of dread.

Chapter Nineteen

Having a date with a mega-wealthy man was an uncommon experience for Sasha. And as it transpired, Lucas also happened to be the son of a Lord – something he'd finally revealed in another phone call later that day. Whilst she was unsure what had prompted him to tell her, it certainly made a few pieces of her Melody puzzle fit more firmly into place.

Accustomed as she was to wearing mostly bohemian or casual garb, Sasha had absolutely no idea what to wear for their Saturday evening dinner date. In fact, it had been so long since she'd been out with a man that she succumbed to some very stiff vodka and tonic's to settle her nerves before his arrival.

In the end she settled on a simple black dress - of course. You could never go wrong with a little black number, and thankfully that essential item was hanging neglected in her wardrobe. Initially she'd bypassed it for reasons of predictability. But predictability was surely better than a kaleidoscopic disaster. In terms of dresses, black tended to say *chic* and *classy*, even if one didn't entirely feel that way. She'd added a beautiful turquoise pendant for a splash of color. And stilettos on a pair of great legs were surely the next best accessory. She thankfully had both.

Giving Lucas address details to pick her up had

caused her some discomfort. Not because she was ashamed of her home, but more because it would potentially build a greater picture of her. Sasha coveted privacy. But in the proper dating sense, Lucas was not the kind of man who you caught the train to meet at a bar or restaurant. She considered him a distinguished type who liked to treat a woman as a lady – except, evidently, when in the midst of a bout of passion. So on this occasion, she'd uneasily dropped the drawbridge to her castle and allowed him to cross her moat.

It was ironic she felt so self-protective, considering she'd wantonly thrown herself into bed with him earlier in the week. Although, technically, they never quite made it *into* bed, just landed heavily atop it. A red rouge color spread across the flesh of her face covering her fine high cheekbones as she recalled the memory.

Never done anything like that before, she thought, dusting some more powder over her face as if that would curb the active chemistry beneath it.

Well, almost never before…

Okay…I should have known better!

Placing the brush back absentmindedly into its holder in a drawer and observing herself with a critical eye, Sasha felt the gloomy return of a weight upon her shoulders. Men seemed to be like some sort of emotional time bomb for her. Stunning at first, yet inevitably exploding like a grenade leaving pieces of shrapnel embedded in her heart and life. How beautiful it would be to have a life-enhancing partner like Amy had. But a love like that was rare and certainly didn't seem to be the case in her life. Not that she'd ever given anyone much of a chance since leaving California.

Still, California was many years ago and perhaps it was time to truly forget and move on. Fiona had bluntly told her she should be out dating. But she didn't have Fee's robust nature – the kind that was capable of bouncing back within a day or two of an unsuccessful love. Although, lately, Fiona didn't seem quite so bullet-proof.

She'll call me. When she's ready. I hope.

Some people needed lots of input in a crisis. Fiona wasn't one of them. She was better left to her own devices to work things out.

Sasha heard the doorbell, the sound traveling through her body in an unpleasant way.

He's just a man, she said, reassuring herself in the mirror.

One I teach yoga to.

Who happens to inhabit an entirely different world to me. She sighed heavily.

Who's also the son of a Lord. Her face screwed up anxiously. *God.*

And someone I now have intimate carnal knowledge of. She cringed inwardly.

'You'll get through it,' she exclaimed to herself in the mirror.

All the same, downing another quick vodka wouldn't hurt.

It wouldn't hurt at all.

***

Opaque light became visible beyond the dark floor-to-ceiling curtains as Sasha's eyelids slowly fluttered open. *It must be late*, she thought. Winter in England meant the sun never appeared brightly until after eight, so it had to be a sunny day.

Those were her first thoughts, followed quickly by confusion about where she was, until recollection creaked painfully in. *'Oh,'* she thought, grimacing. *'Oh, oh, no...No!'* Lucas's bed. *I'm in Lucas Huntington's bed.*

If only she hadn't drunk those stiff vodkas before leaving her place. And the champagne: God...the champagne. *Two glasses over dinner - not much.* Her forehead crinkled with discomfort as a pounding sensation behind her frontal lobe began making its presence known. *And the glass and a half before dinner...on an empty stomach...after the vodka.*

All of that just happened to be added to her previous drunken night out, downing beer and marguerite's with Rodrigo. She was now officially a pit of toxins. What on earth had happened to her discipline and the premise that her body was a temple?! She was a shocking example of the Niyama, Sauca. And about as far removed from inner cleanliness as possible. Not to mention other forms of purity. Flashbacks of the night began to unfold and she cringed with shame.

Dinner with Lucas turned out to be one of the most enjoyable dates she'd been on in years. Having had such a long dating lull she'd forgotten how nice it felt to be wined and dined. As a result of his upbringing and outstanding manners, Lucas knew how to treat a lady in a gracious and classy way. He was intelligent, charming, worldly and well traveled. And after a drink had dissipated some of his British reserve, despite the tinge of formality that remained, he was warm and at ease. Of course, he should be. He'd been married and had also likely dated many beautiful women in his thirty-seven years of life. But a Californian yoga instructor?

Definitely not his norm.

The pounding in her head became louder and more persistent, like a drum beat. She needed water – lots of it. Fast.

As her head rolled slightly on the pillow, she glanced peripherally beyond the strands of blonde tousled hair covering parts of her face. If she was quiet, he might still be sleeping and she could slip away before he woke. But that would be wrong, wouldn't it? Sneaking away, like a guilt-ridden soul after a crime. Besides, she didn't have her car. He'd suggested stopping in at his place for a *nightcap* on the way home for dinner.

Had she learned nothing in her twenty-nine years of life? Nightcap was code for *sex* in man talk. And all she'd done by complying was to likely be deemed an *easy woman* in his eyes. Sex on first dates was a giant no-no. And sex on the first date after having already had sex without *any* dates made her feel like an old-fashioned tart. She should definitely slink away with her little Lucifer tail between her legs. That would be fitting.

Cautiously viewing the rest of the bed, Sasha found it empty. There was no sign of Lucas, aside from the crumpled sheets beside her.

As she sat up, her head suddenly felt as if someone had dropped a heavy object on it. Peering down momentarily at her mostly naked body she realized things were getting worse by the second. Thankfully though, she still had her little black underpants on, which was also confusing. *Think woman, think. What happened?*

They'd arrived back at his house and had another drink – Bailey's. That's what she'd chosen. It was with the idea of lining her stomach, which was a strangely late stage of the night to worry about such things - and an odd choice of drink to achieve it. Everything became a blur. The fridge was holding great appeal for some unknown reason and she ended up beside it. Lucas moved in close behind her and as Sasha turned around, bingo, his lips were on hers. A tongue-exploring passionate kiss, pressed up against his expensive Meneghini fridge.

I could buy a really nice car for the price of one of these, was oddly one of her last known thoughts, along with seeing herself strapped to the top of a fridge and speeding down a motorway.

Who knows how long they'd lingered there. All she could recall was that it felt great. There was something mysterious and compelling about him. And it was great to feel held and touched, kissed and desired…to let go; to not be thinking, hiding or self-protective anymore.

Glancing around the floor of the large and dimly lit bedroom she could see there was no trace of her clothing.

Christ.

Leaning over the side of the bed for closer inspection, a rush of blood surging into her brain cavity caused nauseas bile to rise in her stomach.

Oh, God. She clutched her forehead, moving in slower motion. And there, visibly peeking out from under the bed, was the sleeve and mid-section of Lucas's classy blue shirt that he'd been wearing the night before. For some strange reason, the sight of his shirt caused a flood of relief to wash over her. It was clothing, after all. And finding oneself in a man's bedroom – alone and devoid of an outfit to provide cover - had created quite a disturbing feeling in her gut.

Creeping out of bed as if in hiding, Sasha leaned down slowly, grasping her fingers around the fabric and flushing the shirt out before slipping it on. He was a tall man, so it was a generous size and thankfully hid her torso and backside well.

The pleasant aroma of his cologne wafted off the quality fabric. Momentarily, she sniffed it, as hints of bergamot assailed her nostrils, imprinting his scent upon her. Pulling her long hair out from underneath the back collar, she surveyed her surroundings. The room had a tall ceiling with white washed walls and expensive polished wooden floorboards lay beneath her feet. An infinitely plush ocean-colored rug rested indulgently on the ground at the end of his king-sized bed, which was adorned with expensive white linen and a now rumpled cover that was the softest shade of a perfect blue-sky day. A remarkably elegant chaise lounge was positioned over by the far wall near the door. In the dim light, it appeared to be navy blue with an ornate silver trim and legs that swept outward in a graceful arc.

Sasha made her way to the window, drawing open the thick floor-to-ceiling, navy-colored velvet curtains, as inches of sunlight streamed into the room. Blinking rapidly, she turned away sharply as glaring daylight fired painfully into her bloodshot eyes. It was enough of a view of the back yard outside to recognize she was on the second floor.

With her head thudding madly, she returned to the bed, observing on the way a colorful painting on the wall above it and freezing momentarily at the sight. The work of art seemed out of place in the room, belonging more in a gallery or museum. But there it was, boldly displayed and oozing a deep and lush vibrancy - a magnificent Cezanne. *Le Mont Sainte-Victoire vu des Lauves* was suspended in all its beauty in the sparsely decorated room. The single piece of art shone in splendid glory against the white wall it hung upon.

Peering more closely, she could tell it wasn't a print. It was a full-blown oil-on-canvas piece. But it couldn't possibly be the original - that hung in a private collection somewhere, she was sure of it. And she could be sure, because her love of impressionist art had taken her to many fine galleries and exhibitions over the years in her spare time.

Clambering up onto the bed, she stood hard up near the wall to examine the painting at closer range. This was a breathtakingly good version. The original would sell for millions, not hang openly in some stockbroker's bedroom in the middle of Belsize Park, even if he was the son of a Lord. That would be insanity.

Utterly immersed in the piece of art before her, Sasha did not notice the door open until it creaked further ajar.

'Christ!' She spun about in fright seeing Lucas standing there dressed in jeans and a casual shirt, appearing to have already showered.

'Well, not quite,' he responded drily, appraising her in his shirt as she stood unusually on his bed.

'You startled me,' she said, watching him move slowly toward her and noticing he was carrying a tray with what appeared to be breakfast.

'I would say finding you standing on my bed in nothing but my shirt is a surprise for me, too,' he smiled.

His happy look was reassuring. 'That looks nice.' Sasha glanced down, salivating inwardly at the freshly squeezed orange juice filling the glass. There was a bowl of sliced fruit, yoghurt on the side and cooked eggs and toast, all complimented with a pot of tea and several cups.

'I thought you might need the…replenishment.' He placed the tray down carefully on the ornately carved drawers beside the bed.

'I didn't think you cooked.'

'When I want to,' he responded, gazing up at her with curiosity.

'Cezanne,' she said, observing his brow knit together with a *what-exactly-are-you-doing-standing-on-my-bed* look.

'You like his work?'

'I love many of the impressionists. Of course, he was one of the greatest.'

'He was,' Lucas replied in agreement.

'Pablo Picasso said of Cezanne: *He was the mother of all of us.*'

Surprise flashed across his face. 'Yes he did. You know this piece?'

Sasha turned back to look at the painting. 'I know he painted many views of the Mount Sainte-Victoire. This is not his most known. But it is an excellent…'

'Copy,' he interjected.

'Of course,' she smiled. 'A very good one.'

'Well…it adds something interesting to the wall.'

'Yes,' she said, noticing him downplaying the significance of the piece as she simultaneously became aware of her sparse amount of clothing and disheveled appearance.

'So…do you plan on coming down from there anytime soon?' He smiled, extending his hand toward her.

'Of course. The orange juice looks wonderful.' Feeling a flush of nervousness, her fingers entwined his and their eyes locked together. He watched her with desire as she drew all the way down into a sitting position on the bed. The shirt barely covered the top of her thighs, so semi-folding her knees self-consciously she leaned back onto the plump pillows stacked by the headboard.

Releasing her hand, he passed across the glass of orange juice and observed her gratefully drink it as he seated himself on the bed. 'I've never seen that shirt look so good,' he murmured, running the back of his hand gently down the side of her arm.

An intense awareness of his touch overcame her as she swallowed with relief at the hydration, 'I drank a little too much last night.' Wracking her fogged brain she wondered again exactly what had happened.

'Well, so you know, you were polite and well behaved.'

'I was?'

''Mmm,' he nodded, staring at her. 'We made it this

far. And after you passed out, I put you into bed.'

'Oh.' She hesitated, looking down at the shirt and feeling quite naked as she twiddled with the now empty glass. I couldn't find my dress.'

'Your things are over there.' He indicated to the chaise lounge where the light creeping through the gap in the curtains revealed her clothing folded up neatly at one end. Blushing at the thought of him removing her dress and nylon tights, she wondered, had he slid them off slowly, exploring her body as he did so?

'Great. That's great,' she said, overcome with shyness and releasing her tight hold on the glass. Moving her head absentmindedly, she stared down uncomfortably at the perfect powder-blue bedcover.

'We didn't make love, Sasha. If that's what you're worried about.'

'Worried? Not at all.' The hasty lie slipped far too easily off her tongue. The eight-limbed yogic path had now disappeared entirely, somewhere beneath a torrent of alcohol and into oblivion.

His hand found hers, clasping onto it and allowing her to feel the smoothness of his skin, its softness undoubtedly from a privileged upbringing. 'That's good.' He grazed his fingers slowly and provocatively against hers.

The air became palpable with sexual tension. If she looked at him, it was all over. She had to be strong. There was little time to think this through. Her situation was sudden and unexpected and she really didn't know what she was doing anymore. But it was wrong. It had to be wrong. They were poles apart.

Yet here she was, sitting in a bed, half naked, dressed only in a shirt belonging to a man she hardly knew – one who happened to be her client, and one she'd already had spontaneous sex with a week ago. He was wealthy and powerful. Having been in this kind of position before – albeit a long time ago - she knew it didn't lead to any place good. And where the hell had her professionalism gone? Had her hormones gone mad?! It certainly felt like it. They were buzzing uncontrollably at the moment and wanting only one thing.

Think woman. Think.

But she couldn't think. Maybe it was the hangover that had threaded her brain wildly, but more problematically, she was aroused.

'I'd *like* to make love, though,' he added, his voice dropping into the husky range as his words ended in the place his intention was set on.

'What?' She trembled.

'I want to make love with you,' he reached across, tentatively removing the glass from her hand. His face was so close to hers she could feel his breath, now somewhat erratic…and excited.

Somehow, he'd managed to stretch right around, his long reach returning the empty glass to the tray.

This would be the moment to break away. To spring out of bed and declare she needed to get home and write up a yoga lesson; to visit her friend Fiona; to do anything or be anywhere other than here. But she didn't move. Instead, Sasha waited for his lips to find hers, as she knew they would; and to feel the weight of his body lean over, pressing her more firmly onto the bed.

She felt the soft skin of his hands slip through her hair, grasping chunks of it, as his breathing became more rapid and merged with her own. Eagerness poured through him, along with a need for domination.

Lucas took her that morning and later again that afternoon. And before she fully realized exactly what was happening, Sasha's world became entirely entwined with his.

Chapter Twenty

'Nada Brahma,' the Guru smiled knowingly, as if he'd just divulged a secret they should all be aware of. 'The universe is a *vibratory field*. This is the root of all true spiritual experience.'

Holly, jolted from her thoughts of the toffee encrusted surface of crème brulee and the priceless moment the spoon cracked through the caramelized shell to the delicious contents beneath, tuned in hastily. This was worth listening to. And it sounded as if it was the kind of information she'd been searching for – maybe all her life - without even necessarily knowing it. Her entire being perked up in an alert state.

'Yogis have long observed this field by looking within themselves.'

Have they? Really? A vibratory field. Oh – my - God. And here was me thinking yoga was mainly just about stretching, she thought.

'The *'field'* has been called many things throughout history: the Music of the Spheres, Akasha, the Intelligence of the Logos,' he smiled again, ' and the primordial *Om*.'

'Om. Hmm...I love the feeling I get when I chant Om.'

'Searched for deeply enough, this *field* is the common root of all religions. It is the link between our inner and outer worlds, and', he hesitated, 'it is the mysterious force that moves the Universe...'

Wow. How enthralling. A vibratory field behind everything, thought Holly.

'It is the source behind the divine symmetry in all things – a symmetry replicated over and over...for example, in the replication of cells in all organic life. Ultimately, everything is self-organizing.' He hesitated - she assumed for effect. 'Everything.'

Fascinating.

'In the self-organizing human body, the nervous system contains tree-like structures and patterns. It is an *energetic* system, designed to work in harmony with the vibratory field. If you quiet your mind enough, you can observe this...the subtle energies: Prana, or Chi. Our inner energy, or inner *aliveness.*'

As he continued speaking, Holly felt the distinct sound of a penny beginning to drop in her awareness.

'These tree-like structures, or Nadis, are the subtle wires in the body that carry *Prana.* The Nadis move pranic energy through the Chakra System.'

She was beginning to understand more about the Chakra System – seven energy centers or *vortices* located in key areas up the spinal column of the body and all the way through to the crown of the head.

'The more the Nadis move pranic energy through the Chakra's; the stronger your wiring becomes, the more your energy flows, and the greater your capacity for self-transformation and self-realization,' he said.

Yes, but what exactly is that...self realization? she wondered.

'Self-realization is the understanding and experience that you are *All That Is*...'

Weird – did he just read my thoughts?

'...that you are part of the vibratory field occurring all around you...Nada Brahma...you are One with it.' The Guru pointed his bony finger skyward, as if to emphasize his point. 'There is no separation.' He paused. 'So remember, wherever your consciousness is placed, energy will begin to flow in that direction...and you will manifest experiences and things in your life accordingly.'

Glancing around the room, The Guru's deep-set brown eyes came to rest upon her. A glimmer of dismay flickered across them, bothering her a lot.

'Will the focus of your consciousness and your self-organizing system be one that blossoms toward positive growth? Or will it remain hard-wired by conditioning and negative repetition?'

Holly gulped. Her throat felt suddenly bone dry. He'd used the word *remain* in a way that implied she *was* conditioned and had negative patterns. Was that fair to assume? And was it true? Was she living in a way she consciously chose? She'd never considered the idea before. You just did your life, hoped for the best...and occasionally stuffed it up. As she had. But from what The Guru was saying, it sounded as if there was a way she could actually *direct* her life – *energetically* - if she could gain some level of mastery over her own human vibratory field; over the flow of energy and Prana throughout her body; if she could maximize the health of her energetic chakra system.

'You must be strong and vigilant to break conditioning and any negative patterns.' The Guru exclaimed decisively.

Holly shuddered. *Please, God...bring Jimmy back.*

'Your external world mirrors your internal one. So quiet your own mind and move Prana to manifest your life in the one direction.'

He was watching her thoughtfully. 'Remember, wherever your consciousness is placed, energy will flow in that direction.'

The Guru didn't chuckle. But his eyes flitted elsewhere and her pulse began to slow again.

***

Spring was truly beginning to reveal itself after a long dreary winter. It was evident in the leaves forming on the trees, the buds of unopened blossom appearing, and the first hardy flowers beginning to bloom under the warming weather and lengthening days.

A number of weeks had passed since Sasha had unofficially begun dating Lucas. 'Dating' could be quite an obscure kind of word in the modern age, though - a broad phrase that encompassed dinner and movies, but just as equally, random acts of sexual encounter with the same person. Whilst Sasha knew she didn't slot into the later category with Lucas, she didn't completely fit the former.

Since visiting Fiona, she hadn't seen her again. In fact, they'd barely had contact - just the odd text. The last message she received - a response to hers - had simply requested that she *give her space.* Sasha had respectfully obeyed. Time and distance were best. Sometimes friends just drifted apart for a while. Besides, Sasha was very busy. Her private client business was full and now her weekends included Lucas - at least, some of her weekends. He was often busy working. But she'd been spending a lot more time at his home and had even used his fabulous La Cornue's Grand Palais oven to bake him a vegetarian lasagna. She'd insisted on the stint as chef, if only to get her mitts on the state of the art appliance. Apparently it was, incredibly, only the sixth time the oven had been used in twelve months and at least one of those occasions had been a catered event for business acquaintances. This small statistic might have resulted in her nicknaming him *The Takeaway King*, if he did indeed ever eat takeaways. But mostly, it seemed, Lucas dined in restaurants and café's.

From the time they'd become *involved,* his yoga practice had dropped off and was now a sporadic visitation. Sometimes they'd make it through half a session before he ravaged her and other times his lesson never happened at all. He'd suggest an early dinner and a movie at home instead, inevitably after checking his laptop for emails and market analysis. It was understandable, though, she justified. His role was a responsible and pressurized one.

Of course, the yoga teaching fees continued to roll into her account, despite the variations to his classes – united physical positions being some of them.

She'd had no contact with his secretary, Theresa, since leaving her garbled 'migraine' message many weeks earlier, so Melody was surely none the wiser about them. In fact, she seemed to have stopped being problematic in any way. Except, perhaps, to her own self.

Sasha was now entirely convinced Melody had some sort of serious drug problem. As the weeks drew on, she appeared to be losing more body weight, along with her powers of clear speech. She was also frequently vague, and had even answered the door one day with a glob of white powder sitting partially up her inflamed and wasted nostril. Sasha began to feel sorry for her. Money in the hands of the young and privileged appeared to be a bit of a curse for some. It was evident the pretty model was unhappy. And it was possible she was headed for a major crisis of some sort. Sasha had lived that phase to some extent – thankfully without the downward spiraling effects of drug use. Yet the process of being ground into a personal *rock bottom* was something she was no stranger to. Melody had gone from being someone Sasha didn't like to someone she was beginning to feel a splattering of compassion and empathy for.

As for Rodrigo, they'd barely crossed paths since their flirtatious escapades at the bar. Although, it was true, the first encounter after their Friday night frolic had definitely been a difficult one. Thankfully she'd managed to breeze past any registering of their embarrassing drunken kiss and wriggled her way out of a decidedly awkward moment, thanks to a timely phone call.

At the time, she'd just finished teaching a yoga class at the gym. After chatting to several students about the subtleties of knee positions in poses, she was finishing tidying away rolled mats when Rodrigo strolled nonchalantly in, his emerald eyes sparkling like jewels set comfortably on his obscenely handsome South American face.

She was standing by a cupboard containing all the neatly stacked mats when he cornered her expertly near the wall. 'So how was your head Saturday morning?' he asked with a distinct twinkle in his eye.

'Oh,' she replied, surprised at his tone of familiarity. 'Good. Fine, thank you. I can hardly remember,' she waved a hand indifferently, turning her back on him and continuing to fidget unnecessarily with the rubbery mats.

'I can refresh your memory for you,' he said, stunning her by reaching out and squeezing her arm gently, sending a ripple of shock down her spine.

Turning slowly, Sasha peered down at the large tanned hand now dwarfing her petite but toned deltoid area. 'Probably not a good idea,' she replied bluntly, pretending to refocus on the mats.

'They look straight to me,' he responded, referring to her nervous fidgeting. The warmth in his voice swirled magically like delicious tendrils throughout her body. If she looked, he'd likely have that gorgeous smile wrapped around his perfect snow-colored teeth. There was no way she was turning to face him. Absolutely not.

'Sasha?'

She pushed distractedly on a tightly rolled end of a mat, still refusing to turn. 'Yes?'

'Hey.' He squeezed her shoulder more firmly, nudging her around to face him. 'Look at me.' The softness of his voice and the intimacy of the request caused another warm liquid-like current to run up the center of her chest. 'What are you doing?'

'Just adjusting mats…'

'No. Not that. This.' His free hand gestured between them as he spoke in his lilting Brazilian accent. 'Why are you avoiding me?'

God, *so direct.* What was he getting at? It was difficult looking at him – at those perceptively deep eyes.

'I like you, Sasha,' he added.

Oh, my God. She was speechless. And flustered.

'Have dinner with me.'

Her tongue stuck abruptly to the roof of her mouth as all the saliva particles, fleeing from the invitation, made a hasty getaway from the scene.

'I…'

'You like me, too. I know you do.' Rodrigo moved his free hand up and placed it tenderly onto her other shoulder. 'So have dinner with me.'

He was the best looking man who had ever asked her out. Lucas was attractive, but Rodrigo was something else. He oozed the kind of easy manly charm that let him slope on in to a woman's heart and soul. That quality alone would be enough, but his unbelievable genetics created the kind of dynamite impact that could blow a person off their feet. A woman, to be precise - her.

Sasha was struggling to stand straight as a slight wobbling motion took over in her knees. She bit down nervously on her bottom lip, glancing down at the floor and wrestling with her inner conflict.

'What is it?' He watched her carefully.

'You're...' she swallowed uneasily and her mind went blank.

'Brazilian?' His eyes twinkled.

Searching his tanned God-like face as if she would find some words there, she watched him break into a cheeky smile. 'Because I can't change my nationality for you,' he added. He was playing with her. Light danced on the surface of his sparkling eyes, until he noticed the expression behind her troubled ones. 'What is it?' he asked, taking a deep breath that caused his broad chest to expand even more as his mood shifted to match hers.

'Sasha?' Strong fingers grazed her gently on the chin as he tilted her head up to meet his stare. Their eyes locked together, green on blue, like a swirling tropical ocean, reminding her of their magical dancing...and their kiss. Yes, she'd been drinking, but you could never forget a kiss like that - with a man like this. She should be thinking about Lucas, but instead, she was hovering in the moment, suspended, as if in an enchanted dream.

'We feel good,' he murmured.

If she responded she'd have to disagree, which didn't feel true. Still, he was waiting for her to speak, his green eyes boring into hers.

If I could just have a miracle, right now, she thought nervously.

Sometimes in life, astonishing coincidences occur, just when you really need them the most. Perhaps she'd pre-empted some form of divine intervention that day by switching on her cellphone at the end of teaching her class. But however it occurred, her phone rang – right in that moment. To begin with, it sounded way off in the distance. But maybe that had more to do with where her attention was currently placed. The phone was ringing from within her sports bag over by the wall, but its melodic sound hurtled through the air at speed, slicing a divide between their locked eye contact. Sidling away from his touch, Sasha made her escape.

'I should get that.'

'Sure.' Rodrigo stepped back, a puzzled expression forming on his face as he watched her move hastily across to the other side of the room and pluck out the object of bad timing from her bag. Leaning back against the cupboard he folded his arms across his chest and watched her with curiosity.

She could be a jittery creature; confident one minute, but in the next, snatches of vulnerability would flit across her surface. He'd been attracted to her from the moment they'd met. She had the face of an angel with beautiful hair and a long slender body and he felt mysteriously drawn to her. She was different, somehow. Not only because she was a Californian in a sea of Brits – it was something else. Perhaps it was her reserved nature – she had a kind of crust like the Earth's mantle, occasionally jolting to life as if tectonic plates on the move were about to reveal a smoldering molten layer underneath. He suspected there was a lot of lava flowing beneath her cool surface. It was enticing. But there was something deeper about her, too; something she hid behind those long-lashed and guarded liquid blue eyes.

'Hi,' he heard her voice soften from across the room as she answered the call. He recognized the shift in her tone. It was one he was more used to being on the receiving end of. Rodrigo's ears pricked up, as did his senses. Another man was on the phone with her – someone she was involved with? His body tensed as an uncomfortable drizzle of emotion trickled through him like a small but irritating leak in the plumbing. He shook it off. A phone call meant nothing. Sasha was attracted to him, too - despite her aloofness and control. He was sure of it. Friday night had confirmed that for him. They had danced together like a dream, almost merging into another world. And that kiss... He could feel her. There was so much else to explore beyond that fortified wall.

A small twitch of his jaw occurred as he looked across at her elegant feminine frame. The phone conversation was drawing on. She'd swiveled her body and turned her back on him, lowering her voice as she paced a few meters further away toward the door.

Considering the scene thoughtfully, Rodrigo realized his gut instinct was right. She was not available. Scuffing the floor slightly with his foot, he felt uncharacteristic frustration but shrugged off the feeling. It didn't matter. Besides, it was pointless pursuing anything. He wouldn't be in this cold country forever. It was never somewhere he intended to stay very long.

Before Sasha had finished the call, Rodrigo moved quietly past her and exited the gym.

***

There was no sign of Thomas that morning. In fact, Sasha was so shocked to see Evangeline's face as the large Knightsbridge door swung open that she reeled backwards in fright. Since her partial breakdown and Ganges-like flood of tears, Lady Thornton had become a changed woman – and on a somewhat revolutionary scale. Her thick make-up, heavily penciled brows, eyeliner and garish morning lipstick had vanished. She'd switched to a dusting of mineral powder, a dash of mascara and a stroke of clear lip-gloss. Remarkably, too, the tight beehive bun consistently bound on her crown had been replaced by a new loose low ponytail. And along with wearing a brand new trendy black yoga outfit, she looked a good ten years younger. Strangely, her cosmetics had become more reminiscent of Sasha's own natural look. It was also possible a similar brand was being used as Lady Thornton had recently asked Sasha what she applied to her face. Surprisingly, it was a personal question – and incredibly, one about make-up.

'Sasha, darling,' Evangeline smiled graciously, holding the door wide open.

Remarkably, she'd somehow been promoted to *darling*. Likely handing copious amounts of tissues to Lady Thornton the morning the dam burst on her grief had earned her this endearing phrase. Whatever the reason, it didn't matter. Evangeline had now become *humanized* and that was all that mattered – that, and the reduction of some of the high-pitched shrill previously ejected from her mouth.

'Oh. I was expecting Thomas...'

'I gave him the morning off.' Evangeline interrupted, waving her hand as regally as a queen. 'He deserves it.'

'That's nice.' *And rare, I bet.*

'I've been looking forward to seeing you,' she said a little nervously, as if attempting to become best friends. 'Do come in.'

'Of course.'

Snapping out of her shocked daze at being greeted in person by Lady E Thornton, Sasha wandered tentatively behind her down the hallway, becoming filled with a growing curiosity. Something was afoot in Mrs T's world. The woman appeared nervy like a skittish cat, and fit to burst like a juicy plum, and Sasha strongly suspected she was about to find out why.

The yoga was certainly having an impact on the woman's body, she observed, as they rounded the entrance to *Ballroom*. Evangeline was looking more lithe and toned each week and even carried herself with a new kind of youthful poise and elegance. Somehow, the bullish and self-absorbed crust, along with some extra weight and fuller face, seemed to have steadily dissolved in recent weeks, revealing an entirely different person - one who Sasha suspected was, in fact, quite sweet. It was even possible that had always been her true nature, before it had been buried beneath a mountain of potatoes and the empire born of them.

Having unrolled the yoga mats onto the posh woolen carpet, she was about to commence with the lesson when the first split appeared in the skin of the near bursting Thornton-fruit, now sitting cross-legged on the floor before her.

'Sasha...I wondered if there's something I might ask you.'

'Oh? Of course.'

'You see, there's this...*thing*...coming up. And I'm not quite sure what to do about it.'

To begin with, Sasha thought the *thing coming up* Evangeline referred to was something going on *inside* her, much like a psychological process. Was it possible that Lady Thornton was becoming self-aware? For several seconds, Sasha became excited this might be the case. 'Okay...?' She leaned forward, nodding her head in understanding and in an effort to encourage.

'It's a...ball.'

It took Sasha a little while to compute that the *ball* being referred to was not some sort of dangerous lump in her body.

'A ball? Right.' Sasha continued nodding her head

thoughtfully whilst feeling very confused.

'Yes. It's the Earth Save Charity Ball; an important annual society event,' she responded, staring forlornly off into the distance. 'Everybody goes.'

'Oh…kay.' Sasha raised her brow in pretend interest.

Lady Thornton, buoyed on by Sasha's reassuring gestures, continued. 'You see, Lord Thornton…Harold and I…' She stopped suddenly, a visible lump in her throat being swallowed. 'Well…we always went *together*.'

'Of course,' Sasha responded solemnly.

'Only, this year, I…' Lady Thornton paused with discomfort.

'Would still like to go?'

'Yes.' The tiniest squeak of a word was emitted like a chirping baby sparrow. Tears formed in the back of Evangeline's aging but pretty light blue eyes. 'Yes, I do,' she whispered, hanging her head as if in shame.

'And this is hard for you, because…?'

'Because…he'll be there…with *her.*'

'You know this?'

'Yes. The Frampton's…' she looked up at Sasha, observing the blank expression on the younger woman's face at mention of an apparently noted name. A moment of frustration flashed across Evangeline's face. 'Aioli dynasty…friends,' she waved her hand, indicating supremacy of the mentioned family, 'They said so.'

'Of course, ' Sasha repeated in the appropriate sober manner. 'And you don't think you'll be able to face…seeing her?'

'No, Sasha,' tears welled up like pools, threatening to overflow onto her cheeks, 'I don't think I'll be able to face seeing *him.*'

'Why not?' Their eyes met. Lady Thornton's held a truth that only courage could reveal. Sasha waited patiently for her response.

'Because...I still love him,' she blurted out as her head dropped once more in shame. Sasha heard her sniffle and watched the water begin to run off her chin like rainfall from the guttering overflow of a house. 'I do. I still love him,' she whispered.

Inching within reach, Sasha placed a hand gently on the grieving woman's arm.

'Oh, God,' Evangeline exclaimed, her fruit-like-self bursting fully open. 'I don't know what to do,' she sobbed. 'Whatever shall I do? Please, tell me what to do.'

Pain evident, Sasha comfortingly rubbed Lady Thornton's arm. 'I think,' she responded after careful thought, 'you should go to the ball.'

'You do?'

'Yes. Definitely. I do.'

'But how do I...' Lady Thornton waved her arms fretfully as if fanning air over her face. 'I mean, what shall I do when I'm there?'

Sasha looked deeply into the woman's sad distant eyes, understanding their need to borrow strength. 'Honestly?' She paused. 'I think...you should let him know what he's missing.'

'Really?'

Determination arose from within the pit of Sasha's stomach. 'Truly.'

'You think I can do that?'

'Lady Thornton, I know you can.'

A ray of hope appeared in her rapidly drying eyes. 'Will you,' she hesitated, the suppression of a great deal of pride evident, 'help me.'

'Of course I will. I'd be honored.' Sasha smiled.

'Oh, that's wonderful!' she exclaimed, relief evident. 'Then, dear girl,' she said looking thrilled, 'you must call me Evangeline.'

Chapter Twenty One

'Darling.'

Lucas had never called her that before. These days it seemed many people were using that beautiful adjective for her. Having known him for less than three months, and with barely six weeks of serious dating, things had begun to move at quite a pace and she was now increasingly submerged in his world with little time for anything else, outside of work.

They'd just finished brunch at a local café. Sasha ordered omelet in an effort to avoid carbohydrates, pushing pieces of the chopped egg around the plate and leaving half of it. Being in relationship with a man who liked eating out was proving to be quite a mission for the maintenance of her waistline. And being so tired from late nights and sleepovers, her yoga practice had almost entirely disappeared out the window.

'There's something I've been wanting to ask you.'

'Oh?' she responded, pushing the semi-empty plate away and leaning forward. Her nerves began to fray at the serious look in his eyes. Did he know something? Was it the end?

'What is it?'

'There's an event coming up. I thought it might be nice if you'd come with me.'

Her tense shoulders suddenly relaxed toward the

ground. But was it an invitation or a request, she wondered. 'Really. Thank you. That's nice. What's the event?'

'A ball.'

'Oh?'

'Yes. It's the Earth Save Charity Ball.' He waved his hand nonchalantly. 'Annual thing. Probably frightfully boring. But have to go. You know, keep up appearances...do some good.'

Oh, Christ, she thought, at the idea of bumping into Lady Thornton. But Evangeline had asked for her help. It could be perfect – albeit a fraction outside her social league and current wardrobe ability. She must have crinkled her face. He seemed to notice her concern or be able to read her mind.

'I don't want you to take this the wrong way, but you might like something new to wear...on me, of course. I can arrange for my driver to take you and I have credit at a number of stores. My wife...ex-wife...' his voice trailed off.

'Shopped a lot?' The words fell straight from her mouth.

He hesitated, his jaw twitching with apparent disapproval at her words. 'Something like that,'

'I'm sorry.' Sasha placed her hands on her lap and sighed. 'My Californian directness still pops out at times.'

'No need to be sorry.' Lucas avoided eye contact. Picking up his napkin, he dabbed the corners of the mouth she was now used to kissing, before his eyes finally alighted upon her. 'It's not about you, okay.' His voice softened and his hand grazed hers for a moment. She was getting to know him better. Their trust was building. Surely she could take a risk now.

Shuffling her chair around, she moved to sit closer to him. 'I know it must have been difficult...the separation. And everything that came with that.'

'Everything that came with that? Everything that *went* with that...' his eyes became distant and he shook his head softly as if in disbelief.

'You've never...'

'I don't want to talk about it, okay. Things happened that weren't...good.' he responded blandly.

Sasha paused to consider her response and decided to tackle it philosophically. 'You know, the Buddha said *life is suffering.'*

'That was helpful of him,' he interrupted full of sarcasm. 'And super positive.'

'What I'm saying is...what I think some of his meaning was...was that if we care about anything, at some point we're going to experience loss.'

'So we shouldn't care.' He tossed his napkin back onto his plate with force.

'Of course we should care. It's who we are; it's how we're wired; it's human. I think there's something quite wrong if we *don't* care. But whatever loss experienced inevitably results in some form of *grief.'*

His eyes were downcast, but some part of him was listening, so she continued. 'I don't believe it's caring that's the human trap. I think it's our ability to *let go* that's the great human stumbling block.'

Reaching out for one of the glass salt-shakers on the table, Lucas twiddled it around distractedly. 'And that's why we suffer?' He didn't look up, but a crack in his armor was showing. The words bled from him like a scraped scab. Sasha reflected back on when they'd met and his distant moody self, the crankiness, his inability to sleep and the anger that seemed to simmer beneath his surface. It was grief. She realized that was exactly what was going on inside him; unresolved grief, festering in his unconscious and seeping out of him.

'That's why Buddha said we suffer? Because we

care?' he repeated with a level of exasperation.

'I think Buddha understood the human penchant for *attachment*. We don't grieve what we're not attached to. And it's the attachment that compounds our grief. We cling to what is not; to what cannot be; to what is gone...and this causes deep suffering. And whilst we're in this place, we're stuck in the past. We're disconnected from life now...in this moment. I believe this is what the Buddha meant.'

Lucas leaned back slowly in his chair, crossing his arms as he considered Sasha's words.

'That's what you think?'

'Well...yes, it makes sense. So I tend to agree.'

He pondered a moment. 'So don't care about anything, don't attach yourself – that sounds like the key.'

Sasha could feel the anger behind his words, but steeling herself inwardly, she continued. 'I think that *not caring* about anything is a greater suffering. Care, but understand you can't control everything – control is the ultimate illusion.'

'So we just let things happen that shouldn't?'

'Of course not. We're not powerless. We do what we can, but sometimes even that can't change things. I guess that's something I've had to learn to accept,' she said thoughtfully. 'Ultimate power doesn't always rest in my hands.'

'You're telling me,' he said drily.

'Whatever it is, Lucas, I think you're giving yourself a really hard time. And I feel you could do with cutting yourself some slack.'

His jaw twitched and his eyes avoided hers.

'Hey,' she said softly, tentatively reaching out and touching his arm, 'the simplest fact in life...everything changes. There's not much we can do about that.'

'No. But some things shouldn't change...some

things shouldn't happen the way they do.'

There was pain etched in the recesses of his eyes. She dropped her head quietly in understanding.

'And what the hell are you supposed to do with that?' he said with frustrated defeat. 'Let's just drop the subject. I'll get the bill.' He stood up, moving hastily from the table.

Sasha watched his tall frame and back as he walked away from her. For a moment, she wondered what might have happened in his life that had led to such feelings of helplessness. He'd left her more curious. What was the ending still causing him grief. And what had he cared about so much that continued to cause him such pain?

But the moment had passed and she had to let his vault of emotions go.

Collecting her handbag, Sasha rose gracefully from the table with the distinct feeling that an opportunity to find out more would appear again.

***

The opportunity Sasha was seeking occurred sooner than she thought it might. It happened several days later, after she'd just finished teaching Amy Buckley her yoga lesson. Whilst it was true that Sasha had become a little preoccupied with thoughts of the ball looming on the horizon, what to wear and what was going on in Lucas, she had no idea how transparent her distracted mind had become.

'Everything alright, Sasha?' Amy asked quietly as she rolled up her mat.

'Sure,' she responded with surprise. 'Why do you ask?'

'Oh,' Amy shrugged. 'Probably just a large amount of mothering hormones - protective instinct, I'm afraid.'

She smiled. 'You don't seem yourself lately.'

'Really? How so?'

'Not sure. Can't pinpoint it. But you're a little…distant, somehow.'

'Oh, goodness. I'm sorry – has my yoga instruction deteriorated?'

'No.' Amy shook her head vigorously. 'Not at all, darling. You're quite brilliant.' She stood up with the mat and moved toward Sasha, patting her on the shoulder. 'Look how you've whipped this child-bearing body back into shape.'

'It was never out of shape.' Sasha rolled her eyes looking at her with disbelief.

'I'm sorry, I'm probably just looking for a distraction of my own.' Amy paused. 'Life gets to be a fraction routine with two young children.'

Sasha smiled. 'You absolutely love your life and your children.'

'I know.' Amy beamed. 'I'm quite blessed.'

'I think you are.'

'Yes.' She paused. 'So tell me, how are things going with your boyfriend, Lucas?' Once she'd asked the pointed question, Amy wandered back to the white wicker chair and settled in as if waiting to be told a story. 'I'm being terribly nosy, I know. But humor this married woman. I don't have many adult things to think about.' Her nose crinkled into a mischievous pixie-like grin as she tucked her palm under her chin and waited expectantly. 'I told myself I would mind my own business, but since you told me a little while ago that you're dating him, I must say I've become rather curious to know how things are going.'

Sasha crouched down with the mats, unzipping their carry-bag and considering the request. She was such a private person. But Amy just seemed to be one of those people you opened your heart and soul up to. There was something so *safe* about her. It was why Sasha had let slip to her several lessons ago that she'd started seeing Lucas.

'It's good.'

'Good?'

'Yes. Different from what I'm used to, but good.'

'What are you used to?'

Sasha chuckled. 'Not much, really. In terms of relationship, it was a very long dry spell before…Lucas. So it's nice.' Amy stared at her, encouraging clarification. 'His company is nice,' she finished.

'Nice?' Amy's face drooped to one of disappointment. 'That doesn't sound stunningly exciting. Is he passionate?'

'Kind of. Yes. He's charming, but a little distracted sometimes.' Sasha hesitated. 'He works a lot. And we're quite different in terms of our…lifestyles…I guess you could say. But he's interesting.'

'Interesting.' She nodded her head side-to-side in a *take-it-or-leave-it* kind of way. 'And does he treat you well?'

'Very. In fact, he's just invited me to a ball.'

For a moment Amy appeared slightly taken aback. 'A ball? Now that sounds like a more serious commitment. And exciting. What ball?'

'Oh, it's some Earth Save charity…thing.' Sasha waved a hand casually.

'That's lovely,' Amy said, regarding the floor fleetingly.

'Yes it is. I guess that's quite a step for him – being seen in public with me. Only…' Sasha hesitated.

'Only what?'

'Well…he's not the easiest man to get to know. And he's not fond of me asking about his past.'

'I guess a lot of people aren't. Some people are more private. And some just like to move on and forget.'

Amy sighed. 'But yes, he is a troubled soul...'

Sasha was shocked. It wasn't the words, it was the way Amy had said them - as if she were deeply familiar with Lucas on a personal level. She suddenly felt very inquisitive and more than a little suspicious.

Amy shuffled nervously as if she'd just been caught out, observing the change on Sasha's face carefully. 'I mean, a lot of people are, aren't they...troubled souls,' she added hastily. 'The ones who bury their pasts like they're some deep dark secret.' Her hands moved dramatically to emphasize the point.

Sasha wasn't buying it. It seemed that Amy knew something she didn't. 'I never said he was a troubled soul...Amy?' she added, with a hint of accusation.

Amy looked away, her face awash with guilt.

'Amy? Do you know Lucas?'

'Of course not. No.' She adjusted herself in the chair, clearly filled with discomfort.

'Is that the honest-to-God truth?' Silence filled the air as the two women looked at each other.

'Well...no. Not really.'

Sasha waited quietly for the explanation.

'Okay,' she continued softly. 'Ben knows him. From college days. Cambridge.'

Sasha seated herself in a cross-legged position on the floor and Amy could tell she wasn't moving until she'd heard everything.

'They've been friends for years.'

'So you knew I was teaching him yoga.' Sasha scrutinized Amy's pretty elfin face as she began to put two-and-two together. 'And *that's* how he came to be my student...because you gave him my number.' The penny dropped.

'I didn't, actually.' Amy sighed heavily. 'In fact, I had no idea he was taking lessons with you until you mentioned his name. Then I promised myself I wouldn't bring him up again…that I wouldn't pry…I'm so sorry I asked how things were going.'

Sasha listened perplexed, her blue eyes holding a multitude of questions.

'Ben,' Amy read her mind. 'Ben found your business card in a drawer. I was always singing your praises and those of yoga and how relaxing, calming and good it is for me…so he encouraged Lucas to contact you. Actually, I think he pushed him quite strongly about it. Apparently Lucas's employers were becoming a little…disgruntled…with his state of mind and performance at work. I guess Ben thought the yoga might help him.'

'Help him?'

'Yes,' Amy said softly, glancing down once more at the floor.

'Why? Why was he having problems at work? Why did he need help?'

Amy looked at her thoughtfully. 'Because he's been through a lot.'

'With his marriage?'

'Yes.'

'But he separated from her well over eighteen months ago,' Sasha replied with confusion. 'Why is he still so angry? Is he still in love with her?'

'No. I seriously doubt that,' Amy responded decisively.

'Then what is it?' she persisted.

Rising from the chair, Amy wandered over to a perfectly shaped healthy-looking fern sitting potted in the corner. Momentarily, her hand grazed over one of its dark green fronds as if she were seeking comfort from it. 'At first I was shocked when you mentioned you'd become involved with him,' she hesitated, grappling with her words. 'Then I wondered if maybe that was exactly what he needed…what you both might need.'

Amy spun back to look at her. 'Cupid – striking its healing arrow.'

Sasha unfolded her legs and clambered up to a standing position, now fully focused on the words she was hearing.

'Lonely souls. Two lonely souls,' Amy whispered to an unseen realm. 'But you see, what happened broke Lucas. It broke him completely. And we...Ben and I...don't think he's recovered...remotely.'

'What happened, Amy?'

Tears filled her enchanted eyes as she looked sadly at Sasha.

'Their marriage had become quite...turbulent. They weren't happy. She...wasn't happy. Catherine always wanted more, you know. She was just one of those...self-indulgent, aggressively ambitious types of women. She was a total socialite.' Amy finally smiled. 'Not someone I easily related to. It wasn't enough that Lucas was successful in his own right; that they had enough wealth to live however she wanted for the rest of her life.' Amy turned away from Sasha's piercing look, back towards the comfort of the fern. Her head dropped sadly. 'He's such a lovely man. At least, he was. Before all that...anger. If you really knew him, Sasha. Before then...'

'Before what? You still haven't explained?'

Amy turned slowly. Several tears were trickling down her face. 'She wanted the title, Sasha. She wanted his title. You see, that was all that mattered to her.'

'He mentioned she was a little like that. But I'm missing something. I still don't understand...'

'She didn't really care about him. He could have forgiven her for that. But...'

'But what?'

'She didn't care...about his son.'

'What?' Sasha reeled inwardly. 'He never mentioned

a son.'

Amy's face appeared foreign such was the look of sadness etched upon it. 'He wouldn't, Sasha,' she said, swallowing hard.

'Why not?'

'Because...' her normally happy face was awash with sorrow as Amy struggled to finish the sentence, '...his son died before being born.'

Chapter Twenty Two

'Pratyahara creates the setting for the sixth limb of yoga – *Dharana,'* The Guru explained.

It was Friday. Friday's always reminded Holly of Paul because they'd just about always spent Friday evenings together, usually at his apartment in the city. Every week, she'd spend the day getting excited and thinking about what to wear – something new from the *clothing allowance* he'd leave for her. Friday's were always happy days, until the night she opened that book. That was the day that changed everything: it was the day that catalyzed her being here now – listening to this…strangely wise man.

'Relieving yourself of external disturbances allows you to deal with the distractions of the mind itself. This is no easy task.' He looked serious.

Detaching from the senses…that's what he meant. They'd covered Pratyahara the day before. Unfortunately the lesson on detachment was a little too late to save her from some uncomfortable life experiences. Historically, she'd been way below average at disengaging from her senses. In fact, they mostly seemed to have driven her.

Sex, and her naivety around that and men, were now things she wished she'd mastered a little earlier in life, or had better guidance on. But her parents had been flower-power hippies and very much into free love. And she was so young and impressionable when she'd met Paul; merely aphrodisiac fodder for an older man – one who wielded power and the finery of Ralph Lauren clothing with equal measure. He'd become like a drug to her; one she was blind to - his insipid psychological reach much like an addiction. Somewhere along the way, it stopped mattering that he criticized and spoke down to her; that he objectified her body and made her do things she was never really comfortable with. She felt like she needed him. That was all that mattered. Her world was infinitely more alive with him in it.

'Dharana is the practice of absolute focus that precedes meditation. It is learning to slow down the thinking process by concentrating on a single mental object. This could be a candle, a single energy center in the body – *a chakra* - or the silent repetition of a mantra or sound.'

But he's in the past now. It's all in the past, Holly reflected.

'In the previous three stages: Asana practice, Pranayama; or breath control, and Pratyahara; withdrawal of the senses, you've already begun to develop your powers of concentration.'

I wish I'd known before, though...I didn't know. Her distracted stream of thought continued. *But I should have known. I should've guessed.* A deep torrent of guilt rushed through her as The Guru's hypnotic voice lilted her back into her past.

'Although you pay attention to your actions in both Asana practice and Pranayama, your attention still travels because you are shifting your focus as you fine-tune your posture or breath technique. In Pratyahara you become more self-observant; However, in Dharana you take a further step.'

God, I'm so happy to be here...to be far away from all of that, she thought, focusing on The Guru's lilting voice with great relief and stroking the side of her face at terror-filled memories.

'In Dharana your attention is single-pointed. And extended periods of concentration like this will naturally lead to meditation,' he smiled.

The Guru's face always looked so different when he was happy, she observed. As if he were the sun itself, beaming rays of light. Momentarily, the shock-white hair on his head caught her attention more fully – it suited him, like a crown of wisdom. How many years had this man studied and practiced yoga? She wondered. Had he made sacrifices and walked away from things in his own past? Did he understand what it was to feel shame and guilt over mistakes made? She watched the smile and the brightness behind his radiant brown eyes and began to feel peaceful again. Wherever he'd come from, or whatever experiences he'd had, The Guru glowed with inner peace and a lightness of spirit and he appeared to have achieved something she now yearned for - the freedom of inhabiting the present moment without baggage of the past. The path he'd taken and the vision he had, carried a promise that she could achieve the same. And this meant a new life was possible for her.

She needed that hope.

'From the development of meditative practice and the place of silent listening, you can intuit the best pathway to take in your life. Everything you do can be guided by your own deep well of inner truth,' he said.

'Have courage, dear yogis, to feel and be guided by *truth*...in every moment of your existence.'

Sitting up tall on her cushion, Holly stopped thinking about her past. She fixed her gaze on the sprightly older man and his other worldly eyes, and listened intently to every word he spoke.

***

Exiting her car into the warming air of springtime, Sasha ambled slowly toward the gym entrance. Deep in thought, she was somewhat startled as the door flew open and Rodrigo strode out, looking buff in his tight white t-shirt and navy track pants. It didn't seem possible t-shirt fabric could stretch that far. Still, she had to admit, the look suited him. Some men could simply get away with it.

He appeared to be on a mission headed somewhere in a hurry – or possibly he'd sighted her and was trying to avoid another uncomfortable exchange. It had been over a month since their awkward moment in the yoga room. Since then, she'd caught sight of *Long-Legs-Blonde*, Danielle, lingering around him on a number of occasions and assumed they'd become an item.

With Fiona's *need for space*, Sasha's connection with the gym had diminished and she was now keeping her visits there to a minimum, revolving tightly around her class schedule and as short and sweet as possible. Although he didn't appear unhappy to see her, Rodrigo's face held a strangely cool kind of tolerance as he approached, which admittedly threw her.

'Hi,' her lips curled into a slightly forced smile as his long stride brought him nearer.

'Hey.' His expression mirrored her neutral one as he nodded his head once in recognition.

It wasn't until he was almost parallel to her that she

noticed he'd slowed his pace. Was it possible he was going to stop and talk? Sasha dropped her eyes toward the earth at the precise moment it seemed he would look at her and they glided past one another.

However, several steps later, his voice brought her to a halt. 'Sasha?'

Slinging her sports bag onto her shoulder as if it were an armory of arrows ready for action, she spun to face him.'Yes?'

'How's Fiona?'

Thrown by the question she starred blankly at him as his eyes bored into hers. It appeared he was making a point. 'I…we…' She paused at her own indecisiveness and shrugged dismissively. 'I'm not sure, actually.'

'Not sure?' He took several steps back towards her. 'I thought you two were best friends?' His eyes drilled into hers.

'We are.'

A semi-snort escaped him, one of apparent disgust. It shocked her.

'I'm not sure what you're implying by that.' Sasha cocked her head to one side in confusion.

'You know she's been sick and off work for several weeks, right?' he clarified.

A knot formed instantly in Sasha's stomach. 'I…no. She said she needed space.'

'So you've had hardly any contact with her? For weeks?'

Sasha shook her head slowly, a growing uneasiness beginning to gnaw at her insides.

'None?' he added persistently, disapproval engraved on his face. He'd never looked at her before like this. 'You've had no contact?'

'I told you, she said she needed space.'

'Why did she need space? What was happening in her life?' He took several more steps closer and now stood somewhat confrontationally a meter from her.

'I don't know.' Sasha shrugged. 'She'd broken up from Dave. She was different...distant...angry. She wanted to be alone...to get over him, I guess.'

'You guess?' His Brazilian passion was normally quite attractive, but not this time. 'And you left her alone?'

'Yes. I told you, that's what she wanted.'

'And you think people in pain always ask for what they want? That they know what they need when they're hurting?' His words hit like a blunt object.

Her sense of shock deepened. She'd never seen this side of Rodrigo before – devoid of charm or warmth. And it certainly wasn't pleasant having it leveled at her. 'Look, Rodrigo, I was just respecting her wishes.'

'Respecting her wishes?' His hands began to gesture loosely to match his words. 'Your friend is feeling bad and you *respect her wishes?*!'

'Yes. Yes, of course I respect her wishes!' Sasha launched back at him with force.

'Her wishes? Her wishes, or you needing to spend time with...your boyfriend? The one who likes to beat you up and give you black eyes!' He was talking so fast now that his Brazilian accent was taking over and it was becoming difficult to understand him.

'Oh! So that's what this is all about?!'

'No. It's about your friend, Sasha. Aren't you worried about her?!'

'Of course.' She took a step back in confusion. 'I had no idea she's been off work. And for this long.'

'Well you should know. You should!' he said with exasperation.

An invisible cloak of defensiveness drew over her. She sighed heavily. 'I have a busy life, Rodrigo.'

'Busy? Jesus. I would never use that as an excuse.'

'Well you're a bloody Saint then,' she spat back with

uncharacteristic vehemence.

'No. I'm not a Saint. I just care.' he said, slapping his hand onto his broad chest. 'I care about my friends!' He hit his torso with force again. 'I care about the people I love!'

Sasha reeled inwardly. She'd tried to live her life peacefully, to respect others, to mind her own business. They were lessons from the school of hard knocks and she'd learned them the hard way; how to leave people alone to work through their stuff, like she had to. She'd buried herself in yoga and meditation and acquired the skills to keep her head down and nose out of trouble. What was this? Who was this? This man, right up in her face, implying that it was wrong to be a little detached; that it was wrong to avoid negative vibes and breaking hearts. That it was wrong to protect herself?

Because she had. That's exactly what she'd done.

'How can you be this way, Sasha?' He continued his verbal assault, his eyes blazing as if her presence was like fat thrown onto a hot element. He looked ready to explode completely. 'So...numbed out. I don't understand!' he exclaimed, looking at her as if she were an alien.

Stunned at his display of emotion, she remained speechless.

'I just don't understand,' he said, shaking his head in exasperation.

'We're different, okay,' she finally blurted out. They were the only words she could muster as she beheld his anguish.

Curiously, the anger in his voice then subsided as rapidly as it had emerged. 'Yes we are,' he concluded, taking a last indeterminable look at her before turning away, striding a few steps, then freezing on the spot with his back to her. 'I would walk over coals for a friend. I would even crawl. That's the difference between us,' he said with sadness in his voice.

The words stung in her chest as if a poisoned tail of a scorpion had just unleashed itself upon her. Standing dazed and fixed to the spot, she watched him until he'd walked all the way to his car and driven off.

Wiping away the tear drizzling uncontrollably from her eye and down her face, Sasha took a deep breath and calmed her racing heart. This was not the time to fall apart - she had a class to teach. And then she needed to find Fiona.

***

'Fee?!' Sasha called out, pressing the doorbell a second time.

'Fee!' Her fist banged the smooth cream door. 'I know you're in there.' She leaned on the wall, straining her ears to listen for the sound of feet moving up the hallway.

'Open up!' She paused. 'Please.'

Seconds later, the sound of a latch being removed on the other side of the door broke the horrid silence.

Thank God.

Sasha wasn't remotely prepared for how Fiona looked. The last time she'd seen her she certainly wasn't her usual supermodel self. But this was much worse.

'Did no one teach you it's rude to stare?'

'Oh.' Sasha said, startled at the dull expression staring back at her. 'I…'

'You can stop gawping and come on in, if you like.' Fiona's appearance was really scruffy. Her makeup-less face looked puffy and rounded, as if she'd been on an overeating binge for the past month. And she was wearing old leggings with what looked like a brown sack tunic top. It was coated with patches of…'

'Flour,' Fiona said, opening the door wide and

walking off down the hallway. 'No need to ogle at it like it's a bad outbreak of dandruff.'

'Flour? But you don't…'

'Bake?'

'Yes, bake.' Sasha said, trailing behind her into the living area and detecting the smell of something that had been burnt in an oven. For as long as she'd known Fiona, she'd been a supermarket pre-packaged convenience girl. She watched her move into the kitchen and heard the slam of an oven door.

'People change,' Fiona said in a raised voice from the kitchen. Sasha could have sworn she caught sight of dark brown-black cookies on the tray in Fiona's oven-mitted hand.

'Yes. I guess.' Taking a seat on the lush Italian sofa, she waited expectantly.

'So what do I owe the honor of this visit?' Fiona said crisply, finally returning from the kitchen empty-handed.

Observing her friend's bedraggled appearance, Sasha felt a deep well of concern open up as she watched Fiona move across the living area and seat herself as far away as possible on a single sofa chair.

'I know you said you wanted space, Fee.'

'I do.'

'Okay…well, I've been worried about you. Rodrigo told me you haven't been working at the gym for weeks.'

'Oh, Rodrigo? Your new best buddy now, is he?' Fee avoided looking at her as she focused on dusting down her powdery sack attire.

'No. Quite the opposite, actually.'

Fiona stopped dusting and stared at Sasha momentarily. 'Huh. You've made an enemy out of the friendliest chap I've ever met. Go figure.'

'Look, I didn't come here to talk about Rodrigo. I'm

worried about you, Fee.'

'Well, don't be. I'm absolutely fine.'

'You don't look fine.' The words slipped out of Sasha's mouth before she could catch them. 'I'm sorry. I mean...'

'No, no. It's refreshing to hear you speak honestly.'

'What do you mean, speak *honestly*?'

'I mean it sure beats lying and hiding.' Fiona crossed her arms heavily over her chest in an accusing manner.

'Lying and hiding? Where the heck did that come from?!'

'You've been strange ever since you started disappearing on Saturday mornings.'

'I told you, I teach a yoga class.'

'Whatever.'

'I do!' Sasha said exasperated as she launched up out of her comfortable sofa seat and moved toward Fiona. 'But I didn't come here to talk about me...or to justify how I spend my time. What's happened to you, Fee? This is not *you*.' Her hands gestured expressively toward her appearance.

'Well I'd say not seeing you for a month is not exactly *you*, either,' she responded with a sullen expression.

'Not *us,* I think you mean. Besides, you asked me to leave you alone, remember?'

'Yes, I did.' Fiona said, conceding slightly. 'And of course, I'd do the same if you asked that of me,' she added with a note of sarcasm.

Sasha recalled what Rodrigo had said and her heart sank. Softening her voice, she moved toward the chair Fiona was seated in. 'No, you wouldn't, Fee. I'm sorry.' She meant it more deeply than she could recall having felt in a long time. 'I really am sorry.' Crouching down, Sasha rested her hand on the arm of Fiona's chair and looked into the worn-out red-rimmed eyes staring back at her. The reduced distance between them appeared to make Fiona uncomfortable – she shifted about nervously, withdrawing eye contact. Sasha swallowed hard. 'You wouldn't leave me alone at all. You'd be like…a total pain; like an annoying buzzy bee I'd feel like swatting away.'

Her words almost forced a smile from Fiona. 'Maybe. But you wouldn't swat me away.' She sighed. 'It's okay, Sash. I know I'm a stubborn goat.'

'No, it's not okay. It's so *not* okay. I've had my head up my backside and let my very best friend in the world down.'

'I have needed a lot of time on my own, though. I've never really given myself that before – never had a good look deep inside…not like the last month. But I've needed to…to think about stuff.'

A lump formed in Sasha's throat. 'What stuff? Tell me what's going on, Fee. Please.' Her hand shifted from the chair onto Fiona's knee. 'Is it Dave?'

She took a deep breath before responding, as if considering whether to open up. 'Kind of. But not really. He just…catalyzed some things.'

'What things?'

She looked away sadly. 'You know how little girls daydream, Sash? About living in a castle or being a princess…things like that?'

'Sure.'

'Well I used to daydream. A lot. It's funny how you forget your real dreams.' Sasha was surprised to see tears forming in the back of Fiona's eyes. 'The purest ones – you know? The ones that probably matter the most to you…if you can just remember them… remember who you really are.'

'Who you really are?' Sasha looked at her, puzzled. Fiona always seemed so strong in her self-identity.

'Yes,' she replied, finally restoring eye contact.

'Before life has its way with you. Before other people or events define who you are or how you should be. And you don't even realize that's what has happened.'

Nodding, Sasha replied thoughtfully. 'Yes. I do understand.'

'It's hard to think of myself as anything other than this,' Fiona continued, opening her palms out and glancing in the direction of her body. 'But there was once a time, long ago, when I felt differently about my life.'

Listening keenly, Sasha became filled with curiosity. Fiona always tended to skate on the surface, never revealing anything too deep about herself. So this was something unusual.

'I knew what I wanted; really wanted.'

'And what was that?'

'It's funny…' A small smile creased Fiona's lips. 'You'd never guess it.' A single tear tracked slowly down the side of her face as her eyes locked fully onto Sasha's. 'I was such a…*robust* little tom-boy, as a child. But you know, Sash, my deepest dream was always to actually…have children,' she said, forcing back the emotion threatening to overcome her. 'Lots of them.'

Sasha, taken aback, smiled in surprise. 'Really?'

'Yes. It's funny, isn't it? Good old staunch Fiona, spending her life training like an Olympic athlete, when really, she always just wanted to be a mum.'

Sasha stood up and perched herself on the side of the chair, resting her hand on Fiona's arm. 'That doesn't sound funny to me.'

Fiona visibly relaxed. 'I was doing fine without that dream, though. I was…in control. And then I met Dave. Happy, easy-going Dave, and my biology just went *whammo.* You know?'

Sasha didn't know, but nodded her head in agreement anyway.

'And now I'm this.' She glanced down at her body with a look of semi-disgust.

'What do you mean, you're this? Fee?' Sasha stared back at her with shock and disbelief. 'You mean you're…'

'Pregnant.' She nodded her head as tears began to stream down her face.

'Christ.'

'No, I don't think he's involved here.' There she was again, joking in the midst of a crisis. Whilst stunned, Sasha couldn't help feel relieved at the positive sign.

'But that's impossible. It means you must have got pregnant straight away - the first time!'

'Or second, or third…or fourth,' she said sheepishly. 'They were in pretty quick succession.'

'And unprotected, from the sounds of things.' Sasha nudged her shoulder into Fiona's.

'Well, Dave and I just had a certain kind of chemistry, right off the bat. It was hard to…'

'Cover with a condom.' Sasha couldn't help the quip. They both chuckled.

'I'm paying the price now, though. Jesus, Sash, what am I going to do?'

'Have you told Dave? Talked with him about it?'

'No. And no.'

Sasha popped her arm around Fiona and leaned into her. 'That sounds like the first step, doesn't it?'

Squirming a little in discomfort, Fiona looked away, concern evident on her face. 'I'm not sure. I'm not sure I should tell him.'

'But you must. He has a right to know.'

'Not if I don't have it.'

Sasha lurched inwardly. 'What do you mean? You just said you always dreamed of having kids, Fee.' She looked at her with concern.

'I know. But that was before…my horrid and bitter

old grandmother...'

'What do you mean?' Sasha cocked her head, perplexed. 'What's your grandmother got to do with this?'

'Everything!' Fiona replied with force. 'Everything about me; about my life. It's taken me weeks to figure out what's going on in myself. It didn't come to me at first – I just felt hideously bad for a long time, and so fearful. But then I remembered. I remembered it all.'

'What?'

'How much of a bitter and sad old woman she was. Devil's spawn...' A spontaneous snort of disgust escaped her. 'That's what she said – about babies. I was five years old. What a stupid and cruel thing to say to a five year old. I had nightmares for a long time. They were terrifying.' Fiona's face filled with sadness. 'And that dream I had for myself as a little girl...it just vanished, completely. Because of that one stupid thoughtless moment.'

Sasha remained silent, listening deeply with compassion as Fiona continued. She shared the story of her childhood, revealing the trapped tears, anger and sadness. She talked and talked until she was emptied of it all. And when she'd completely finished and every last tear was dry, Sasha gently took her hand.

'So, Fee, now do you know what you need to do?'

'Yes,' she responded, nodding her head solemnly. 'I need to talk to Dave.' A long quiet pause filled the air. 'You know I could never get rid of it.' Sasha acknowledged the comment as Fiona's hand grazed over her belly and lingered there. 'I wonder how he'll respond?'

'He'll be okay.' Sasha hesitated. 'But before you see him, there's something I really think you should do first.'

'Oh? What's that?'

Sasha sighed heavily. 'Take a super long shower. Wash your hair. Shave your damn legs and put some decent clothes on.'

A small chuckle escaped Fiona's lips. 'That bad, huh.'

'I can hardly recognize you.'

'I know. I'm certainly not a pretty sight…unlike you. You're positively glowing.' Fiona took a good long look at her as a light bulb appeared to go on in her brain. 'Okay. Who is he?'

Feeling suddenly flustered, Sasha eased herself out of the chair. 'No one.'

'What bullshit. Look at you, you're blushing! Come on, it's your turn to spill the beans!'

Exhaling heavily, Sasha realized it would now be impossible to leave without sharing the story about Lucas. For several seconds she considered telling her everything – about *all* of her past. But then thought otherwise. 'You better put the kettle on,' she finally said.

Launching up at haste, Fiona appeared infused with instant energy and immediately more like her old self. Grabbing Sasha by the shoulders, she declared, 'Honey, you don't need to ask me twice!'

'Calm down, Fee.'

'Can't!' she exclaimed. 'I'm so excited I'm about to pee myself!'

'Well, get used to it - that's only going to get a whole lot worse.'

Pulling a fake grimace Fiona moved toward the kitchen.

'How about you pee and I'll put the kettle on,' Sasha added helpfully.

'Bloody perfect!' she responded, veering sharply in the direction of the bathroom.

'One more thing, Fee.'

Turning to face her, she stared expectantly at Sasha. 'What's that?'

'I seriously wouldn't give up the supermarket baking just yet.'

Chapter Twenty Three

Evangeline sat cross-legged on her delicately sewn and blinged-out Indian meditation cushion that was covered in sequins of various shades of pink and purple. The cushion, more a work of art than a mere pillow, had been ordered six months ago from an ayurvedic yoga center in southern India, after some painstaking research by Thomas – despite the Internet not remotely being his area of expertise.

After attempting to suggest it would be easier to try a shop or yoga center in London, and even having provided ideas, Sasha finally gave up offering to help. Evangeline had insisted on sourcing a cushion herself.

Why, of course it must come from Indiaahhh, she'd shrieked.

But eight months after walking through her large front door to begin teaching her yoga, Sasha had noticed the spectacular transformation of Lady Evangeline Thornton. Serenity was now imprinted on her face; tension lines had softened; she was breathing easily all the way into her belly and her diaphragm moved in a deep rhythmical fashion. Her eyelids no longer twitched when closed, but lay resting calmly. And her spine was stacked ramrod straight, with her shoulders softened down and breastbone elevated up, all in perfect alignment. No longer saturated with thick make-up, her skin glowed with oxygen-enriched breath, and she shone peacefully and radiantly with an appearance ten years younger than the sad and uptight older woman who had greeted her all those months ago.

Yet the most wonderful thing of all, the screeching words ejected violently from her mouth had mostly disappeared. As a result of the recent critical mass of emotion bursting forth from within her, like a geyser in full force, a major turning point in Evangeline's evolution appeared to have occurred. The hideous high-pitched tones sounding like very bad opera had declined markedly in recent weeks. It was a vastly softened and graceful voice now detectable behind much of her dialogue.

Watching her thoughtfully, Sasha brought the lesson gently to a close. *'Om...Shanti, Shanti, Shanteee...Omm ...Peace, Peace, Peace...'*

The first time she'd finished the lesson like that, Sasha had glanced up to see Lady Thornton looking back at her with an expression of obvious distaste, as though Sasha were completely weird. Despite this, she'd persisted over the months with the closing mantra and times had now thankfully changed.

'Namaste.' Evangeline bowed her head with her hands pressed together in prayer position at the center of her chest and a surprising sincerity in her voice.

'Namaste,' Sasha responded, nodding her head in acknowledgment. They were both merely reflections in a mirror.

'You've changed my life, you know,' Evangeline said quietly.

Sasha dropped her eyes modestly. 'I can assure you, it wasn't me that changed your life.'

'But it was, dear girl. I could not have got this far without you.'

'Oh, on the contrary, I believe it's *You* that you

couldn't have got this far without.'

Evangeline smiled softly in understanding. 'I suppose I did have something to do with it.'

'Of course you did. It was all you. I merely opened the door,' Sasha responded humbly. 'You stepped through it. You made the commitment; you showed up twice a week for the past eight months; *you* made the change happen, Lady Thornton.'

'Evangeline,' she reminded her.

'Evangeline.' Sasha smiled. 'It is *you* who deserves the acknowledgment.'

'Thank you, Sasha. Do you think I've come far enough,' she hesitated.

'For Lord Thornton to notice the changes if your paths cross at the ball?'

She smiled somewhat shyly. 'Yes.'

'I'm positively certain,' Sasha replied, moved by the woman's vulnerability.

'Really?'

'He'd be a crazy foolish man if he didn't notice.'

'Thank you, dear girl.' She reached out, touching Sasha's hand gently. 'You're an absolute Godsend. I'm actually beginning to feel quite excited now about the ball. I even have my dress picked out.'

'You do?'

'Of course! It's barely a week away,' she said, stretching her legs gently and slowly standing up. 'Have to be prepared well in advance for these things, you know.'

'Why, that's wonderful!' Sasha said enthusiastically, suddenly remembering she was attending the same event and still hadn't thought about shopping for a dress, even if it was courtesy of Lucas.

'Can I show you what I'm wearing – I'm so excited. I haven't been able to fit a gown like this since...forever!'

Sasha stood up. 'Of course! I'd love to see it.' A troubled frown furrowed her brow fleetingly. Lady Thornton was not yet aware she was also invited to the event. The realization caused Sasha to shudder at the possible reaction. 'Evangeline...'

'Yes, dear?'

'There's something I need to tell you.'

Piercing light blue eyes scrutinized her face for a moment. 'What is it, Sasha?'

'It's about the ball.'

'Yes?'

'Umm...well...I've actually been invited myself.'

Lady Thornton's eyes suddenly grew large in her head. 'To the ball? The Earth Save Charity Ball? You've what?!'

'Been invited.'

'My.' She spun about, appearing overwhelmed and beginning to pace like a nervous cat. 'Oh, but dear girl, that's wonderful!' she exclaimed, turning back to face her. 'If my nerves get the better of me, you'll be there...right beside me. That's the best news I've heard all day!' Evangeline declared with excitement.

'Honestly?' Sasha replied with total surprise.

'Of course!' Moving directly to her, Evangeline gripped Sasha's shoulders and stared her in the face. 'But how? Who's the charming gentleman who invited you?'

Discomfort surged inside Sasha as she saw the searching look boring back at her. 'Well,' she shrugged nervously as the words froze inside her.

'Spit it out, dear girl. He can't be all that bad.'

'He's not. He's Lucas...I mean, his name is Lucas Huntington.'

For several seconds it seemed Evangeline could not register the words fully. She appeared confused, and then somewhat out of breath. 'Lucas Huntington.' The look was one of complete surprise. 'Lord Huntington's estranged son?'

'I'm not sure about the estranged part. But I think that would be the one,' Sasha replied nervously.

'But he's…' she stopped herself.

'He's what?' A wave of concern swept over Sasha.

'He's…'

'What?'

'Oh, dear girl, I don't want to be the one to speak such things to you.' Remnants of the old Evangeline surfaced in her widening blue retina's. 'And I'm not one to gossip…'

Sasha almost choked at the blatant lie. Despite Lady Thornton's recent positive transformation, old habits died hard. She refrained from disbelieving eye rolling. 'Say it. Please.'

'I shouldn't'

'But you must.'

'Well…quite frankly, the man is a playboy. A cad and a heartbreaker.'

Having heard Amy's heartfelt words, Sasha couldn't equate the description she was hearing with Lucas. Shaking her head, she stared back aghast.

'No. He's not. He's not like that at all.'

Evangeline sighed, turning and pacing a few steps away before spinning dramatically about again. 'I rather regret he is, Sasha. By all accounts.'

'Whose accounts?'

'Many, it seems.' She shrugged. 'I recall my friend, Mrs Jackson-Jones, saying he treated poor Catherine, his ex-wife, appallingly towards the end of their relationship. And Mrs Jackson-Jones should know – she is the dear woman's second cousin…' she hesitated momentarily, '…twice removed, perhaps.' Evangeline took Sasha's silence as complicit approval to continue, so she did. 'I understand that after one of their arguments Catherine fled permanently to France – away from his bad temper - apparently,' she shuddered. 'After that, I hear he dated a string of silly model's for a while. Then, rumor has it, he exploded at his office a few months ago, acting like a crazed man and he verbally abused some of his colleagues.'

Evangeline watched Sasha's face fall and added. 'From what I've heard. Of course, I'm also aware they lost their child,' she finished quietly.

'Maybe a lot of what you heard wasn't the true or whole story.'

'Well, whatever the *story*, the silly man should have known how to behave better and avoid terrible publicity. Poor Lord Huntington. It must have been outrageously embarrassing for him – his son acting so badly.'

'Perhaps his father never considered what he might have been going through?' Sasha responded defensively, feeling deeply troubled by Lady Thornton's storytelling version.

'Dear girl, you really don't understand.' A hint of patronizing crept into Evangeline's voice. 'Lucas Huntington is the son of a *Lord*. He has great social standing and a family reputation to protect. People like us...' She stopped, clearing her throat to check herself before continuing. Sasha was finding it hard to recall the much nicer woman who had, only minutes ago, been sitting angelic-like before her on the blinged-out Indian cushion. 'What I mean is, when you're raised with privilege you really don't have the luxury to lose control. You must bury whatever challenging emotions are there and soldier on, for the sake of not only your own reputation, but also that of your family name.'

'And how did that work for you?' The words fired out of Sasha's mouth without thought. Instantly clapping a hand over her mouth, she froze. 'I'm so sorry.'

Evangeline remained silent – quite speechless – the vivid blue of her eyes looking as if they'd just seen a ghost. Walking to the nearest chair, she slowly maneuvered herself down into it. A long and deathly-silent minute passed before she looked back up - her glassy eyes carrying the sheen of moisture and sadness. 'Don't be sorry. You're quite right, Sasha.'

'No. I shouldn't have…'

'Shush.' Evangeline hushed her. 'I owe you an apology. I just regressed into being someone I don't enjoy being anymore. I probably never did enjoy it, if I'm honest. Not really.'

Sasha listened quietly.

'Family reputation and name is a heavy burden to carry, it's true.' Her shoulders slunk forward as her words flowed in somber reflection. 'I never really had my own identity. Nor even much of a childhood. Most things in my life have been about *duty*. Upholding the family name and being seen to be doing the right thing. People look on and probably think *what a life of ease*. But really, it's rather suffocating, you know. It's funny – so much wealth and so little…happiness. Gossip is all I've had to hold onto…to feel any sense of *aliveness* or community, I guess you could say.'

Sasha continued listening carefully, compelled to take several small steps toward her.

'But the last couple of months I found myself forgetting all of that: thinking different thoughts; becoming someone else - quite possibly my real self. And so much happier.' Tears welled up in her eyes. 'All these years I lived up to social reputation and high moral standards and action, like I've been taught to. And the very cruel irony is, that in the end, my husband clearly didn't give a jot about any of that. He didn't care about embarrassment – mine or his.' Tears began to trickle down Evangeline's cheeks. 'I think he just wanted to be happy in the end. And he did exactly what he felt like doing.'

'Then maybe he did you a favor,' Sasha said gently.

'What? You mean like turning me into some tearful wreck who cries at the drop of a hat?'

'Maybe that's part of it. Tears *are* the river of life, after all. And it sounds to me like it's *life* you've really been seeking,' Sasha paused. 'To feel again - even if occasionally it hurts.'

Evangeline considered the words carefully as she gazed directly into the younger woman's bright oceanic eyes. 'It's scary, Sasha. It feels so…daunting…waking up, way past the middle of your life – alone. And realizing you may be someone else quite different from who you've been being for much of your life.'

'Yes.' She nodded in understanding. 'But perhaps it can be exciting, too…exhilarating even.'

'How?'

'Well, for starters you get to go to a ball looking more fabulous, svelte and…sexy…I might add, than you may have looked and felt in years.'

'Or ever,' Evangeline added, wiping her tears away in a flurry of exasperation.

'So enjoy that. Let yourself *feel* that. Celebrate it!'

'You mean, by squeezing myself into a *tube* of a ball gown and having Harold's eyes pop out of his head at the sight of me.' She finally managed a smile.

'That's exactly what I mean.'

Sighing heavily, Evangeline gathered her thoughts. 'Sasha, I'm sorry I shared all that silly gossip about the Huntington boy. It really wasn't fair. You're so right, I don't know the true story…and what does that matter anyway. It's all in the past.'

Wise words were not usual for Evangeline. It was another revealing sign of her transformation and an impressive leap. A hint of pride formed in Sasha. 'I think you're in danger of not needing me anymore, Evangeline.'

'Nonsense!' she declared, standing up from the chair and restoring herself to a strong posture. Moving gracefully past Sasha, Evangeline lingered briefly, touching the younger woman's arm gently as she did so. 'I will always need you,' she said quietly before moving toward the door.

Sasha's heart swelled in her chest as she watched the very dignified woman hovering momentarily by the door of *Ballroom* and appearing quite reflective.

'Now, dear girl,' Evangeline said, finally turning to face her with decisiveness and warmth. 'It seems we *both* have a ball to prepare for.'

As she glanced back up the passageway, Sasha caught the glint of renewed determination set deep in Lady Thornton's eyes.

'Thomaaasss. Briiing the dress,' she commanded, trumpeting down the hallway.

***

Sasha felt like skipping into the gym the next day. She was feeling so much happier. Her friendship with Fiona restored, and with Lady Thornton's miraculous morphing from caterpillar to butterfly, the colors in her world took on a brighter hue. Although his words had hurt, it was an undeniable fact that Rodrigo was the catalyst for the repair and reconnection with her best friend. What a shock it had been to find out about Fiona's pregnancy. But at the same time, it seemed like a wonderful thing – especially after hearing of her dreams and how her childhood nightmares had affected her.

Sasha was more than curious about how things were progressing with Dave and was looking forward to a good catch-up with Fiona over the weekend. Booties and baby clothes had now galloped to the forefront of her mind, almost overtaking her pressing need for a ball gown.

Please God, let me find something great to wear this afternoon, she thought, wandering through the busy reception area at the gym.

The flush of a sixth-sense sneaking suspicion passed through Sasha at the sight of Danielle *Long-Legs-Blonde,* clearly visible inside the entrance of *Sleazy Ian's* office. It was hard not to recognize a figure like hers; legs like spaghetti and a slim sporty frame. Was she hitting on *him* now? Sasha wondered. Peering through the doorway, there was Ian, sitting perched on his desk as he had been with her weeks ago, a happy and sleazy expression etched on his face. Catching sight of Sasha glancing in, he promptly got up and slammed the door shut.

Moving to the entrance of the training room, Sasha stole a glance around the weights area and spied Rodrigo chatting to a male gym member, a broad smile emblazoned across his handsome face. Pausing for a moment to watch him, she observed his charismatic ease. He radiated a rare combination of confidence without arrogance. She'd mistaken his genuine South American warmth and been wrong about him – something she now felt very humbled by. He cared greatly about people. No wonder they gravitated toward him like iron filings to a magnet – both men and women alike.

Feeling her heart soften, Sasha thoughtfully watched him. His passionate words in the car park, fired at her like missiles, were the necessary wake-up jolt she needed. Ever since she'd left California, cultivating detachment had been her way of dealing with emotions. She'd managed to conveniently hide deeper layers of feeling behind her curtain of *spirituality.* It was easy to pretend you didn't need anyone when you were focused on divinity and self-improvement; easy to ignore your humanness. But there was also something difficult to ignore about *truth* rocketing toward you like a blazing arrow through the night sky. Light tended to make a glaring mark in the darker and more confined spaces of the self. Rodrigo's talent was wasted - he perhaps belonged more on an archery range for the soul, not in a gym.

Catching sight of Sasha standing at the doorway staring at him, Rodrigo felt a ripple of surprise. Politely excusing himself from the club member, he wandered across to her.

As his long graceful strides brought him closer, Sasha felt her cheeks redden slightly as she realized she had no idea what to say to him.

'Sasha? What's up?' he said, the cool note in his voice obvious.

'Oh. I just wanted to have a quick word with you about the other day.'

'What about it?' he replied, visibly bothered.

'I wanted to thank you.'

He shrugged. 'For what?'

'For everything you said to me in the car park. You were right.' Glancing down, she found herself unable to meet his fixed gaze. A tangible awkwardness hung between them like a dense cloud. 'I should never have left Fee alone like that. I wasn't being a great friend, at all.'

'Uh-huh.' His indifference was evident as he looked back over his shoulder at the club member, checking the man's technique was okay as he raised heavy weights.

'She's going through a lot.'

'Yes. It's called pregnancy,' he said quietly.

Sasha was thrown. 'She is...how did you...?'

'Dave.'

'Oh.'

'And I suspected so, too. Fiona told him yesterday and he phoned me last night. I guess women aren't the only ones who need someone to talk to.'

'No, of course,' she said surprised. 'How was he?'

'Stunned. And...happy.' A slight smile creased Rodrigo's lips.

'That's great. I'm sure they can work it all out.'

'Yes. They're so new, but I think they love each other.' He finally looked at her, breathing in her special scent; observing the shape of her body in her yoga gear and noticing the long, blonde, perfectly tied-back ponytail trailing behind her. 'That seems to help.' A strange form of discomfort settled like silt within him. It was a feeling he was generally unaccustomed to having around women. Glancing back at the man heaving weights, a strong desire to move away from her formed inside him. 'I better get back to my guy over there.'

'Okay,' she said softly. 'Thank you again, Rodrigo.'

He hesitated. 'I'm sorry I was so blunt,' he added scratching his jaw awkwardly.

Sasha felt an overwhelming desire for him to stay and talk. She didn't want to see that broad back of his walking away from her. 'Maybe...' she started to say, but stopped herself.

'Maybe...what?' He gazed at her, the fathomless depths of his eyes momentarily holding her spellbound.

'We could grab a coffee or a drink sometime? I'd love to thank you, properly – you did save me from ruining my best friendship,' she smiled tentatively.

'That's really not necessary, Sasha.' He paused. 'Besides, I'm leaving in a couple of weeks.'

For some reason her heart sank completely. 'You're leaving the club?'

'No. I'm leaving England. I've decided to head back

to Brazil. To some sunshine.'

'Oh, God.' Disappointment wracked her body. 'That's such a shame.'

'Is it?' A look of happy surprise crossed his face.

'Of course. We really must…have a farewell drink.'

'I doubt your banker boyfriend would approve of that.'

Sasha reeled inwardly. Fiona must have mentioned something to Dave. But why did that make her feel so uncomfortable? It was the truth, after all. It wasn't as if she needed to hide the fact she was seeing Lucas. Yet, for some reason, she found herself suddenly dry-mouthed and speechless, as well as sad.

Rodrigo, suddenly overcome with the unfamiliar sensation of jealousy, recognized the unmanly feeling as if being struck by a mighty blow. It was one thing to challenge Sasha on her friendship with Fiona, but quite another to bring up her boyfriend. His response was undignified and he'd gone too far. 'I'm sorry. That was unnecessary. I should get going.' Their eyes met briefly. 'Have a nice time at the ball.'

He knew about the ball as well? Had Fiona spilled the beans on absolutely everything?! As if telling Dave about their child wasn't enough to fill their conversation. She could talk the ears off an elephant. But that was Fee – a woman prone to *banter*. Besides, adding to that she was now also full of raging baby hormones. The realization caused an instant feeling of forgiveness and understanding to form within Sasha. If she wasn't so bothered by the strange and aloof expression on Rodrigo's face as he turned away, she might have smiled at the thought of her best friend having a child. Instead, her eyes were glued to his triangular shaped back as he walked off.

A surge of dismay moved through her and she frowned. *Didn't go as I'd hoped.* The bright beaming

Brazilian sun was covered in cloud. *Quite the opposite.*

Rodrigo felt her eyes following him as he returned to the man floundering with his weight-lifting technique. By the time he glanced back at the doorway, she was gone. A feeling of flatness overcame him. It was strange and rare, but it was as if some of the light in his life had suddenly been extinguished.

Chapter Twenty Four

As the end of her lengthy yoga training was drawing to a close, Holly was feeling so much better for it all. A greater stability and balance now existed more inside of her; her body was supple, lighter and infinitely more limber; and thoughts of the past no longer haunted her so badly. Remarkably, too, she hadn't daydreamed about unhealthy food in days. Not only that, she'd grown to love listening to The Guru. Any fear of him had left her – he was now simply *Jimmy*, as far as she was concerned, and regardless of how he got his point across. Jimmy was all about love and so was The Guru. They were different faces of the same coin. But she liked the nickname *Jimmy* for him – it was approachable somehow. There were no scary monsters in the room anymore. He was simply speaking about Truth and Love - a love that began within her own Self.

Holly was getting it. Hanging off every word he spoke, she absorbed Jimmy's words into her core, hoping like crazy she'd learned enough to create a new life beyond this sacred shelter; that she could hold this new ground within herself; anchor it in and keep her new path ahead safe and trouble free.

'Dhyana is the seventh limb. This is to do with meditation or contemplation,' Jimmy was explaining. 'It is the uninterrupted flow of concentration.'

Seems the same as the sixth limb, Dharana, Holly thought.

'At first, Dharana and Dhyana may appear one and the same,' he said, smiling.

Surely that man had extrasensory perception and could read her mind.

'However, a line of distinction clearly exists between these sixth and seventh limbs,' he continued. 'Dharana is the practice of one-pointed attention. But Dhyana is the state of being keenly aware *without focus*.'

Ahhh, she thought, the penny dropping. *Awareness without focus.*

'At the stage of Dhyana, the mind has been quieted and is still. It produces few or no thoughts at all,' he said, waving about his long elegant finger to emphasize the point, as he was prone to do. 'It is most impressive, the strength and stamina it takes for a yogi to reach this state of stillness.'

The idea of bringing her mind to a place of complete stillness and silence was daunting - given it was incessantly busy, forever chattering away about something, and trying endlessly to figure things out. She'd noticed it was also often seeking control or ways to get needs met, and frequently filled with righteousness, judgment, self-attack, self-doubt or condemnation. Considering how long it had taken her to begin to tame her addictive thoughts about food, Dhyana may as well be a space flight to Mars!

Jimmy's warm feeling brown eyes found her intensely curious blue ones. 'While it may seem a difficult or impossible task, remember, yoga is a *process*. The picture perfect pose or ideal state of consciousness, for most, may be attained sporadically or momentarily at best. It is important to understand we benefit at *every* stage of our progress.' His features softened. 'Don't give up.'

Pondering Jimmy's words deeply, Holly contemplated Dhyana for much of the day. However, it was only later, as she awoke in the dead of night, a disturbing realization occurred to her: If she persisted, what would she find in the stillness of Dhyana?

And If she wasn't her mind or thoughts…who exactly was she?

***

'So you have your gown for the ball?' Lucas asked her. The charity event was looming rapidly ahead at the end of the week.

It was Sunday and they'd just finished breakfast at his house. Light streamed through the tall kitchen windows that looked out onto the perfectly mowed back lawn, surrounded by immaculately trimmed miniature shrubs.

'I do,' Sasha said absentmindedly, glancing down at the tabloid newspaper with utter disinterest as she sat perched at the breakfast bar in his kitchen. He was fiddling with an expensive coffee-making machine that had been installed a number of weeks earlier - the one she'd hardly ever seen in action, despite it being fit for café patrons, and despite having had a lot of sleepovers at his home.

'So you've found something suitable?' He glanced out the window without turning around.

'Suitable? I've picked something out and they're adjusting it slightly for me.'

'Don't you think you should be collecting that soon, darling? The ball is less than a week away.' He spun about, a concerned look evident in his eyes that she observed with interest.

'There's plenty of time.'

'Is there?'

'Yes,' she said, surprised at the tone of disbelief in his voice. 'I can pop in and pick it up on Wednesday, between clients. It's just a dress. No need to panic.'

His eyes appraised her carefully. 'I'm not panicking.' He hesitated. 'You understand the ball is just one of many important events I attend throughout the year.'

'So you're saying I should get used to shopping? Expand my wardrobe,' she quipped.

'There's no need to be flippant. You know I'll pay for everything.'

Sasha flinched. 'You mean like a *clothing allowance.*'

'Well it's not exactly an *allowance* when it's unlimited.'

'I like the clothes I wear.'

'Sasha, I'm only suggesting the clothing for events and functions. Please don't be like that.'

Defensiveness prickled her insides. 'Like what?'

Taking several steps to the opposite side of the breakfast bar from where she was seated, Lucas leaned his elbows down onto the marble surface, searching her eyes as he did so. 'You always look good, whatever you wear.'

'Thank you.' The compliment helped. 'So why suggest I should like shopping more then?'

'I have a lot of public events,' he stood up straight again, shrugging his shoulders.

Scratching her neck nervously she stared back at him. 'And I need to look great for them…right? Like good eye candy.'

'Look, this is going somewhere it really doesn't need to,' he paused. 'Why don't you like shopping?'

'I do like shopping. Sometimes.'

'Well?'

'I just...don't like doing it to suit someone else,' she finally admitted.

A puzzled expression formed on his face. 'You wouldn't be shopping to suit me. Buy things you like – as long as they're...respectable. I don't understand. I thought most women loved to shop.'

'Well, I guess I'm not like most women then – I'm sure least of all like your ex-wife.'

A troubled frown flickered across his face. She'd struck out at him needlessly and instantly regretted it.

'No. You're not.' He turned back toward the coffee machine as if signaling the conversation was over. Tinkering once more with it, he added. 'You still like looking good, though. I know that.'

'Yes, I guess I do,' she agreed, recognizing they needed space. 'Hey, I'm going to head upstairs and hit the yoga mat.'

'Okay,' he responded, barely moving his head.

Padding quietly out of the kitchen, a strangely sick feeling formed in her stomach. It seemed that lately they were becoming like an old married couple – or possibly that he was assigning her the role of *wife*...or *social spouse.* Some women surely thrived on having a credit card thrown at them, but Sasha found herself feeling quite uncomfortable. Her taste included looking good, with simplicity, not opulent decadence. And she enjoyed her independence.

An echo appeared to be rippling through time into her present. Disturbingly, she found herself recalling what it was to feel like a commodity.

He didn't mean it like that, she reminded herself. They were very different people, though. That was evident.

Entering the upstairs room, Sasha turned on the heater. Despite the weather being warmer it was still only early Spring. Grabbing one of the two rolled up mats that now lived permanently by the door, she wandered to the center of the room, unraveling it flat on the floor.

Beginning her practice with a few simple Downward Dog stretches and deeper breathing, she suddenly stopped, distractedly glancing about and allowing her attention to alight on the screen at the end of the room. Not normally the nosy type, she found her curiosity getting the better of her and left her yoga mat, moving barefoot toward the boxes shielded from her for a number of months. There were three, stacked one upon the other. The top box appeared so full it couldn't quite close.

Sasha tentatively lifted a side of the lid and peered in at the contents below. There were a number of paper documents on the top – they were legal, and full of boring looking jargon. Ignoring those she lifted the paperwork up, spying several framed pictures underneath. Sliding the top one out, her breath halted momentarily as she stared down at a wedding photo of Lucas and Catherine.

He looks really happy.

Despite any resistance Lucas had toward his wife's desire for him to take his family place, he appeared to have loved her. In fact, he looked very much *in love*, which both surprised and bothered her. She plucked out a number of other pictures, all with him smiling – an expression she rarely saw on his face these days.

Sasha appraised the woman in the pictures. She was stunning looking. Slim and smiling with an air of confidence, elegance and extravagance about her – her clothes, hair and jewelry, all immaculate, in every shot. She oozed class, and the look of wealth and privilege. Lucas had given the impression they were ill suited. But it was clear this was not the case. They looked like the perfect pair…albeit, perhaps, in the arena of ambition.

Glancing down, she caught sight of the corner of an unframed photograph and carefully slid it out. It was another picture of the two of them, but this time Catherine was wearing a loose gown with a swollen baby-filled belly. Sasha guessed she must have been about seven or eight months pregnant. Lucas had his hand wrapped protectively around his wife's waist and resting on the top of their unborn child.

'Sasha?' Lucas's voice cut the air like a knife.

Christ. She dropped the photo promptly back onto the top of the pile in the box.

'Are you okay? What are you doing?' he said, his voice becoming suspicious as he walked toward her.

Spinning nervously to face him, she had no idea how to explain. 'I…umm…was just…'

'Being nosy,' he said in a frosty tone, joining her by the boxes.

'Yes. I guess I was.' There was no point denying it. 'Catherine's very beautiful,' she said, reaching for the photo she'd dropped onto the top of the pile. But before she could retrieve it fully, Lucas slammed one of the sides of the lid down, almost trapping her hand along with the picture.

'That's private.' A glare of anger flickered in his eyes.

'I'm sorry,' she said, meaning it. 'I shouldn't have looked.'

'No you shouldn't have,' he said, fussing about with the other sides in an effort to close the box. 'That's my personal business.'

Sighing heavily, Sasha took a few steps away from the box and his frustrated endeavors to close it.

'How did it end, Lucas?'

'I don't want to talk about it,' he replied sharply, persisting with his attempts to shut the box.

'It obviously still affects you. Maybe it would help if you talked about it.'

'I doubt it,' he said gruffly.

'How did it end?' she persisted without thinking.

Slamming a side of the box down forcefully with his fist, Lucas erupted with fury. 'Damn it, Sasha! How the hell do you think it ended?!' He glared at her full of rage.

'I don't know,' she stammered, nervously taking several steps backward, but still wanting to hear him tell her.

Striding two long steps he moved right up in her face. His jaw was clenched tight and his eyes had turned cold. She saw the bitterness before it lashed out at her.

'Badly! Okay! It ended badly!'

And there, in the depths of his anger and the faraway place he'd just flown off to, she saw all his unresolved pain. 'I'm sorry,' she said, feeling a source of strength arise from within her and recalling Rodrigo's passionate words about people hurting. 'I'm so sorry for your loss. Truly,' she whispered, as gently as she could. 'But don't you think you've held onto this pain long enough.'

Lucas was trembling. His cheeks were flushed red and it looked possible he might explode, lash out at her, or fall apart. She prayed for the later and waited.

It felt like an awfully long time before he spoke, such was his effort to curb his shaking. His eyes remained off in the distance somewhere. And when the words eventually came, they fell out all staccato-like, in little short sentences, with great pauses in between. Gratefully, thanks to Amy's revelation, she was able to interpret them.

'She was drinking. Wouldn't stop. Always socializing. Selfish. Dangerous. Unfair to…' Tears formed like pools that thickly covered the entire surface of his eyes. 'She wouldn't listen. We argued.

Incessantly. She was angry. Wanted a Lord.' He swallowed, his voice sounding choked up. 'One day she came home…quite drunk.' The first pool plopped out of one of his vacant eyes, landing on the wooden floor. Sasha steadied herself, staying fully focused and listening deeply. 'I couldn't believe it. Why would she do such a thing?' he added, placing all ten of his fingers onto his forehead in clear distress. 'How could she do that to…' An exhalation of despair escaped his lips. 'We argued,' he whispered. 'Climbing the stairs. Yelling. She tripped.' The second plump pool fell out of his eye, followed closely by another. He staggered slightly. 'She just…tripped…'

He was right there now. Right in that hideous moment that lay at the root of the darkness that was eating at him. Wobbling, Lucas took a step back, reaching out to the boxes for support. 'She fell. Badly. Rolled.' His face contorted with anguish as his breathing became more rapid. 'Too far away. Nothing I could do,' he whispered. The watery pools in his eyes appeared to be blinding him. He blinked again, ejecting the fluid obstacles. Clutching onto the top box as if the weight of his own body were too much, his lip trembled uncontrollably. 'Ambulance came. She was so drunk she wasn't hurt. But the baby…' He slid helplessly to the floor. 'My baby. My baby boy…'

The first choked sobs left his broken soul. Then others. They came in waves as his long upper frame folded over his knees. His arms clasped firmly about them and his head dropped in shame and pained resignation.

Curled up like a ball by his boxes of memories, Lucas felt his canyon of sorrow - and wept.

***

'Bellisimo, why so long? It's been...' Basilio glanced toward the ceiling, gesturing widely and dramatically with his hands, 'an eternity.'

The air in the café was warmer than the morning spring air outside. Fiona kissed Basilio warmly on each cheek then removed her light jacket, revealing an uncharacteristically loose top that hid her tiny swelling belly. 'Cool your jets on the Cary Grant routine, Basilio,' she quipped.

'Cary Grant?' He raised his brow.

'You know – the actor. Your...generation...' Fiona's voice tapered off at his look of confusion. 'Never mind,' she said, tucking the jacket over the back of the chair and sitting down.

'And Bella, darling.' Basilio grasped Sasha by the shoulders theatrically. 'Mama Mia, boyfriend is gone, yes? No black eye,' he said, examining her face closely.

'Ah...' Sasha wasn't quite sure what to say.

'Yes?' He asked hopefully.

'Mmm...'

'No.' He shook his head in despair. 'Bella, you break my heart. So beautiful. And so tragic.' He tut-tutted, turning away. 'Coffee is on me.'

'No, Basilio. You can't run a business that way.'

'Utt.' He waved his hand dismissively, turning back with a smile. 'I am a wealthy man. Two coffee's for two beautiful women, coming up. Exactly as you like them.'

'Thank you, Basilio,' they both chimed sweetly.

'God, we're like Charlies-bloody-Angels chatting to Bosley,' Fiona quipped.

'Without the big hair,' Sasha added, chuckling as she sat down.

Fiona laughed heartily. 'God, I've missed you, Sash.'

'I've missed you more.' Reaching out, she placed a hand upon Fiona's.

'Two dummies, huh.'

'Sure were,' Sasha responded, smiling.

'What's a good drama amongst friends every few years or so, though?'

'One drama too many, I think, Fee,' Sasha replied, meaning it. 'How've you been feeling?'

'Fat,' she screwed up her face.

'What rubbish. You must be like only seven weeks pregnant?!'

'Can never be sure about these things.'

'Well, some women can. The one's who remember the event.'

'Who's grown a sense of humor while I've been out of their life?'

'You've never been out of my life,' Sasha retorted.

'No?' Fiona looked at her sheepishly. 'I hope not. Because you're my best friend in the world and I'd like it to stay that way.'

'So would I.' Sasha paused. 'Now you know I've been dying to know…how did it all go with Dave?'

'Amazing,' Fiona sighed, her face lighting up brightly. 'He was amazing. Ecstatically happy, actually.'

'That doesn't surprise me.'

'Why's that?' Fiona searched her face carefully.

'He's one of the good ones. Warm, kind, caring, loves you to bits.'

'You think so?'

'I do. I can tell.'

'That's good. I think so, too.' She smiled. 'And what about your man? The mysterious Mr Huntington?'

'Oh, I don't know,' Sasha shuffled about nervously. 'He's nice.'

'Nice?' Fiona's expression changed to one of distaste.

'Why does everyone always do that whenever I say *nice*?' Sasha said, recalling the look on Amy's disappointed face.

'Because *nice* doesn't sound very *alive,* or very romantic, does it!'

Sasha snorted. 'Romantic. What's romantic?'

'I'll tell you what bloody romantic is,' she said, leaning right in close to Sasha's face and eyeballing her with great intensity. 'It's getting goose bumps when you see him; when you look into each other's eyes. It's when you could swoon in his arms and have him hold you as if nobody else in the world mattered…with time standing still.'

'You just gave Basilio a hard time for his Cary Grant routine, but you're giving him a real run for his money at the moment,' Sasha added drily.

'Shut up.' Fiona stared at her with a deadly serious look. 'Let me finish.'

'Okay,' she replied quietly, slightly taken aback.

'It's when you're dancing together as if you're under a spell and you're mesmerized by each other. Your bodies move in perfect union because you *feel* one another. And you're so close and it feels so good that you fall into a deep and passionate kiss…'

Memories of the night in the bar with Rodrigo began to resurface.

'…and when you pull away, you can't take your eyes off each other, because you know,' Fiona said, her eyes locked onto Sasha's.

'What are you talking about, Fee? Know what?'

'You know what magic is. And you know that the chances of ever connecting with anyone like that again are slim or none.'

Sasha felt distinctly uncomfortable. 'That's hardly realistic, is it.'

'Is it?' Fiona replied pointedly.

'Sounds a bit like a Disneyworld dream.'

'Well, lucky you then.'

'Why? Fee, what on earth are you talking about?'

'You know exactly what I'm talking about.'

'No. What?' she shook her head. Had Dave seen what happened that night in the bar? He must have. It was the only explanation. Sasha considered her recent encounters with Rodrigo and how strange and aloof he'd been with her at the club the other day. Was it possible he'd really liked her?

'A certain drop-dead gorgeous Brazilian man in a bar one night - ring any bells? Or has Prince Huntington been dazzling you with too many diamonds?'

'I'm not like that. And neither is Lucas.' she said, recalling with sadness the broken man she'd listened to a few days earlier.'

'No? Well, he's no gym instructor.'

'That has nothing to do with it.'

Fiona's expression softened and she leaned back slowly in her chair. 'Probably not, knowing you. I guess it doesn't matter anyway,' she said, a hint of gloom creeping into her voice. 'Since Rodrigo's leaving.'

'I know.'

'How do you know that?'

'We talked,' Sasha responded dismissively, her mind awash with troubled thoughts.

'Oh? When was that?' Fiona peered at her.

'The end of last week. He said he's heading back to Brazil. And finishes at the gym in a couple of weeks.'

Fiona nodded her head in affirmation. 'I'll be really sad to see him go.'

'Yes.' Sasha couldn't bring herself to add that she would too. A curious cocktail of emotions was whirling about in her that was hard to mask.

'You know how his parents have a place over here in London where he stays?' Fiona added.

'One of the staff mentioned.'

'Well it's because they're filthy bloody rich. They

have a big gym franchise across Brazil. And that's a pretty huge country, in case you hadn't noticed, Sash.'

'I know it's a big country.' She shrugged. 'So why's he been here? Surely he has *an empire* to oversee. Besides, he doesn't like the cold.'

'Dave said Rodrigo heard a lot about London from his parents. They love visiting. That's why they keep a house here. So he wanted to experience it for himself. He told Dave he thought working in a gym for a summer would be a great way to meet lots of people, as well as research other models of gym operation and management.'

'Really,' she replied, feeling strangely flat.

'Yes, because he's used to setting up gyms. He's not really a personal trainer at all – although I'm sure he's completed the training and knows what he's doing. Dave said he's more like a Franchise Operations Manager. He understands every area.'

'Dave seems to know an awful lot. A bit of *pillow talk* between you, too. I bet.'

'Yes, we talk a lot.' Fiona smiled, oblivious to Sasha's comment. 'I'm so glad I have that back in my life again. God I missed him.' She fixed her gaze on Sasha adding, with strange pauses in between each word, 'he does – tell me – a lot.'

Ignoring another pointed look, Sasha continued. 'Well Rodrigo can't like London much at all. He didn't even make it to summer. Perhaps he just chewed through all the available women in record time.'

'I don't think you know him as well as you think,' Fiona said quietly.

'I guess not,' she shrugged, pretending not to care. 'And never will, since he's leaving in a week.'

'No.' Fiona glanced down sadly at the table. 'Such a shame. Dave will miss him. They were becoming good friends.'

'They did seem to get on well.'

'Anyway, let's change the subject,' Fiona added, resting her hand maternal-like on her stomach. 'I don't want my child picking up sad vibes.'

'That's very New Age of you, Fee.'

'Well, I've changed. Ever since a good friend told me about the Yamas and Niyamas,' she winked. 'Now you, darling, have a ball to go to tomorrow night. And I haven't even heard about the dress!'

'What dress? What ball is this?' Basilio said, approaching their table and gently placing their coffee's down.'

'Our girl is being taken to a fancy ball tomorrow night.'

'Bella, have you met your Prince? Basilio smiled. 'Don't tell me – it's the Prince of Black Eyes.'

Fiona guffawed.

'Hysterical. You two are hysterical.'

'No. No. Don't be like this, Bella,' Basilio reached down and touched her gently on the shoulder. 'I am happy for you.' His other hand moved to his chest. 'Sad for me, because you not have nice Italian boy who treat you well. But he take you to a ball and he make your heart sing. Si?'

'Does he?' Fiona interjected. 'Does he make your heart sing, Sash?'

They were both staring now. Waiting in suspended silence for a response. Sasha felt decidedly awkward. 'I haven't really known him that long.' The frothy cappuccino surface suddenly held infinitely more appeal than the two people staring at her.

Basilio and Fiona stole a glance at each other. It was Basilio who finally broke the uncomfortable silence. 'Well, Bella, the main thing is that you are happy.' He looked at her thoughtfully. 'And you have a ball to attend, with a Prince of a man. Mama Mia, you shall look Bellisimo!' Pressing several fingers to his lips he kissed them before extending his arm in a grand manner.

'Thank you, Basilio.'

'Divertitevi…enjoy.' Bowing his head graciously before departing, the gentle smile on his face reflected a deeper wisdom.

Sasha sat quietly. For a few moments she contemplated telling Fiona the truth about her past - about everything. After all, Fee had found the courage to be honest with her. So had Lucas for that matter – and about their most painful hidden places. It was wrong to hide so much from her best friend for so long. But to be that honest with Fiona would require her to be that honest with herself. And she wasn't ready for that. That was the problem with lies: the more you layered over things, the bigger the pile you had to dig yourself up from.

Glancing across the table, Sasha caught the quiet knowing look in Fiona's eyes as she watched her carefully. It was unsettling and made her want to run from the café. The problem was, the moment Fee spotted Sasha's discomfort she changed gear like a cyclist navigating a hill.

'How about you tell me what your ball dress looks like, Sash,' she asked softly.

Chapter Twenty Five

'Darling,' Lucas tapped on the door, 'we'll be leaving in twenty minutes.'

'Okay. I'm almost ready.' *I think.* Sasha stared at the woman in the mirror who appeared to her like a stranger.

'I'll be downstairs…having a drink,' he added.

A little *Dutch courage* wouldn't have gone astray. Maybe three, she thought, sweeping a critical eye over herself. But even she had to admit she'd never looked better - or more glamorous. There was something about the cut of a designer dress and beautiful quality fabric that could easily make a woman feel like a million dollars.

Twenty million.

A striking ivory sequined gown had caught her eye in the shop that Lucas's driver had taken her to. No sooner had she caught sight of it the super efficient shop attendant had hurried it over to her. Knowing it would suit her hair, eye color and skin tone, she didn't hesitate in trying it on and had promptly made her decision within minutes.

The dress was now form-fitting – the result of having had a slight adjustment of a centimeter or two. Gathered fabric at the waist showed off her beautiful toned and feminine figure to great advantage. It was the longest item of clothing she'd ever worn, flowing elegantly to the floor and covering the three-inch ivory-colored Jimmy Choo's. The attendant had insisted upon the stiletto's, despite nobody able to see them beyond the yards of fabric. With such dazzling service, it was hard to refuse such a divine pair of shoes. Sasha guessed there was something compelling about a woman waving a credit card belonging to a man with lots of money - it evidently demanded the best of attention and sales advice. There was also something momentarily enthralling about being the one whose hand the credit card was held in.

The dress was classy and strapless and accentuated her long neck so beautifully that it required no adornment around it. Clear Swarovski crystal drop earrings were the only sparkling extra. An excellent fake spray tan the day before had lifted her skin tone to her former Californian glory. Whilst a nearby salon visit, pre-booked and visited a few hours ago, had her blonde tresses drawn over to one side with stylish feminine waves cascading down over her collar bone. A make-up artist had visited her in the house the past hour and had transformed her face so much it looked like she belonged on the cover of a magazine. Sasha seldom wore that much in the way of cosmetics – generally a splash of tanned mineral powder and a dash of mascara. But her blue eyes now appeared super enlarged in her head, her lips full, and her cheekbones high and accentuated.

Spinning slightly, she spied the dress's subtle train extending several feet onto the floor behind her. So graceful, so stylish…

Perfect.

Taking a deep breath – probably her last for the night since it was so hard to inhale properly with the cut of the dress – Sasha collected the small satin ivory clutch purse containing a few make-up provisions and her cellphone, then quietly exited the room.

Moving tentatively in her high heels, she assumed Lucas would be in the kitchen. But as she rounded the last bend in her descent down the stairs, there he was, waiting at the bottom and oh so dapper in his black tuxedo. He watched her carefully all the way down to the base step and didn't speak until she'd stopped three feet in front of him.

'Utterly breathtaking,' he whispered, taking a couple of steps forward, leaning over and kissing her softly on the cheek. 'You're an absolute Goddess.'

'Thank you,' she smiled, feeling suddenly shy at the large compliment. She'd never been so dressed up before. 'You look very handsome yourself,' she added sincerely.

He appraised her further. 'We need to get you out of that yoga gear more often.'

'I thought we already did.'

His lips curled into an easy smile. 'Well, that too. But you look dynamite in a dress. Come on,' he gestured. 'Champagne?'

'Wonderful. I'm in need.'

Lucas threw her a quizzical look as he guided her into the open-plan living area extending beyond his modern marble-surfaced kitchen. 'You're not nervous, are you?'

'A little.'

Nearing the center of the spacious elegant living room, they stopped beside an expensive bottle of champagne sitting open and chilling in an ice bucket atop an exquisite antique cocktail table. Sasha had often admired its most elegantly curved legs. 'Surprising,' he said, removing the bottle and filling several long-stemmed flutes. 'You always seem so...calm.'

'Well, teaching yoga tends to connect you a little

differently to people than…' she looked down at herself, 'this,' she added, gesturing toward her dress.

'Out of your comfort zone, huh.'

'A fraction.'

Lucas placed the bottle back in the ice bucket. Collecting the two glasses, he handed one to Sasha. 'You stretched me out of mine. Time to repay the favor. Here's to new comfort zones.'

Smiling at each other, they chinked glasses. As the alcohol began to flow quickly through her bloodstream, a flood of relief surged through Sasha. It was just a charity ball. No big deal. Yet she'd been increasingly anxious as the day wore on and had no idea why. Except, for some reason, a strange and uneasy feeling about what lay in store lurked in the pit of her stomach.

'We'll have a great time,' he said. Placing his champagne glass down he reached into the inside pocket of his tuxedo and withdrew a small box. 'Your earrings look beautiful, but I thought I'd take them up a notch.'

Taking a quick glance down at the small velvet blue box sitting closed in his hand, Sasha looked back at him with surprise. 'You shouldn't have.'

'Of course I should. What's the point in having all this wealth if I can't gift a beautiful woman.'

'I can't…' She was filled with discomfort. The last time a man had given her something expensive it had come at a very high price. The memory stole some of the magic of the moment.

Lucas smiled wryly, shaking his head at his own private joke.

'What is it?' she puzzled.

'Oh, I was just thinking, one woman who this kind of thing was never enough for…and one who doesn't seem to want it. Here,' he placed the box carefully into her hands, closing her fingers around it. 'Please, take it,' he added, his eyes filled with sincerity.

Nervously pursing her lips together, Sasha slowly opened the box. Before her, glittering in magical splendor, were the most beautiful pear-shaped diamond drop earrings. 'My God, Lucas,' she gasped with astonishment. 'They're spectacular. This is too much. They're…'

'Perfect. And they'll look perfect with your dress,' he interrupted. 'Diamonds go with everything.'

'Thank you,' she finally conceded. 'It's incredibly generous of you.'

Lucas gently touched her chin. 'Beauty deserves beauty,' he said, leaning down and softly kissing her cheek. But she only partially absorbed the compliment.

It had been such a whirlwind few months and her life seemed to be taking a dramatic new direction with her barely having a chance to assess it. Looking back into his trust-filled eyes, she wondered at her worthiness and felt a ripple of uneasiness. Was this the life she wanted for herself? Was it where her heart lay? She was a yogi, after all. Her path was one of detachment and greater simplicity in life, wasn't it? Who would she be or become in a world surrounded by such opulence – such wealth and privilege? She'd fallen into bed with him and the relationship had followed. But had she really chosen it? Had she truly and consciously chosen him, or was she merely fitting into a space that had opened up before her?

As she watched Lucas cautiously removing the beautiful diamond earrings from their ornate box, Sasha realized she wasn't very sure of the answers.

**

The Great Room at the Grosvenor had been especially decorated for the Earth Save charity event. It looked spectacular. Stunning and beautifully lit floor-to-ceiling photographs of the Amazon, Antarctic, oceans, flora, fauna and several shots from space looking back at Earth, all adorned a full section of wall.

A huge overhead screen showed beautiful images of Earth and nature – each one slowly dissolving into the next. Decorations overhead were themed in blue and green, and a giant glittering model of the planet rotated spectacularly in the center of the venue, throwing out rays of sparkling light and revealing each glorious continent and ocean from its bright interior. Gorgeous white and gold candles twinkled atop every table, while attendants with trays laden with champagne buzzed about amidst lavish and beautiful leafy white-floral arrangements that were dotted everywhere.

Amy would love this, thought Sasha. The Buckley's would have been at the event, but they'd decided take the children away for a holiday in sunny Spain. And as much as she would have enjoyed seeing Amy, Sasha was quietly thankful. It was better she attend her first public event with Lucas in relative anonymity.

The dance floor rippled like a patch of ice-blue ocean, with ritzy white lighting underneath and all around it. A live band was playing off to one side. The soothing sound of it's lead vocalist helped Sasha relax as they moved throughout the throng of attendees, most of whom were milling about by the multitude of round banquet tables that filled the huge space.

There were hundreds and hundreds of people, all dressed in elegant splendor. Many of the women's ears dripped with expensive jewels that equally garlanded their necks. Glitz and glamor surrounded Sasha at every turn.

Momentarily, she wished she were sitting relaxed in her regular spot on Fiona's sofa, with a nice bottle of wine and wearing comfortable clothing. Taking the only kind of breath her body-hugging dress would allow she promptly dismissed the thought. This was the place and moment her inner self had brought her to – this ball. And this man. She simply needed to be present, enjoy it, and see what unfolded.

Lucas walked close by her side, occasionally touching her elbow to direct her. He emitted unmistakable ease, as if he were a creature who'd suddenly found his own natural habitat. Somehow he seemed bigger: larger than life - or at least the more subdued life he led at his Belsize Park home. Charismatic and charming, people appeared to approach him with great respect. Although cynically, Sasha also wondered if there were those who simply wanted something from him...fawning with fake smiles. It could be an odd world, that of money and title.

Politely she greeted everyone, wondering if they were curious who this stranger of a woman was on his arm. But after reflecting upon Evangeline's recent *gossip*, she realized it was likely Lucas had towed a raft of models to previous events over the past year. So who would bat an eyelid at her being on his arm...or bother to converse with her? The occasional person who did strike up a conversation, only to discover she was a yoga instructor, tended toward slight brow-raising, sudden silence and disengagement. Sasha tried not to mind, but for some reason failed dismally. On the whole, she felt as appreciated as the Earth pictures on the wall undoubtedly were by many – superficially, without depth, reverence, or any genuine connection or concern.

Finding their table, Lucas continued to mill about and chat with people. Feeling somewhat displaced, it became clear she needed a distraction fast. And there was only one possibility.

Locating Lady Thornton would be like finding a needle in a haystack amongst a crowd such as this.

There must have been easily over a thousand people who had showed up already. But thankfully, as it transpired, she didn't have to look too long or too far.

'Sasha, darling,' Evangeline trilled softly from behind her.

Turning at the familiar voice, she stared in awe at her now svelte and sublimely dressed student. 'Evangeline. You look absolutely breathtaking. Stunning.'

Lady Thornton could have given most of the younger women at the event a run for their money in her divinely feminine, floor-length, gray-silk, vintage couture gown. Drawn in gracefully at the waist by a glittering wide belt, embellished with silver sequins and lots of *bling*, and with elegant soft elbow-length Grecian style sleeves and a low plunging v-neckline, she looked every inch a Goddess. Her hair color had been softened, closer to a glossy ash-blonde shade, and it was now cut and styled to a flattering shoulder length with wavy curls. Crimson red lips and smoky eyes were almost enough to detract attention from the diamond-encrusted necklace, set off by a beautiful large ruby at its center. She was a vision of elegance, class and mature sexiness.

'Thank you, Sasha. I couldn't have done it without you,' she responded graciously, gently touching the younger woman's arm. 'And you look most spectacular yourself,' she added warmly.

'Lady Thornton?' Lucas interrupted them, approaching with an amazed expression.

'Lucas, dear boy. How are you?'

'I'm very well, thank you. You look exquisite.'

'Thank you, Lucas. Eight months of yoga, with this dear woman working me to the bone.'

'Really?' He darted a surprised look at Sasha.

'Of course. She's an absolute Godsend.'

'Yes, she is,' he flashed her a charming smile.

'Certainly not one to let get away, dear boy.' Lady

Thornton's laser-like gaze could have punctured the most robustly defended look.

Lucas ignored the remark, turning to Sasha. 'Darling, there are a few people I must briefly catch up with. Do you mind?'

Having felt decidedly self-conscious at becoming the subject matter, Sasha was entirely relieved. 'Of course not.'

'Come join me at my table for a while, Sasha dear,' Evangeline added. 'I'm sure Lucas has more than a few people demanding his time and attention.'

'Thank you, I'd like that,' she smiled with genuine relief.

Lady Thornton turned quickly to Lucas, firing a parting question before he departed. 'And how is your father, dear boy?'

Lucas's face seemed to glaze over like shutter blinds closing. 'I understand he's quite well, thank you. I believe he's even here somewhere. You may be able to enquire directly,' he responded coolly.

Scrutinizing him carefully for a moment, Evangeline considered his words. 'I do hope so.'

'I'll be back shortly, Sasha,' he said, leaning over and planting a light kiss on her cheek. Then politely acknowledging Evangeline, he moved toward a cluster of guests and rapidly disappeared amongst them.

Sasha promptly sat down, thankful to be out of the fray for a time.

'Here,' Evangeline said, holding two glasses of champagne she'd swiped at remarkable speed from a nearby attendee's tray and extending one of the glasses to Sasha. 'You look like you could use one of these.'

'Thank you.' Sasha received the bubble-filled flute with relief.

Sitting down in the vacant seat next to Sasha, Evangeline gave her fragile silk dress a rudimentary check before speaking. 'Here's to yoga, Sasha. And a better body, better health...' she hesitated, appearing thoughtful, 'and a better life, with great new beginnings.'

'A better life, with great new beginnings,' Sasha repeated softly, looking her in the eyes and nodding her head slightly as they gently chinked glasses.

'Lady Sasha Huntington...perhaps?' Evangeline peered at her.

'Oh,' she responded, shocked at hearing the words. 'I don't...I'm not...'

'Shush, dear girl. You're an absolute delight. He'd be a lucky man to have you.'

'Eve?' A deep male voice suddenly interjected from behind them.

Sasha couldn't see to whom the voice belonged. It was a surprise, though, to hear Lady Thornton referred to in such a familiar way. Apparently stunned, Evangeline's eyes grew wider as she starred up at the man.

'Harold!' she said with shock before composing herself. 'Harold,' she repeated more calmly and graciously the second time.

As Lord Thornton moved alongside them, Sasha glanced around to see a tall and distinguished looking older man with a finely trimmed graying beard, salt and pepper hair, pale skin and warm brown eyes. 'Eve,' he repeated, as if in mutual astonishment.

'Harold,' Evangeline said a third time, maintaining dignity and poise as she rose up out of her chair. Sasha observed Lord Thornton extend his hand in a gentlemanly way to assist her. 'What a surprise to see you,' she added.

'More the surprise to see you. You're looking stunning.' Taking a step back, he appraised her fully with genuine admiration. 'An absolute vision, Evie,' he said softly. 'I don't know what you've been doing, but you look incredible.'

Sasha caught Evangeline's composed façade drop ever-so-slightly at hearing him call her *Evie*.

'Why, thank you,' she smiled, the glint sparkling in her eyes making her appear as radiant as a youthful bride. Harold was looking totally entranced. It seemed as if he was about to say something else. However, before he could speak there was a tap on his shoulder by a curvaceous blonde woman wearing a satin-pink gown that ballooned out below her waist like a meringue. Sasha did her best to be non-judgmental, but the dress looked wrong on her - as Cinderella-like as the idea may have been. It became quickly apparent that the young woman - not more than ten years older than Sasha - was Lord Thornton's scandalous match. Her cheeks were rouged a little too pink and her lips were boldly crimson in color, giving her the unfortunate appearance of an enlarged Barbie Doll.

'Harry, darling, let's get a drink,' she said, glancing briefly at them all in relative ignorance – either that, or she knew exactly whom Lord Thornton was talking to and was not letting him out of her sight.

Harry darling? Oh, my God...I bet that felt like an arrow shot straight through Evangeline's heart, thought Sasha.

'It's nice to see you...Evangeline,' Harold said more formally, nodding his head graciously before departing with his pink meringue-cake, but looking back over his shoulder with a longing in his eyes as he did so.

Lady Thornton whimsically watched them wander off through the crowd.

'Are you okay, Evangeline?'

'Yes. Quite,' she responded, appearing deep in thought as her eyes trailed after them.

'Are you sure?'

'No. Not really,' she paused, slowly shaking her head. 'That dress…it's utterly wrong on her.'

Sasha began to chuckle. She couldn't help it. The more she looked at the total indignation etched on Evangeline's face, the less she could suppress the feeling of laughter. 'Why, it looks like she's put on a large pink marshmallow,' she continued, still clearly piqued.

For a second, Sasha felt as if she was listening to Fiona, such was the humorous effect Lady Thornton was having on her. Her chuckling became louder.

'I mean, really! What on earth was the dear girl thinking?!' Evangeline continued, finally turning toward her with a look of great seriousness on her face as Sasha did her best to suppress the feeling of hilarity. 'Why, he could take her camping and roast her over a fire for dessert,' she added aghast.

At this point, the laughter burst fully and uncontrollably from Sasha. It seemed to puncture Evangeline's solemnity and she finally smiled. 'Why Sasha, he's dating a giant pink meringue,' she chuckled. Then she tittered. And before long, they were both hooting and hollering together in uproarious laughter.

***

It wasn't until later in the evening, well after the banquet meal, that Sasha saw her.

Melody Trenton had been wasting away the past couple of months and was now stick thin, aside from her famous voluptuous breasts. Garbed in a sleek, black, cleavage-revealing dress that looked a little like something out of the Flapper era, and with her long dark glossy locks trailing down to her rear, she looked stunning in a photo-shopped super-model way. But ever so boney.

324

Having enjoyed a good evening, with just the odd social snub, Sasha relaxed more as the night wore on and finally persuaded Lucas to hit the dance floor with her. However, as they threaded their way past tables toward the band, by some strange chance, Melody now loomed directly in their path. But not so strange upon closer inspection, as she'd hastily and strategically repositioned her stick-like self several feet in front of them.

'Lucas,' Melody exclaimed with fake surprise and enthusiasm, almost pouncing on him. Wrapping a gangly arm around the back of his neck and pulling him into a semi-embrace, she planted a ruby-red kiss on his cheek, leaving the telltale print of her lush lips. Sasha wondered if Melody was drunk, observing the formerly Amazonian model weave slightly backwards as she unglued herself from him.

'Oh, Lucas. You're with my yoga instructor. How sweet,' she gushed in a clearly patronizing way, causing Sasha to experience a rare rush of anger.

Taking a breath, Sasha forced herself to focus fleetingly on emotional detachment. *If I could just practice compassion toward Melody...*

Lucas was clearly a little embarrassed and uncomfortable. 'You two know each other?'

'Of course. My private yoga instructor - Sasha Devine.' Melody stared at her briefly with a smug look. 'Such an intriguing name, don't you think, Lucas? So...catchy. Remarkable coincidence for someone in such a *spiritual* profession.' She stared at Sasha, cocking her head thoughtfully to one side and pouting her flaming red lips as one of her hips suddenly jutted out in a catwalk-like pose.

Lucas gazed carefully back at them both as if he were assessing the situation.

A deep well of discomfort began to open up in

Sasha. It wasn't just the pointed words, but also the way both Melody and Lucas seemed so *familiar* with each other.

'I see your yoga tuition must be going…splendidly. So much personal attention,' Melody continued, her eyes widening as she blatantly treated Sasha as if she were invisible. '*Limbering up* really does get you going, doesn't it,' she smirked. 'I wish Damian, here,' she gestured to a tall good-looking young man behind her, 'could give me some private yoga sessions.'

Looking into the strangely large cavities that Melody's eyes were set in, Sasha realized she wasn't drunk: Melody was high on something, or stoned.

'Okay.' Lucas said firmly, 'We'll be on our way to the dance floor now. Nice to see you, Melody,' he added unconvincingly, whilst attempting to move past her.

Melody reached back and grabbed her unsuspecting partner, dragging him toward them. 'How about you go and have a dance with Damian, Sasha. There's something I need to have a quick chat with Lucas about,' she chirped innocently. 'Damian, darling, be a good man and take dear Sasha for a twirl on the dance floor.'

'Sure,' he readily replied, leering at Sasha's body as he grabbed her hand.

'Melody, stop this,' Lucas said annoyed. 'I don't wish to have a *chat* with you about anything.'

Damian yanked at Sasha, drawing her several feet away into the dancing crowd. She could barely make out their conversation over the noise of the music.

'Of course you do, ' Melody was saying. 'I have some very important information you should know.'

'I'm not interested!' She heard Lucas reply, as Damian - an underwear model with a cheesy grin and little evidence of a brain - swept her onto the flashing dance floor and proceeded to gyrate his financially favorable pelvic region against her.

As he twirled her Latin style, Sasha strained her neck through the gaps in the crowd in order to keep her eyes on Lucas. Catching a glimpse of him, she saw an irritated scowl darkening his face. Damian began to grind his now semi-firm groin hard into her as he wrapped his arms around Sasha's waist and leered down at her cleavage. Sweat was trickling down the sides of his face as he gyrated rhythmically.

Swinging about again, she caught a clear view of Lucas with an expression of intense concentration fixed on his face. He was now listening carefully to Melody. She was leaning right in close to him with her hand placed intimately on his stomach.

She's one of his ex's, realized Sasha, feeling a sudden wave of insecurity. *Explains a lot.*

Pushing her forcefully back over his arm, Damian dipped her amidst a cluster of legs, bringing the lower half of expensive dresses into view. Clamping his hand down in the gap between her breasts, he held her down, his teeth one of the few signs of light. Then once more he flung her up and twirled her about, providing her with another clear line of sight to Lucas. But this time, she saw him gazing through the crowd directly back at her, his face holding an expression of deep annoyance and moodiness. He looked much like the man she'd met on the stairs at Belsize Park in the rain on the morning of his first lesson.

Whatever Melody had been telling Lucas wasn't good. He wasn't happy at all. For some reason, Sasha had the awful feeling the tongue wagging in his ears had conveyed something very personal about her that disturbed him deeply. Could it have been the very thing she'd been running and hiding from for years?

Damian spun her away again and wrapped his arms tightly around her, wedging his pelvis hard into her backside as he groped the base of her breasts. Catching one last sight of Lucas staring back at her, she saw the look of deep distrust now etched firmly on his face. It was in that moment Sasha knew for certain that Melody must have found something out about her past and revealed it. For as her eyes locked onto Lucas, he dropped his gaze and, turning swiftly, began to stride away.

Sasha, now overcome with fear, broke free from the grasping of *Supercrotch Damian* and bolted from the dance floor after Lucas. Moving at speed, she zig-zagged her way past clusters of people. Thanks to the height of her three-inch Jimmy Choo's she was able to follow Lucas's bobbing head through the crowd, eventually catching up with him by a wall at the side of the Great Room.

'Lucas!' she exclaimed, grabbing one of his arms and causing him to turn and face her. His eyes blazed with anger. 'Where are you going?'

'I need some air!'

'Why? What's happened?' she asked, desperately wanting to know, but not wanting to hear it.

'I don't want to talk about it.'

'What is it? What did Melody say to you?'

'I said, I don't want to talk about it!' He gritted his teeth.

'Tell me. Talk to me, please.'

'Do you honestly want to know?' He glared at her.

'Of course.'

'She said my girlfriend is not remotely the person I think she is.' He leaned into her, his eyes fiery with accusation. 'Is that the truth?'

Sasha reeled inwardly. She couldn't lie, but to tell the truth was far too much to explain and a bad option. It was better to say nothing.

'Is it?! Did you destroy a top banker's life and

career…his family?!'

'No!' she exclaimed, feeling confusion and the past spill over her like a torrent from a burst dam. 'No.' Her eyes welled up with tears. 'It's not how it looks.'

'Well, that's how it sounds. Like I need more crap, Sasha! More bloody bad press!' He ripped his arm away from her. 'Jesus, she said that's not even your real name. 'Is that the truth, too?'

Hesitation could speak an unfortunate volume.

'Christ. Who the hell are you?!'

'I'm…' she stuttered, her eyes filling with tears. 'It's not what you think. It's not how it looks…'

'How it looks?! It looks like a damn great lie to me!' Lucas spat out vehemently. 'All of it. You…' He looked her up and down with disgust. 'You're a lie.' His eyes blazed with bitter disappointment as he grasped her angrily by her shoulders. 'You're nothing but a lie.'

'I'm not,' she whispered, recalling painful memories of anger vented toward her. Tears began to pour down her cheeks.

'I have no idea who you are,' he released his hold on her and composed himself.

'I'm exactly the person you've come to know,' she said, sadness overwhelming her.

'I wish I could believe that.' Lucas sighed heavily, his shoulders slumping. Taking one last disappointed look at her he turned and marched angrily away.

'Lucas…!' She moved to follow him.

'Don't!' He held up a hand with finality, barely glancing back at her. 'Just don't.'

Sasha's world was derailing rapidly as she watched him stride off.

'Oops.' She heard the smirk in Melody's voice before observing it on her face. Sasha looked around at the bone-thin wasted looking model, noticing her gleeful eyes rolling in her cocaine-fueled head. 'Told you, I have spies everywhere,' she wobbled, reaching out to the wall for support. 'A lying yoga instructor…go figure.' Melody chortled like a hyena, the hideous sound filling the air in a most haunting way. 'I bet your *Guru* wouldn't like that,' she poked Sasha's arm and turned to watch Lucas's disappearing frame. 'As if a man like that would ever choose someone like you…over me,' she added, prodding Sasha in the shoulder again. 'It was never going to happen. You must have known that.' Melody licked a snakelike tongue over her plumped out glossy lips. The million-dollar model could not have looked less attractive in that moment as she arrogantly tossed her drug-induced head and wove her way along the wall, disappearing into the ladies powder room.

It was hard for Sasha to breathe. It wasn't the dress anymore - it was her lungs. It was as if all the air had been blasted right out of them. The sound of a kind voice was the only thing that preceded her first sob.

'Dear girl, let's get you home,' Evangeline said softly, before an avalanche of hurt - both old and new - began dismantling the façade Sasha had spent years carefully creating.

Chapter Twenty Six

'Let me remind you,' Jimmy said, 'Yoga is a *spiritual* system. The Western world may apply it more for physical or athletic purposes, but in reality, the Asanas are designed to affect the subtle body for the purposes of *spiritual transformation.*'

Having burst into tears on the yoga platform a number of times the past week, without any known reason or clarity as to why, Holly was beginning to comprehend this.

'Physical fitness, physical health and relaxation...yes, yes, these are all great byproducts of yoga. But ultimately, its greatest purpose is *spiritual development.*'

Okay, but how does that work? Holly thought, accustomed by now to waiting for a response to miraculously eject from The Guru. Once again she was not to be disappointed.

'This *spiritual development* depends on breaking through places in the subtle body that are blocked with unresolved issues and energy. When you work with the body, you are also working with the mind and energy system. Emotional breakthroughs can be like markers of progress on the road to personal and spiritual growth.' Jimmy smiled broadly. 'Although they may not always appear or feel that way at the time.'

Why do we get blocked, though, pondered Holly. *What happens?*

'Emotional pain and trauma are difficult for the human system to bear. In these situations, the body comes to the defense of the *whole being*. And in this defending, the body will do things to stop the pain from being fully experienced, until the system is strong enough to process it.' He paused, glancing around at them all with a serious look on his wise face. 'Emotional pain is overwhelming. We all know this, yes?'

Observing most of the students nodding their heads, Holly felt a strange and deep sense of relief. For some reason, she'd always felt she had to pretend she was strong in the face of emotional pain and suffering...that somehow it was wrong to cry or express it. She was so used to burying her true feelings that half the time she wasn't even really sure what she felt anymore. Holly realized, in that moment, that there was a deep sense of shame attached to her experience of revealing sadness and grief...perhaps even joy. The awareness caused tears to spontaneously sting the back of her eyes.

'Emotional overwhelm is even more potent in children. Without the resources to deal with feelings, the body shuts off. It stores the emotion like a survival feature. It has to, because...' The Guru paused for the longest moment, 'the body can die from emotional pain.'

Several blobs of salt water balancing precariously on the rims of Holly's eyes now teetered over the edge and rolled down her cheeks as she listened.

'Even long after a painful or traumatic situation ends, the body continues its physical protection.

However, in doing so, it binds the individual to the past. Memories and experiences are held and stored in the mind, body *and* the spirit.' The Guru scanned the room somberly. 'And these are powerful.'

Holly considered recent events in her life and sighed heavily as she continued listening.

'So perhaps this begins to help you understand the yogic view that there is no separation between the mind, the body and the spirit. Emotional turmoil is carried in all three and is intricately connected, as is the health of the entire human system. Symptoms may appear in the physical body that link with emotions from a time long passed – a time that deeply impacted your mind *and spirit*. Although it can be difficult to accept, these symptoms or manifestations actually belong to the past.'

Now he was going to explain how to resolve the past, she was sure of it. He simply had to.

Jimmy continued. 'Asana practice can help you access awareness of energetic distortions in the body; help you release old and stored inner tension and emotion. However, this does not come ahead of its time. The student of yoga must be ready to receive the awareness necessary. And this may take years.'

Ready to receive the awareness...hmm, Holly contemplated.

'As teachers of this ancient practice you will have to find your own way in communicating a range of understanding from details related to a more physical level - such as the lengthening of the hamstring in the Pigeon pose, or other aspects like keeping the knee and hip joints safe - to the true yogic view of *enlightenment* or inner equanimity,' he said. 'The Universe as Oneness.'

The world seemed suddenly very *vast* to Holly, who had not felt so inspired and excited for some time. Suddenly the possibilities of healing and levels of self-mastery truly existed.

'Know this,' the expression on Jimmy's face held deep understanding, 'the truth you will find is that we are *not here to fix or change ourselves.'* He scanned the platform before his eyes rested firmly upon hers.

'We are here to meet ourselves...exactly where we are.'

***

'It's a mess,' sobbed Sasha. 'It's all such a mess.'

'My dear, it is no such thing,' Evangeline said, bobbing about in the back of the vehicle, as she handed another tissue to the teary young woman. 'Thomas, slow down, for goodness sake. It's not a Formula One race!'

'Sorry, Maam.' He glanced into the rearview mirror. 'Just worried about the girl.'

Even in her sadness, Sasha felt touched by the comment. Thomas had finally acknowledged her in a human way, albeit as a *girl.*

'She's not dying, Thomas!' Evangeline glanced across at Sasha with a look of concern fixed on her face. 'Are you, darling. But you've had a terrible shock. And I saw it all.'

'You did?' Sasha planted her nose into the soft tissue and blew hard.

'Yes of course. I watched that scheming little cocaine-addict tramp accost you and Lucas on the way to the dance floor. I watched the entire thing play out. Why, she practically ambushed you both before pouncing on dear Lucas. But you know...' Evangeline paused to consider her words carefully.

'Know what?'

'Well…the silly boy *did* take her to an event last year, if I recall. It seems he must have made quite the impression on her. She clearly wasn't going to let a nice juicy Lord-to-be get away.'

'No, I guess not,' Sasha said quietly, knowing the hole was so much deeper than that.

'Obsessed with him, I would say.'

Silence was her best option.

'But it doesn't make sense to me,' Evangeline continued detective-like. 'Why would Lucas storm off and leave you there on your own? That seems terribly rude and uncalled for. He should have been protecting you, not leaving you hanging out to dry with that she-wolf!' she added, clasping her hands together and leaning back thoughtfully onto the fine leather upholstery in the back of the Bentley. 'I'm quite appalled at his strange behavior.'

'It's really not so strange at all,' said Sasha, feeling an ounce of courage as she clasped the tissue tightly in her hand.

'Why ever not?' Evangeline replied, shuffling around in her delicate dress, filled with curiosity as she gazed at Sasha. In the seconds that followed it was not hard to spot the guilt and self-blame oozing from every pore in the younger woman's body. 'Sasha? Whatever have you done?' Evangeline added carefully.

'I can't…say.'

'Are you in trouble, dear girl? With the law? Have you done something quite illegal?'

'No.' Sasha said, staring down solemnly at her perfect dress.

'Well it really can't be all that bad then, can it?' Evangeline observed the somber silence for some time before reaching out and gently tilting Sasha's chin to face her. 'You know, you remind me a lot of me,' she said softly, staring into eyes filling rapidly as if they were hydro lakes requiring dam release. 'When Harold left me for…that woman…I blamed myself. I didn't really know that's what I was doing at the time, but I was being very hard on myself. I pushed everyone away. Even dear loyal Thomas.'

A gentle look of understanding spread across Thomas's face as he glanced momentarily into the Bentley's rearview mirror,

'And then, almost nine months ago, this remarkable young woman walked through my door and changed my life. She helped me find the courage to truly face those feelings…to embrace the place that life had brought me to. To see perfection behind the imperfection.'

Sasha stared back at her, speechless, feeling a large teardrop glide slowly down her cheek as she listened.

Evangeline continued softly. 'Not long ago, when I very much needed to hear it, you told me that every moment is a new moment - that we can be reborn again in every second if only we have the eyes to see it, and the compassion to allow it. *You* said that, Sasha.'

'I lied,' she whispered, as a second large tear fell straight from her eye and landed splat on her beautiful dress.

'You didn't lie.' Evangeline's steely blue eyes blazed back with certainty. 'It was one of the greatest truths I have ever heard. And look at me now – I'm a new woman.'

'Don't,' Sasha's hand rose slightly and her voice was barely audible as she shook her head in pain.

'Don't what?'

'Change,' she whispered.

'Why of course I had to change. I was miserable. Trapped in a self-condemned prison of my own making. Not even dear Harold was worth doing that to myself over. Don't you see, Sasha?' She squeezed her arm. 'You helped set me free. And if you can do that for me, you can do it for yourself. Regardless of how badly you might be feeling in this moment.'

Glancing down at the hand now wrapped around her forearm, Sasha felt the full rush of feelings as her two worlds began to collide. 'I'm such a phony,' she murmured, her head bent in shame.

'I don't understand, dear girl. Whatever have you done that could make you feel this way?'

'I'm not the person you think I am. I'm a fake,' she whispered.

'Are you saying you're not actually a qualified yoga instructor?' Evangeline replied, filled with confusion.

'No.' Sasha inhaled sharply as she reviewed her past. 'I'm saying it's one of *the only* things about me that's the truth.'

***

Standing subdued at Fiona's closed door, Sasha watched Lady Thornton's posh Bentley cruise off quietly into the night. Feeling suddenly very alone and quite exposed, without the comfort of Evangeline's caring concern, she nervously wondered how she could explain her story to her best friend.

As the front door finally creaked open, Fiona gazed at her in alarm. 'Sash? What's happened? You said in the text it was urgent?' Quickly opening the door wide, Fiona gestured her inside as mascara-smudged panda eyes looked sadly back at her. 'What the hell happened to you?!' she said with concern, grabbing Sasha's slim wrist and pulling her stationery frame inside. 'You look awful! And amazing!' she exclaimed with a look of awe on her face as she gawped at the gorgeous dress.

Unable to find any words, Sasha remained mute as Fiona closed the door behind them. Shuffling her down the short hall into her warm and softly lit living room she guided her toward the sofa.

'You're alone?' Sasha finally spoke, glancing nervously around.

'Yes. Well no, actually. I sent Dave out to get a pizza and some fries when I knew you were coming.'

'It's a little late for that, isn't it?' Sasha said, realizing it must be close to midnight.

'Not late enough for this one.' Fiona rubbed her belly affectionately. 'I'm telling you, Sash, who'd have thought you'd get cravings this early in pregnancy. I feel like I'm eating for six.'

Sasha couldn't help smile. Being around Fee was the best tonic and she found herself instantly begin to relax. It was her first smile in well over an hour. 'That's because you're only used to eating the amount of food needed for an Olympic athlete…and burning it off on the treadmill by running a half marathon most days,' she replied.

'True,' Fiona responded, patting the sofa and gesturing for Sasha to sit beside her. 'It's hard to tell anyone this, but the other day I actually craved dirt.'

'Strange.'

'Weird, huh. But apparently it's because of the minerals in soil.'

'Couldn't you just get them from a bottle?'

'I can. And I do.' Fiona tapped Sasha affectionately on the knee. 'But we're not really here to discuss nutrition, are we honey?'

Staring down at her gorgeous Lucas-funded dress, Sasha watched the brief respite from feeling terrible rapidly dissolve. 'No. We're not.'

'So hit me with it. I'm all ears.'

Hesitating for the longest time, Sasha thought carefully. 'I know it was a number of years ago, but do you recall the first couple of weeks after we met, Fee?'

'Of course.'

'Sometimes I'd ignore you when you spoke to me.'

'That's right. I thought that was odd…and a little rude.' Fiona paused. 'But at-the-time I put it down to you being a self-absorbed Californian.' She chuckled watching Sasha appear slightly taken aback. 'I'm kidding. You know I love that you're Californian,' she added.

'I never responded to you back then because I didn't recognize my name, Fee.'

'I don't understand.'

'My name was not my real name. I mean, it's *not* my real name.'

A long silence permeated the air and hung like a dense cloud as Fiona crinkled her nose and registered the information. 'Fuck. Really?' She flopped from her upright position onto the back of the sofa.

Sasha nodded in response, her face awash with sadness.

'Why isn't it your real name?'

'I never really wanted to go to College,' Sasha reflected. 'I was never interested. So I dropped out after my first year. And - I know this will surprise you - but, I became a personal trainer.'

'You're kidding me?' Fiona's eyes popped wide open as she simultaneously sat bolt upright.

'No, I'm not,' Sasha remained tentative. 'I was doing really well as a personal trainer and building a great private client base. And then I met this man…'

'Who fucked everything up, right?'

'Well, in fact, I did. Because I got involved with him.'

'As we do.' Fiona grimaced, leaning back again.

'He was a lot older than me. Handsome. And one of those charming charismatic types.'

'The asshole variety?'

Sasha shrugged. 'I'd meet him at his apartment – at

first for personal training sessions, and then…'

'Things got hot, right?'

'We got involved, yes,' she paused. 'I was so young and naïve. I never stopped to question things. He was seventeen years older than me…intelligent and powerful.'

'Cunning and manipulative, ' Fiona countered.

'He told me he was a lawyer.'

'Yep. Cunning and manipulative.'

Sasha sighed heavily. 'It's funny, looking back now I can see how gullible I was; so young and impressionable. What easy pickings I must have been for him.' Sadness blanketed her face. 'Anyway, over time he became like some sort of drug for me. I was so hooked I couldn't see straight. I didn't use my head. And then one day, while he was taking a shower, I happened to pick up one of his books. I remember there was a small shelf of them at the apartment. I'd never bothered to look at any of them before because they all seemed so boring. Statistics, finance and accounting books…and oddly, just one law book.'

'So this book, this book,' Fiona said, hastening her along.

'Yes. The book. Well it fell open to a page with a photo inserted.' Sasha hung her head in shame. 'Of his wife and two children.'

'And you didn't know?'

'Of course not. I'd have never got involved. Seriously, he seemed like the ultimate single man. Until I saw that photo there were no real clues. Except that he seldom took me out. We generally just stayed at his apartment.'

'That's a pretty big clue, Sash.'

'Not when you're twenty-three years old and love struck.'

'You never did a bit of online stalking?'

'Initially I did. But, of course, he'd given me a different surname from his real one. He never wore a ring. He lived in an apartment…'

'No. He *kept* an apartment. How convenient for him.' Fiona's voice dripped with sarcasm. 'So what did you do when you found the photo…besides freak out.'

'I did freak out, for a few minutes. But I managed to pull myself together and decided I'd check out the whole truth before I jumped to any conclusions. So I started digging around. And following him.'

'Clever girl. And?'

'The trail led to a plush suburban house on the other side of the city where his wife lived…with his children. I climbed the fence, hid in the bushes and watched him with them one evening. Looking back, I can't quite believe I did that, but I did.' She hesitated. 'Anyway, he didn't look like a loving man with them at all. Not remotely. In fact, it was horrible to watch. His wife looked caring and sweet. And he appeared almost… hostile - hard and cold. Given the man I knew, he could have been two different people.'

'How horrid,' Fiona added.

'Then I found out he was actually a very successful banker.'

'And you didn't know that?'

'Jesus, Fee. How could I? Aside from the fact he'd lied about being a lawyer, I wasn't remotely interested in the news, the banking world, politics, or any other sneaky entity.'

'Except, you happened to be in bed with one.'

'Yes, I was.' She shrugged in acknowledgment. 'He'd quizzed me about my interests early on in his personal training sessions. All that time I thought he was interested in me as a person, and really, he was just doing calculated research…I guess to see if I was the kind of woman that he could get away with being such a deceptive man.'

'You mean, get away with being such a deceptive bastard. It's disturbing.'

'Yes. But not the most disturbing part.'

'It gets worse?'

'Unfortunately, yes. The point came when I told him it was over. I didn't say why – just refused to see him. But the very next day I went to his house to tell his wife.'

'You went to tell her?!'

'Of course I did. It was wrong of him. And me. She was being deceived and deserved to know. And it seemed like the right thing to do.' Sasha's eyes became moist. Fiona gently laid a hand on top of hers.

'So what happened next?'

'Well, she wouldn't open the front door for the longest time. And I knew she was there because I'd seen her moving about through the windows. In the end, I pretended I was a courier delivering something and she finally opened the door.' Sasha's voice cracked.

Fiona squeezed her hand tightly.

'She was like a timid little sparrow. And her face…God, her face, Fee. She had black eyes and red welts. She'd put makeup over it all, but it was so obvious.'

'You mean that asshole beat her up?!'

'Yes,' she replied anxiously. 'I think he'd taken his anger about me leaving him out on her.' Tears finally flowed freely from Sasha. 'And when I told her the truth, she barely said a word. She just stood there looking so…defeated…so scarily passive, as if she knew all the time.' Shaking her head in disbelief, Sasha finally looked Fiona directly in the eyes. 'I don't understand that. I don't understand it at all,' she sobbed quietly. 'Why she wasn't angry at me. Why didn't she yell at me, or say something? Anything.'

'Maybe she knew he'd done it before. He could have been a serial...prick. In fact, he sounds like a first-class prick.'

'She should have been angry, though. She deserved to be.'

'Absolutely, she did. But not at you. It wasn't your fault.' Fiona rallied toward Sasha pulling her into a warm hug. 'It wasn't your fault at all.'

'Well it was, really,' she wept. 'If I hadn't have got involved with him...'

'He would have simply found someone else.' Fiona interrupted. 'He was a cheat. He was a lying, controlling and abusive cheat. You didn't make him that way, Sash. That was all him. And she probably knew he cheated on her, or suspected it. Which is why she never snapped at you. She was used to it and too disempowered by her life with him. It sounds as if she lacked the strength or security to walk away. Maybe he threatened her. It sounds as if she was a very broken and disempowered woman.'

'She *was* broken. It was horrible. And her face – her beaten face still haunts me. But more so, it was the utterly sad and dead look in her eyes. I felt terrible,' Sasha said with despair. 'I still feel so bad.'

'For something that's not your fault?'

'He was so angry, Fee. At me.'

'Did you see him again at any point?'

'Just once,' Sasha said, beginning to shake uncontrollably. 'He must have waited outside my apartment. I had this terrible and uneasy feeling about him after I'd been to see his wife.' Finding it hard to express the words, she stopped speaking momentarily.

'Do you need some water or something, Sash?'

'No,' she exhaled heavily. 'I'd already decided to leave Los Angeles after I'd been to his house and seen what he was capable of. But I had to go back to my place and pack up my things. Silly me. Of course, he came after me. With a knife.'

'Good God. What happened?' Fiona asked, looking horrified.

'A couple of nights after all of that happened, I left the gym and drove home. It was nighttime. I parked the car and was approaching my apartment when he grabbed me from behind. He put the knife to my throat and said I needed to pay for what I'd done.'

'That's terrible!' Fiona gripped Sasha's hand, shocked.

Sasha nodded her head quietly. 'Then he threw me violently on the ground like a man possessed and...' She swallowed hard. 'He just kept saying I needed to pay. Over and over. I could see the knife in his hand and I thought I was done. Then some guy came up the street, thank God. He saw what was happening and ran shouting towards us.'

'Then what happened?'

'I guess Paul...'

'You mean, the prick?'

'Yes, well, I guess he saw the guy sprinting over to us. So he ran off, thank God. But before he did, he looked at me one more time with pure venom in his eyes and told me he'd hunt me down. He said *you'll pay for this, you little bitch!* Those were the last words I heard him say to me in person. I've always remembered them. And the look on his face,' she said quietly. 'He meant business. So after that I called a friend to help me, went home and packed. And that was it – I was pretty much straight out of Los Angeles.'

'You poor thing.' Fiona put her arm around Sasha to comfort her. 'What a lot to go through.'

'God knows what else he did in anger to his poor wife. That haunts me,' she sighed. 'And he left me some threatening abusive phone messages, saying he'd get me back…that I'd pay. I was petrified. He had the power, the money and probably the connections. So I left California, really fast. I jumped on a plane, went straight to an Ashram and dived into a yoga teacher training course that I'd been thinking about doing. Then I moved to London and began working as a yoga instructor…and changed my name.'

A flash of understanding crossed Fiona's face. 'So he couldn't find you.'

'Yes. And maybe so I couldn't find me either,' she reflected sadly. 'Because I felt so bad.'

'*You* felt bad?!' Jesus, Sash, you were young and naïve. That's not a crime. Him wielding a knife, threatening you, cheating on and beating up his wife…those are the crimes. That's the real disgrace.'

'Thanks, Fee,' she replied quietly, glancing down at the vibrant red rug covering the floor. I think I finally understand that now. I've been so lost these past years.'

'I bet. A lot of things about you make more sense to me now.'

'They do?'

'Of course. For starters, your reluctance to get involved with a man.' A troubled expression formed on Fiona's face as she glanced thoughtfully at Sasha. 'You realize…' she hesitated. 'It's really quite odd but…'

'What, Fee?'

'Well…you realize you've been dating someone in the banking profession. And he's given you black eyes. Weird. It's almost as if your guilt brought Lucas into your life and those bruises onto your face.'

Recognition and discomfort passed through Sasha at hearing the words. 'But Lucas didn't mean it, honestly. Maybe it was just my Karma.'

'Karma?' Fiona balked. 'Christ, Sash, would you let up on yourself. It wasn't Karma! If anything it was your damned wasted sense of guilt that manifested that.'

Sasha registered the insight in Fiona's words about the power of her guilt, but still the resignation settled in. 'It doesn't matter anymore, Fee, because Lucas has gone. He's gone.'

'Well, maybe that's for the best. I don't see him sitting here supporting you right now. And I did wonder how you got the black panda eyes tonight, albeit by running mascara. But it was him - again.' Fiona nudged her shoulder into Sasha's. 'So you better tell me what happened at the ball. And then *I just know* you're going to tell me where you spend your Saturday mornings,' she winked.

'I think we'll be needing a tea break before that.' Sasha sighed.

'In my case, I think you mean a *pee break.*' Fiona slowly stood up. 'Phew. Tea would be good, though. It's been a marathon thriller…worthy of an Oscar.'

Sasha smiled, feeling some weight already beginning to slide off her shoulders. 'Thank you for listening and being such an amazing friend.'

'It's just *stuff*, Sash,' Fiona said, shrugging. 'We all have it in our own ways. We all have our things to work through. And some have bigger, more painful things, and sometimes they're uglier than others. But we're all vulnerable.'

Sasha nodded in agreement. 'Yes, we are all vulnerable…and life can be a bit perfectly imperfect.'

'Sure can. I mean, look at me,' she continued, gesturing to her belly. 'This is *not* the picture perfect life I imagined for myself. Jesus, I barely *looked* at Dave and *bingo*…baby jackpot.

'I think you did a little more than just look at him.'

'Okay, I can't disagree with that. And I've given myself a really hard time over it. But should I still be punishing myself two or three or more years down the track after the event? Being miserable and filled with pointless guilt? What kind of a waste would that be?' Fiona added pointedly, extending her hands to Sasha and hauling her off the sofa.

'I get it,' Sasha sighed. 'It would be a huge waste. It's time in life when you could just be happy – choosing and creating happiness.' She placed her hand gently on Fiona's stomach. 'Besides, something tells me this is perfect.'

'You're probably right about that. Because you bloody yogis know everything, remember?' Fiona said with an apologetic look on her face. 'I'm really sorry I was rude about your yoga, Sash. Sometimes my mouth has a life of its own.'

'It's okay, Fee. Honestly, no apology needed at all. You're my best and most wonderful friend in the world. You've always been incredibly supportive. You make me laugh and I love you.'

'I love you, too,' Fiona responded instantly, giving her a big warm hug before drawing back with a serious expression. 'And I have to admit, I actually secretly admire how committed you are to your health and to…' her eyes glazed over with moisture, 'being a good and decent person. Because you really are, Sash. You have an amazing big heart. You care so much about people. And you inspire me.'

Sasha's eyes misted up. Fiona noticed and decided it was time to lighten things up. 'There is something important I need to mention, though.'

'Uh-huh,' Sasha nodded.

'You know this eight-limbed yellow brick road of yoga that you've been telling me about.' She suppressed a cheeky grin. 'I've a sneaking suspicion you're more than a tiny bit off track.'

Several seconds passed before they both erupted into laughter, chuckling heartily until they were interrupted by the sound of the front door opening.

'Christ, that's Dave back already. You haven't even spilled the dirt on the ball, yet!' Fiona exclaimed.

'And you don't even know my real name.'

'Oh God,' she waved a hand about nonchalantly as if it meant nothing. 'I was happy to wait for that.'

'Why?' Sasha asked, perplexed.

'Timing is everything, honey.'

'What on earth do you mean?' she said with surprise, finding it hard to believe the Fee she knew could be so relaxed about it all.

'Are you kidding me?!' Fiona finally exclaimed, grinning ear to ear as Dave wandered in with his hands full of paper bags and a deep-fried aroma trailing after him. 'I can't have an announcement as huge as that without a drumroll, now. Can I!

Chapter Twenty Seven

Despite Sasha's dignity stinging for several days after events at the ball, her spirits were slowly beginning to lift. Having never spoken about her past to anyone before, the talk with Fiona had been like the release of a gigantic weight from her shoulders. And although it was sad she hadn't heard from Lucas since he'd dramatically stormed off at the ball, she realized it was perhaps for the best. Their lives were poles apart.

Reflecting on the past couple of months as she parked her car and made her way into the club to teach, Sasha realized she felt more herself than she had in a long time. She'd even managed to hit the yoga mat for her own practice this morning – something that had well and truly slipped off the radar the last month or two.

Pushing on the familiar glass door and entering the gym, she had the strangest feeling that something was different about the place, but couldn't fathom what it was. Walking past a number of members milling about in reception she made her way into the locker room, changed quickly, and was just stuffing her sports bag into a locker when Danielle *Long-Legs-Blonde* arrived. It was odd, though, she was only carrying a handbag and wearing a smart navy dress and boots – not her usual sports gear. In fact, it seemed like she was paying a purely social visit. And surprisingly, it looked as if the person she was calling on, was Sasha.

'There you are,' Danielle smiled warmly as she approached. 'I saw online you were due to be teaching a class about now. You're just the person I was looking for.'

'Oh, really?' Sasha glanced around the near empty locker room, feeling suddenly nervous. Why was Danielle looking for her? The last time they'd spoken she had a black eye – several actually – and they hadn't connected well at all. In fact, it had been a weird conversation. But here she was, now bounding up to her like her new best buddy.

Strange.

Stopping short a meter from her, Danielle seemed surprisingly sincere. 'Yes. I really just wanted to apologize to you. Before I leave.'

'What?' Apologize, why?' Sasha replied confused.

'Well, the last time we spoke it was a bit…difficult between us.' Danielle's expression softened. 'Which was my fault entirely. I asked you some strange questions and put you on the spot. And I'm really so sorry if I made you feel uncomfortable.'

'Thank you. Yes, it was a little uncomfortable.' Sasha conceded quietly, relieved at the mutual honesty and the courage she felt to speak the truth.

'The thing is,' Danielle said, brushing a hand through her long loose blonde locks and looking very relaxed, 'I wasn't completely honest with you. But it was my job, you see.'

'I'm not sure what you mean,' Sasha replied puzzled.

'Well, I'm not who anyone here thinks I am.' Danielle considered her own words. 'At least, I wasn't,' she added.

It was the strangest thing hearing a person echo back similar words about their identity that only a few days prior she'd spoken herself. And here was Danielle saying it all so simply: so devoid of any guilt. *I lied about who I am.* Just like that.

'I'm sorry? I don't understand?' Sasha reacted with confusion.

Danielle chuckled, as easily as if identity fraud were an innocent carefree thing – as if she were a child who'd swiped a lollipop from a store counter without paying because she didn't know money was critical in the process. 'I'm actually a reporter, Sasha. I write a column for a magazine.'

'Oh, God,' Sasha blinked, completely taken aback.

'I've been doing a little *undercover investigation*, I guess you could say,' she explained.

'Undercover?'

'Yes. For *City Woman* magazine. Do you know it?'

'I do,' Sasha replied, recalling Fiona's private client, Diana Smithwood. And the whole bathroom debacle.

'I had an inside tip,' she paused. 'Actually, I was *instructed* to come here and write an article based on my research. Reaching into the large tan-colored handbag strung over her shoulder, she rifled around briefly before removing a rolled item and handing it to Sasha. 'Here. It's not even on the newsstands yet. A small gift for you.'

The smile was so open and sincere that Sasha couldn't believe she'd ever considered Danielle as being anyone other than a nice person. 'Thank you,' she replied, not knowing what else to say as she grasped onto the magazine.

'There are two copies. Diana asked if you could get one to her personal trainer, Fiona, thanks.' Danielle paused, a thoughtful expression forming on her face. 'She said it was important to tell her *the sisterhood is alive and well, and we're looking out for each other.*'

Curious, Sasha began slowly unrolling the magazine bundle.

'It's my first full cover piece,' she added, beaming with pride. 'I think it's an important story to share. I hope it helps.'

Staring down at the cover image and main article title, the penny began to fully drop for Sasha.

Danielle gently patted her on the shoulder. 'In fact, I believe it already has.'

'Oh, my God,' Sasha whispered, staring at the front of the magazine in shock.

'I have to dash now, sorry. Another deadline to make,' she said moving purposefully towards the door.

'Thank you, Danielle.'

'It's Jill,' she said, looking back over her shoulder. 'My real name is Jill.'

'Jill.' Sasha smiled, nodding her head in acknowledgment. 'Thank you.'

'You're welcome. Oh, and by the way,' she added, pulling on the door handle, 'I hope I didn't get in the way of you and Rodrigo. He really likes you, you know. It's quite obvious.'

Sasha flinched inwardly.

'He's not just a pretty face – he's a very nice man. You should give him a shot,' Jill winked as the door closed softly behind her.

For several moments Sasha barely moved, before eventually seating herself on a locker bench. Tentatively opening the magazine to the page of the cover article, she began to read.

Ten minutes later, having completely finished the article, she quietly located her phone and dialed her most popular number.

'Fee,' she announced calmly at hearing her best friend's voice, 'I hope you're sitting down. You're not going to believe what I have to tell you.'

***

Sasha was still in partial shock as she left the locker room, clutching the magazine in her hand. Sometimes when bad things were in writing they could be seen warts and all and as plain as mud. They became what they truly were: a dirty coating covering an unclean truth that only a full beam of light could penetrate and wash. A determined and clever reporter by the name of Jill had been that beam of light.

Glancing across the reception area on her way to teach her class, Sasha spied the wide-open door to *Sleazy Ian's* den and strolled toward it. The blinds on his window, normally always tightly shut, were now partially open. Behind them she could make out someone moving about in his chair. Nearing the office entrance, she was overcome with curiosity and quietly peered in.

There, hunched over in the chair, rummaging around in the desk drawer was another man – clearly not Ian. It took only two seconds to work out who he was. She could tell because of the size of his shoulders, the fit of his t-shirt, and those incredibly strong looking biceps.

'Rodrigo?'

At the sound of her voice, he sat up with a start, clearly interrupted from an intense search for something. 'What are you doing?' she added.

'Sasha.' He stared at her with surprise. 'I'm looking for the operations manual.'

'No Ian?'

'No,' he said, frowning. 'Ian was forcibly removed from the premises this morning by the franchise owners…and the police. Deserved treatment.'

'Because of this, I expect,' she held up the publication.

'You have a copy?' he gestured toward the magazine, standing up and moving around the desk toward her.

'Danielle…or rather, Jill, gave it to me.'

A couple steps more and Rodrigo was in front of her. 'May I?'

'Of course,' she replied, handing over the magazine. 'You knew about this?'

'Only after they took Ian away. Jill phoned to cancel Danielle's lesson,' he smiled. 'And then she told me her true identity and name. She said she'd been on a *special assignment* here and had written an article due for release today.' He tapped knowingly on the front page that contained a sneakily taken picture of Ian, crouched down in his work uniform near reception, staring up at a woman's backside and looking very predatory.

How Safe Are Our Gyms? Sleazy Manager Prays Upon Members and Staff, the article said.

'Accurately blunt heading,' added Rodrigo with narrowing eyes. 'He's lucky I didn't see this before he was thrown out. It would have been more than the article title that was punchy.'

'I'm mortified he had a hidden camera in the ladies locker room. That was a huge shock to me,' Sasha responded.

Rodrigo shook his head in disgust. 'Unfortunately, it's probably a blessing. Because of that he'll be criminally convicted and go to prison. So it will keep women safe from him, at least for a while.'

'Did you have any idea what he was like?' She asked.

'Just a little. He had a strange kind of vibe. But I wasn't aware of the extent of his behavior and I wasn't in a position to do much about it.' An angry expression formed on his face as he looked up from the magazine and scrutinized her face with concern. 'I hope he didn't lay a finger on you?'

She shook her head, surprised by his protective words. 'No. Fiona was one of his main targets. And obsessions. With me it was just the general undressing with his eyes…and I used the changing rooms, of course.' She cringed at the thought.

'I'm sorry,' he said softly.

'So am I,' she replied as their eyes met briefly. But it was as if they were both apologizing about something else. Sasha broke contact between them first. 'I have my class to teach. I better go.'

'Right. Yes. You should have this back.'

'No, you keep it.' Without thinking she placed her hand over his, pressing the magazine more firmly into his grasp, but was jolted by the sensation of his skin. 'I've read it and once is enough,' she said, feeling embarrassed by their physical contact and hastily removing her hand.

'So I'll see you at the local for drinks on Friday evening?'

'Drinks?'

'Yes, my…'

'Oh, God.' Sasha interrupted. 'Your leaving drinks. Of course, I'd almost forgotten.' Sadness tugged at her heart. She really wished the farewell drinks weren't happening and that he hadn't mentioned them. For some reason the thought of his departure from the gym and her life made her feel strangely lonely. And did she really need more endings at the moment. First, Lucas had rapidly exited her life; then Fiona would be moving on as a busy mother; and now Rodrigo was heading back to Brazil. But she was just feeling sorry for herself – a moment of weakness. Ignoring the feeling, she switched on a bright face. 'Definitely. I'd love to pop in.

'Good,' he smiled warmly. 'Sasha,' Rodrigo added, noticing she was about to disappear out the door.

'Yes?' She nervously glanced back at him.

'I never asked, but,' he appeared uncomfortable for a number of seconds, 'how was the ball?'

'Oh,' she waved a hand dismissively, fighting the rush of bad memories, 'a complete disaster, actually.' Momentarily, her face dropped its façade and the briefest flicker of sadness washed over her. 'I really have to dash. Goodbye, Rodrigo.'

'I'll see you later,' he said, perplexed by her response.

But Sasha had already disappeared at haste.

***

It was both a great surprise and a disturbing one to hear the voice message left by Evangeline that day. Having taught her yoga class, Sasha quickly changed and left the club, offering little more than a cursory glance at Ian's former office in her hasty exit out the door.

On her drive to the private hospital, she contemplated the stunning news about Melody Trenton – the model had collapsed from a drug overdose in the ladies toilets at the Earth Save Charity Ball. Upon reflection, Sasha realized the incident must have occurred after their horrid encounter, the thought of which caused an odd mix of hurt and guilt to flood through her. It didn't make a lot of sense that she'd go and see the one person who'd treated her so maliciously, yet she still felt genuine concern and a strange compulsion to do so.

Having stopped in at a florist's to collect some colorful spring flowers she parked her car at the hospital and made her way, somewhat worriedly, into the building.

At reception, she was told the location of Melody's room and headed straight up to the second floor. Any hospital she'd previously been in always had a cool clinical feel, but of course, Melody was comfortably ensconced in a private facility, one both inviting and pleasing to the eye.

The door to the private room was closed. Although, upon peering in through a slim glass panel, Sasha could see Melody was alone and asleep in bed with her nose heavily bandaged and several tubes attached to her body. With a number of days having passed since the ball, she was thankfully well out of the critical condition she'd arrived in. Still, a wave of compassion arose in Sasha at the sight of the slim and fragile woman lying in such a vulnerable state and she became filled with empathy for Melody's current plight.

Pushing on the door and quietly entering the room, Sasha approached the bed, squeezing the bouquet of flowers onto the bedside table beside several other vases filled with long-stemmed roses and leafy fronds.

Melody looked skeletal. At the ball she'd looked extremely slim, but now she was positively emaciated. Her long bony arm lay stretched out on the bed beside her, much like long sticks of wood placed by charring embers of a fire. Sasha observed her pale facial skin and quiet breathing as she reached down and gently touched Melody's hand. However, to her surprise, the young woman's eyelids flickered open immediately, causing her to reel backwards with a start.

'Sasha?' Melody said, finally becoming cognizant of who was beside her.

'I'm sorry. I thought you were asleep.'

'Just resting.' She licked her dry lips and appraised Sasha momentarily, her expression devoid of warmth. 'You're the last person I expected to see here.'

Sasha wasn't entirely sure how to respond so she simply patted Melody's hand gently. 'How are you feeling?' she finally added.

'Quite hideous,' Melody answered bluntly, rolling her head away and gazing absently toward the window.

'Your nose is very bandaged. Does it hurt a lot?'

'I lost the septum,' she responded matter-of-fact, but with a subdued voice. 'And probably a lot of modeling contracts along with it.'

'I'm really sorry.'

Rolling her head back, Melody's worn and glassy blue eyes gazed doubtfully at her. 'Are you?'

'Yes, of course. It's terrible seeing you this way.'

'I don't deserve that, Sasha. Least of all from you,' she said coolly.

'Of course you do,' she responded gently, her feet shuffling awkwardly on the super clean floor.

Tears appeared fleetingly in Melody's eyes but she forcibly blinked them back. 'I'm the one who should be sorry.' She turned her head back toward the safety of the tinted window and stared at the dull skies outside.

Sasha squeezed Melody's thin and veined looking hand in lieu of a verbal response.

'Here you are visiting me…after how I treated you,' Melody continued. 'It's no wonder he's so taken with you,' she added with a hint of bitterness.

Taking a deep breath, Sasha remained silent, despite the temptation to add *was taken with me.*

'I was jealous.' Melody paused, considering the past and dropping her guard with a rare and spectacular display of honesty. 'I kept thinking, how could someone like that be so interested in someone like you.'

Flinching at signs of the old and rude Melody, Sasha dropped her gaze to the floor.

'He's such a charming and generous man, Lucas. Treated me so well – even if it was brief. We kept in touch a little.' She thought for a moment. 'Or rather, I did. I thought how perfect it all could be, if I just got to spend more time with him. And I waited patiently. But then you came along.' Melody rolled her head back, facing Sasha with an expression of restrained frustration. 'And what an unbelievable stroke of chance you mentioned his name at my lesson that day.' A hint of glee flickered across her damaged face. 'I figured you'd have something to hide...and I suppose I wanted you to have something to hide. So I hired a private investigator to find out more about you...this mysterious Californian yoga instructor. And he followed you – everywhere.'

Feeling abruptly uneasy, Sasha quietly removed her hand. 'I should go.'

'No, don't.' Melody grabbed at her hand with a strange and sudden kind of desperation, gesturing toward the visitor's chair beside her. 'Please,' she implored.

After some hesitation, Sasha finally sat down.

Swallowing, Melody licked her cracked dry lips. 'The investigator revealed to me your affair with the banker.'

Startled at the blunt delivery, Sasha attempted to explain. 'I didn't know...'

'I know,' she interrupted. 'You didn't know he was married with children.'

She nodded her head solemnly in response.

Melody carefully considered the words she was about to say. 'You probably didn't know he was also a bigamist.'

'What?' Sasha stared at her in shock.

'Yes. He had a second secret wife and child. Quite a pig of a man,' Melody conceded. 'But thankfully, he was prosecuted for some kind of serious banking fraud several years ago and put away for a while,' she stared at Sasha's paling complexion. 'Which I gather you also knew nothing about?'

'No.' Sasha replied quietly.

'So you didn't wreck a marriage. Although,' a tiny smile escaped Melody's parched lips, 'you may just have wrecked two. But in this case, even I have to say *well done*.' She paused, a begrudging note creeping into her voice. 'I'm sorry I lied, Sasha. I'm sorry I twisted the truth. You didn't deserve the hurt and embarrassment.'

The unexpected apology caused Sasha's heart to soften as she considered all the new information and the situation. 'You know, in a funny sort of way, Melody, I'm actually quite grateful for what's happened. I've been carrying a load of guilt about that experience...for years. I'd have never known the truth if this,' she gestured between them with a flick of her hand, 'hadn't happened.'

'Is that why you changed your name?'

'Yes. It is,' Sasha reluctantly admitted, squirming inwardly at her great deception. 'He was very threatening toward me. And I was afraid.'

'Well, you kind of blew your cover with your little Saturday morning secret. But I'm glad you know the truth now.' Melody glanced down quietly at the starched white cotton sheets, her face suddenly appearing sad and very tired.

'Why don't you get some more rest. You must be quite exhausted.' Sasha stood up, preparing to go. 'I brought you some flowers.' She indicated to the pretty bouquet.

'That was kind of you.' Melody's eyes welled up as she clung to a shred of pride. 'Particularly when I acted like a crazy person. You must think me silly.'

'No, I don't.' Sasha responded decisively. 'I made mistakes when I was your age, Melody. You know this now. So who am I to judge? What kind of person would that make me?'

Melody shrugged. 'I guess all that cocaine didn't help much,' she admitted, opening up a fraction. 'But, you see, after spending time with Lucas I became a little obsessed with him. It's no excuse. I was just lonely. I am lonely…a lot. People must look at me and think I have this great life gallivanting around the globe doing modeling shoots. And in many ways it has its good points, but in truth, I'm so tired of it all.' She sighed heavily. 'I'm just so tired.' She rolled her head towards the window once more. 'Sometimes I feel like the loneliest person on the planet.'

Sasha nodded in understanding.

'I hope you can forgive me,' Melody said quietly.

'Of course I can.'

A long silence filled the air. 'I'm not sure I deserve it after the way I've treated you,' she finally said, turning her head back and exposing signs of genuine remorse in the recesses of her jaded cornflower blue eyes.

The young woman's life was now in quite a mess. Sasha looked at her with sadness, but forced a bright smile. 'Of course I forgive you. The main thing is that you're okay. And hey, there are always new beginnings,' she said reflectively. 'I really should leave you to rest,' she added, gesturing toward the door and noticing Melody affirm with a nod.

After taking a few steps to leave, however, Sasha stopped and turned back. 'Melody?'

'Yes?'

'Did the private investigator ever say what happened to his wife? I mean the wife who lived in the Hollywood area?'

'Yes, he did.' Melody finally smiled, revealing dazzling white teeth that dominated her gaunt and sunken face. 'She left him, quite a few years ago, after lodging a domestic abuse complaint and putting a restraining order on him. That was well before his fraud charges came to light. Then she remarried a year ago – to a heart surgeon, if I recall.'

'That's great news,' Sasha replied, relief flooding

through her. 'It sounds as if she got the right man for the job.'

'Yes, it certainly had to be an improvement.'

'It did. Well…goodbye Melody,' she added, moving to the door.

'Thank you for visiting me, Sasha.'

She heard Melody's words but couldn't fully absorb them. Merely tipping her head in response, Sasha left the hospital room, trudging down the immaculate corridor, deep in thought and filled with overwhelming emotions.

By the time she'd reached the car park, the first tears were streaming down Sasha's face. They flowed readily and didn't stop until she'd made it all the way home.

Chapter Twenty Eight

'The personal virtues and observances of the first few limbs of yoga are followed by the *mental practices* of the fifth, sixth and seventh limbs.' Jimmy was summarizing. 'But ultimately, all of these are designed to culminate in the eighth limb – Samadhi. The union of the busy thinking mind with its deepest most silent self: the unified field of consciousness.' His face beamed.

Holly was already sitting upright and alert, hanging off his every word with complete fascination.

'In life, day after day, you will meet circumstances that are outside your sphere of control, or that don't meet your expectations. When your happiness is determined by the world around you, it will deteriorate time and time again.' He paused. 'I'm certain that over the years each and every one of you has felt helplessness about this.'

Many heads nodded.

'What can one do to cope with the myriad triggers to your emotional world in any one day: the moods and emotions of others around you, and events outside of your control?'

Holly considered the scenario. *Run away and hide*.

'Separate yourself from the rest of humanity?' Jimmy suggested, searching the sea of heads on the yoga platform.

Thank God. We finally agree about something. My thoughts entirely.

'Unless you wish to live like a monk in the mountains, this really isn't possible.'

Holly's heart sank.

'And why would you, when we're all One. There is no separation,' he added.

You can only truly progress in yourself as you grow in the understanding and consciousness that there is a common unity of all things – a unified reality that lies behind and within everything,' he said, waving his hand about for good measure. 'This eternal field is where the bliss consciousness of Samadhi is found and experienced.'

Sounds amazing, Holly thought.

'You see, what you're seeking most is *inner peace* - to no longer be reactive to daily events and challenges; to avoid being pulled into stories and dramas around you; to be your Self, your true Self. Your most evolved and joyous *You*. And to be at one with the unified field of reality...with All That Is. This is *Moksha*, or freedom. Freedom from the bindings of everyday life.' Jimmy's smile was dazzling. 'This is bliss.'

Wow. Holly wanted whatever he was on.

'Bliss consciousness is the highest level that yoga is intended to take you to - Samadhi.'

Okay, then that's where I'm headed. Samadhi.

'So is your thinking mind – the small self – ready to experience union with cosmic intelligence – the big self?

Yes. Holly thought. Although in truth, she wasn't one hundred percent certain. After all, the big self did sound awfully big, if it was indeed Cosmic Intelligence.

Couldn't she get lost in, or absorbed by that? And what would that make her as a person? If she opened herself to that, would she still actually exist as her own separate self? Or would she be just become some blur of light and energy merging with everything and then have no personality?

'When you are in *Samadhi,* the intensity of happiness and the bliss of this state eliminates any sadness. No darkness or sorrow can enter bliss consciousness.'

Okay, cool your britches, sister. Holly coached her now nervous self. *It's just a state of consciousness - a state of Being. And from what I'm hearing I can't be negatively affected in this state. So that's my pathway; that's where I'm headed...Samadhi.*

Jimmy looked across the platform at her with a beaming face full of joy.

Bliss - a life of happiness where I'm deeply connected with All That Is. Where I can be free in every moment, she thought, captivated by his radiant smile.

'To cultivate this topmost and eighth yoga limb is the greatest nourishment for the whole tree of yoga,' he said. 'Samadhi is both the end and the beginning, and the most essential ingredient of a truly blissful yoga path.'

I wonder if it's really possible, though? Her mind responded. No sooner had she experienced excitement, her head had begun its doubt-filled chatter. *It does sound like a bit of a dream...not something the average human could achieve...*

'If you're wondering if you can attain this blissful state,' Jimmy said, interrupting her disbelieving thoughts as he stared beyond the surface of her eyes and deep into her very soul. 'You can. Of course you can. Anyone can.'

A ripple of relief spread throughout her like a soothing breeze on the hottest day.

Jimmy chuckled. 'Having said all of that, however, I can only add that Samadhi is almost impossible to describe in any meaningful way. You will simply have to experience it for yourself,' he said, his eyeballs glued to Holly's. 'After all,' he added, 'it's what you really came here for, isn't it?'

***

It was Friday.

Sasha sat on her sofa staring out at the small patch of grass that was her back yard and noticing the light outside just beginning to dim into a smoky shade of gray. She should have showered and been ready by now to go to the bar for Rodrigo's farewell drinks. Instead, she was glued to a suede-covered cushion thinking about Amy.

For some reason she hadn't been able to face her favorite client's lesson this week. News of her fraudulent identity, via Lucas, would have likely reached the happy Hampstead home upon return from their holiday. Sasha was convinced of this – or deeply paranoid. Despite her sensing Amy would forgive her, or at least try to understand, she'd left a message cancelling the lesson under the guise of sickness...the *litany of lies* type of sickness. Of course, that was actually another lie, too. Recently they'd flowed from her mouth as thick and fast as the thundering Niagara Falls. But it was time to change all that now.

How had she expected her life to move in any favorable direction when it was so utterly peppered with falsehood? All these years of yoga practice and endeavoring to follow truth and the virtues and observances of the eight limbs and yet she'd turned out to be some kind of spiritual and human sham. So she simply wasn't able to be in the presence of Amy's goodness whilst acting like her polar opposite. Besides, Amy was bound to ask about Lucas and the ball, and Sasha couldn't bear to relive the whole embarrassing event.

At least her horrid, abusive and philandering ex, was now safely tucked away in a Californian prison and his poor ex-wife happily remarried and no longer at the mercy of his beatings. Sasha didn't have to live with all that terrible guilt and fear. She didn't have to feel like she had to hide anymore. She was free. If only she felt that way, though: if only that awareness was nestled firmly inside her.

It was a tough realization to discover that a cage, however large or small, did represent some form of safety. And all of a sudden, Sasha felt the distinct discomfort of being outside of hers. Something was clearly missing in her path to feel so attached to a life so incubated and imprisoned - something essential. Or was she was missing it?

The shrill tone of the doorbell rescued her from her mental mire, but it was certainly odd to hear the sound on a Friday night.

Lately, any night, she reminded herself.

Still dressed in her yoga gear from the day of work, Sasha unfolded her lotus positioned legs and wandered to the door, ensuring the security chain remained on as she slowly opened a two-inch gap and peered beyond it.

'Lucas?' He was the last person she expected to see. Particularly as all her time spent with him had been at *his* house – not here at her place.

'Hi, Sasha.' He peered through the small opening in the door as the moments passed in silence. 'Do you think you could..,' he gestured toward the chain.

'Oh, of course,' she said, finally snapping out of her trance.

Although dressed in a formal suit, Lucas appeared more relaxed to her than she'd ever seen him. He was lighter somehow, as if a weight had lifted from him. There was even a soft smile on his face. And was that kindness in his eyes? Removing the chain, she drew the door open fully, catching a glimpse of his car parked across the road and his driver installed behind the wheel.

'I'm sorry it's taken me so long to come see you,' he said, the blue of his eyes peering intently into hers, 'I owe you a great apology.'

She listened quietly.

'I treated you appallingly at the ball. And I'm deeply sorry for that and any hurt I caused you.'

'Thank you,' she said, admitting the apology was welcome.

'You didn't deserve that. At all,' he said softly, reaching out and touching her shoulder. 'In fact, you should be slamming the door in my face...rather dramatically...but I know that's not your style, or nature. I should have ignored Melody.'

'Except the bit about my name,' she said quietly.

'I know,' he replied.

'You know? What?'

'About your past.'

'What do you know?'

'Well, Melody phoned me yesterday. She said you'd visited her in hospital after her...'

'Drug overdose?'

'Yes.'

'And you decided to listen to Melody again before talking with me?' Sasha's frustration was evident.

Lucas appeared momentarily troubled and removed his hand from her shoulder. 'At first I didn't want to speak to her. But she insisted she had to tell me the truth …about everything.' He shuffled his feet a little awkwardly, leaving Sasha with the intuition that Melody had also revealed her feelings for him. 'I'm sorry. I know it's *her* version of *your* truth, but she did seem remarkably sincere. I think it was her way of making amends to you somehow…as I also wish to do.' He gently tilted her chin so her lowered eyes would look at him. 'I'm sorry for all the things you've been through, Sasha. What happened to you - in California - was wrong. And I'm very sure it wasn't your fault. Any of it.'

'It wasn't,' she responded firmly, finally acknowledging that was the truth.

'I never asked you much about your past: about you. I've been really quite self-absorbed.' Lucas lowered his hand fully, allowing his arm to fall back by his side. 'You know, as I left the ball - somewhat like a petulant child,' he added, 'I ran straight into my father at the entrance.'

'Oh, really?'

'Yes. But I kept walking, of course.' He smiled. 'Or rather, striding fiercely. But still he followed me. All the way out to the street, I might add. I've never seen him act so determined like that with me before.'

Sasha finally smiled at the sight of his face lighting up.

'By the time he caught up with me he was quite…' Lucas paused to reflect.

'Out of breath?' She offered.

A small smile appeared on his face. 'Well, he was passionate. Something I've seldom seen in him before. I think that's part of the reason I dreaded taking up the family mantle – becoming the walking dead. But when I saw him like that the other night. So…alive, I did something I haven't done well in my past. I listened. I

listened to what he had to say. And what he had to say
surprised me greatly.'

'In a good way?'

'Yes. Very much. You know, I never spoke to my
family at all after what happened with Catherine. I
figured they'd just hear things through the great gossip
grapevine and make their own assumptions. And I
didn't really care what those were – at least, that's what
I told myself. But you see, my father figured out the real
truth. Not because he investigated the gossip, but
because he knew his son. It turns out he trusted me more
than I gave him credit for.'

Sasha nodded in quiet understanding.

'He's a proud man. One of the reasons why he never
communicated well.' Lucas paused. 'Proud and
stubborn. And I think there's a lot more of him in me
than I've ever cared to admit.'

'It seems that as children we often find that out
eventually,' she added.

'You think you know someone. And then,' he
smiled, 'you can be pleasantly surprised.' A look of
peace rested in his eyes. 'He really just wants his son
back.'

'That's wonderful, Lucas.'

'Yes it is.' He paused, considering his words. 'Sasha,
there's something I need to tell you.'

She could already feel what was coming. 'You're
going home, aren't you? Returning to the land. You're
going to take the title and responsibilities of Lord
someday.'

'Yes,' he responded softly, gazing into her eyes.

Nodding quietly, a little sadness moved through her
chest as she felt the reality of the situation. 'It's the right
thing to do,' she finally replied, feeling the peace he'd
made with himself. 'And I think the best for you, too.'

'Well,' he shrugged, 'I'm not sure I'll be any good at

it. But perhaps I can *modernize* things a little. Bring yoga into the family fold. Maybe the eight limbs?' He smiled, searching her face hopefully.

Sasha remembered the moment they'd met on his rain-soaked front door and all the special times and memories they'd shared, affectionately recalling their months together, 'You know I can't,' she managed a half smile.

Reaching toward her, Lucas wiped the stray tear away that had begun to slide down her cheek. He lowered his head. 'I had a feeling you might say that. It's not the life for a beautiful free creature like you, is it,' he said sadly.

Blinking back any further tears, she reached out and took hold of his hand. 'You will make a great Lord, someday.'

'Thank you,' he smiled. 'I hope a more *flexible* one, thanks to you.'

Momentarily, their eyes exchanged a look of deep knowing about the journey they'd traveled together.

'I mean it, Sasha. I can't thank you enough,' he said. 'I was so lost. I have no idea how I would've ever dug myself out of that vast hole if you hadn't come into my life. You saved me.'

'No,' she shook her head. 'You saved yourself.'

'Oh, God, I simply will not accept that.' He glanced up at the sky with mock despair before fixing his powder blue eyes back upon her. 'Perhaps it's time you begin to accept credit where credit is due, Sasha. Accept appreciation. And support. Let people in. Take some of your own wise advice, I might add.'

She shrugged, as if brushing away his words.

'Like Amy, for example. I know you missed her lesson this week.'

Sasha's eyes held the question as she searched his face.'

'I didn't tell her...everything. But you can. And I know she'll understand. She cares about you greatly.'

'She's such a good person...'

'So are you.' He stared into her eyes with a serious expression. 'She's worried about you, Sasha. So am I,' he added.

'I'm fine, really.'

'Well *fine* is not good enough. Because I happen to know you're amazing. Here,' he said, reaching inside his jacket, removing an envelope and handing it to her.'

'What's this? She responded, taken aback. 'I can't accept...'

'It's not a wad of cash, if that's what you're thinking.' He chuckled. 'I'm not paying you for *services*, my darling. It's a gift.' His hand closed over hers as she clutched the envelope. 'And you deserve it. It's the least I can do. You helped give me my life back. Let me do something in return for you.'

Puzzled, she watched him reach down by the wall outside the door.

'Here,' he said, picking up a large rectangular and weighty looking package and moving it inside her apartment as she stepped out of the way. 'For you, with love and deep gratitude.' For a long moment he looked at her tenderly before leaning in, kissing and holding her close one more time. 'Beauty deserves beauty,' he whispered in her ear.

From across the road his driver sounded the car horn. Drawing away, he sighed, rolling his eyes. 'Have to go. Duty calls, already.' Touching the side of her cheek, he added softly. 'Keep in touch.'

'I will, Lord Huntington,' she smiled.

'Not yet,' he winked, before striding purposefully back across the road. Reaching the car, he turned and waved, his hand lingering in the air briefly before he disappeared into the back seat and the vehicle sped off.

Sasha glanced down at the large package and frowned. Whatever could it be? Tearing an end of the envelope open she carefully removed the paper contents inside. On top of a formal looking document, a small note was attached.

Dear Sasha

I can't apologize enough for the hurt I've caused you.

Whatever choices you make in life, know that I will always care about you.

Every now and then, one stumbles upon a miracle in their life. You have been that for me. Thank you for the peace you have brought to me. There is no price a person can pay for this.

I thank you, eternally.

With love, Lucas

As Sasha slowly lifted the note, she peered underneath at the legal document attached behind and scanned the words with confusion. Gasping, she stared down at the package, then back at the letter.

'Oh, my God.'

There in her hands, with her name imprinted clearly upon it, lay the title of ownership to the expert copy of the *Le Mont Sainte-Victoire vu des Lauves* painting that had hung in Lucas's bedroom...including its sizeable valuation. Sasha's eyes grew large in her head.

Unbelievable.

Shutting the door at haste and moving quickly to her mobile, she phoned Lucas, to no avail. He didn't pick up.

For several minutes she paced nervously, finally freezing on the spot in the center of her living area. Thinking carefully, it became very clear to her what to do in that moment...and exactly where she would extend a great portion of Lucas's grand generosity.

***

By the time she sat on her cushion, a deep stillness had already arisen within Sasha. She sensed something new was before her. Having experienced so many challenges with meditation for so many years, she unexpectedly felt differently about it now, as if a doorway she hadn't seen before was finally within her reach. There was a deep feeling on some level that an important pathway was now clear.

How would it be without any scary monsters in her mental closet leaping out at her?

As Sasha began her breathing technique and dropped into a deeper state of awareness, her mind became awash with multiple streams of surface thought, like birds dive bombing the ocean surface for food. But, eventually, as the deluge of thought began to dissolve into a gentle drizzle, her body settled and she descended steadily into a space of peace. It was usually at this point her trial would begin - a blast of bitter words leaping from the shadows and jolting her from serenity. But this time none of those dark fears from her past appeared. This time she found herself diving even deeper as a bright light began to permeate everything. The light was so pervasive she began to find it difficult to discern herself as separate. She was part of it; suspended light particles, hovering then moving. Dancing. Energetically swirling like a ballerina right out of her apartment, her awareness flew up into the air, moving over rooftops and flying like a bird, higher and higher.

London was beneath her now, the buildings becoming smaller and smaller like tiny speckled dots as she moved higher and faster through air and space. Suddenly the entire planet was below her, the blue-green majesty of beautiful Earth. There was nothing but exhilaration and delight all around and throughout her. What a miracle: what a divine miracle the Earth was: a place with so much grace and life, beauty and color. She could see and feel it all now – every pulsating incredible heartbeat of this bountiful radiant planet. There was so much life on Earth; so much love. And now she was one with it all. If she were just a body she would have simply burst with the awareness. She was everywhere. She was everything.

Rocketing further into space, whilst at the same time feeling as if she were drifting like a feather, Sasha began to explore the galaxies and stars far beyond Earth. Time had disappeared entirely. There was nothing but vastness; incredible expanding and ever-evolving creativity, life...and love. Love infused everything. It was behind and within all things. As was she - her immortal soul.

There is no place I am not.

It was as if her awareness had whispered the words in unison with the universe, the galaxies, the suns and the moons. Everywhere...she was everywhere. She was the ecstasy of all things.

There is no place I am not. The whisper echoed again, through all eternity.

And then whoosh, the whisper became her breath; and the steady mesmerizing beat of her own heart, returning her serenely to her body.

Sasha sat for minutes, maybe hours, as the dark of night descended all around her, just listening to the perfection of her every precious breath.

Her face beamed with a joy she'd never known before and she was filled with utter bliss. She had finally come home, to her truest self, to her deepest knowing.

She had arrived at the eighth limb. And discovered her very own Samadhi, at last.

***

The next day, as Sasha watched the remaining few women drop their rolled mats back into a storage box and amble slowly out of her Saturday morning yoga class at the Women's Refuge Center, she breathed a sigh of deep contentment. It felt as though all the darkness of her past had lifted completely and she was entirely free of it.

Had her positive action to assist other women to find peace and recovery from abuse contributed to that?

Perhaps, in some way.

She'd probably never know for sure, but there was a feeling it had certainly helped - not only in her own life but also in the ripple-on effect in the lives of others.

Feeling a deep sense of fulfillment inside, she glanced around at the tired looking venue and imagined the place modernized and upgraded, as a broad smile spread across her face.

Finally, she gathered her bag, checked everything was switched off and was giving the room a final scan when a familiar face appeared at the exit door.

'Rodrigo,' she said startled, staring at him with surprise and noticing the shadow of stubble on his face making him appear even more ruggedly attractive.

He gazed at her, a serious expression masking his face as he replied somewhat soberly. 'You didn't show for my leaving drinks last night.'

'No, I'm sorry,' she said with discomfort. 'Something came up.'

'Uh-huh,' he nodded quietly. 'Fee told me last night that I'd find you here today.'

'I see,' she shrugged, surrendering to the reality her dear friend was inclined to blab. 'So you've come to say goodbye, I guess.' She toyed nervously with the strap of the bag slung over her shoulder.

'Actually, I just wanted to check out where you mysteriously spend your Saturday mornings,' he answered, the faintest of smiles lighting up his face.

'Oh,' she replied, surprised and confused.

Taking a few steps inside the door, he moved within meters of her, causing her skin to flush and her heart to beat faster.

'I didn't have leaving drinks last night.'

'Oh?' she said taken aback. 'Really?'

'No. I've been offered Ian's job, so I thought I'd stick around for a while.'

For some reason his words caused a surge of great relief and happiness to flood through her. 'Wow. That's good,' she said, hiding the extent of her enthusiasm.

'Yes,' he finally smiled. 'So the drinks turned out to be celebratory ones in the end.'

'I bet. I'm sorry I missed them. I gather Fee made it okay?'

'Yes, she was glowing. And it's the most contented I've ever seen her drinking water.'

Sasha chuckled, relaxing as she did so.

Rodrigo searched her eyes for a number of seconds before breaking contact and glancing around the old room. 'So, this is what you've been up to. Teaching women at the refuge, yoga. That must be rewarding for you?'

'Yes, it's wonderful,' she smiled at his nice understanding.

'It's really high time I checked out what yoga is all about. So many people have raved to me about how good it makes them feel. I've spent too much time focusing on the weights.' He tapped one of his sizeable biceps, once again trapped inside a super fitted t-shirt that was a military shade of green. There was a screen print of something emblazoned upon it, but she didn't want to stare at his broad muscular chest. That would just be rude.

'I guess you'll just have to try a class sometime. 'Have you ever?'

'No.' He smiled. 'But I *have* read the Bhagavad Gita.'

'Really?' she replied, shock evident.

'Yes. I heard of it's connection with yoga.'

'Right,' she smiled. 'Wow. I can't believe you read that. When?'

'Oh, I've whizzed through it over the past month or so,' he replied matter of fact. 'I thought a bit of inside knowledge might help me with a certain intriguing yoga instructor.'

Freezing inwardly, Sasha realized the pointed remark was about her and was suddenly struck by shyness.

'But it was odd,' he continued.

'What was?'

'There were no women involved. And it was all set on a battlefield. So I didn't really get it.' He grinned, shaking his head good-naturedly.

She felt so light around him. His warmth was infectious. Glancing down at the floor, she smiled.

'I thought it might be a romantic love story...since so many women do yoga.'

'But it is a love story,' she responded.

Rodrigo shook his head. 'I didn't get that. That dude...Arjuna...I mean, hell of a journey to take and not meet the love of his life.'

'Yes, but he did, in some form.'

He chuckled. 'I'm telling you, there were no women in that book.'

Sasha was about to explain what she meant when Rodrigo swiftly held up his hand to stop her. 'Wait. Please,' he said, his expression changing to one of seriousness. 'There was a lot of deep wisdom and truth in the book. And I kind of get it. Maybe not all of it, but

I think I get it in essence.'

'That's wonderful.'

He hesitated momentarily. 'Yes it is. I get that the journey we're all on is ultimately a spiritual one. That the deepest love we can ever hope to find is a spiritual love. A divine love…and guidance.' His voice softened. 'And that's what you're doing, isn't it. Searching for that. It's what you've been looking for.'

Moisture formed in the back of her eyes. It was the most unexpected thing he could have said. Taking another step toward her, he reached out and gently took hold of her hand. Sasha's legs shook slightly. She bit her lip and shuffled nervously. Her mouth went to move but no words came out.

'But it's not in a book, is it,' he added. 'You could read a million. You could study every sacred text, religion, philosophy and ideology. But I doubt you'll find it there. Because it doesn't exist in knowledge alone.' Guiding her hand, he placed it softly onto his snugly fitted t-shirt, splat onto his chest and the screen-printed picture, which she now recognized was a surfer riding a wave. 'It's right here.'

Riding the waves? She puzzled for a moment.

'In the human heart,' he continued. 'So your search is really all about *this*. It's about love.'

The moisture in her eyes was beginning to prickle. She seemed to have become a lot more prone to tears lately. Scanning a spot on the ground again, her gaze remained fixed there. It was too hard to look at him: into those vibrant green eyes, so open and feeling.

'It's about letting people in,' he continued. 'It's about being seen. Being vulnerable. Being known. Being loved and loving. Because *love is the greatest truth there is*. It's all that matters. And I don't know if that guy, Arjuna, or any kind of God would agree with me, but that's *my* version of spiritual love.' Lowering her hand, Rodrigo gently released it by her side and remained silent for the longest moment. 'I'm not sure if that's where you're at…' his voice softened.

Was it possible someone so…*manly*…could be so tender? It was unbelievably attractive.

'..but if it is, then I'd love to love you, Holly Devon.'

That was what he said. He said he'd *love to love her*. And then he lingered, waiting.

It was a risk, saying what he had. Rodrigo knew that. His honesty could win her, or it could scare her way the hell away from him. But she'd already been a distance too far and with someone else, so he had nothing to lose.

Yet she didn't respond. A long pregnant moment passed in silence. It spoke to him in a loud volume. He waited a few more uncomfortable seconds. 'Look, I'm going to take off,' he finally said, masking his great disappointment. 'I've got a football game I have to get to.'

It was just a few extra moments that he lingered. He waited for her to look up from the ground she seemed fixated upon. But she didn't move or make a sound.

Eventually, turning, Rodrigo walked slowly toward the exit and disappeared outside.

He said my name. He must have seen it on the Refuge board, or Fee told him… But he said my real name. That's who I am…I'm Holly. Holly Devon.

Her breath moved slowly through the back of her throat. It was labored. In and out, the hypnotic sound of her inhaling and exhaling; of life happening right here and right now. Before she knew what had happened, she was transported instantly back in time - back to the Ashram and her last day there.

She saw herself walking down a little side path away from the yoga platform; walking through trees and lush tropical foliage toward the beach. Crashing waves were off in the distance. Birds were chirping joyously and colors of radiant tropical flowers were as bright as flamingo's and rainbows all rolled into one. It was then that Jimmy suddenly appeared, strolling straight toward her. Wouldn't you know it, she was leaving in a mere two hours and here he was, right in front of her – the only human being she'd ever met who could see straight into her soul.

Dressed entirely in white, a long flowing tunic-like top draped knee-length over Jimmy's pants and momentarily the brightness of his snowy-colored clothing and shock-white hair dazzled her. Or was it something else? Was it the luminous energy about him?

He was so close now. Their paths were almost crossing – at least, they were about to cross up until the point he stopped. He stopped right in front of her. Dead quiet, Jimmy stared directly into her eyes, as he'd done on so many occasions before.

'It's Holly, isn't it,' he said without smiling, but there was a hint of a twinkle in his wise eyes.

It transpired the two of them were the same height. Having spent most of her time around him sitting cross-legged she'd never really noticed that before.

'Yes. Holly Devon.'

'Holly Devon,' he paused. 'Perfect.'

'Why do you say that?' she asked, curious as ever.

'Because every name is perfect.' The tiniest of smiles made the corners of his mouth twitch.

She looked at him with bafflement.

'Why did you come here, Holly?'

Shuffling self-consciously before him, she wondered where his question was headed. 'To learn yoga, of course. To learn how to teach it. And to understand more about myself and life, I guess.'

'No. Why did you come *here* – on this path, at this precise moment, to be standing before me now.'

'Well, I didn't. What I mean is, I was just heading to

381

the beach. I happened to take this pathway. I didn't expect you to be here.' Confusion rippled through her.

He finally smiled. 'You just happened to take this path and you met your teacher.'

'Yes?' she replied with uncertainty.

'You will find this a lot in life,' he said, breaking into a giggle.

'What?'

'On every bend in the road; at every twist and turn and fork, and on the straightest and narrowest stretches of your journey, you will meet your teachers, again and again.'

'Oh.' She began to get the gist of what he was saying, but still wasn't quite sure why she was currently privy to a private discourse.

'You are a sincere student. I see you thinking much. Working so hard to figure things out; to get it all so right in your mind.' He reached up and tapped her ever so gently on the side of her head. 'So many things you need to know.'

Holly felt more perplexed by the second. 'Yes, I do. And the Eight Limbs of Yoga,' she hesitated. 'I've been wondering, how long do you think it takes to learn them properly? To reach the eighth limb.'

He chuckled again, quite heartily this time, then looked at her with quiet sincerity. 'How long?' he reflected. 'I would say, as long as it takes you to get to the beach. And to know you're always there.' See,' he said, pointing down the pathway toward the ocean. 'Just keep heading in that direction.'

Feeling a little uncertain about what he meant and how on earth that related to her learning the eight limbs, Holly inwardly gave up.

'One day, you'll understand there is nothing to know and nothing to get,' he finally added. 'And in that moment you can be free, here.' He tapped her playfully on the point between her eyebrows. 'Surrendering in every moment…how long do you think that takes?'

She shook her head the tiniest amount, more like a twitch, and partially in despair that she was missing something important.

'Because that is the answer to your question.'

'I'm not sure I under…'

'That which you seek is seeking you, Holly Devon.'

It was surely his most enigmatic remark, ever. Whatever was he on about?

Jimmy beamed broadly. 'And that is why we have met on this path, at this precise moment in time.'

Because he's seeking me?

'And one day, you will meet me again.'

Did he mean that he knew she'd come back to the Ashram? She thought, baffled. 'Perhaps he could tell she'd make such an appalling instructor that she'd have to return and repeat the entire training.

'And when you do,' he continued, 'you will not recognize me. Not straight away,' he giggled his oh-so-Jimmy giggle. 'I will appear in other forms. And then a moment will come when you see things differently. Clearly. A precise moment will come. You see?' He said, giving her a gentle tap on the center of her chest.

'I'm not sure I…'

'The time will come when you will understand so many things all at once. Here,' he tapped the center of her chest a second time. 'And here.' He tapped her head again.

'You will find yourself when you meet and embrace yourself fully, Holly Devon. In this moment and the next.' Gliding past her, Jimmy smiled serenely. 'Remember always, love is the greatest truth there is.'

Love is the greatest truth there is, she echoed in her mind.

His sparkling brown eyes stared so deeply into her

soul. They bored into her being with so much light and understanding.

You will meet me again.

Warmth emanated from his heart.

You can be free, here. His hand moved to his chest.

Joy is the essence of spirit.

It was strange. He reminded her of someone.

Love is the greatest truth there is, Holly whispered, feeling herself drifting away from the Ashram memory and the little path to the beach; drifting back into the present and the words that Rodrigo had not long ago spoken.

The tropical bush had vanished. She was back at the Women's Refuge Center...with her heart beating ever so slowly and her breathing almost stopped; and she was right in the moment of clarity that her beloved teacher had spoken about all those years ago. It was a moment of total awareness - of her whole self, as she'd just experienced in her meditation. But this time she was right here, in her body, feeling it all. The exquisite knowing that she was one with all of life and her essence of consciousness was unchanging throughout it all. Eternity – that's where she existed: forever at the beach, whilst walking the path toward it.

Her heart soared wide in sudden understanding as she exhaled for the longest moment, feeling vibrancy and a radical aliveness in every cell of her body. An acute awareness existed inside her of exactly where she was – in another extraordinary moment of her life.

Love blasted through every molecule in her body.

You will find yourself when you meet and embrace yourself fully. That's what Jimmy had said.

'Oh my God, oh my God...I get it!' Sasha began springing about in the hall, leaping with joy and spinning endlessly around the floor.

'I get it!'

Her two worlds had collided completely at last; her past and her present; her mind and her heart. Integrated. Married. One. She was love overflowing – bursting with it. And now all she wanted to do was share it. Share that divine joyful feeling; share her happiness.

I'd love to love you, Holly Devon.

Rodrigo, she remembered with a start. How much time had passed? Had he driven off by now?

'Rodrigo,' she said out loud, becoming aware of something similar about him and Jimmy.

You will meet me again...

Rodrigo!

Suddenly energized beyond measure with the realization, Sasha bolted for the door, clutching her sports bag more firmly over her shoulder as the door clanged shut behind her. Yanking out her tight hair band, she part-stumbled down the rickety wooden stairs, searching the horizon of the car park in vain through the glare of the late morning sun. There was no sign of his car. No sign of him.

'Rodrigo!'

Running past all the parked cars she made for the roadside pavement, bounding over a small railing fence in her haste.

'Rodrigo!' she yelled again.

Spinning left and right in her search for him, her heart raced. Was she too late?

But there, a little further down the pathway she could see his tall tanned figure drawing to a halt beside his parked car, not fifty meter's away.

Rodrigo heard his name being yelled down the street but was slow to turn. Surely it couldn't be Holly? She didn't seem the kind of person to shout so loudly.

But it *was* her.

And not only was she hollering his name, she was sprinting like a gazelle down the street toward him, with her long blonde locks flying loosely behind her and the sun beaming directly onto her lightly-tanned ever-so-pretty face. Rodrigo saw the shine in her eyes and an unfamiliar carefree innocence radiating from within her, as if some happy joyous creature had suddenly morphed into her body. It was a priceless moment - one he would always remember: this divine Goddess, galloping happily toward him, filled with such trust and lightness of spirit; this beautiful creature, so utterly her own woman and so free.

'Rodrigo,' she stopped up short in front of him, panting from the quick dash.

'Holly?' he smiled inquisitively.

'I was wondering,' she took a few more panting breaths, 'if I could come watch the football game with you.'

'Watch it *with* me?' He grinned. 'Honey, I'm playing.'

'You're playing?'

'I'm Brazilian.' He shrugged his shoulders, full of cheeky charm.

Holly smiled with delight. 'That's great then.'

'It is?'

'Sure,' she beamed. 'Nothing better than a man of action.'

'Well, in that case, while I'm on a roll, can I take you out for dinner sometime?'

She took a good long look into his soulful shimmering emerald eyes. 'I'd like that.'

'When I say sometime, I mean this evening.'

'This evening sounds perfect.'

'Phew,' his hands gestured dramatically. 'That was only three months of hell.'

They both erupted into laughter and he drew his arms around her, wrapping her into a warm bear hug.

'What made you change your mind?' he asked

huskily into her ear.

'I didn't change it,' she responded, affectionately recalling the conversation with Jimmy, 'I lost it.'

He leaned back, looking deeply into her eyes. 'I approve.'

'Do you now.'

'Uh-huh.'

She chuckled. 'I think my old yoga guru would approve, too.'

'Really? What's their name?'

'Jimmy,' she smiled broadly.

'Jimmy? That's an...unexpected name...for a yoga guru.' He grinned, leaning back and searching her face with a mischievous twinkle in his eyes. 'But the big question is...'

Holly felt his arm shift down to her waist and her upper body falling as Rodrigo stepped nimbly away from her with a deft movement. For the tiniest split second she tensed against him. But it was as fleeting as the blink of an eye. His action was as swift as her synchronistic response and as natural as the movement of the tides. Holly's arms fell fluidly toward the earth as her supple vertebra rippled like a well-oiled chain and folded back over his arm. Exhilaration flowed through every cell and every neural pathway in her body and a long surrendered breath escaped her lips as he dipped her, right there on the sidewalk, with the birds chirping cheerfully and the spring blossoms blooming. He dipped her and her heart flooded with ecstatic joy.

'...could Jimmy do this?' he said in a throaty voice, his face lighting up with happiness as he leaned down over her.

Holly wasn't sure if it was the memory of him, but she could have sworn she heard Jimmy's sweet giggle on the breeze, clear as day. He was nowhere in sight. But then she heard the sound of his voice one more time, whispering through the air.

And when you do get lost - because this is certain - return to your practice. Return to your mat; return to your meditation and your breath; time and time again, over and over. Then one day, before you realize what has happened, you will be living your life wide AWAKE. You'll have come home, to yourself. You will be at one with All That Is. Your life will be lived consciously, with choice, in every moment. And you will inhabit it so fully and completely, and you will take up so much space, that The Divine will move aside and marvel at the miracle created.

That's exactly what she heard before Rodrigo's lips found hers. Then nothing else in the world or that moment mattered.

Nothing at all.

The Eight Limbs of Yoga

(Eight Limbs – Union)

Sanskrit Word	Common Translation	Description
1. Yama	Moral Code; Universal Morality (Ahimsa, Satya, Asteya, Brahmacharya, Aparigraha)	Restraints (non-violence, non-lying, non-stealing, non-waste of vital energies, non-greed)
2. Niyama	Personal Conduct (Sauca, Santosha, Svadhyaya, Tapas, Ishvarapranidharna)	Observances of self (purity, contentment, self-study, discipline, surrender)
3. Asana	Postures	Postures; positions
4. Pranayama	Breath	Life energy (Prana)
5. Pratyahara	Sense Withdrawal	Withdrawal of the senses
6. Dharana	Focus	Concentration of life energy in one place; Inner perceptual awareness
7. Dhyana	Meditation	Meditative state
8. Samadhi	Union	Unified state of mind; freedom and joy

The Bright New Dawn

Louise Beker

Isadora Bright has had enough of life. At her lowest point, a dramatic intervention and a series of 'coincidental' encounters radically alter her path. In a quest for faith, her spirit awakens and she embarks upon a mystical journey, capturing the intrigue of an ancient civilization.

From Ireland to London and a magical encounter with Egypt, Isadora's adventure leads her not only to deep personal healing and love, but also a profound discovery.

Her journey will captivate and inspire you. It is a transformational story of hope and finding the courage to face our deepest wounds. Enchanting and thought provoking, it reminds us of the power we have to create our lives in an age of rapid change.

"A parable for our times…a must read."
Mike Alexander, Journalist, New Zealand Sunday Star Times

www.louisebeker.com

ABOUT THE AUTHOR

Louise Beker has previously authored *The Bright New Dawn*. *Her Eight Limbs of Love* is her second fiction novel.

Louise has spent over twenty years discovering, exploring and experiencing, core healing principles with gifted teachers and practitioners from around the world. She resides in Auckland, New Zealand with Izzy, her much loved SPCA rescue cat.

A certified Yoga Instructor, Louise can occasionally be found standing on her head, viewing the world from upside down…and contemplating the nature of life and this remarkable Universe we live in.

To find out more about Louise and her novels, visit her below. She would love to hear from you.
www.louisebeker.com
info@louisebeker.com
www.facebook.com/louisebeker.author